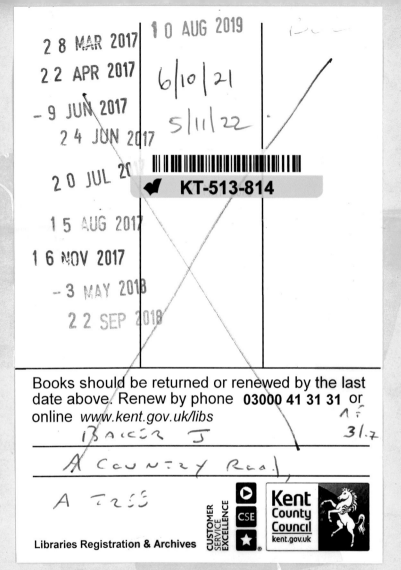
'This exquisitely crafted novel re-creates the World War II peregrinations of Samuel Beckett and the volatile Frenchwoman who became his life's companion.' *Oprah Magazine*

Praise for *Longbourn* by Jo Baker

'A genuinely fresh perspective on the tale of the Bennet household . . . Baker confronts the darker elements of eighteenth-century life . . . The result is engrossing – and a lot of fun.' *Sunday Times*

'Intoxicating . . . a joy in its own right, a novel that contrives both to provoke the intellect and, ultimately, to stop the heart.' *Guardian*

'Delightfully audacious . . . a work that's both original and charming, even gripping.' *New York Times Book Review*

'A novelist with a gift for intimate and atmospheric storytelling.' *Financial Times*

'An Austen lover has the satisfaction of matching the novels chapter for chapter. Lovely.' *Observer*

'To twist something so familiar into something quite fresh is impressive . . . *Longbourn* is not just nicely packaged fan fiction, or an Austenian *Downton Abbey*; it's an engrossing tale we neither know nor expect.' *Daily Telegraph*

'*Longbourn* is a really special book, and not only because its author writes like an angel.' *Daily Mail*

'Superb . . . The lightest of touches by a highly accomplished young writer.' *Mail on Sunday*

'This clever glimpse of Austen's universe clouded by washday steam is so compelling it leaves you wanting to read the next chapter in the lives below stairs.' *Daily Express*

'The much-loved *Pride and Prejudice* is shaken up and given the grit that Jane Austen could never include – with great success.' *Evening Standard*

'What bravery to take *Pride and Prejudice* as the springboard for a new novel! Jo Baker takes a fresh angle on a story that millions of diehard fans know inside out.' *Sunday Express*

'Debut novelist Jo Baker takes the reader on a journey back to a version of Regency England that is as much about poverty and war as social comedy and romance.' *Metro*

'Just enough Darcy to delight, as well as being a fascinating insight into the harsh working conditions of life in a grand house 200 years ago.' *Good Housekeeping*

'A freshly egalitarian reimagining of *Pride and Prejudice*.' Vogue

'*Longbourn* is a fantastic feat of imagination, unflinching in its portrayal of war and the limitations of life for a servant – a novel you will want to shelve with the original classics you plan to read again and again.' *Psychologies*

'*Pride and Prejudice* reimagined as a mysterious manservant stirs up passions in the Bennet household both upstairs and down.' *Woman and Home*

'A must-read for fans of Jane Austen, this literary tribute also stands on its own as a captivating love story.' *Publisher's Weekly*

Also by Jo Baker

Longbourn

and published by Black Swan

A Country Road,
A Tree

Jo Baker

BLACK SWAN

TRANSWORLD PUBLISHERS
61–63 Uxbridge Road, London W5 5SA
www.penguin.co.uk

Transworld is part of the Penguin Random House group of companies
whose addresses can be found at global.penguinrandomhouse.com

First published in Great Britain in 2016 by Doubleday
an imprint of Transworld Publishers
Black Swan edition published 2017

A CIP catalogue record for this book
is available from the British Library.

ISBN 9780552779524

Typeset in 12/15pt Adobe Garamond by Thomson Digital Pvt Ltd, Noida, Delhi
Printed and bound by Clays Ltd, Bungay, Suffolk.

Penguin Random House is committed to a sustainable future
for our business, our readers and our planet. This book is made
from Forest Stewardship Council® certified paper.

1 3 5 7 9 10 8 6 4 2

'When some went out, others lit up.'

Molloy, Samuel Beckett

Cooldrinagh

Spring 1919

THE TREE STIRRED and the sound of the needles was *sshh, sshh, sshh*. The boy swung a knee over the branch, heaved himself up, and shifted round so that his legs dangled. The scent of the larch cleared his head, so that everything seemed sharp and clear as glass. He could still hear the faint sound of piano practice, but he could also see out across the fields from here; he could see for miles and miles, and the sky was wide open as a cat's yawn.

He heard the side door of the house, and then her voice go calling out for him, sing-song: 'It's ti–ime.'

He chewed his lip and stayed put. The door propped open, he could hear more distinctly the bright ripple of music, a stumble, and the phrase caught and begun again. Frank was trying hard to get it right. He, though, would not oblige. With her watching, he couldn't lose himself while playing; and if he couldn't lose himself, then what was the point of playing at all?

'I'm wai–ting.'

He didn't move. She gave out a sigh and the door clacked shut behind her, and she came down the step, out into the garden, looking for him.

He dug at a scale of bark with a thumbnail.

'Where have you got to now, you wee skitter?'

But it was herself that she was talking to as she marched through the garden, searching him out. He shuffled in against the trunk, wrapped an arm tight around it.

He watched her pass under his dangling tennis shoes – the white dividing line of the parting in her hair, her skirt snapping out with her stride. Her feet moved like darting arrows, pointing the way. The wrong way, but she wasn't going to give up on it. If she were to stop, and plant her feet and crane her head back, that would be that. But it didn't cross her mind: he simply couldn't be where he was not allowed to be. Up there, he had climbed out of her imagining.

The music ended. Frank had finished the piece. He was waiting to be excused.

She was out across the lawns now, and there was just the spiral stair of larch branches down towards the brown earth, the mat of fallen needles, and the sound of her voice, calling again and fading round the far side of the house.

He waited until he heard her footsteps return, and then the click and clack as she opened the side door and shut it again behind her. A moment later and the music started up again. Poor old Frank, he'd been lumbered with it; Frank was paying for his little brother's escape.

He too would pay for it, he knew, and in spades, when she found him; his mother had a strong arm. But for now, he had disappeared, and it was a miracle.

He shuffled forward on the bough, tweaking the legs of his shorts down, one and then the other, between the rough bark and the tender backs-of-knees. Gravity tugged at him now, teased at his core, making it lurch and swoop. A bird was singing somewhere – a blackbird, pouring its song up and out into the Easter air.

He sucked in a breath. It tasted of sap, and of spring, and of his rubbery tennis shoes. He let go of the branch; he let go of the trunk. He lifted his arms and spread them wide. The pause on the cusp, the brink. He dived out into the empty air.

Gravity snatched him. Air stuffed his mouth and ballooned his shirt and his shorts and pummelled him, and it was stacked with branches and they smacked and scurried past; twigs whipped his cheeks and legs and arms and belly and tore at his shirt.

The ground slammed up. It knocked the breath out of him, knocked the light out of him. Made him still.

He lay, his cheek on hard earth. No breath: empty, red and pulsing, and no breath. Gaping, but no breath; then, in front of his eyes, the dust stirred and the fallen needles shifted: he dragged in a lump of air and heaved it down him, and then pushed it out again. It hurt.

He felt too a hot pulse in his hand, a burn on his thigh: he noticed these particular discomforts, alongside the tenderness of bruised ribs and the hard weight of the earth pushing up against him.

He creaked up on to hands and knees as his breath became normal again. Then he sat back on his heels and brushed the needles off his palms. After a moment, he twisted himself round to stretch out his legs. He considered the scratch across the ball of his thumb, which was not so bad after all, and another on his thigh, which wasn't bleeding much, and the pink bald patch where an old scab had come off a knee. He licked the ooze off his hand, tasting not just blood but the salt-sweetness of unwashed skin and medicinal pine. He brushed down his shins and tied a trailing lace. Then he eased himself upright, unfolding like a deckchair, all angles and joints. He tugged his shorts straight, and they more or less covered up the scratch on his leg, so she wouldn't notice that.

His head swam, just a bit. But he was all right.

He looked over to the house: the windows stared straight back at him. The music laboured on. No doors were flung open, no one came thundering out to grab him by the scruff and drag him in and thrash his backside blue for doing something so very dangerous indeed, for putting himself in harm's way, for risking life and limb, when it had been impressed upon him so soundly not to do such an idiotic thing again. She must be standing over the piano, her stare flicking from Frank's hands to the score, the score to his hands, making sure that Frank, at least, was going to get something right.

And knowing the piece, he knew he had a good while yet before Frank would be done with it.

He glanced up through the helix of branches to the sky, where clouds bundled and tore towards the mountains from the sea. On the lowest branch, near the trunk, the bark was polished smooth with the wear of his own hands. He reached for it, grasped it in his stinging palms, and heaved himself up till his elbows locked and his belly was pressed against the bough. Then he swung his right knee over the scaly bark, making the blood bead again. He stretched a hand up for the next branch, where it hung just above his head. He began, again, to climb.

This time, this time, *this* time, he would skim up to join the clouds. This time, he would fly.

Part One

The End

1

Greystones, County Wicklow
September 1939

H IS STOMACH IS oily and heaving. His hand shakes and there's a mean little headache between his eyes. The sun, slanting in through the harbour window, catches in the cut glass and kicks off the silverware. It makes him wince. Everyone else has already breakfasted, and what's left has gone quite cold.

'Shall I ring for more bacon?'

He shakes his head; it hurts.

The drink always seems necessary; it seems like the solution. That certainty fades with the actual drinking; he drinks himself into disgust, and now, a few parched and sleepless hours later, he's prickling with it, sweating whiskey, scraping butter across cold toast and swallowing sour spit while she watches every movement, notes every flicker. She seems to scent it off him, the whiskey and the misery. It makes her scratch at him and scrabble round for solutions.

'Eggs? Would you take some eggs?' Half-getting up: 'I'll have Lily fry some for you.'

He speaks too quickly, over the heave of nausea. 'No. Thank you.'

She sits back down. 'Well, you have to eat something.'

He bites the corner off his toast, sets the remainder back down. He chews and swallows. He *is* eating.

'I mean something substantial. Something with some nourishment in it. Not just toast.'

'I like toast.'

'You eat like a bird. Are you ill? You're not ill.'

Eating like a heron or a puffin or a gannet: all that stabbing, scooping, struggling and gulping; eating like an eagle or a hawk that smashes its prey into the ground and tears it into messes. Owls swallow their dinners whole and cough up boluses of bones and fur. He picks apart his toast and eats a fragment: is he eating like a penguin, perhaps?

Something lands hard overhead: a hairbrush or a shoe hitting the floor above. He flinches but doesn't look up, while she, distracted for a moment, peers at the cracks in the ceiling, and her face softens. There are voices, a clattering of footsteps. A door slams.

'They'll bring the whole place down around our ears.'

It is precarious, this little rented house by the harbour, with its rattling windows and fireplaces that smoke. So she stuffs the rooms with guests, to keep the walls from buckling in, to stop the roof from collapsing down on top of her. Sheila and Mollie, his cousins; Sheila's girls, Jill and Diana: all the daughters that his mother didn't have. And she won't hear of them leaving, however old the season grows. The cold winds do not blow. The summer will not end. There are no clouds.

'Those girls.' She smiles and shakes her head.

He swallows down another bit of toast; she pours herself a cup of milky coffee. A slick drip gathers on the lip of the pot and they both watch it fall. He is just about to push away his chair when she looks up and says, 'Oh, I saw a friend of yours the other day in town. Lovely boy. Medical man. Can't for the life of me remember his name, now. He would have been a couple of years below you at Portora.'

He knows who she means. 'That would be Alan Thompson, I'd imagine.'

'Ah yes. Doctor Thompson, that was it. He's doing very well.'

'So I believe.'

And had been a pale frog in the peat waters of the Erne; in whispering huddles in the library, cricket whites, a naughty caught-red-handed smile. Later, in the middle of the medic crowd at Trinity, crossing the quad in a gaggle with wine bottles and a whiff of cigars. Always seemed to be at the centre of things, to simply know how to *be*. Encountered since and drunk with; helpful, when help had been needed. A good man.

He lifts the skin off his coffee, a greasy caul, and drapes it into his saucer. He shouldn't do it to her, but: 'Unless it was his brother Geoffrey,' he says.

She folds her lips. Geoffrey is a psychiatrist. 'I'm not sure that I would consider that medicine.'

But it is a palliative. I do sleep sometimes now, he thinks of saying. I can breathe: air comes in and out of me as required. You might consider that a good. You might think it money well spent. Is that not medicine, after all?

'Well,' he says. 'Good for their old mam; she must be very proud.'

He lifts the little silver lid on the marmalade and picks the spoon out of the jar.

'Were you getting anything . . . written, in Paris?' she asks.

He watches the marmalade drip. It is thin and slides off the spoon like spittle. He feels her discomfort and her desire. Could he not, for once, write something respectable, something that she could leave out for her visitors to admire? He sets the spoon back in the pot, fits the little silver lid back into place around it.

'No,' he says. 'Nothing much.'

'Well then, you may as well stay here.'

He looks up at her strong-boned face, its feathering lines. 'Is that right?'

'You'll get so much more done here, with us to look after you. You can write those articles for the paper. I know Paris is cheap, but that's no real help at all if it just encourages you to be spendthrift; if your allowance—'

He goes still. She has become accomplished at this. The incision is precise, as is the pause.

'—if you can't live reasonably well on your allowance there, and there are too many distractions from your writing, then there is nothing for it but to stay here. For your own good.'

And be begrudged. As if he were not keenly enough aware that the food he eats, and the air he breathes, and the water – and the whiskey – that he drinks, that the space he takes up in the world is most dreadfully squandered.

'If nothing else, you could help your brother in the business.'

'He wouldn't thank me for it.'

'He could do with the assistance.'

'The last time I got involved, I made a right hames of things. Frank can do without that kind of trouble.'

This makes her wince, as if it tastes sour.

'I know that if you would just make the effort, if you would exert yourself, if you would . . .' She trails off. 'You did so well at the College. Everybody said.'

Having arrived at that, she must be almost done.

'I'm sorry, Mother.' His long, lean frame unfolds, the chair shunting backwards.

'Where are you going?' she asks.

'Fresh air.'

'Sure, you haven't finished your breakfast.'

'I've had enough, thank you.'

He is followed from the room by the sound of her long, deflating breath; his shoulders rise at it.

But quietly, alone, surrounded by the meal's debris, with the sound of young voices from the upstairs rooms, she presses at her eyes. It is just all so sketchy, so insubstantial, the way that he is living; it's all hand-to-mouth and day-to-day. That crowd in Paris: she doesn't know the half of it, she suspects, and, really, she doesn't want to know. But the sight of him in that hospital bed, his chest in bandages, the nurses jabbering away in French: she blinks, her eyes wet. When she thinks what he could have been. Her brilliant, beautiful boy. Throwing it away, just throwing it away. Until he has the heart turned sideways in her.

Because it doesn't even make him happy, does it? If he could just be happy.

The girls thunder down the stairs into the hallway to greet their almost-uncle; his voice is warm and cheery in reply. A glimpse of him at a distance. Of why he must always be leaving.

All shiny buckled shoes and neat cardigans, Jill and Diana are to take themselves out for the morning. He feels seedy and liverish and guilty; the two of them are so glossy and clear-skinned and lovely, and full of skittish energy, like ponies.

'Oh, hang on two ticks,' he says.

He fishes out coins, drops a clutch into cupped palms. 'Get yourselves some toffees.'

'Gosh, thanks!'

He follows as they clip down the front steps into the street. They are chattering, gleeful, sounding so English; they will stride along the seaside pavements, heads together, past the folded papers in racks, the honesty boxes and the crates of apples and plums and tomatoes; in the sweetshop the shelves are cheerful with jars of pastel bonbons, chalky mints, glossy toffees, boiled sweets like stained-glass windows. They'll slaver and suck and crunch on the quayside, watch the boats lean in the wind, the waves jostle, hear the rigging slap. He feels solicitous for these moments, their accretion. That they be strung together like beads on a thread, to be counted through in later times.

He leaves them to it, turns the other way along the beach, the stones shifting and sliding underfoot, his narrow Italian boots useless for this, for anything more challenging than urban flags and cobbles. He follows a belt of rotting seaweed for the slippery comfort of it, stalking along like a wading bird, ungainly and in a hurry. Striding up through seakale now and bleached-out thrift, all its little heads tossing in the wind. He follows a worn bare line in the salt-grass that takes him up towards the road and the last houses of the town. The sun is low. The shadows are long. The wind comes bundling down from the mountains.

Ahead lies the little graveyard. The gate draws him over and he pauses at it. You can see this spot from his mother's window. She could be watching him right now: like a figure in a Seghers landscape, rendered insect by the bulk of the mountainside.

They lined the grave with turf and moss. He and his mother, working together. As though they were making a garden. As though they were planting a seed.

His father had always been his companion in this, striding out from the old house, Cooldrinagh, the two of them marching along the suburban streets, and then country lanes, and then scrambling up through the heath, till they reached a point, only so far away and no further, the limits of the wound-out thread. They would sit, and scuff up stones, and pluck at cotton-grass and stare.

And then his father would say, 'She'll be wondering where we are.'

And they'd heave to their feet and begin the long trudge that would bring them down and round and back and all the way to the grey box of home. Not Ariadne's thread. Nothing so gossamer as that. Sinewy, this pull she has, and tough.

And now he is alone, and his father planted in a trough of moss, and nothing grew from it at all except the ache of missing him. He turns away from the gate and walks on. The lane climbs between fields, shaded by high hedges that drip with fuchsia like blood, and every bit of gravel is felt through his boot soles as he goes, and sheep call and gulls weave and hang overhead.

He swings over a gate and out into the open ground beyond: gorse rattles its seed pods in the wind and his own breath rattles in his chest, and with exertion now the scar pulls. But he carries on and up through the grey scabs of limestone, and as he reaches the crest the ground falls away to reveal the sweep of the coastline beyond, the fungal growth of suburbs crawling up towards the rust-grey city. To the left, the mountains swell, and the wind pummels down from there and snatches at his jacket and makes his eyes water. He turns his back on it and blinks out towards the wrinkled slate-grey sea, and the old world that lies beyond it.

. . . You hear the grating roar
of pebbles which the waves draw back, and fling . . .

24

But you don't, do you? Not from here: there's just the wind, and his own blood pulsing and the rasp of his own breath. The sea far below mouths silently; a sly lick towards the town, the graveyard, the roots of this dark hill. And over there, out over the horizon, beyond that wedge of Britain and deep into the expanse of Europe, a tidal wave is gathering, and any moment now will come the tipping point, the collapse and rush, the race towards destruction.

He turns to pick out the rooftop, the particular skirl of smoke, where his mother waits by the fire and looks at seed catalogues and can't bear to have the radio on.

He knows he cannot stay. He can't help Frank. He can't write articles to order for the *Irish Times*. Sleep would fail him; he would drink to calm the shake in his hands, to soften the thud of his heart. Soon it would be a conscious effort to breathe at all. There had been nights, and even days, before he went to Paris, when he would have unwrapped a new razorblade and neatly opened his wrists and had done with it all, if it were not for the mess that he'd leave behind him. The bloodstains on the floor. Her outraged grief.

He will have to tell her that he's going, though he cannot tell her this.

He tugs his cuffs down straight. He pushes the glasses back up to the bridge of his nose. He begins the inevitable lope back down towards the precarious little town, to all the things that can't be said.

*

25

'Will you be joining us, May?' Sheila asks.

His mother's reply from the dining room is a deal more soft than it would have been, had it been he that asked.

'I am fine here, thank you.'

Bent into the smell of hot dust and electricals, he twists the dial through squeals and fuzz until he catches and settles on the signal from the BBC in London. He goes to lean against the sideboard, arms folded.

Sheila sits herself down; Mollie perches on the arm of her chair.

'Where are the girls?' he asks.

'Still out,' Sheila says.

The three of them gathered here know what's coming, more or less; they know how the pieces stand on the board. The broadcast begins, and the British Prime Minister speaks, in his precise, quavering way, from London. They each stare at the carpet, each lost in the darkness of the transmission.

This morning the British ambassador in Berlin handed the German Government a final note . . .

There is movement outside the open door. His mother stands there, in profile. Behind her Lily holds the dishes, halted by the gravity of the moment: the moment that has been drawing everything towards it now for years.

. . . by eleven o'clock that they were prepared at once to withdraw their troops from Poland, a state of war would exist between us.

His mother raises a hand to her mouth.

I have to tell you now that no such undertaking has been received, and that consequently this country is at war with Germany.

Sheila sits back at this; Mollie rubs her arms. His mother reaches for the door frame. Chamberlain's voice continues to spool out from the wireless and tangle on the floor.

'Well, there we are now,' Mollie says.

Sheila reaches for her sister and their hands clasp. His mother still stands in the doorway, hand to the jamb. Her face has gone grey. He pushes himself upright, crosses the room to her. He takes her hand and slips it through his arm.

'Here,' he says. He brings her over to her armchair. She is trembling.

He switches the radio set off. Then there is just the little parlour, and the morning sunshine through the window, and the sea wind blustering, and you could tell yourself that nothing had changed, but these words have changed the world.

The girls, though, their cardigans ballooning, their hair blown into tats. They'll be huddled on a bench to finish up their lemon bonbons, coltsfoot rock, liquorice; they are still free from it. They're a gorgeous empty spell of wind and hair and sweetness.

'Can I get you something?' he asks.

His mother shakes her head.

He glances over at Sheila – pink cheeks, pink nose, a smile forced over a dimpling chin – and even as he watches, her smile thins, her lips pressed tight and trembling, and she turns to her sister and crumples into her.

'Buck up now, darling,' Mollie says, rubbing her arm. 'Don't spoil your face.'

27

After a moment, Sheila sniffs and nods and leans away, and dabs at her eyes with the flank of a hand. Because the girls must not see that she's upset.

'I'll have to see about an earlier crossing,' she says.

His mother blinks up now. 'Whatever for?'

'We must get back, May.'

'No, indeed you must not. You heard what he said – there's to be another war. You'll be much safer here.'

Sheila straightens her shoulders, touches her hair back into place. 'You are so kind, May, dear, but you know, the children will want their father. Donald has to join his regiment, and we shall want to see him first.'

'Well, Mollie,' May now says. 'You'll stay.'

Mollie makes an apologetic moue. 'A little while, May, but then I'm afraid I shall have to go too.'

'Whatever for?'

'Work. They're expecting me.'

May is left with nothing now but to turn her face away and be silent. She must swallow it down in one hard lump, this unpalatable truth that everyone has been chewing on for months. They may not like it either, but at least they have grown accustomed to the taste.

He lays a hand on her shoulder. He feels the bones of her. She turns her sharp blue eyes on him.

'I'm sorry,' he says.

'This is hardly *your* fault.'

From that frozen moment, the household stillness breaks into a cascade. Voices bounce and spin around the place like spilled ball bearings. Stairs are hammered up and down. Telephone calls are placed, timetables consulted, sketched-out plans become solid and concrete.

Lily turns out the hot press for the girls' balled-up socks and folded vests and blouses; Sheila and Mollie discuss – at varying distances and volumes – the need for this item or that, the possible location of the other. Where are the girls' good shoes? (They're wearing them – which becomes evident on their return, all tangled hair and stickiness, dustily shod.) What about these books? Have you seen the hairbrush? Whose hairbrush? My hairbrush, the tortoiseshell hairbrush. Is this the one you mean? Feet clomp back and forth across the landing and up and down the stairs, then the voices become softer, closer, as the work begins to come together and be set in order.

He stays out of their way; he can't be of any help. His head still hurts; he's liverish; he's wary of questions, doesn't want to share his plans. He hides behind his book.

When they are done and the taxi is ordered, he carries the luggage downstairs and lines it up in the hall, the girls' neat little cases and their mother's larger one. Everybody waits, since that is all there is left to do now, the girls sitting side by side on the upright hall chairs, one set of white socks and buckle-shoes dangling and swinging slightly, the other set neatly instep-to-instep on the parquet, their owner made grown up by the gravity of the day.

Time stretches and slows; the clock ticks. Mollie expresses concern about the taxi. May is worried about the weather: they'll have a rough crossing ahead of them, she dares say.

They cannot say anything worth saying, but that does not stop them talking, and the soft words accumulate, like sand trickling through an hourglass. They are up to their knees in it and yet still they can't stop.

Then there's the sound of a car bumbling along the harbour road, which makes conversation break and scatter.

'Is that—'

'Ah, that must be—'

'Have you got—'

The motor idles in front of the house. Sheila has the front door open; the driver gets out of the cab and comes to help with the luggage.

The girls smell of wool and boiled milk and soap, when they are kissed; they are solemn and excited, knowing this is all so very serious now; their cheeks are hot against his cheek, and they smell no doubt his guilty adult reek of cigarettes and sweat and last night's whiskey.

Sheila hugs him sudden and hard. Words fail him.

'God bless you, dear boy.'

He manages, 'God bless.'

And then Sheila slides in beside the girls, who shunt themselves across to make room, and the door slams on them, and the driver gets in the front seat, and the car turns and moves away, grinding alongside the slate-blue harbour water.

He goes indoors. He lights a cigarette. 'Boy' is right. Child. Bear-cub that the dam didn't bother licking into shape.

The house feels dim and cold. A limestone pebble has been left on the hall console. It's greyish, skin-smooth and about the size of a peppermint. It had sat in the girl's creased and grubby palm, revealed to him like a secret that she knew he would keep, then tucked away again with a little gappy smile. Abandoned now, forgotten, its meaning shed. He lifts the stone. It's cool to the touch. He cups it in his palm a moment, and then he slips his hand into his pocket and drops the stone in there.

He lopes along like a broken-down hound at Mollie's side. Mollie has taken his arm to tether him to her pace. Her body is compact and soft in her Irish tweeds. It is a glorious afternoon, breezy and blue, a mockery, the low sun making them squint.

'So are you going to tell me?' she asks him.

He peers down at her. 'Tell you what?'

'Ach, come on now. Sheila and I could see it straight off.'

'See what?'

'Who's the girl?'

Her arm hooked through his, they stumble on together. He says nothing. Seagulls wheel overhead; waves suck and spit.

'Come on, spill the beans.' She tugs his arm.

'What makes you think there are beans to spill?'

'You know what you're like. Left to yourself, you're a liability. You get ill; you get thin; you even got *stabbed*, for goodness' sake! You can't take care of yourself, can you? But look at you.' She stops and drags him round to face her. 'Just *look* at you.' Rosy-cheeked in the wind, she studies him. 'You're clearly being taken care of.' She peers in closer,

31

frowns. She flicks the back of her hand against his chest. '*Somebody* has fixed a tear in that shirt.'

He peers down. His lips twitch. Then he offers Mollie his arm again; she takes it and they walk on.

'There's a girl,' he says.

'I know.'

He doesn't offer anything more, holds a smile at bay.

'And . . . ?'

He shrugs.

'Ach, come on!'

He smiles. He says, 'Years ago, we used to play tennis, mixed doubles, when I was at the École Normale. But I didn't see her again until last year, after the attack. She read a report in the newspaper and remembered me. She came to the hospital and, well, that's when.'

'That's when you fell in love.'

It is to be supposed so. He does not confirm, correct or contradict.

'She made curtains for my flat.'

Mollie laughs.

'They're actually quite fine.'

'Sorry. I'm sure they're beautiful . . .' She waves a hand. 'I didn't mean – I just never thought of you – being the fellow that you are, I didn't think you'd care about things like that.'

'I didn't say I cared. But when it gets dark,' he says, 'one has a need of curtains.'

That's what Suzanne had said, anyway, lying naked on the tangled sheets, looking out through the high window of the sleeping loft, her dark hair tumbled, moonlight on her skin. He'd agreed, but had determined that on no account would he ever get any; if there were curtains then they would lie together in pitch black, and that would be a shameful waste of her nakedness.

And then, when she had presented him with curtains, he'd thanked her, and had even participated in their hanging.

'I don't know what all the fuss is about.'

'I'm just happy for you. Thrilled. That you've got a nice girl who'll mend your shirts and make you curtains.'

'That's not all she is. She's a musician. She studied at the Conservatoire. She is a writer, too. She writes.'

'God help you then, the pair of you.'

The curtains are drawn that evening in the little house, even though it's not yet dark. The radio crackles and shrieks as he hunts out the BBC again. When it's tuned in, he goes to stand beside his mother, a hand resting on the back of her armchair. She has steeled herself to listen now.

At the back of her head, grey hair frizzes out from its pins. Her old hands clutch the armrests. Mollie is huddled in the seat opposite, her legs drawn up underneath her, chewing on a nail. Lily stands by the sideboard, included but separate, eyes downcast.

At five o'clock today, France declared war on Germany.

His mother fumbles a hand upwards. He takes it. It is cold. They listen to the continuing bulletin, but little of it sinks in. Because the pieces are all in play now, are moving out across the board. He strokes the back of her hand with his thumb. One traces the possibilities out from here and ends up – where? Wire and trenches, is that what is coming all over again? He could volunteer for the ambulance corps, grind an old taxi over mud . . . Back in France, could he enlist? It is all so grim. His head buzzes as though the lid has been taken off a jar of flies. His mother twists round in her seat and looks up at him. Her hand grips tight and she pulls him down a little closer.

'Well, that's that,' she says.

He nods. That is indeed, as she says, that.

'You can't go back now.'

He looks down at her face, the sharp angles, the lines of it. But he can't stay. 'I've told everyone I will be back.'

'Everyone?'

'All my friends.'

'Your friends.'

He nods.

She looks at him for a long moment, her throat in an uncomfortable twist. Those shady, disreputable people with their unimaginable lives, they are drawing him away from her. From security and comfort and a decent life.

'And what possible use,' she asks, 'do you imagine you would be?'

2

Paris
Autumn 1939

I<small>T'S RIDICULOUS</small> to be happy now, Suzanne thinks. It's outrageous. But she can't help it.

She slips her arm through his. He shortens his stride for her, and this synchronization makes her smile. She breathes the warmth of tobacco and shaving soap and wine. Their footfalls clip across the Place Saint-Michel. The two of them are heading out in the hope that the cheap little café on the rue de la Huchette will have held its nerve and still be open, even though so many of the fancier bistros are battened down and shuttered now.

He didn't have to come back. But here he is. Shoulder, throat, jaw and cheekbone, blue eyes following the passage of a car along the street. She leans in against him, and all is well.

In the morning, she slips out of his bed and into her clothes and out into the streets, threading through the bin men and the delivery boys and the market traders, back towards her own apartment and out of his way. There is a gauze of mist lying in the air and Paris is new again, and beautiful, after years of going almost unnoticed.

He has his work and it is important: she must not get under his feet. She has her own work to go to anyway, those fruitless hours with plump children in the bourgeois *quartiers*, plonking away on pianos that are far too good for them and of which she finds herself feeling jealous. She keeps her quiet hours alone in her own apartment too – she is finishing a new jacket, with little bone buttons, in anticipation of the colder weather to come. She goes to the market and she goes to the library; she takes herself off to see her friends. She keeps busy. She measures out her company carefully. A drop here, a drop there. She won't make a nuisance of herself.

Whenever she goes to see him, she brings small comforts with her. A pastry to share, a bar of chocolate, some small item of needlework to soften the edges of his austerity. In the little kitchenette, there is usually only coffee and dust. She wants to make him comfortable. More comfortable than he can make himself.

The pale and wounded Irish man, his chest in bandages, strapped down by hospital sheets. She has been trying to make him comfortable ever since.

Nothing happens.

Late September days soften and cool and Paris is still lovely. The children walk in crocodiles in the street; confined for the day, their voices hang round school buildings in a haze: passers-by walk through clouds of rhyme and times tables, into billows of song.

There is a radio in the apartment next door; at the weekend, the thumping left-hand rhythm of popular songs, waves of laughter, jazz leak through the wall. The neighbours' baby cries.

Someone comes to wrap the street lamps in blue paper; at night the cars go by half blinded with blackout strips. The rue de Vaugirard becomes a deep-blue river. It washes past his own backwater, the rue des Favorites. He closes the shutters, draws the blinds and lights a lamp, and pours just a drop of Jameson's for himself, because it must be made to last. He settles into a book, or into his work, into the translation of *Murphy* into French.

Suzanne comes and goes. She twists her treacle-coloured hair back and stabs it with pins and throws him a brilliant smile. He's always startled by that smile, as though a ball has dropped out of clear air and landed smack into his palm. The thing is, of course, to lob it back into play, but he's often a fraction too late; she's tidying away the newspapers, she's heading to the kitchen, plumping up a cushion, she's half gone already. But he knows she's wanting something. It's as though there is a cat around his ankles, silky and twining, but making him anticipate a stumble, expecting to do inadvertent harm.

He tries for her. He sets coffee warming on the gas ring, spreads rillettes on bread, fishes cornichons from the jar.

They eat in bed, their feet slipping together. She brushes shards of crust from the sheet. Her limbs are brown from the

37

summer, her breasts and belly white where her swimming suit covered her; before he came to France he'd never seen a body patched like this, in a slow sepia exposure. Running a hand along her back, from tan to white to tan again, he feels grateful. She lifts her cup and sips her coffee. He turns away to hide his face. No point pinning this with words. Let it flutter by.

She goes with him to the Irish Legation, because his status here must be sorted out once and for all. And *if you want to get something done,* she says, *ask a busy woman.* She walks with him to the Place Vendôme through the drifting plane leaves, and she takes his arm. They pass the Opéra. It has gone dark. The building is shut up and locked tight, the windows shuttered, the gates wrapped in chains.

'Oh,' he says.

'We'll go back,' she says, pulling him close, 'when they reopen.'

'You think they'll reopen?'

'Of course they will,' she says. 'Eventually.'

Inside, the Legation is all polished wood and marble and dust-motes drifting in shafts of autumn sun. They join the back of a stationary queue. The Irish voices here, the conversations, tangle the air and make him breathless. He keeps his mouth shut, eyes down, to avoid the small-country connections, the friends of friends and cousins of cousins that there inevitably are in such places.

'I'm sorry, I – but you wish to remain?'

The clerk is a bluish-pale boy he has not dealt with before.

'Yes.'

'The two of you. Mr and Mrs . . .'

'No.'

'But. Well.'

He watches the clerk's expression, the questions that are not being asked. *Why stay? What good will it do you staying here?*

'We are processing exit permits right now . . .' The clerk looks at him a moment longer, then frowns down at the passport, picks through the pages; he purses his lips, peers up again. 'Just let me, um.' He gets up unevenly from his desk, shuffles some documents together, tucks the passport in alongside them. 'I won't be a moment . . .'

And they're left standing there at the desk together, in the light from high windows, with the smell of beeswax and tobacco smoke and with a parched, half-curled plane leaf at his foot that has tumbled in along with them. Her mouth twists up with impatience.

After a while, the clerk returns and hands the passport back. 'He says you'll need a certificate confirming your profession. That, along with your passport, should be sufficient for you to be granted leave to remain in Paris. Under the current dispensation.'

'How does he get one of these certificates?' Suzanne asks in her brittle English.

'By applying to us.'

She opens her lips. The clerk forestalls her: 'We need a formal letter of application. With references.'

'How long will it take to process once you have the letter?'

'I can't say. We have a good deal on our plates here at the moment.'

He nods, pockets his passport. 'Right,' he says. Then, 'Thank you.'

They turn away, and Suzanne tuts and shakes her head.

Outside, the wind blundering around the Place Vendôme has a new chill to it. He offers Suzanne his arm and she takes it, and they walk along, huddled together against the cold.

'When we get back, you must write to your publisher. They will send references. They will say what you are.'

'I shall,' he says, though he does not feel the confidence that this suggests.

'And then you will be in good standing here at last.'

He nods. 'I hope.'

The words, in French, do not sound quite so unlikely, so uncomfortable. *J'espère.*

In the Tuileries Gardens, fallen leaves bundle across the gravel. The dust, as they walk, whitens their shoes.

He writes his letter of application; he writes with some discomfort to London to request a brief reference from Mr Read at Routledge. He stamps the envelope and sends it. It seems dreadfully importune of him. As though he is asking the man to take part in a deception on his behalf.

But nothing happens.

Or rather, things keep on happening, but to other people. Nothing happens to him.

When he heads out for morning bread, there's a green van standing by the kerb on the rue des Favorites. It's the type of vehicle that the locals call a *panier à salade*. You get packed in, shaken up and spun round in them. They are police vans.

His shoulders stiffen. He does not have his papers yet.

But it's next door. He sees the *porte cochère* shoved open and a *flic* stepping over the sill on to the pavement, and a young man stumbling after, his dark hair rumpled and his shirt misbuttoned, straight from bed. A second policeman comes after them. People stop, stand back, so as not to become entangled. He finds himself amongst the bystanders, watching, without ever having meant to watch.

The young man gets into the back of the vehicle, looking baffled and angry; the door is shut on him; the officers get in too, one in the back, one in the front, and the van rumbles away over the cobbles, and that is that.

'Who was it?' a woman asks near by.

'Foreigner.'

'What has he done?'

'Don't know.'

'Where will they take him?'

Another woman leans past him to answer; he smells her breath. 'The Préfecture, the Santé, maybe.'

'Seems a shame, doesn't it?'

'It's what they'd get up to, left to themselves, isn't that it?'

He keeps his own mouth shut. And he does nothing. It all seems at one remove from him, untouchable: someone has been lifted clean out of the everyday. And from that moment on, these people become ubiquitous, unmissable: the shabby-smart, the hounded, the dispossessed. When overheard, their accents vary, but there is a definite type: educated, thoughtful, softly spoken, terrified. They are the jetsam of half a dozen different nations; they're fragile and exhausted. They've been washed up here by the floods at home.

Sometimes, like bus drivers raising a hand to each other in passing, he sees the moments when they notice each other: there is an uneasy snag and tear of the gaze, an urge for companionship, but an undertow of fear. Who would want to be associated with, who would want to belong to this community of un-belonging?

The autumn is gentle at the start, and things go on as normal, more or less. He tries to work, to make it matter that he be here. He plays a bit of tennis with Alfred Péron; they meet at cafés or the Pérons' apartment to work on his translation. Mania greets him warmly and does not seem to mind Alfy wasting all this time on his Irish friend. Alfy has become a trusted companion in futility. They inchworm through the text of *Murphy*, sipping coffee or wine, smoke spooling round them, deep in the problem of turning his own particular English into his own particular French. There is about as much point to this as there is to the completion of a crossword puzzle: there is from time to time the pleasing shift and click of a problem solved, but that's the sum of it. Once they're done, all they'll have achieved, he suspects, is a book that, having gone unread in English, can now go equally unread in French.

The heating still functions; there's still hot water when he turns the tap and scrapes a razor; in the day the lift still churns up and down; there's still the sound of the neighbours' wireless set coming through the wall, tuned to *Le Poste Parisien*, and now and again that baby cries. He'd like to see Joyce, go out drinking with him, lose himself in the wash of booze and talk, but the Joyces are all out of town, and then they're back again, and then they are away, and though a message is left it has not yet been returned, and it's impossible to keep track of them.

'The sheets need washing,' Suzanne says.

'I know.'

'They're starting to smell.'

'I know.'

'They feel greasy to me.'

'Yes.'

'Do you think the line will hold?'

Her thigh over his thigh, her hand on his chest, his scar underneath her thumb a purplish, ragged line: this damaged man is also the boy she recalls in tennis whites, starfished for a ball. The space between those moments sometimes seems just a tick, a tock. Sometimes it seems vast.

'What?' he asks, but he had heard her.

'Do you think the line will hold?' she asks again.

He rolls away and fumbles for a cigarette. He had been thinking, by association with the sheets, *washing line*, seen linen billow and snap. But she means Maginot. 'I have no idea.'

'They put too much faith in it,' she says. 'I think.'

'I daresay.'

43

'The generals go on as though it's the answer to everything. For them it's the last war all over again. But it's not the same war, is it? So that damned line is not the answer.'

He lights up the cigarette, draws on it, then offers it to her. 'It might be the same war. More or less.'

'Times have changed,' she says. 'Things have moved on, haven't they? The world goes faster now. The war will too.'

He watches as she takes a sip of smoke. Her lips, with the dip of a seagull in flight.

Over a cloud of outbreath, she says, 'They'll go round, won't they? Load up in their Volkswagens and just motor on through.' A pause. 'Perhaps you should have stayed in Ireland.'

He blinks at her, then rolls his head away and looks up at the ceiling, where a cobweb trails in the draught. He is not necessary here, though here is necessary to him. 'Do you think so?'

'It won't go on like this for ever, nothing happening. It won't last. The *drôle de guerre*. It'll stop being funny soon enough.'

'It's not really funny now.'

'The Legation would help you if you were to leave.'

Mr and Mrs, the clerk had said.

'I can hardly breathe back there in Ireland. I certainly can't write.'

'Well then.' Eyebrows up, lips pursed. 'You must stay, whatever comes.'

He takes the cigarette back and smokes it.

She sits up, swings her legs out of the bed. 'If I strip the bedclothes,' she says, 'would you take the sheets down to the *pressing*?'

*

Two streets away from the apartment, on the Place Falguière, one of those strays asks him politely for the time; he stops, consults his watch, tips it towards the other fellow, who nods. He also offers a cigarette. Eager thanks; a match is struck; he offers out the flame: the old man dips his head towards it.

To the rusty crown of a once-black bowler hat, he says, 'You're not from round here, are you?'

The old man looks up at him from under the brim, made wary. 'What makes you say that?'

'Your accent.'

'You've got quite an accent there yourself.'

'It's not me that worries me.'

The old fellow grins, reveals quite the worst teeth he's ever seen. 'Maybe it should be, my friend.' A phlegmy sound, which might be a chuckle. 'We're all dangerous, we're all contaminated. We're all *sales métèques* as far as they're concerned. And if they lock you up now, when those Nazi lads get here you're dinner. Kaput.'

He baulks at the hard words, casually used: dirty foreigners. 'I'll have my papers soon.' His own voice sounds confident.

The old man lets smoke go, touches a thread of tobacco from his pale tongue, wistful. 'I had papers once.'

'You don't any more?'

The old fellow shakes his head. 'All obsolete; all gone.'

'Can you get new ones?'

45

'There's nobody left to grant me them. I have no country now; no rights. No one will hear me.'

'Oh God.'

The old man nods, drags again on the cigarette and it crumbles to a coal. He lets out an appreciative huff of smoke.

The urge to assist is visceral . . . *the oldest hath borne most* . . . but what can he do? This is massive and abstract and there is no way to get even a fingernail into it. He peers into the cigarette packet, shakes it, taps: there are three cigarettes left.

'Here.' He hands the packet over. He waves aside the thanks.

The old fellow fumbles the pack away before the offer can be retracted. 'God bless you, sir.'

'God bless you.'

He turns away, rounding the corner on to rue d'Alleray, chewing at the inside of his cheek. The weather's turning; it's getting cold. Things can only get worse. His fingertips find the round limestone pebble from the shore at Greystones, smooth and cool as a mint between his fingertips. He lifts the stone and slips it between his lips. He watches his feet swing out ahead of him in his scuffed-up, exhausted boots, and sucks on the stone, while music rises and swells inside his head, the sad loveliness of the *Winterreise*.

> *Wunderlicher Alter!*
> *Sol lich mit dir geh'n?*

He has an answer for his mother now, at least: *no use whatsoever*.

46

3

Paris
Winter 1939–40

ALFY IS MADE strange by uniform, his flesh somehow transfigured, made more solid; his kepi rests on
the café table, between the half-empty glasses, beside the
half-full ashtray. His fingers play with a coaster, a cigarette
smokes between his knuckles. He keeps his voice low and his
eyes averted, as if he is himself abashed by his new state, by
the thick green greatcoat around his barrel body. He is doing
what he can do. He has enlisted. The professor will be shov-
elling out the stables for the cavalry.

Cavalry. It makes his eyes fall shut, his head shake in slow
negation, just to hear it, just to think of it, obsolescent, an
insane word for a modern war. For dear Christ's sake: *cavalry*. It may as well be Calvary, for the sacrifice and slaughter
that shadow it.

'I wanted to ask you,' Alfy's saying. 'While I'm gone, if
you could keep an eye out for the family, for Mania and the
boys.'

'Of course.'

'I know,' Alfy says. 'I know you would anyway. I just needed to say the words. And if I don't come back . . .'

'Ah God now, Alfy, don't.'

'Because it doesn't look good, if we are to be honest about it.' Alfy tilts his head, taps his ash into the ashtray. 'So. If I don't come back . . .'

'Alfy, no—'

'Consider them family, would you? Mania and the boys. That's all I wanted to say. Would you do that for me, if I don't come back?'

'Of course. Count on it. But do me a favour too.'

'Anything, my friend.'

'Come back.'

Alfy flashes his big grin; they part with a hand clasp, a kiss on the cheek. At the street corner he glances back at the stocky, uniformed figure, and his throat aches at the parting.

Alfred, his old friend, his new brother, leaves for his regiment; he, though, returns to his notebooks, to his desk, this pointless, circular work. Maybe he should try to enlist. He could shovel dung as well as anyone. It would be more worthwhile than this.

His friends drift.

Rootless anyway, the winds make hay with them; they are bundled up and off, tumbling and in disarray. They come and go; you wouldn't know where anyone would be.

The Joyces are back, James and Nora arriving at the station in a noisy huddle cluttered round with bags and cases. Both he and Paul Léon are there to meet them, to help, but still it is all short temper and frayed nerves, bloody-mindedness and frailty. Mr Joyce with his smouldering cheroot and his stick and his dark glasses, questions for Léon about what's going on with Giorgio, enquiries about books: the man is entirely disengaged from the moment and its imperatives. Nora's complaining is a constant exhalation like the steam engine. They have been in Brittany to make arrangements for their daughter, to see her settled out of harm's way. Though whether harm's way can ever be quite avoided by Lucia is uncertain, since she carries so much harm around inside herself.

Léon goes in search of a porter and they head towards the cabs. Following the bickering couple, his own face flushes at the recollection of fractured, thwarted Lucia. His blunt failure at love.

He and Paul get them settled in the cab and then return across the concourse, heading for the Métro.

'They are to pack up the apartment, do you know?' Paul says. 'Nora insists on an hotel.'

Paul is so benign, so mild, and yet there is a sweet one-upmanship to this; an almost-schoolboy *I know something you don't know.*

'Switzerland, then,' he says, expecting to annoy.

'It's an obvious choice, isn't it? They could both get the proper treatment there – the father and the daughter. Perhaps the situation is not all bad, since it will force the issue for them.'

They're approaching the entrance to the Métro; he glances round at Paul's milk-smooth face, its gentle intelligence. That his admiration for James Joyce extends to this – that a benefit to the family could add a hint of silver to the thundercloud of war. They descend the steps, and their boots clip *allegro* down the worn wooden treads. Paul's are the same style as his, he sees, though shiny still, and stiff; there's a flinch to his walk.

'New boots?' he asks. 'Do they pinch?'

'Still wearing them in.'

'Mine wear out before I can wear them in.'

They step in parallel from the bottom tread on to the tiled floor, and their boots swing along together. Joyce's favouring of the style has made them popular.

Paul says, confiding: 'Oh, my feet, good God.'

Not everyone is in transit. Mary Reynolds stays on in her house in the rue Hallé; she and Marcel Duchamp have their gatherings still; they have cards and conversation. Parties still happen. In one room, a wall is painted dark blue and stuck with pins and a tracery of string; her globe stands smooth in the shadows. There are maps and books and paintings and bright fires, and with the conversation and the glass of *fine* and the little dishes of olives, you would think this was for ever; you wouldn't know that the axis of the world had already tipped and that everything was sliding towards disaster.

But even on the rue Hallé, there is talk of departure. Marcel talks of it. Mary doesn't bring up the subject herself, but then neither does she contest it. Head south, Marcel says, which they would do anyway in summer; but go early, be gone before the dam breaks. Because Paris will bear the brunt and break the wave of the advance. So they will head to the south-west, to the coast, to the house in Arcachon. Distance will protect them.

'And you must come and see us there,' Mary says. 'It will be a long summer if you don't come.'

It sounds pleasant and strange, to spend the summer in Arcachon, while the war goes on elsewhere. It is impossible to think of it as real.

He just keeps ticking on, ticking over. He tries to work, but with Alfy gone, the translation, previously inchworm, now swallows its own tail. He cannot make it matter even to himself, not any more.

The weather turns bitter; the wind is thin, the temperature plummets. He hunches into himself. He is always cold.

In the street, strangers have an uncanny knack of looking like old friends, like people who have already gone. His sight is far from perfect: the number of times he's raised a hand in error and, on realizing his mistake, has had to blunder on, resettling his hat, adjusting his glasses, trying to act as though nothing had really been meant by it.

Suzanne's friends do not disperse. The younger men have joined up; the card-carrying communists have been interned for carrying their cards. But those who are still at liberty do

51

not drift away. They belong, they're rooted here. And they stand staring dead ahead at what is coming. They meet now with discretion, these friends, at each other's apartments, arriving in ones and twos, leaving in a similarly staggered fashion. The government's swiftness to intern is stunning. One does not have to do, one simply has to be.

She takes herself off to these meetings, her collar turned up and scarf wrapped against the chill. He watches her go with a needle-thin interest that he would not quite describe as jealousy. He goes along with her sometimes, when she asks him to. She doesn't always ask him to, and he wonders if that means there will be someone there she doesn't want him to meet, or to witness her meeting. There are former lovers drifting round the place; one doesn't get to their age unmarried without chalking up a few. Her tennis partner in mixed doubles, for example. That fellow.

If there's a piano in the apartment when he goes, he'll play it. As the evening wears on, she becomes voluble and insistent and she taps the tabletop with a finger and corrects people, and even in these anxious times there are bright moments when she throws back her head and just laughs. This is her without him, unsolicitous and assertive, and he feels uneasy at it. What is he doing, letting her saddle herself with him?

Cigarette smoke blues the air, a fire glows in a grate, ashtrays fill, glasses empty. He picks out a few tunes, though listlessly, because music is not really required and he has no desire to draw attention to himself. And they talk.

Just a little fellow then, but I remember the last time round; they got within a whisker of the place. The bombing, good God, do you remember? But a whisker is not Paris: they *were* held at bay; they had to bomb us because they couldn't get close enough to shoot us in the streets. Yes, but the siege of '70, yes, it was a while ago, but the restaurants were reduced to serving rat and cat and dog and the menagerie from the Jardin des Plantes, the elephant and the giraffe and everything slaughtered there for food. There's good eating on an elephant; I wouldn't say no. That's not the point: we could be there again before you know it. But things are different now! We have the line, the Maginot. Pfft. The line! Don't talk to me about the line. The Germans are prepared, that is the thing nobody seems to understand, that while we've been sitting on our arses behind the Maginot Line playing cards and scratching ourselves, Germany has been farting out smoke and shitting artillery. They'll be here before you know it and they'll fuck us properly this time. No no no, that's alarmist nonsense: the line will hold, the army will stand its ground; the line will hold. The line will hold.

He glances up to his glass, perched on top of the upright piano. There's just a smudge of purple in the pit of it; he glances back towards the table, and the bottles are empty. They talk in circles and wind themselves up like watch-springs. But what can they *do*?

She goes to speak, and when the noise doesn't falter she just raises her voice and continues, till the other voices fall away and she goes on. The key is to do *something*. Because that's better than sitting around doing nothing. And so they have to figure out what they can do. Even if it's only to ensure the fair distribution of elephant steaks.

Someone gets out a notebook and pencil, licks the tip; the mood shifts and becomes purposeful. But not for long, because they know that the moment they show their faces as communists they'll be locked up, since their loyalties will be assumed to lie elsewhere. But where else now can they lie? They are on their own. Stalin has thrown his lot in with Hitler and will look the other way. There is just the queasy idea of England peering across the Channel and biting her nails, while America stands, arms folded and whistling, pretending not to notice what is going on at all.

People fall silent, and then they start to talk of other things, of their children and their grandchildren and the music and the bitterly cold winter that this is turning out to be. And they must be going. They don't like to stay late, not nowadays. They make their farewells, pull on gloves and caps and leave in dribs and drabs, heading off into the night, hunched and blowing clouds of breath to disturb the fog.

Nora, in her blurry way, is moving around the apartment, carrying a coffee pot. Joyce is playing the piano and singing 'The Salley Gardens'. Nora sets the coffee pot down on the hall console, then picks up a vase and moves off again on another of her aimless peregrinations. He watches her as she goes, then he picks up another book, peers at the spine, and sets it in the tea-chest. Joyce finishes the song, lights a cheroot and leaves it to smoulder, then starts to pick away at another tune. 'Croppy Boy'. He is feeling sentimental. His voice sounds weak today.

The Joyces are moving out of the apartment and into an hotel. It's supposed to make things easier, but it isn't making anything easier yet. Paul Léon has overstepped the mark; it's easily and inadvertently done. Just an unwelcome word about Giorgio and he has plummeted out of favour as precipitously as if he had fallen down a well. And so his help is no longer wanted here, though help is always wanted here: nothing very much gets done unless someone else does it.

Joyce's voice trails away; his hands fall still. He closes the piano. He fishes for his stick, rises to his feet. 'You'll take a drink?' he asks.

He sets aside a book, straightens up, brushes himself down. 'Mrs Joyce won't mind?'

'We shall be discreet. Where's my coat?' A hand extended, a hesitant step, head cocked like a blackbird, the better to see out of the edge of his remaining vision.

At the café, Joyce orders white wine. He drinks as though it's for the good of his health, sucking away at his glass with a pained expression. He talks, he drinks, he frowns, he drinks, he talks.

'What, anyway, is the use of this benighted war? I cannot see that there is any point to it at all.'

Well, there are Hitler's incursions—

A dismissive puff. Lines on maps are there to be redrawn. The Brits can hardly get up in arms at that, now, can they? They've pinkified half the planet.

His persecutions.

But the Jews have always been persecuted. There's nothing new in that at all. Old as the hills, that is. I don't see why we should have a war about that now.

Joyce doesn't want to hear; there is no point in insisting. Instead, in the little local café on the rue des Vignes, under gaslight, the two of them foxed and yellowed by the old mirrors, their two heads bent, his a dark brush, Joyce's pomaded and streaked with grey, he drinks. He drinks and lets the older man talk; the old accent and the light voice feel like home, and he finds himself thinking of Germany before the war, cool light, heavy pale flesh, solitude, the paintings, the bare spaces on the gallery walls. He opens his mouth sometimes and words fall like stones, and he closes his lips and resolves to keep them closed. Because Joyce is eloquent tonight, for all that he's exhausted, and whatever he is saying there is always wonder in it, in being in the flow of his talk. Outrage at this state of affairs, the effect that all of it is having on Nora's nerves, and Lucia's . . . nerves. And Giorgio may be conscripted if he doesn't get out of France, and the fact that his book, his book is not news now, not any more, because of this, this, this *politics*, and how galling it all is.

'You know the *Wake* better than anybody else. You know it inside out. You've been up to your elbows in it, up to your oxters; you were there all along. So you know what it is, and what it should be seen to be.'

He nods. He knows. He knows. Of course he knows.

'What will you do?' Joyce asks him suddenly.

He pauses, caught off guard. 'Drive an ambulance, I rather thought.'

'They'll have you, will they?'

'I'll have to look into it.'

'Ah well, yes,' Joyce says. 'Well, of course, you see, yu young.'

He nods. He swills the wine that the other man has chosen, and lets the other man talk, and does not speak any of the sentences that clot and collapse and disperse inside his head.

They make their way back just a shade before ten. It's a damp, still night, and it's difficult in the blue underwater light, and at the corner Joyce hesitates; he feels his way forward with his stick.

'Filthy night.'

'It is indeed. Here.'

He offers his arm. The older man turns his head blindly.

'My arm . . .' he offers again.

He guides him down off the pavement; they cross the cobbles together. He curtails his stride.

'Here's the kerb,' he says.

'And here's the steeple.'

The two of them push into the lobby of the Joyces' apartment building. It is brighter there, a small gas mantle glows. They make their farewells, Good night, God bless, all the old reflexes. Joyce taps across to the lift, his good coat draping warm around him, his hat tamped neatly into place, doing a fair approximation of sobriety. Half-cut, the rush of love for him is overpowering. That James Joyce would consider his company acceptable, when he himself can hardly bear it.

57

...d pulls the cage across. But before
..., and I have a little something for

... round.'

...m is gone, hauled up through the dark
storeys o... building towards the apartment stacked with
boxes, with dust rings on the sideboard from where the ornaments are gone. He is left alone, on the bright-tiled lobby
floor, in the cold. Nora will be cross. And she'll consider him
responsible for her husband's absconding and his state on his
return. As though he had bought the wine and held the gentleman's nose and poured it in.

He pulls his jacket collar up and shoves his way out again.
The night streams past him, is wet in his face. He leans into
it, as if there's a wind blowing, though the air is perfectly
still. He is drunk, of course; he has no papers, his friends are
leaving left and right; Paris is deserted; he is no use to anyone at all. He feels, for once, and only briefly, quite
content.

The Joyces depart Paris finally at Christmas time. In the
breathy quiet of the platform, beside a stationary steam
train, he shakes hands with the son Giorgio and the father
James, accepts also Nora's forgiving kiss: sometimes he is
held to blame for her husband's delinquency and sometimes
he is not, but while Mr Joyce is on his best behaviour then he,
too, can hope to be approved. He hands her in; she moves

stiffly, troubled by her joints. He can still be useful to them, that much is clear: he can lift cases into the carriage; he can offer a hand to the man himself.

'Come and see us,' James Joyce says. 'At Saint-Gérand-le-Puy. Come and see us in the spring.'

'Thank you.' It's at once a pleasure and an anticipated awkwardness.

The older man nods, settles himself, legs crossed, toe tucked under instep, hands folded on the head of his cane. 'Well then,' he says. 'Until the spring.'

All the warmth and gratitude, all the unease and discomfort. And of course he just says, 'Until the spring,' and shakes Shem's hand, and then Nora's, then clambers down from the carriage.

Alone on the platform, he kicks his heels and looks off down the train in the direction of their going.

And then there is the engine's sigh, the greased shift of pistons and the slow haul into movement, and the train is leaving. It is peeling past, and it takes with it all of those entanglements, and that real and honest awkward love.

He walks through the Gare d'Austerlitz and out into the low sun. As he makes his way home through the streets, the sunlight is sharp between buildings, the blue shadow sliced into wedges. The city seems more stark, more sharply angled, the sky more distant. It seems more beautiful, if that were possible. It seems more dangerous, and more prone to harm.

A bitter bright cold day. The lift is out of order and the seven flights leave her out of puff. Suzanne lets herself in, closes the door behind her and eases off her shoes. Her nose is cold, her hands are frozen. She's already fumbling in her shopping bag, drawing out a little crocheted rug.

'Darling . . .'

He needs his peace, his privacy. But he also needs to be taken care of, since he can't be trusted to do it himself. He can put this over his knees as he works; it'll keep him warm while he is writing.

'Are you there?'

She has spent a good deal of time on it. There is, as her mother would say, a lot of love gone into that rug.

'I have a present for you.'

There's no reply. She stands, silent, listening to the empty apartment. Disappointed, she lays the rug over the arm of the settee, smoothing out the crocheted squares.

He has left his notebook lying on the table. She stands looking at it.

He will be back at any moment. She'll make some coffee. She'll give him the rug. They will have some time together, and she will leave him to get on with his work.

She stands looking at the notebook. She doesn't go to the kitchen. She moves closer to the table and touches the book; she lifts it. Her whole body's alert for a foot on the stair, the creak of a board, the shift in sound as the main door opens from the street below, any hint of his return.

It has never been forbidden, that she look at his work. But then, it shouldn't need to be forbidden.

She opens it.

The pages separate on a mess; they're thick with scribbles, scratchings-out.

Her skin bristles in unease.

She leafs back through to see what came before. The notebook is three-quarters full; the completed pages are densely covered. But every clear French phrase that has been achieved is barricaded all around by crossings-out and scribblings. He has filled pages, he has written his pen dry and refilled it, he has covered sheets and sheets, but very little is let stand. It seems that all that has been achieved here is the consumption of paper, ink and time.

Baffled, she frowns down at the mess of it.

The hours they'd spent in cafés, he and his friend Alfred, before Alfred joined up, going over this. And now the hours alone. And this is all there is to show for it.

She turns another page. On the verso, he has drawn a little picture of Charlot, the tramp with his bowler hat coming down over his eyes, his toothbrush moustache like Adolf the peacemaker's, his sagging trousers, his splayed feet in broken boots. What does he think he is doing? Why can't he simply write? Why can't he just get on with it?

And then there's a yell – from outside, in the street. She drops the book and turns to the window, peers down at a scuffle. Is that him? He doesn't have his papers, oh my God, they'll lock him up.

And then she sees the ball.

Just a kickabout in the street. Her fear contracts. A bad-tempered game, all elbows and shoving. The ball is sent

61

spinning crosswise on to the pavement, where Monsieur Lunel shuffles along under his black fedora, his body foreshortened by the angle, and one of the lads runs over and scoops up the ball and apologizes, and another comes up and up and stands too close to the old man, his skinny chest puffed out – she can't hear what he says from up here – and spits upon the ground. Then his mate shoves him, and there's another scuffle, and the ball bounces off the cobbles, and they chase after it, and Monsieur Lunel, after standing frozen for a moment, shuffles on.

This is what they don't see, the Amerloques and the Irlandais, the writers and the artists and the wives who come here for the cheap living and the cheap wine and the distance from their mothers, all his fly-by-night friends. They skate over the shining surface; they don't see the murk beneath.

She peels her forehead from the window, rubs the mark with a sleeve and turns away. She sees the notebook lying there on the tabletop. How exactly had he left it?

She meets him at the door and gives him quick kisses, one cheek and then the other. He has brought a parcel home with him; he drops it on the settee. She hands him a cup, laughs at herself – a tussle in the street, I thought they were arresting you! She shows him the rug that she made for him, though it has already lost half its loveliness: she had thought that they were both, in their own ways, working on the same thing. On his success.

'What's in the parcel?' she asks.

He touches the rug, pressing a little moss-coloured square of wool with his fingertips. 'This is very nice. Thank you.'

He takes the parcel over to the table and lays it down to open it. 'It was left with the concierge.' She sees him notice the notebook. 'Have you been here long?' he asks.

'No,' she says, a shade too quickly. 'Not long. What's in the parcel?' she asks again.

'Soon find out.'

He opens a drawer and slides the notebook in. Then he turns the package over so that he can get at the knots. The bundle is soft and bulky and he has already noted Nora's girlish handwriting, but he can't make sense of it at all. He undoes the knot, tugs the string away and unfurls the waxy paper. Inside there is a bolt of dark twill. He still can't make sense of it. And then he sees. He lifts it out. It is a coat.

'A coat,' she says.

It brings with it a cloud of scent: pomade, cheroot smoke and lemon soap. A cloud of associations, of time dispensed in cafés and books and drink, the gut-punch of guilt about Lucia. A note tumbles from the folds and lands on the floor. He stoops for it and peers, holding it close up to his face to read. This from the man himself.

'Who's it from?'

'Mr Joyce.'

For all of everything, this is what he's worth. He gets to wear the great man's cast-off coat.

'Oh,' she says. 'Well. That's handy.'

He folds the coat and lays it in the paper, and fumbles it all back together again. He sits down. He takes out pen and paper.

'What are you doing?'

63

'A thank-you note.'

'Ah.'

His hand flicks across, leaving loops and curls of blue behind it, then whisking down to traverse the page again. The white swiftly fills with clean blue. Her lips bunch and twist. She turns and moves away to the little kitchenette, where she rummages irritably in the cupboards, drags out tins and packets, shoves them back. She feels as though she has been taken for a fool.

4

L'Exode
June 1940

ANXIETY MAKES THE air thick; the urgency is a dream urgency, where there is a desperate need to run and yet the limbs are heavy and entangled. The earth shudders when the bombs hit. The sky is greasy with smoke.

The ticket officer doesn't look up. 'Where do you want to go?'

They've been queuing for hours; they're footsore and twitchy to be gone. He has two bags and she has her backpack. Trains have arrived with their plumes of steam and they've left with their plumes of steam, and the concourse remains congested still, suitcases drawn into little settlements with joggled babies and fractious kids and tired old women, and the queue weaves round and through it all, a ragged line of anxious faces and sweated-through summer clothes; it has been skin-crawlingly slow progress to get even as far as the ticket desk. It has been an age. And not once in all that age did it occur to him that this might come up. The only thought so far has been *Away*.

'There's a choice?'

The ticket officer looks up now. 'Well, no. But people tend to say, and then I tell them what I can give them.' The fellow glances past them at the never-ending queue. 'It's usually over quite briskly.'

Suzanne huffs in irritation. He touches her arm. 'So, what can you give us?'

'There's a train for Vichy in a couple of hours.'

'Vichy . . .' He turns to Suzanne. She nods, whisks a hand to hurry things along. The old spa town will do; anywhere will do; anywhere away from here.

'It's a four-hour journey, under normal circumstances,' the ticket officer says. 'But these aren't normal circumstances.'

A thought leaps up: Joyce is now at Vichy. They'd shifted there from Saint-Gérand-le-Puy; there was a postcard from a hotel, the Hotel . . . Beaujolais. Maybe they could get a room there themselves. So they'll go to Vichy and they'll see Joyce, and it's a feeling something like home. A little landslip of images: white wine and talk, and together they're leaning over a copy of the *Wake*, and he is reading out the commas and the full stops while Shem frowns and nods and determines what corrections must be made. He can swallow down his chagrin about the coat; he can swallow it down like a gannet. The war will blunder past their windows and bowl along the high street and they'll barely notice that it's happening at all.

'Vichy it is, then.'

While the tickets are torn, he counts out his francs. Their little store of money is dwindling at an alarming rate. He tries to gulp the worry down along with the shame, but it twists and flicks and shivers inside, very much alive.

'What will we do in Vichy?' Suzanne asks. They weave through the crowds, lugging their bags, in the hope of finding a quiet corner to settle down and wait.

'Work out what to do next,' he says.

The train doors are slammed open; there's a surge forward through the ticket barrier and down on to the platform. The two of them are pushed along with it. He wants to stand back, to let people in ahead, to wait for the crowds to clear. Good manners are worn deep into the grain. And yet a more atavistic edge shoulders forward too – *me, I, need* – and he is pushing ahead, his heart beating faster, his body seething with adrenalin. Guards yell and bellow and are ignored. Children cry. Suzanne falls behind, dragged away by her backpack in the crush as though she is being pulled out to sea. And there is also *we,* also *us.*

'Come on—'

He reaches for her and she grabs his hand and hers is small and sweaty, and he pulls her up to join him, and they are at the dirty flank of the train, just a yard from an open door. He shoves forward, hindered and frustrated by the bodies ahead of him, the crush that moves into any space behind, the grimed hat and greased hair of the man in front, the solid flesh and the smell of it all. He glances back at

Suzanne; strangers' shoulders press between him and her. She is struggling on, scowling at the nuisance of it all.

'Are you all right?'

She nods, grim. Their hands are clamped tight together between the flanks of others, their fingers intermeshed. His hand stretching back to hers, he steps on to the first tread up into the carriage and drags her with him, insistent.

'Excuse me,' she says, pushing through.

Face tight against the knapsack of the man in front, he gets up the second step and she heaves herself out of the crush to climb up behind him. They are on board.

They are lucky. The concourse is still full. The station doors are bolted. The grilles are locked down; the ticket clerks are gone and the offices are shut. And behind the closed gates and grilles and doors, there are people still waiting, still hoping: once the crowd inside has cleared, perhaps the station doors will be unlocked again, perhaps the Gare de Lyon will reopen and they too can make their way out of the threatened city and go wherever it is still possible to go.

The train is an adder, barely warmed by the early sun; it moves by inches, eighths, sixteenths. It hardly moves at all.

A layer of smoke hangs over the city; it rises in plumes here and there, sickly-looking and unsettling.

'Do you think that's an air defence, to screen the people as they leave?'

'Maybe. Or they're bonfires.'

'Why would they have bonfires?'

'To be rid of stuff they wouldn't want the enemy to get their hands on.'

They sit shoulder-to-shoulder on the hard wooden bench. There are passengers packed, standing, down the length of the corridor. He chews his nails when he isn't smoking; when he isn't chewing his nails he smokes. She stares out of the window, her hands in her lap, knees sloped together; his long legs are tucked uncomfortably in. His two bags are wedged behind his heels; her overstuffed backpack is on her lap.

The train creeps past streets; it begins to pick up a little speed. Passengers strike up conversations. Children chatter, swing their feet. A road swerves towards the line and for a moment the two run side by side. The road is a rubbish dump, a mound of junk and clutter. But then it separates itself into movement, individuals, men and women trudging burdened like ants; into cars, donkeys, handcarts, prams, horses, suitcases, bicycles, frying pans and mattresses, birds in cages, briefcases. A child lugging a baby. An old woman in a pram, legs dangling, pushed by an old man who squints in the bright June sun. His eyes catch on the woman's white, sharp face above the bundled body. The train pulls past the two, the old woman and the old man scraping along together, and then a fence ticks past, breaking up the image like an old zoetrope, and he closes his eyes, and reaches in behind his spectacles to press on them.

When he looks again, a brick wall ghosts alongside and Suzanne's head is resting against the window; her eyes are closed and she is breathing softly and asleep. He is glad that she's asleep. He feels as though he could never sleep again.

When Suzanne wakes, they are out in the countryside and the train has picked up speed. He sits glaring out of the window, across the copses, the wide planes of farmland, at the dotted villages and church spires.

'What is it?' she asks.

'The people.'

'What people?'

He nods across the open land, towards the main road south. The way is packed still, cars nudging along, edging past the pedestrians and pony carts.

'Name of God,' she says. 'That must be the whole of Paris.'

He says, 'Yes. And . . .'

'What?' She glances round at him,

'And, I think, the army,' he says.

'What?'

'I think I saw uniforms. Before.' He raises his shoulders. His sight is not that good. 'I can't be sure.'

Her face goes still. She turns back to the window. The train skims across a bridge over the road. And then she sees them too. It's just a moment, and then the train is past and they're gone. But a pocket of infantry was slumped on the verge, filthy and unkempt, legs stretched out in front of them in the long summer grass.

'But no,' she says. 'What are they doing?'

'You see them?'

She nods.

70

'It must be a rout.'

She sits back, swallows. After a moment: 'Maybe there won't be so much fighting in Paris. If they are running away.'

'That's one way of thinking about it.'

'Hmm.'

'But the other way is, with the army there, that makes everyone a target.'

'You think they'll come?'

She turns her gaze up; she searches the sky. The sky remains, for the time being, innocent and clear blue.

The train stops unpredictably, and in awkward places. Time ticks by, and people murmur, and children cry.

They are marooned. An hour; an hour and a half. Her stomach rumbles, and she folds her arms over it. The sun glares on them. Her face is pale and sweaty.

'If we were at a station,' someone says, 'we could nip out and buy some bread.'

Further up the train, someone thumps open a carriage door and climbs down on to the track. She watches the dark figure pick his way across to the embankment, then stand there at the edge of the grass. It takes her a moment to realize that he's pissing, and then she looks away. Soon others are climbing down from the carriages to stretch their legs and relieve themselves; women share a cigarette, or clamber further up through the long grass and off into the bushes. Children hopscotch from sleeper to sleeper; a toddler blinks sleepily in the daylight as his mother holds him, pants around his ankles, and he puddles the gravel.

And then there is a whistle and a rush and a general rebut-toning and regathering, and a flurry to get back inside.

The train grinds back into motion, and for a while is clip-ping along again, stopping sometimes as other trains whistle past, and sometimes stopping for no obvious reason at all.

Vichy is cursed; leaves and tendrils and blooms and branches have been bewitched into stone and steel, and forced into service as buildings and street furniture. There is clean cold light here; the streets are glistening and chill.

Together they head down one of the main boulevards. Every step becomes a conscious effort, and he feels as though he is tacking and lurching along like a golem. They're being watched – discreetly from café terraces, from the security of linked arms, from behind the defensive barrier of a shopping basket or a yapping dog. Children simply stop and stare. Because Vichy is not used to visitors like these: scruffy, exhausted, travel-worn visitors who flood out of third-class carriages with their belongings bulging from their bags and without the means to make themselves comfortable. Wealth, in Vichy, is as normal as the bubbling warm water; here, nobody carries their own luggage.

One bag slides against his thigh as he walks. *Murphy, Murphy, Murphy.* The other bag drags on his shoulder, stuffed with clothing, shaving gear, tinned food: the body's barest needs make for a heavy load. If he could just be rid of one of the bags; to shed either his manuscript or his belong-ings would be such a relief. But he heaves one strap up his shoulder and hooks a thumb under the other, and drags himself along. Suzanne, craned forward by the weight of her backpack, trudges beside him, silent. They carry on, past the *tabac* on the corner and the pharmacy with its display of Vichy pastilles, the tins piled in a pyramid, and past the milliner's shop where the hats are ranged like dead birds in a cabinet.

'The Hotel Beaujolais,' he says. 'It's on this street, it can't be far.'

She nods. Mr Joyce, it turns out, will be here. She hadn't known that Vichy would also mean Joyce, would also mean hard drinking and unhappiness. Whatever he might think, Joyce is not what he needs.

There is, thank goodness, a room remaining at the Hotel Beaujolais. Suzanne lets her backpack slide from her shoulder and hit the floor.

Dark panelling, cool tiles: a couple of comfortable-looking armchairs. He is desperate for news, but the only paper is a folded copy of *Action Française* and he's not going to stoop to that. Though it needn't mean anything about this place – anybody could have left it there. For the moment at least, they must assume that this is a decent establishment.

And then the receptionist mentions the price of the room. 'Ah.'

The receptionist's expression – he is a pale fellow with a neat moustache and clear skin – remains neutral, but then the cost is neither here nor there to him.

'You have nothing less . . . expensive?'

A minor shrug. 'No, Monsieur.'

Because at whatever price they're charging for a broom cupboard nowadays, there'll be no difficulty in filling it, with Paris emptying itself out like a toppled-over bucket. Vichy can afford not to be cheap. They'll have to keep on going, find somewhere more suited to their finances; the Joyces' hotel was always likely to be too grand for them. He glances round at Suzanne, who has left her backpack on the floor where it fell. She is grey with fatigue.

'Problem?' she asks.

'No,' he says. 'It's fine.'

And so, definitively, he prints his name on the page and signs, committing himself to a sum that he really can't afford.

'Monsieur and Madame Joyce are staying here, I believe?' he asks, and clears his throat.

'There is a gentleman and lady of that name, yes.'

He thanks the receptionist, and hates him. He takes the key and turns to lift Suzanne's backpack, brushing off her protests, which are hardly meant. There are too many stairs; they just keep on going up and up until they reach a narrow landing, a corridor and a small dark door, where the number matches the number on their key. Inside, he drops their bags and the two of them fall on to the bed. It sinks beneath them, springs creaking. They lie there, parallel, feet trailing to the floor.

'Are you hungry?' she asks, a little later.

'I am, yes.'

'I'll get those biscuits,' she says. But she doesn't move. After a while, he sits up, strips the laces from his boots and toes them off, wincing. Then he unties her shoes for her too, and eases them from her feet and rolls down her stockings for her. Her toes are patched with red, her ankles swollen.

'Put your feet up,' he says.

She heaves herself round with a grunt and falls back on the pillow. He winces his way around the bed and lies down properly beside her. The shutters are closed. His eyelids are heavy. He thinks, I will just rest my eyes for a moment, but the next moment it is tomorrow.

He is returning from the bank. Where they will not cash a cheque – not his cheque anyway, not on an Irish bank. The hotel won't take them either. He doesn't know what he's going to tell Suzanne. On a whim he ducks into a *boulangerie* and buys brioche, the smell making his stomach clench tight like a clam. This is money that should be used to pay for the room, but he doesn't have enough to pay for the room and so it hardly seems to matter if he dispenses what little he has in dribs and drabs. Food. Shelter. Money. Shelter. Food. Money. It is all so simple and yet so unresolvable, and he is frowning over it, as though there were some obvious solution that he had missed, when his gaze snags on a dark figure across the street. He pushes his specs up, peers, and his face softens. There he is. The man himself. The crowds part around his strangeness as he fumbles along with his stick and glasses, oblivious and uncanny and sharp as you like.

He lopes across the avenue to him, up on to the far pavement, addresses him in English. 'Mr Joyce, sir.' He reaches out a hand, stops short of touching the sleeve. 'Good morning to you.'

The head goes up, searching. The eyes are concealed by his dark glasses. He tilts his head.

'My word,' Joyce says. 'Is it yourself?'

He says, 'It seems so.'

'Ha! At last, thanks be to God, somebody to talk to.'

'Have you had any news, sir, from Paris?'

'No, no. Not a word. No one tells me anything.'

Joyce gropes forward with his stick; he turns his head to catch what he can in what's left of his sight.

'Is that a dog?' – and an old hand fumbles into a pocket.

It's a fluffy, perky little thing going by on a lead, tail up, arsehole on show, totally oblivious to the pair of them.

'Yes.'

Joyce has brought out a handful of stones, is picking through them with dry fingertips. 'Where is it?'

'Gone,' he says, perturbed.

The old hand closes, slides back into the pocket. 'Filthy creatures. They have no souls, you know.'

'Is that so?'

'They run loose all over the village. That place where we were staying. *Saint Machin Truc*. They bark at me.'

'Do they?'

He watches Joyce quite openly, knowing that he is not himself observed. It has been, what, six months since he saw him last? But it looks as though as many years have passed for the older man. Shem has stepped over a threshold, is suddenly old. He is crumpled-looking, his hair slick with pomade, but the white now shines through. His skin is slumped; he

76

looks as though he's wearing a mask of himself, of his own skin. The rings roll loose around his fingers.

'How are you, though?' he asks.

A shake of the head, a sigh, and then there falls a cascade of words. 'I don't know what we are coming to, I really don't. All the books I want are still at the apartment in Paris, and I can't get hold of anything I want down here. People say that they'll send me books, but no one ever really sends me books, or not the right ones. Madame Jolas is pestering us to come back to the village, where we are safe, but you know what country life is. Anything is preferable to that, there's no one to talk to, and the flat's so small you couldn't kill a cat in it—' A pause, a moment. 'Vichy is a hole, but it is not as deep a hole as Saint-Gérand-le-Puy. I'm very glad, you know, that you have come. You will be an asset.'

To be noticed like this has its brief effect; it makes him more real, it makes him mean something. But the talk goes on and on as Joyce continues with his litany of complaint, and it need not really be him at all that hears it: the lack of notice of his *Wake*, the pointlessness of this war, the failure of others to see what is really necessary and important, Nora's impatience, Lucia's distractedness, Giorgio's absences – the Lord knows what he is up to. Family concerns, family, family, family.

He nods. Of course. Family is what matters most at times like these.

But family is his mother sitting alone in the house by the harbour, watching the sea wind tear across the water and the cemetery and her husband's grave. Family is Frank squinting out across the golf course, or hunched over his desk, doing capable things with account books and a slide rule. Is Mollie and Sheila, the tousled girls; is dispersed through Ireland, Wales and England and the Lord knows where. And he can't go back to that, to family, because there is nowhere to go.

'Did you ever drive that ambulance?' Joyce asks.

'We were somewhat overtaken by events.'

At the hotel, they part with a handshake and a promise to meet later; they will go out for a drink.

And then, the thin old mouth parting on false teeth: 'It'll be just like old times, eh?'

He leaves Joyce waiting for Nora in the lobby and climbs the heavy stairs. Joyce exerts such a deliberate gravity; he draws one in, he buffers one away. One's kept in orbit, circling.

He is woken by a rapping on the door. Suzanne sits up. Her face is lined by the pillow. He stumbles off the bed. In the doorway there's a red-faced boy in livery, confusing just by being there, and then by being apologetic and in too much of a hurry to make sense.

'What? Sorry? Say that again.'

The boy redelivers his lines. He's an unconvincing actor, distracted by what's going on offstage. This is only one of many times today that he will have to blunder through this speech.

'What?' Suzanne says, shaking her head to clear it. 'What is he saying?'

'The manager apologizes, we understand that this must be very inconvenient, but we are unable to continue to provide accommodation for you here.'

'What?'

'You must vacate the hotel in the morning.'

'But we've only just arrived.'

The boy looks off down the corridor. 'It can't be helped. It's out of our hands. Government orders.'

'I don't understand.'

'Paris has fallen,' the boy says, a little too loudly and quickly. Then he pauses, straightens his shoulders, clears his throat. 'Paris has fallen, and so the government is to move here. They are to take over the hotel. All the hotels.' Though the boy holds himself straight, his young eyes are brimming.

'If you would settle your bill in the morning, sir, and then vacate the premises.'

He doesn't move.

The boy gives a little bow, and then turns abruptly and marches a few steps down the corridor, to the next room along.

He closes the door. He can hear the boy, the conversation he's now having with the other guests, which follows much the same pattern as their own. The rumble of the man's voice, the higher pitch of the boy's. His lines sound surer now; by the end of the day he might even have convinced himself.

Suzanne says, 'What shall we do?'

He says nothing. He still faces the door, his head bent. His hands in his pocket, he runs the coins through his fingers and his mouth twists.

'But what shall we do?' Suzanne asks. 'Where shall we go?'

He still stands there, his gaze on the wood panels and brass fittings. If he could just stop. Give up. Have done with it all.

Suzanne lets go a long slow breath. He hears the springs creak as she heaves herself to her feet. 'I'd better pack.' But then she doesn't move any further; after all, there's hardly any packing to be done.

He turns back to the room. He fishes up his boots and sits to drag them on.

'Where are you going?' she asks.

'Have to sort something out,' he says. 'I'll be back soon.'

It's the act of a child, he knows it is; he's reaching up to tug a sleeve, to slip a sticky little hand into his father's hand.

Joyce, gaunt, his dark glasses on, rests his paws on the head of his cane, and turns to stare blankly for a waiter, and seems more in need of help than able to provide it. The Joyces, just like everybody else currently lodged in the hotels of Vichy, must move on. They must go back to the village, to village life, however unwelcome that must be. They do, though, have somewhere to go, and that is something.

'Get the boy's attention, would you?'

When the waiter comes over, Joyce orders a *pichet* of the local white, and taps his fingers till it arrives. When it does he takes a mouthful, winces, then takes another sip.

'The old stomach trouble,' he says.

'You have had another attack?'

He tilts his head. 'More a war of attrition. I find that white wine helps. That and Pernod; both are good.'

'Ah.'

'It's my nerves,' he says. 'It's just a nervous disorder. I've had several doctors agree on that.'

He murmurs sympathy, but can only think how much he doesn't want to ask what he has to ask.

'Well, it seems that we're to be off,' Joyce says. 'And in short order. So that's that. No wonder my nerves are playing merry hell, faced with a return to that backwater.'

To the village where the dogs are not on leashes and they bark at the strange old blind man fumbling his way down the street, muttering to himself because there is nobody to talk to and throwing stones.

He wants to offer rather than ask. He wants to say, I'll help you. I'll come with you to Saint-Thingummy-Bob and spend the days correcting the whole of the *Wake* again for you. I'll read out every comma, dash and full stop and you can sit and consider each and every one of them for days, and drink white wine, and think, and change your mind, and change it back again, and there will be time enough and more for all of it; that would be a life well spent, filling your glass, playing the piano or listening to you play and sing; throwing stones at dogs on your behalf.

'Then I suppose we shall try for Switzerland,' Joyce says.

'Ah, yes.'

Then the words come falling out of the old thin lips: 'I think that's the only choice that we have left now, because

Switzerland was kind to us before, in the last war. Lucia could come to us there, the best treatment she could hope for is in Switzerland. And Giorgio would be out of the way of conscription. And whatever he is up to in Paris.'

'Good,' he says.

The old man drinks. His Adam's apple rolls down and up, re-arranging the soft folds of his throat.

'I hope you won't mind me asking . . .' he tries now.

The black glasses are shiny; they kick off light. He is being considered, head tilted. Peered at in peripheral vision.

'We are . . .' he says, and clears his throat. The words are burrs, difficult to shift. 'We find ourselves in some difficulty. It transpires my cheques are not acceptable here, and we are running very low on cash.'

'I don't have any money,' Joyce says.

He swallows. 'No, of course.'

'I have my family to think of, you know. Expenses.'

'I understand.'

He just wants this to be over. The embarrassment is acute. He'll feel it for ever.

'Getting all of us to Switzerland will leave me overstretched.'

'Oh yes, indeed. Well, we shall manage . . .' Though he has no idea how. He scoops up his cigarettes, straightens his jacket, his face hot. What will he say to Suzanne?

Joyce turns his head, birdlike. 'You'll wear it out,' he says.

'What?'

'Love.'

'Love?'

'What's left at the end, it's threadbare, you can see right through it.'

The older man lifts his glass again, and his throat spasms as he drinks. He, though, leans away from the table and the glasses. He watches, suddenly clear, wondering how it happened. That the old man should be so diminished. That his gaze should have become so narrow. His skin comes out in gooseflesh as old Shem talks on, about the seat of love and where it lies, rather lower than the heart, and the failure of it always in the end, how it leaves him in disgust even to hear talk of it.

Shem is not what he was; he is not what he achieved. How could he be?

'Well,' he says eventually, 'I had better go.'

'Eh?' Joyce raises his head. 'Yes. I suppose so. So many departures, after all.'

He reaches into his pocket for coins that he can't afford to part with. He feels light and empty and one step away from himself, almost elated. This sense of loss, the openness that is offered by it. He has not even been abandoned; he was never held that dear. The world is different and brilliant and empty.

Joyce drains his drink, and then sets his glass down and nods quietly, agreeing with his own thoughts.

He counts out his weightless coins.

'D'you know Larbaud?' Joyce says, out of nowhere.

He blinks. 'Valéry Larbaud, the writer?'

'Yes, yes.'

'I know the work,' he says, nonplussed.

'Get the boy's attention, would you? We must have another *pichet*.'

'Oh, I'm not, no.'

'Nonsense, I insist.'

So he turns in his seat, catches an eye and gestures for more wine, while Joyce talks on.

'Larbaud's an old friend of mine; he lives round here. You should go and see him. He might be able to help you out.'

'Do you think?'

A nod. 'Larbaud is on the side of the angels. And he's rich. Which is only sensible, if you must be a writer.'

A hand-me-down coat, a favour done by proxy. He drains his glass, and humiliation rinses through him, and it is cleansing.

'Yes, good,' Joyce says. 'I'm glad I could be of help.'

Madame Larbaud greets him at the door; she is courteous, with a quietness about her that doesn't invite conversation. This is welcome.

The house is dim and cool and lovely. She leads him through the lobby and the scent of lilacs and the sound of trickling water – in Vichy there is always water – and it is as much as he can do to put one foot in front of the other.

He carries a letter of introduction in his breast pocket, addressed in Joyce's own hand. It lies there like a plaque over his heart. He doesn't know what the letter says and he doesn't want to know. The experience is mortifying enough already.

Her heels click along the floor; his leathered tread is softer on the tiles.

'You know, I imagine,' Madame Larbaud says, 'about Monsieur Larbaud's state of health?'

'I understand that he has not been well.'

'You know that he cannot speak?'

He did not. 'I'm sorry.'

She pauses at the door, a hand on the glossy wooden panel, as though she is going to say something more, but then thinks better of it. She pushes the door open.

The wheelchair is placed in a shaft of light from the French windows; Larbaud is reading, the book flat on his lap, his left hand holding it open. Madame crosses the room to her husband. She touches his hand, lifts the book from his lap and moves round to stand behind him. Larbaud lifts his left hand to the newcomer to be shaken.

The hand is cold and soft in his; Larbaud's eyes are heavy-lidded, his face half-fallen.

'It is kind of you to see me, Monsieur Larbaud.' His hand feels strange with the softness he had gripped. He fumbles in his jacket and produces the letter. His face burns. 'This is from our mutual friend, Mr James Joyce.'

Larbaud does not smile, is perhaps unable to smile, but his face somehow lightens. The letter is suspended there between them, hanging from his fingertips. The seated man doesn't move to take it – he can't, of course. Awkward, he moves closer, but then instead Madame darts forward, relieves him of the letter, opens it, retrieves spectacles from a pocket, helps her husband on with them. Her silence is a kindness; it softens her husband's, makes it less stark. She hands Larbaud the unfolded sheet; he holds it left-handed;

85

he peers through thick lenses, while she looks off and away, leaving him to read privately.

Larbaud's expression as he reads is itself unreadable behind those shining lenses. He turns away too, towards the high windows, and endures the silence and the shame. The husband passes the letter up again to his wife's smooth hands. There's a look, a touch between them. She glances over the letter. She murmurs a few words to Larbaud and he nods. Then she refolds the paper and slips it back into its envelope as she moves over to his desk.

'We should like to help you.'

He swallows. 'Thank you.'

'How much do you need? Not just to resolve your current troubles, but to see you on to wherever you are going?'

He shakes his head, not in negation, but because he has no answer for her. It's a calculation that he cannot make, and a gratitude that is beyond articulation.

The money is a thick pad in his breast pocket. His throat is thick too, as he goes with her down the hallway. Their footsteps syncopate.

She opens the door for him. She smiles.

'Thank you,' he says again. The words are entirely insufficient, but they are all he has.

'It's a little thing,' she says.

It is not a little thing at all. 'I shall return the money to you as soon as possible.'

'Well, don't make things difficult for yourself.' And then she says, 'Good luck to you, Monsieur, and good courage.'

She closes the door on him; he catches a glimpse of her face as it turns away, back to that closed room, and the silent man in the wheelchair, and the wordlessness.

Don't make things difficult for yourself.

He stands there in the blue evening. He lets a breath go. They are saved. For the time being.

He lights up a cigarette and sets off back through the cool residential streets. A proper meal, he realizes, is now possible. He peers in through café windows as he passes, at the neatly laid tables, at the soft old ladies already poking at their salads there. He and Suzanne will find a nice little place; they'll have dinner tonight. They'll sleep in a decent bed, and then tomorrow set out again, into whatever follows. They'll head for – well, for the coast, for Arcachon, if that is possible, if Suzanne is willing to give it a try. They have, after all, an invitation there. And underneath everything is a taint of unease. He is ashamed, he does not deserve; why him, why should he be saved?

On the wider roads and avenues there are carts and cabs lining up along the pavements. The lobby of the Beaujolais is filled with piled bags and trunks, with anxious, tired women settling their bills, with drooping children, and old men monopolizing the chairs.

And you must come and see us there, at Arcachon. It will be a long summer if you do not come.

But the station at Vichy is closed to passengers; it is rammed with government traffic and only official travellers are allowed through. If they are heading west, to the coast, they should try one of the stations further down the line. Gannat, say; that's probably their best bet.

'Is there a bus to Gannat?'

A blowing-out of the lips, a shake of the head: who's to say?

And so they walk. Bags on back, on shoulder and on hip. Through the town, and then the suburbs, and then out of Vichy itself, the mountains rising fat and green ahead of them, the streams bumbling under ancient stone arches below.

'How far now?'

'A little less far than when you asked before.'

The day is soft and cool and there is a springtime feel to it, and there are people strung out in little clots all along the road, as though they were setting out on a pilgrimage. Little traffic passes: the odd truck, the occasional Citroën, a farm cart. It's not too bad for now: he and Suzanne are rested, fed, and that's something. But they are right in the middle of France; this is the core, the omphalos. They must cross half of France again to reach the sea.

'Not that we'll be walking all that way,' she says out loud.

'No,' he says. 'We'll get on a train. At Gannat. The man said.'

She nods; she watches the mountains for a moment, the birds circling in the updraught. Then her eyes are on the curve in the road ahead, and then down at her feet, swinging out, one after the other. Somewhere, a bird is singing. She doesn't know what kind of bird.

It's all right for now; maybe it will continue to be all right.

'But then,' she says, 'you know what the trains are like.'

*

This train stops altogether at Cahors. And there is nothing to be done but to descend, stiff and gritty with fatigue, and follow the stream of crumpled passengers out into damp air. The station guard points them along to the reception centre – beds lined up in the hall, hot soup. But they can't go there, not without the proper papers: if someone asks and he can't produce them, he could be arrested. So they nod and say thank-you, and she takes his arm, and they peel away, off into the dark.

The rain keeps the streets quiet, makes them conspicuous. No one stays out in rain like this unless they really can't help it. He turns his collar up, winces as the water runs down his neck. She tugs at her bag strap. He offers her an arm. She shakes her head. It will just press the wet through to their skin.

The rain knocks the blossom from the trees and the pavement becomes slick and treacherous with petals. Their feet squelch inside their shoes. At the first hotel, the lobby is warm with gaslight. Unhappily, the receptionist informs them, the last room has just been let: she was just about to turn the sign over. They are directed on to a guest house, where the board is already up in a window. *No Vacancies*.

'I'm tired,' she says.

'I know.'

'I'd settle for a stable now. A shed.'

But no star, no kings, no virgin birth. He takes his glasses off and rubs the lenses on a sleeve. They're still too wet to wear, so he pockets them, presses his tired eyes. But that's when she staggers, sways. He reaches out to steady her.

'All right?'

She nods.

Her face, though, is white and running with water, and her eyes close in a slow blink. She would be safe, if it were not for him; she would at least be safer; she would be holed up in the countryside with her mother. She would be staying with a friend. Even now she could be tucked up in a reception centre. There's nothing wrong with her papers.

'Come on,' he says. He hauls her upright. 'There'll be something round the next corner . . .' Even if it is just slick pavements, bolted doors.

They carry on. It's getting dark; the rain continues. They are in narrower, winding streets, which circle in upon themselves, repeating and changing like a melody, at once familiar and different. A thin wind throws the rain right into their faces; their eyes sting. The church looms above them. The street curves away in both directions, a commercial street with all the commerce done and everything locked up and shuttered for the night. Have they been this way before? Are they walking round in circles? Would it even matter if they were, since there is nowhere to go but on? Then Suzanne pulls away from him and stumbles off across the wet cobblestones.

'What—?' he follows her.

She sinks down on a public bench.

And now they've stopped. Somewhere a clock chimes ten. He stands beside her, puts a hand on her shoulder. The wool is cold and wet. She leans against him like a dog, eyes shutting, half asleep although still upright. His eyes could close too, and then the sting would be less, of water, and the salt that water picks up off the skin. But he doesn't trust himself to close his eyes.

'We can't stop here,' he says.

She nods, her cheek grazing up and down against the cloth of his coat.

'You have to get up. Suzanne. Listen. We have to move on.'

She turns her face up to him, opens her eyes. Her skin is bone-white; her eyes are black.

'Where'll we go?' she asks.

He blinks and looks away. He wipes his face.

'I don't know,' he says, 'but we have to.' And music winds through and out of the tumbling rain, and his head is filled with the brilliant hallucination of song.

> *Vom Abendrot zum Morgenlicht*
> *Ward mancher Kopf zum Greise*
> *Wer glaubt's? Und meiner ward es nicht*
> *Auf dieser ganzen Reise!*

His head feels full and overflowing. It seethes with music and fatigue. Her body leans heavy against his; he feels it through him when she shivers. It is deep and hard, a palsy through her bones.

Terror has wormed its way into his. He wipes his face and the wet is cold with rain and warm with tears. There is another voice now in his head. It cuts through the music, the night and the rain, through everything with its sharp incision:

What possible use do you imagine you would be?

91

'Come on,' he says to Suzanne.

She slowly shakes her head.

'Come on,' he says, and reaches for her arm.

Suzanne mumbles and softly resists his pull. 'I feel quite warm now.'

'No,' he says. 'You can't do that.'

He leans down and wraps his arms around her; he lugs her to her feet. For a moment they sway together. Exhaustion has made them ridiculous: they could be toppled with a push. Soaking, they cling to each other, all legs and arms, like a creature of the moon.

Then they are spotlit. The green fleck in her coat, the cold pink of her throat. He leans away to look at her and she blinks like a baby at him, confused.

Who's watching them?

He scans round. On the far side of the street, above a shop, a window is illuminated. Then a figure looms up against the pane and draws down the blind. Blackout now. They're back in darkness. It turns out nobody's watching them. Nobody's interested in them at all.

'Come on.'

He shifts his grip round her and half carries her across the street, to an unknown door.

They eat, huddled in the upstairs room in front of a low fire. Suzanne's cheeks are hot, and from time to time a deep shiver runs through her. She is capable of nothing beyond the necessities of courtesy. If her eye is caught, she smiles. It's the best that she can do. She is not yet herself, but at least she has the chance now to become herself again.

The window is misted; it runs with drips. They have been found two rush-seated chairs and given cushions. There is a liquorice liqueur in chipped coffee cups that they both sip at compulsively. There is perfect bread and perfect ham. These are extraordinary comforts.

They wear stale-smelling, borrowed sweaters. Their coats steam over chair backs, their shoes are stuffed with newspaper, their socks and stockings hang above the fireplace to dry.

The lady of the house, who is the keeper too of the shop below, asks about what's going on in the north. Paris has fallen, she heard that from the radio, but you can't be certain of what you are told, not the radio, not the newspapers, not any more. They keep telling everybody to stay calm, but why should we be calm? Things must be very bad indeed if people will up and leave their lives behind just like that.

'We don't know any more than you,' he says. 'We left before the Germans got there.'

She widens her eyes, considers this. 'I suppose you'd have had to,' she says, 'or you couldn't have left at all.'

There is no space for them in the flat, the family is already packed in like cigars in a box. They will have to sleep downstairs in the shop. They can borrow blankets.

He watches Suzanne down the narrow stairs; he carries the bundle of bedding. She is doing what she's told without demur, she's uncertain of her footing. She holds tight to the handrail, like an old woman. He is still worried about her.

The shop below sells religious paraphernalia. It is populated with plaster saints. Christ hangs, his ivory flesh crucified over and over again, all around the walls. Sacred hearts flicker in the light of their little candle. This is the *deus ex machina* by which they have been saved.

They huddle down behind the counter, backs to the panelling, the counter-top a narrow ceiling above them. The little shop is riddled with draughts. He fumbles a borrowed blanket over her shoulders, draws the other up over his knees. They sit shivering side by side. There's a steady drip from the blocked guttering and the tumbling rush of water down the street outside. He huffs out the candle and the saints blink out of sight. In the darkness, she huddles closer, her face pressed into the covers. Her voice comes muffled through the blanket.

'It smells of feet.'

'Want me to turn it round?'

She shakes her head.

After a while, she says, 'I'm so cold.'

He fumbles his blanket loose and lays it over her knees too. Stiff, she pulls her blanket out in a wing and slides it behind his shoulder, draping it round him.

'Well,' he says. 'This is not so bad.'

She tuts.

'You'll be missing your lovely bench, then, and the rain?'

He can just about make her out in the light from the street: her white face, beautiful and alien as those plaster saints. He should never have burdened her with him; he should never have let her make herself a part of what he did. Her head sinks down to rest on her knees.

'You see, you've got these great long legs,' she mumbles. 'And mine are only short.'

The warmth gathers between them; their outer edges are still cold. Blinks slow; breath softens. Now and then there is a shiver. In the hallucinatory slip towards sleep, it seems to him that the statues swell and shrink with breath. Blood wells from wounds and drips, drips, drips. And below, on the bare floorboards, human bodies share the almost nothing that they have, and go on living.

5

Arcachon
Summer 1940

T HE WAVES CREEP up and crash on the far side of the rue de la Plage. The breeze is cool from the Atlantic and takes the sting out of the sun. The two men sit on the terrace, under the shade of an awning. Their hands are brown as they reach to lift and shift the veined marble and speckled granite pieces.

It has been – who would deny it? – a beautiful summer, full of ugly news.

Studying the chessboard, a cigarette smouldering between his knuckles, he tries to conjure all the futures he and Marcel Duchamp might summon up between them here. Marcel lifts a piece, and sets it down, and a web of potentiality collapses and falls away to dust: the future refines itself. He follows threads of possibility. He thinks.

Marcel tweaks the brim of his white straw hat low, to shade his eyes. Mary reads on the sunlounger, soft-limbed and tanned, and every so often he hears her sigh and turn a page.

He takes a long drag on his cigarette, and lets the smoke go, and lifts his knight.

When Suzanne joins them, after her swim, all slicked wet hair and lean tan, Mary looks up with a smile and sets her book aside. Drinks are proposed and the game put in abeyance till the following day. The stone figures cast long shadows as the sun sinks, and everything is softened by the Charentais-pink light. They drink and talk and laugh and it is all apparently quite lovely. But it is also a bubble. Everybody knows that it can't last.

'There is Spain, of course; we could go to Spain.'

'Why would you go to Spain?'

'A friend of mine's in the British Consulate there. And it's not far.'

'That's no reason to go anywhere. You don't want to go to Spain. Spain will be shit.'

'Marcel!'

'Sorry. My apologies. The ladies' tender ears, et cetera. But it will be shit. You know it will.'

'You'd need a car to get to Spain.' Mary turns to him, speaks in sudden English.

'Do you think so?'

'Well, it'd be a hell of a walk.'

'Oh, he could walk it,' Suzanne says, and they are back in French. 'He could walk the legs off a mule, you should see him walk, my God.' Suzanne lifts her glass; he looks to her,

97

but she doesn't catch his eye. He has offended her, it seems, but he doesn't quite know how.

'You don't want to go to Spain.' This is Marcel again. 'Bloody fascists.'

Mary's tone is emollient, explanatory: 'I don't think he is suggesting they settle there permanently.'

Marcel tilts his head at this now. 'America?'

'Ireland,' he concedes.

'Ah, you're going home.'

'I wouldn't quite say that.'

Suzanne looks up at him, his heron profile, his shadowed eyes. His spectacles have been tucked carefully away. He turns his head and meets her look with that startling blue gaze.

'What would we do,' Suzanne asks, 'in Ireland?'

He shrugs. 'We'd get by.'

Suzanne looks at him, then down at her glass. She turns it round and round on the tabletop, watching the light caught there, the way it stays put no matter how much she twists the glass. Her cheeks feel hot.

'Better off in America,' Marcel says. 'Ireland won't last. Not after England falls.'

Mary gives him a look.

'I'm telling you. America will be all that's left. Anywhere else will just be more of the same, and it will be shit.'

A bruised silence. Suzanne watches as Marcel drains his glass, and pours himself another drink, and starts talking about New York. He, though, has reverted to wordlessness; she can hear him breathing, and that is all; breathing, thinking, unfathomably thinking. While Marcel goes on: New York is the future; New York is where they should all be heading now; New York will soon be all that's left of Europe.

'I miss Paris,' Mary says lightly.

'You'll always miss Paris.' Marcel lifts his cigarette case from the tabletop. 'From now on, all of us who ever gave a fig for it always will. Paris won't be Paris any more. Paris can never truly be Paris again.'

He, now, leans away from Marcel; he folds his arms, glances over to the chessboard.

'Well, Paris is my home,' Mary says. 'It's where my books are.'

'You can make more books,' Marcel says, over a huff of cigarette smoke. 'You always do.'

There's a silence after this, and it extends just a little too long before Mary speaks again.

'I'll go see what's holding dinner up.'

She gets to her feet and pads off inside the house.

Later, the two of them walk home together along the promenade. She slips her bare arm through his; it is cool silk, and heavy.

'Earlier, what you said about us going to Ireland.'

'Yes.'

'Do you mean it?'

'I dare say.'

'You said you couldn't breathe there, couldn't sleep, you couldn't write.'

He nods.

'But you would go. We would go.'

'If we had to. But, you know, you'd hate it there.'

'You think so?'

There is a long pause, in which their feet crunch along the sandy boards and the wind blows her hair into her eyes. She tucks it back behind her ear, looks at him sidelong, waiting for what might come.

'I'm at a loss, to tell the truth,' he says. 'There's nowhere left to be.'

They walk on, arm in arm, through the summer night and the sound of waves breaking on the shore. The world is ending, and it is exuberantly, ridiculously beautiful.

The year turns, and the shadows lengthen, and they do not go to Ireland, or even Spain. The Atlantic wind blows chill, and Mary and Marcel's arguments heat up. America, Marcel says. America America America. New York. Mary just says Paris, and Home.

But Marcel does not leave, and neither does Mary. Nobody leaves. Nobody goes anywhere at all. The bubble holds, shimmering in the end-of-summer cool.

He, though, at least writes letters; he sends off enquiries and tries to find out what could be done. Replies come from Madrid. He hands one such to Suzanne, watches her face as she sits reading it in the dim little *salle à manger*, where the furniture is too big for the room and must be edged and shuffled round and leaves bruises on the hips and thighs.

She lays the letter down. 'Well. Should we?'

'I think so. Probably we should.'

She considers the letter again, the official stamp, the friendly-but-cautious tone. Safe passage through Spain is still possible. Once in Portugal, finding a berth to Ireland would be relatively unproblematic, since commerce continues between the neutral countries more or less uninterrupted.

Daylight gleams on the tabletop. His expression is null, withheld, his back to the light. She cannot make him out at all.

'Well,' she says.

He shrugs. If they go, everything changes. They would have to get married. *Mr and Mrs*, the clerk at the Legation had said. It's the only way Suzanne could travel with him. They'd take ship, dock in Dun Laoghaire in November. His mother would be happy to have him grown up and respectable, would try, for a while, to like Suzanne. Frank would give him a job. He would knuckle down; he would loathe every ticking minute of it. Suzanne's English would improve; she would use it to complain about everything because it isn't French. And that would be it, for ever. And he can't face it.

'If you want to,' he says.

She raises her eyebrows, pulls in her chin, assesses him. 'We're getting by, though, aren't we?'

'In Cahors, that night,' he says, 'I thought that you would die.'

'Well, I didn't. Neither of us did.'

'If you had, it would have been my fault.'

'Don't be stupid.' She pushes her chair back, edges out and round the table.

'But what will we do?'

She hands the letter back to him. 'Look at you. Like a dog that's had its bollocks cut. I'm not going to Ireland with you, not like that.'

Pétain delivers his quavering speeches to the nation over the radio waves and he is not to be believed. But still, the news from Paris, when it trickles in from other sources, from friends of friends and newcomers in town, is not so terrible after all. The city seems to have fallen softly: it's occupied, but it hasn't been destroyed. The government has graciously stepped back and ushered the invaders in, and little material damage has been done to the capital. There have been skirmishes in the streets, but as yet there have been no massacres. Cafés and cinemas and shops are reopening already; the Opéra is lit up again. There is still wine to be drunk and dinner to be eaten and films to be seen, if you have the money and if you can stomach the company. They come and go as they please, the occupiers, cameras dangling round their necks, gawping at the sights, cluttering up the place, buying knick-knacks. If you can live with that, then you can live in Paris; you can live in what has become a resort town of the Reich.

It's worth a try, isn't it? It will still be Paris, won't it? More or less.

6

Paris
Winter 1940

THE SPINE OF a small fish lies picked quite clean between them. Suzanne is busy with the *décorticage* of the fish's head: her slender, quick fingers and little knife pick the flesh from the cheeks, then tease out the eyes and brain. Capable. That's what he thinks. She is so capable. He is lucky that she is.

'I'm sorry,' he says.

She gathers the bits together, then presses and smears them on to two coins of bread.

He has his papers at last. He has his letter of certification. The return to Paris has enabled this much. His presence in France is now legitimate; he is allowed to stay. The fact of the occupation seems to have finally added a degree of efficiency to the Legation's work, which the mere threat of invasion never did. He is entitled to the same rations as any French citizen. So he has his fourteen ounces of bread a day. These two pieces are the last of it. They are a reminder of three hours of queuing, with a book in hand, shifting his weight from foot to foot. Trying not to think of cigarettes. Of which there is a dearth.

She hands a disc of bread to him.

'Is there anything we can do?' he asks.

She pulls her bread apart now, having so carefully assembled it. 'I don't know.'

They have twelve ounces of coffee a month. Twelve ounces is not even close to enough, not even for a week. Twelve ounces cannot in any reasonable way be made to stretch to a month. He is in constant want of coffee. The headaches are blinding.

'Do you want to go down to the Commissariat and ask?'

She breaks a fragment of crust in two, and slips one half between her lips.

'We could just ask.' He bites, and carefully chews, and an eyeball pops between his back teeth and he tastes salt. 'If they know people know that he is there, and are concerned about him, it might help.'

'You think they would treat him more kindly?'

'Maybe.'

'Maybe I will, then.' After a moment: 'I see you've been reading that dreadful stuff again.'

His copy of *Mein Kampf* lies face-down, splayed out upon the table. He does not usually treat his books like this.

'I don't know how you can bear it,' she says.

He swallows carefully, licks his lips. 'It's important.'

'It's dreadful.'

'Yes, but it is important.'

These words have redrawn the map of Europe, they have leached out the different colours of the world. They have sucked up rights and liberties. These words kill. The world is different because of them.

'But does it help?'

'I don't know if it *helps*.'

She teases her bread into crumbs, her lips twisted. To choose a word is to force feeling into shape. To speak that word is to hand that feeling and that shape over, and watch the other person turn it round and find colours and contours of which one had not been aware. And that is what Suzanne is struggling with now. Because these feelings do not have an easy fit with words, they are ugly and clumsy, like phlegm in the throat. Language becomes a fumble, a blunder, sputtering. It fails her.

Because a friend of hers, someone she's known since she studied with him as a youngster at the Conservatoire, has gone. Just gone. She found the flat empty and the door sealed and the neighbours twitchy and boggle-eyed in their doorways, wanting the conversation over and the door shut and her *gone*. No, they didn't have a clue why he was taken; no, there was no sense to be made of it at all; such a sweet man, such a gentle soul, never a moment's trouble from him and they've been neighbours for a decade. No, it was not the Germans; it was the French police.

Her friend was a communist. That's all that she can imagine that they had on him. They are awkward things to carry round with you these days, principles.

And her friend is not alone in his disappearance.

Old Monsieur Lunel also seems to have dropped out of existence. First the yellow sign went up on his draper's shop. That itself wouldn't stop his regular customers from shopping there, but the Boche, the Green Beans, were the only ones with any money, so it hardly mattered if anybody else wanted to do business with him. Then one day the place just didn't open, and then there were new managers, and the yellow sign came down, and nobody knows where Monsieur Lunel went, who used to make such a pet of Suzanne, who'd throw in thread and tape gratis when his wife's back was turned. Whose daughters would chat with her, would shake their heads and laugh at the old man's flirting. Whose grandchildren would learn their spellings behind the shop counter, would use buttons as counters to do their sums. Nobody knows where any of them went.

She still hopes it could be a magic trick of their own devising. A disappearing act.

'That graffiti is disgusting,' she says. 'Did you see?' There's a deep line between her brows.

'At the Lunels'?' he asks.

She raises a shoulder. 'They're scrubbing it off. The new people. Do you think you could put that away while we're eating?' She flaps a hand towards the German book. 'Or, better, chuck it out. Throw the damned thing on the fire. It gives me the shivers.'

He closes it.

'I don't know how you can stomach it at all.'

He pushes it aside.

'I hate it. It makes me sick.'

She shoves it off the table. It tumbles, lands with a thud on the boards, pages fluttering.

He leans over to pick it up.

'I'm living on my nerves here,' she says. He straightens with the book. 'I'm living on my nerves and you're acting as though everything's normal, as though it's nothing, as though there's nothing to be said.'

He closes the book, gets up and shelves it. 'Not at all.'

She glares at him. Then she stands up and stalks to the door and shrugs herself into her coat.

'You're impossible,' she says.

She claps the door shut behind her, clatters down the stairs.

He picks up the plates and takes them to the little pantry to be washed. He could have said, perhaps, that he is try-ing; to get a fingernail into this, to get a foothold.

It is a brutal winter. The wind cuts to the core and whips snow.

Shortages are sudden and hard and unpredictable: one day there is no milk to be had, another there are no matches; he goes to buy razorblades and it turns into a tour of the quarter's pharmacies: he finally gets hold of them in a drab little corner shop near Saint-Sulpice. Coffee becomes avail-able again, but it's a ghost of what it was; it's no longer made of coffee beans, but roasted barley corns. The butcher's shop closes at noon, because there's nothing left; the meaner cuts are now expensive, but they disappear as quickly as the steak, since they're still off the ration and so can be simply bought.

The shelves in the *épicerie* are empty. Rationing quite quickly becomes abstract: it doesn't really matter what your share of nothing is.

He lights the gas under the cold coffee pot, lights a cigarette from the gas to save on matches. He heats up the liquid, sloshes it into a cup, drinks it black. It looks like coffee but it tastes like watery burnt toast. He dreads the day when they start to ration cigarettes.

At the table, he holds his ink bottle up to the light, sloshes the fluid from side to side. The glass base is domed and thick. It's deceptive. He pulls out a pocketful of coins and drops them on the table, sorts them into heaps, tidies the heaps into columns. He writes the word *ink* on a scrap of paper torn from a cigarette packet. That itself, he thinks, is a waste of ink. There may not be any more ink to be got.

On the corners there are new signposts; there are new signs on the shops. It's obvious they're in German even before you read them – the print shrinks to fit all the letters of lengthy compound words. On the front of the neighbourhood *cinoche* it now says *Soldatenkino*. So the locals cannot go to see a film there any more.

Bread, though, remains the most pressing issue. They take it in turns to roll out of bed and heave on layers of clothing and go to join the queue. Before the shop opens, the line has grown behind him; it now stretches down the street and round the corner. The press of bodies before and behind, the stink of old clothes. He pulls his collar up, wraps his arms around himself. Stamps his feet in his thin boots. Closes his eyes and does his best to take himself elsewhere.

Consider well the seed that made you. You were not made to
live as brutes, but to follow virtue and knowledge.

When he surfaces again, there is Lucie Léon, struggling home in a buttoned-up coat with a muffler wrapped round her mouth and chin. He hails her and she tugs the muffler down and they talk. She and Paul have been back in Paris for some time now, with the family. She's a journalist, she has her work, and work is work and must go on. He feels an ache of anxiety for her. It is not going to get any easier for them. The family is Jewish.

'How are the children?' he asks.

She shrugs, smiles. 'Always hungry. Outgrowing their clothes.'

She, herself, looks translucent in the winter sun.

Suzanne has unravelled an old sweater. She is knitting him mitts, the fingerless kind, so that he can continue to write despite the cold – so he can at least hold his pen. It's complicated work, the separation of the fingerholes, the angling of the thumb. She's counting stitches, tongue protruding from the corner of her mouth. She will not allow him any excuses: there can be no reasons not to write.

'I saw Lucie Léon today,' he says.

She lets her hands fall, the knitting bundled in her lap. 'Lucie! How is she getting on?'

'She seemed all right.'

He gets up, prowls out to the pantry, where he opens cupboards, stares at the bare shelves. A quarter-full bag of barley-coffee, an inch or so of brandy, a small packet of sac-charine. A tin of toothpowder.

'I bought a swede,' Suzanne calls. 'And there are two car-rots left. I'll make a purée later.'

He nods, in the little pantry, where she cannot see him; he calls back to her, 'Thank you.' But it wasn't his own hunger that he had been considering.

The next morning, they wake to an apartment of ice. They fumble into their clothes, clumsy, skin bristling, their breath clouding the air. The heating-pipes are cold to the touch.

'The boiler must have packed up.'

Huddled in her little cubbyhole off the lobby, the con-cierge just shakes her head, her hands stuffed into her armpits. She has her husband's old coat pulled on over layers of sweaters, wraps, aprons and cardigans. She has a blanket over her knees.

There's nothing wrong with the boiler; the boiler's com-pletely fine, or it would be, if they had anything to feed it with.

This is, she informs them, the drop that made the vase overflow.Simply put, there is no coal. There is none to be had. Not from their usual supplier, nor from any other, and believe her, she has tried. Between them, she and her hus-band have telephoned to or trudged round every coal yard in the quarter, and there's nothing in them but horse dung and black dust. The coalmen are in trouble: it should be their busiest time of year, but they have nothing left to sell.

Suzanne's not having it. 'That's ridiculous.'

110

The woman shrugs. 'That's the way it is.'

'But why?'

'The coal's gone the way of the potatoes and the wheat and all the blessed wine.'

'What way's that?'

'To Germany.'

But life is not impossible, not yet. There's a fireplace in the apartment, though he has never thought to use it before. Suzanne crouches to peer up the chimney, pulls out damp balled newspaper, which is followed by a fall of soot and twigs and the mummified body of a bird. They drop the corpse in the waste chute, then flatten out the paper and read the news from March 1936. There in grey and paler grey is news of the remilitarization of the Rhineland, an obituary for Jean Patou. That one could feel nostalgic for that!

Stiff with cold, they scavenge fallen wood and fir cones in the parks and squares and from the trees that line the avenues. They build inexpert smoky, spitty little fires in the grate and huddle close to them, wrapped in blankets. But the parks are soon picked clean; all the lowest branches are torn clear off the lindens and the plane trees; the boards are dragged down from the windows of boarded-up shops. People – people who are clearly much better equipped for this than they – start to cut down trees, so that there is nothing left but sawdust, and the disc of a stump, and an absence up into the air that the tree had used to fill.

*

She gives up her apartment: impossible to keep both places.

He tries to work. There's a tickling at the back of his brain, an irritation, something squirming and wanting to be noticed, but there's too much else going on for him to feed it, to grow it, to tug it out into the light to be examined. The complaints of the body can't be dealt with, and so become insistent, intrusive, far noisier than the quiet need to write. Hunched at the table, the little crocheted blanket over his shoulders, mitts on his paws, his empty stomach whines and pops; his feet are a torment of chilblains, his nose is ice. He finds himself staring for he doesn't know how long at the blank page in front of him, or out of the window at the grey sky, his thoughts caught up in his body's and his friends' distress. His being here has merely added to the general burden. Another mouth. He is disgusted with his hunger, with his needs.

'Sorry, I didn't want to disturb you, but . . .'

He holds the door wide with one hand, grasps his blanket at his throat with the other. Suzanne is carrying a bundle of something; she lugs it into the apartment, dumps it down on the floor.

'I'm going to need your help with this, if you don't mind.'

She is shifting furniture now.

'It's too cold to move,' he says.

'It's too cold to stay still.'

She's lining up chairs, backs turned to each other, six foot or so apart. As though they're about to march away across the rug, then stop, and turn, and fire.

'What's all this?'

'I had an idea.' She jerks her head towards the bundle. 'Just lift that for me, would you? Help me shake it out.'

The bundle unfurls into a hefty sheet of canvas; it smells of damp and is spotted here and there with mould. A forgotten dust sheet, or a tarpaulin used in some long-ago *déménagement*. When they shake it out, dust motes spin into the cold winter sun.

'Where'd you get it?'

'It was in the basement.'

'Isn't it somebody's?'

'Yes,' she says. 'Ours.'

She gestures for him to move round to the far side of the chairs. Between them they spread the fabric over the ladder-backs, so that it drapes down to the floor on either side. She straightens out the edges, tucks them in under the chair-feet to hold the fabric taut. He crouches down on the other side to do the same.

'Did you ever do this as a child?' she asks.

He's still not quite certain what they are doing. 'Eh?'

'Make a den.' She lifts a fold of canvas, glances inside.

He takes a step back, squints at it. Oh yes. 'No.'

'We did. Once in a while. On a rainy day.'

She ducks in underneath the canvas; he follows.

Inside, the air is frowsty; the light glows through the fabric. Beneath them is the old rug, with its faded Turkish patterns. He arranges himself uncomfortably, draws up his knees, feels ridiculous.

'You can work in here.' Suzanne blows on her hands. 'It'll be warmer.'

113

'Yes,' he says. 'I see.'

She is pleased with herself. He smiles for her. It makes sense, of course it does, and it's also utterly absurd. The two of them are hunched there in a tent on the rug, as though this is a game. As though later there will be nursery tea and bath and pyjamas and prayers and bed, and not just more cold, more hunger.

'Do you want your book?' he asks.

'Please.'

'And coffee?'

'Oh yes, please.'

'It's horrible coffee.'

'*Comme d'hab.*'

He scrambles out, unfolding his long limbs. He finds her book; he finds a cup and rinses it. He dawdles over these little tasks, leaving her tucked away out of sight. She keeps doing things for him unasked, her kindnesses weave a mesh of obligation. He stirs in saccharine and watches the ersatz coffee spin and then fall still. No question now of milk. He brings these things back to her, passes them through the opening of the tent and crawls in after them. He folds himself up, knees and elbows. It's warmer, yes, inside the shelter, in their shared warmth. They are toe-to-toe. The fabric drapes above his shoulders. His neck is bent. He can feel her breathe. The world has closed down to this. To body and breath. Ridiculous.

He carries it with him like the stone in his pocket, cold and hard and unassimilated; it jolts against him with each footfall. He's aware of very little else. James Joyce is dead.

His stride takes him without thinking through the streets and through the fog, as it used to take him along the lanes and tracks and paths up into the mountains back at home, away from his mother and her blue scrutiny and all those domestic entanglements. It's a January afternoon and it hasn't been properly light all day. He passes braziers where men shuffle chestnuts, and the damp posters on the flank of a building, and graffiti, and the smell of drains, and the *pâtisserie* with one solitary *galette des rois* in the window, and the warm chatter from a café by the Métro Charles Michel – *And so I told him he could go to hell,* and *Excellent idea, I was just thinking that myself* and *It really is the most extraordinary thing* – that he realizes only afterwards was in German. The Boches. The Chleuhs. The Haricots Verts. And German is still and always beautiful.

He finds himself where he should have realized he was going: the rue des Vignes; he stares up at the Joyces' old apartment. The windowpanes reflect the fog and look opaque. This is the last place of their own in Paris: Shem's books, he said, were still in there; maybe they still are. He recalls rubbed wallpaper, fingerprinted light-switches, the greasy brown telephone set: all of them polished by Joyce's hands, grazed by Joyce's shoulders, haunted by his breath. The people living here will have no idea that they're buffering up against this extraordinary ghost.

Because James Joyce has died in Switzerland. But it's Paris that he'll haunt.

Police, gendarmes, coming round the corner from the rue Bruneau. It doesn't do to be seen loitering. He steps down on to the road. He feels the weight of an arm on his, catches the click of a walking stick, a voice whispering in his ear. The inconvenience; what a panic over the latest *bobard*, he doesn't believe a word of it, not a word. Can the world not get by without another war? His *Wake* may as well have been published in secret for all the notice it's received.

All that brilliance tied to a failing body, to be dragged round like a tin can on a string.

He walks on.

In the cold, in the fog, his feet measuring out distances, he tugs at his cuffs, turns his head against his collar. Still, faintly, there is the scent of the old man's pomade and cheroots and lemon soap. There's a song in his head, 'The Salley Gardens', sung in that astonishing quavering voice, and the taste of whiskey at the back of his tongue, and, and, and – that thrill in the blood at finding himself favoured, at being accepted into that charmed circle. Of being useful to a man like that. And then the sick lurch of the hand-me-down coat, and the favour by proxy.

He rubs his hands over his head; the hair stands up in fuzz.

He walks on.

But Paris isn't Paris any more. He walks past the closed shops and the stripped trees, and a *confiserie* with a display of pasteboard confections, an *étalage factice*, and the quiet, skinny kids on their way back home from school, and the off-duty German soldiers strolling past in their good coats, and the lean women with their shawls and baskets and their pinched looks, and the potholes in the road and the red banners hung like washing from the balconies, and the nervy scavenging dogs and the flights of shabby pigeons and the sandbags stacked on the pavement, where policemen stand and watch him pass. Let them ask for his papers. He has papers. He doesn't care who sees them.

He walks on.

It is a cold world, and Joyce has turned away from it and finally woken from the nightmare.

And with Shem gone, everything is different. After Joyce, what is the point of writing? What else is there to say?

He keeps a tally in his head; he keeps an eye out. Neighbours, acquaintances, familiar faces: he ticks them off when he spots them in the street, in the *boulangerie* queue or in a café. There are so many people, too many people to keep track of – the shop girls and the young *curé* and the old fellows who play boules on the square, and the new mother with the child strapped into a second-hand baby carriage, who has that anxious jostling air because the baby's needs are so much more urgent than her own. And the two ladies at the *pressing* whom he passes, and the office-bound functionary. This, for the moment, is something he can do. He can notice. He can keep a kind of reckoning. That, and one cigarette, even now that cigarettes are rationed, for that shabby-smart old fellow, the *sale métèque* who'd asked him the time on the Place Falguière. He's saving it for when he sees him again.

It's easier with friends, with people he actually knows. He can ring them up. He can call round to their apartments; he can drop by their haunts. No, no, he can't stay, no, he won't take anything. He happened to be passing and thought he'd look in and say hello: so, hello. No, really, he can't stay. No, really. Well, maybe just a small one.

Alfy has been demobbed. He is back teaching at the Lycée. Still the sturdy cheerful presence that he always was, but his cheeks hollow now and his eyes haunted, after the defeat. Always ready for a drink, a chat, sometimes a game of tennis; but also always glancing discreetly at his watch. Yes, they must get together and make some headway with that translation; how has he been getting on with it alone? Himself, oh, busy, busy. So busy, really; it breaks his feet; never a moment's peace. Will have to dash, because. Has to go and meet someone. Right out of the way; pretty much the opposite direction to where you're going. Wherever you are going. So he'll make his farewells now.

Alfy's not necessarily lying, but there's a lot of flannel here, a lot of bluff. Something is not being said. And since Alfy clearly prefers not to confide, he doesn't really feel that he can say anything more than a platitudinous *Take care*. They part at the corner; he watches till Alfy reaches the next crossroads, and turns away. No backward glance.

Well, that was Alfy, and he was, for that one moment, there. He marks his friend off, on the tally in his head.

Tick.

He walks on, all the way to Mary Reynolds's house on the rue Hallé. It is calm and dim and cool after the bright street, and she draws him inside as though these are the first steps of a dance. He follows her into the shadows, with her pale nape and the cornsilk of her cropped hair. She pours him a *fine*, offers him a seat. She puts on a '78 and he melts into the chair.

For a while they just listen, sip. But he must know how she is faring, so 'How are you getting on?' he asks.

She laughs, shakes her head. She had thought that she'd get so much work done here, back in Paris, that'd she'd just hole up at home and make her books. That there'd be nothing else to do. But the reality is that she is getting nothing done; she can't bring herself to do it. She can't make it feel important any more: it has no context, it makes no sense, it just doesn't matter.

'Does it have to matter?'

'I'm used to it mattering.' She shrugs. 'And then everything is such a fag, these days! Just the bare essentials take up so much of one's time and energy. Living is a vocation now; life's an art. One must carve it out for oneself every day.'

She moves to lift her glass; her long earrings catch the light. At least she is good at it, at this carving out of life. She does it with conviction.

'Any news of Marcel?'

Her face puckers up, half smiling, half a frown. 'He's quit,' she says.

'Quit?'

'Quit work.'

'No.'

She nods in contradiction. 'It's not that he *can't* work – it is simply that he has decided not to.'

'And that's that?'

'That's that. All he'll do now is chess.' She has heard it far too often, has got it by rote, is bored of it. 'Art has become shop-soiled. You can buy and sell a picture or a sculpture, but you can't own a game of chess.'

The purity of that. That's something.

'Yes, he's right, of course, I know,' she says. 'But where does it take you, in the end?'

Through a complex web of potential, towards an end-game that is at once foreseeable and shifting, into silence, stillness. 'It's rather beautiful.'

'It's a shame, is what it is. He was in Marseilles for a while, and Sanary-sur-Mer. He's still planning to go to New York.' She lifts a shoulder. 'I'm staying here.'

She parts her lips to say something more, but then the needle shifts into the hiss and fuzz at the centre of the disc, and she goes over to lift the arm and slide the record away. She has no notion of what an indulgence it has been to him, the music. More so even than the glass of brandy.

She speaks over her shoulder: 'Would you abandon your home because you had house guests who wouldn't take a hint? I'm not leaving. They can go.'

'You're right, of course. It's dreadfully bad manners.'

A delicious smile. 'Shocking.'

When he leaves, she kisses him on both cheeks. He catches the scent of her powder, feels the coolness of her hair. He should be glad that she continues just the same, when so much else is changed; but he can't quite work out why he's so unnerved by her. Her words have stuck with him like ink on the skin, smudging in and creeping along tiny creases.

'You take care of yourself, now,' she says.

'And you,' he says. 'God bless.'

Stepping back into the street is like coming out of a matinée. Dazzled, heady with brandy, he ambles along, chewing on their conversation, her gestures, that cheeky defiance, all the way home.

But where does it take you, in the end?

I'm not leaving. They can go.

Later, he lies awake, his back turned to Suzanne's soft breathing, his toes twisted in the sheet, his shoulder denting the ticking and his ear pressed into the pillow. He can't sleep: he is haunted by absences, by things unsaid. He can't keep account of everyone; he can't accommodate it all.

7

Paris
Summer 1941

IT'S STRANGELY COOL for August. The sky is grey; the city is grey. There are grey-green uniforms on the café terraces around Odéon; German officers swing out of shops with little luxuries; they walk three abreast and take up the width of the pavements. Paris is a luxury they have allowed themselves; they indulge in it. They fill the city with their grey.

He makes his way through all of this as if it is not real. The occupiers are silent images projected upon the city. They slip over him without touching. He holds his own pictures, his own images of Germany, in his head: the cool spires, the mist and stillness of early morning, the fug of beer-halls, strong paint-spattered hands, a crook's smile.

Remember this. The Germany you love.

He takes out his cigarette pack, touches the tip of his last cigarette. This morning – in one of the Jewish neighbourhoods – the police made a mass arrest. They have taken hostages for the new French State. He is scanning through that tally in his head, for friends who might have been at risk. He must go and check on the Léons, at the very least. He puts the cigarette packet away and turns the other way down the rue de Vaugirard, and it seems quite ordinary, workaday, but normality is now a skin stretched thin and it can split at any time.

He's walking briskly, urgent with concern for his friends, when a young woman brushes past. She does a little half-skip to make headway. Her body doesn't quite fill her dress and she has no stockings on, but she's swinging along the pavement as though she's glad to be alive. Charming, that, if quite deluded.

She falters, slows. He peers past her to see what she has seen.

There's a hulk of grey-green on the corner. A knot of soldiers. For the time being they're occupied with some lad who's failed to show sufficient respect: he's jostled, barked at; some German, some ugly French. His cap is sent spinning into the gutter. He scurries after it, ducks to scoop it up, then darts off down a side street; he's gone. And then, amongst the soldiers, a fist knocks against an arm; a head jerks, a chin juts; eyes swivel round and watch the young woman approach.

An arm swipes at her. 'Mademoiselle, your papers, if you please.' And she can't refuse or turn away. She has not that right.

He's in a rush, but fear slows time, so that one could feel the sluggish thud of one's own blood as the papers are presented, shaking, and thick fingers receive the document. She is addressed in heavy French; the comments underneath are in German. He watches, approaching, as she blinks back and forth from one face to another.

He is passing her now, and her eyes follow him round, watching as she might watch someone else's balloon drifting free up into the air.

His hands flex, grip. His thin boots plant the pavement and he is past her, and he has done nothing and is still walking on, and he can hear her voice crack with frustration: her papers are in order, she has to get home, she's expected, her mother will be worried. These arrests, you see. And the heavily accented voices, the suggestion in French that they meet later to clarify the issue, perhaps over a drink. The German, muttered underneath, is a more intimate suggestion.

And he just keeps on walking. Against all instincts. Because what good would it do to intervene? *What use do you imagine you could be?*

No use whatsoever, Mother. No use to anyone at all.

He rounds the corner, teeth stinging, his jaw is clenched so tight. He blunders straight into another man.

A fumbled readjustment.

'Ah, excuse me—'

'Oh, hello—'

And it is Paul Léon himself, his light summer jacket neatly buttoned over a pristine shirt and a blue silk tie. He looks as though he has stepped straight out of those satellite years before the war.

'Paul.' They shake hands. 'Thank God. I was just on my way to see you.' He touches Paul's elbow, exerting gentle pressure, steering him away from the checkpoint.

They cross the road together and continue in the direction Paul had been going, but now on the far side of the street. They pass, with the expanse of cobblestones between them, the knot of soldiers and the young woman. She is really arguing now; her voice is shrill and insistent and the soldiers are getting fed up, shuffling; it's not exciting now that she's scolding them like a furious little sister. He sees the papers offered back and her grab them and stuff them away. She stalks off.

'I was worried, when I heard about the round-up,' he says.

Paul's lips compress. 'We plan to leave.'

'I'm sorry.'

'It's not your fault, my friend. We'll leave as soon as the boy's got his *bachot*.'

'When's that?'

'Tomorrow.'

He nods. Good.

'Though I have to say, we're not best pleased. Lucie particularly hates these *déménagements*. There is so much to organize, and it is so disruptive for the children, and for our work.'

'I know,' he says, though he knows he does not really know. Work is one thing, but children are entirely another. How one could look a life's worth into the future and consider the prospect good enough to throw small people out to flounder round in it, to pin exams to them and think that it will matter. Instinct is powerful, he supposes. Blood and spunk and all of that, it pushes against sense. Love, perhaps.

'I still expect to see him,' Paul says.

It takes just a moment. 'Do you?'

He tries to see Joyce here, now, a blind man with a stick, feeling his way along through Paris under occupation. Outraged at the inconvenience of it all.

'I knew he wasn't well, but it just didn't occur to me that he would die.'

'Fifty-eight,' he says. 'It's not old.'

'I thought maybe we would have another book from him,' Paul says.

'Really?' He can't imagine what this book would be.

They approach the junction with the rue Littré. This is where Paul must turn, it seems, because he slows and offers out a hand.

'Ah well,' Paul says. 'It's good to see you, my friend.'

'Be careful,' he says. 'Please.'

They clasp hands. Paul gives him a smile and turns away, and ambles off. The stooped pale shape diminishing down the dim street, under the grey August sky.

It is the fascination of disgust, the way his attention is fixed on her and her lips as they move. The disgust of the green and pink twist of mouse innards left on the doorstep, the slime-thick hair teased from the plughole, the way that nails sink into the flesh of an overlooked pear. The lips forming on the words: those *sales métèques*. With their dirt and disease and lice and their disease and their dirt and their scheming, and their insistence on being where they are not wanted, their insistence on just being.

He turns himself away, watches the posters as the wind tugs at their corners. The easy lines of a dancer's leg, the yellow and blue of a southern beach. Fresher, more recent layers of the palimpsest: children clustered round a stolid man in uniform: *Populations abandonnées faites confiance*, it reads, *au soldat allemand!*

The queue shuffles itself forward. He turns his collar up against the wet and tugs his hatbrim down and shuffles forward too. His boots are leaking, unrepaired; his feet squelch.

Look at us, mugs that we are, queuing for hours in the rain, and in August, would you believe it! Dreadful summer that it's been. And even then the bread not what it was.

Sawdust in the flour, her friend says.

Chalk.

Bad year for the grain.

But in the camps, oh ho, they just get everything handed to them. Out at Drancy and at Royallieu. They don't know how lucky they are: three meals a day, all the bread they want, nothing to worry about, not like us. They don't know they're born.

Bad year for the grain, in that all the grain has been carted off to Germany. Bad year for the potatoes. And for the wine. And for the coal. He has a choice, of course; he doesn't have to stay and listen to this. He could just step out of the queue. He could just walk away. And he could have a good go at tearing that poster off the wall as he passes. He

127

could just keep on walking, walking like he used to, the long miles winding into the mountains, the wide spread of silence, with its markers of distant birdcalls and a farm-dog's bark and sometimes a solitary car, the wind in their ears and their feet planted one after the other on the mac-adam, and then gravel, and then narrow trails of worn earth. The escape up to where everything was fresh and clean and clear.

But now the war is everywhere and he cannot walk away.

And – this of course bears consideration – Suzanne will tear strips off him if he comes home without their bread.

So he turns aside, his back against the wall, and smokes a cigarette. He thinks, you shall find out how salt is the taste of another man's bread, and how hard is the way up and down another man's stairs.

Dante is a consolation.

'But. No.'

Suzanne's lips are compressed and her face is tight with distress. She nods. It's true.

'But how did it happen? When?'

'There was another round-up this morning. He must have thought it was safe to be out, that it was all over and done with. So many people must have thought as much.'

'Christ.' He sits down. 'Where've they taken him?'

Suzanne shakes her head. 'Drancy, maybe?'

The world can collapse to this. To the inside of a truck, rattling across the cobblestones of Paris. To the crowded pre-cincts of a camp. To the locked door and the barbed wire coiled across the sky. And the vile ignorance of fellow citizens, who begrudge you even this.

'How's Lucie?'

Just another shake of the head.

His jaw is tight, his teeth stinging. He can feel the pressure of Paul's hand in his, the lightly worn intelligence, that civility. The stooped figure diminishing down the street. They can't do this. How can they do this? It's just ridiculous, to lock up Paul Léon. It is an outrage. He's on his feet, rebuttoning the coat he hadn't yet removed, and is heading for the door.

'Where are you going?' Suzanne blinks at him, her eyes big and wet.

'I'll go and see Lucie.'

'What can you do?'

'I'll find out.'

Lucie has been crying. Her eyes are puffy and her mouth is smudged, but her face has been washed and powdered and when she speaks her voice is careful and measured. She holds herself erect.

She does her best to smile. She ushers him into the apartment, offers him a seat, has nothing else to offer. The children are not at home. Whatever else they are denied, they are still obliged to go to school.

'I'm so sorry, Lucie.'

In the sunny room of Shakespeare and Company, years ago: she was on Paul's arm, her belly huge under a blue coat, and they were talking with Sylvia, and Lucie had laughed, he remembers the sight of her, and she had seemed almost

129

luminous then, extraordinary beside her gangling husband. She's a journalist, Sylvia had informed him in one of her gossipy confidences after the couple had left; she's on the Paris desk of the *Herald Tribune*. And the husband has a couple of books under his belt too. Now the woman is creased and dimmed, her mouth twisted to a knot. And then her face crumples and she buries it in her hands. He reaches out towards her, then stops short. He tucks his hands between his knees, looks up at the unbleached square on the wall where a painting used to hang.

'Do you know where they've taken him?' he asks.

She wipes her cheeks, blows out a breath, composes herself.

'Drancy. He's been taken to Drancy.'

It's on the edge of Paris. A nasty unfinished little housing project that they have looped around with wire.

'Have you seen him?'

'I went out there, but they wouldn't let me see him.' She rolls her lips in, biting on them; her eyes brim. 'But I have heard that he's been tortured.'

'My God.'

She closes her eyes; tears run. She shakes her head. 'He's done nothing, he's got nothing to confess. If he could give them something, if he had something to give, then perhaps—'

'Oh Lucie.'

She takes a breath, swipes away tears again, making an effort to still herself. She says, 'He's quite weak, I hear.'

'But you haven't seen him?'

'No. There's a woman. She told me.'

'Oh?'

'She lives out there, near the camp. It's just a shell, that place; there's no proper food, everyone's ill. But she says that if I can get a food parcel together, she can get it to him.'

She pushes away a curl that has fallen loose. Her smile is brittle and it does not last.

'So that's something,' she says.

He sits back. Blows out a long breath. Now, at last, there is something he can do.

The concierge peers at him, back again so soon. She is dark and squat and there is a fleshy growth on the side of her nose the size of a collar stud, which the eye snags on involuntarily; it must happen to her all the time because she doesn't seem to take offence. She follows his passing with a blink and an upward tilt of the chin that he takes for approval. He'll assume that she is decent. That's all that can be required of anybody: decency. Everything else follows from that, or from its absence.

His knock is followed by a moment's anxious pause. But then there is the clack of shoes on the parquet, and the door inches open and Lucie's pale face appears again: anxiety melts into bafflement. She opens the door wide and goes to usher him in.

'I'm not stopping.' He holds up a grubby canvas shopping bag. 'Just wanted to leave this.'

The bag is shaped by tins and packages. A baguette pokes grey-beige out of it. She looks at the bag, the bread, at him. She doesn't move.

'Actually,' he says, and holds up a finger. 'Two ticks. Suzanne will miss the bag.'

He pulls out the baguette and the pack of cigarettes, and a tin of anchovies and one of corned beef and a waxy block of cheese wrapped in paper. He passes the things to her, and she takes them off him to be helpful, filling her arms automatically, not yet really understanding.

He bundles up the bag and stuffs it into a trouser pocket. 'I'm sorry it's not more.'

The groceries are too much to hold – the baguette's crushed under an arm, a tin is slipping. She tries to hand them back to him. He wafts the attempt away.

'They're yours,' he says.

'No . . .'

'It's for Paul; for the parcel.'

She shakes her head, a kaleidoscope shake, to make a pattern out of chaotic bits. 'But. No. Because you need it yourself.'

'Get it to Paul.' He gives her an awkward pat. 'I'll see you soon, Lucie.'

He heads along the brown corridor and down the slow spiral of the wooden stairs, past the woman with the little button on the side of her nose, who, being decent, gives him a half-nod. He nods back and opens the door on to the street, the grey sky, Paris, straight on to the crunch of uniform boots and the skim of green-grey jerkins. He stands frozen. The soldiers pass as a chill in the air. When they are gone, he steps over the threshold, easing the little *porte cochère* shut behind him, and turns in the opposite direction, for no other reason than it is the opposite.

He only once looks back, when he comes to the corner. The street is void, as though the people have dripped through the gaps between the cobbles and oozed into the cracks between the paving stones.

His head swims; the street seesaws. His hand, when he reaches out for balance, has become his mother's hand, crabbed and veined and shaking. He wants rillettes and cornichons, a boiled egg, a piece of bacon, a bowl of steaming moules. Bread and butter.

He leans back against the wall. He's sweating. Cold.

A smoke.

A smoke will have to do.

He rifles for his cigarette packet, peers in at the remaining cigarette. Dry filaments of tobacco curl from the open end; the paper is ragged and softened. He looks at it for a long time. He touches it with a fingertip. Then he slips the packet back into his pocket. He pushes away from the wall and begins his long walk home.

'Here's something you never see any more,' she says.

He rolls his head round on the pillow to look at her, eyebrows raised.

'Spoiled fruit,' she says.

He studies her profile, the soft nap of her skin. Despite the lines at her eyes, there's still something of the girl about her, even now, even in the middle of all this, with her hair all fallen anyhow, and her gaze vague and turned towards the ceiling and her thoughts freewheeling and ravenous.

He wets cracked lips. 'True.'

'Or vegetables.'

He nods.

'Because you'd see it all the time, wouldn't you, on a market day. There'd be bruised apples that'd rolled off a barrow. Or oranges, on the cobbles, burst open, wasps on them; kids would kick them around. Sometimes you'd see an old fellow, a *clochard* would be picking them up, stuffing them in his pockets. Fallen fruit, all bruised and gritty.'

'I remember.'

'But you never see that any more.'

'No.'

'Or the tramps, for that matter.'

'No.'

'They're all gone too.' She considers this a moment. 'The days when you could pick up an orange off the street, can you imagine? God, I'd love an orange. Even if I had to fight the wasps for it.'

'Or the tramps.'

She smiles. Her teeth show. Her gums are pale.

'A bad orange is really bad, though,' he says. 'I'd take a bad apple over a bad orange, any day.'

'Depends how bad.'

A long pause, in which both of them consider the relative merits of spoiled fruit. Then: 'No one feeds the pigeons any more.'

'One might, if one thought it might get one close enough to catch it.'

A moment passes, and then she says, 'Pigeon pie. I could eat a pigeon pie, couldn't you? With potatoes in it, and carrots.' She still stares up at the ceiling. Her lips compress, her chin crumples.

'Potatoes aren't rationed yet,' he says.

'But you can't get hold of them anyway.'

'Or carrots, or radishes, or turnips, they're not rationed.'

'I know.'

A silence.

'It will be all right . . .' he says.

She doesn't roll her eyes. But she can't stop herself from expelling a huff of breath, almost a sigh, and twisting her head round on the pillow to give him a long look.

'I'm not that bothered anyway,' he says. He wets his lips again. There's a sharp catch on the tongue there, and a taste of blood where the skin has split. His voice is dry too, and sounds dusty when he speaks.

'I don't expect you . . .' he says. 'Just because I . . .'

She does roll her eyes now. Heaves up on to an elbow, the better to glare at him.

'That's not how it works,' she says. 'Of course that's not how it works. You know that. I'm not going to stuff myself with bread while all you've got to eat is turnips.'

After a moment, he says, 'Lucie was desperate.'

She blinks, sighs, flops back down on her pillow. 'I know.' Then she says, 'I keep thinking of omelettes. What I'd give for a mushroom omelette. The kind where the mushrooms are cooked almost black and there's that inky juice seeping out of it, and the eggs are a bit crisp on the outside, but still soft and oozy in the middle. You might get the mushrooms, if you were lucky, but where would you get the eggs for it now?'

'A gorgonzola sandwich,' he says.

She nods keenly, as though this is a particularly insightful observation. After a moment, she says, 'We are in real trouble now, you realize.'

'But what else could I do?'

She parts her lips, is going to speak, because there are a few valid responses to this. But then he starts to cough. And doesn't stop. He heaves himself up, away from her, his legs swung over the side of the bed, and he is curled over like a C, his backbone a line of knuckles, his belly hollow and his chest heaving. His scar slides and strains over his ribs; it's livid against his white skin. Suzanne fumbles him a handkerchief and shifts round next to him, her hand on his back. He clutches the handkerchief to his lips. Gradually the fit subsides and he manages a shaking breath. He wipes his eyes.

'Sorry.'

'It's all right.'

'I just need a cigarette.'

She rubs his back. 'I know.' They don't have any cigarettes. 'I'll make you a cup of tea.'

'Have we got any tea?'

'I think we've got a little left.'

'Thank you.'

'Rest.'

He eases himself back down as she gets up off the bed. She pads her way down to the tiny kitchen, and lifts tins from the cupboard, and puts the water on to heat. He lies and looks up at the ceiling, his breath raw.

The way it nails one to one's body, this dearth. A battle to think about anything at all beyond the discomforts of the flesh, a battle to do anything more than attempt to deal with its demands. Which is, presumably, intentional. A canny weapon, hunger, the way it turns one in on oneself.

'It'll get better,' Suzanne says. She hands him a cup of pale and milkless liquid. He shifts up on his pillows to take it from her.

'Shamrock tea,' he says.

'How's that?'

'It's got three leaves in it.'

She smiles.

'What you're doing,' she says. 'For the Léons. I am proud of you.'

He looks up at her. She strokes his shoulder, her hand cold over gooseflesh, her expression grave.

'But remember, you, yourself, you matter too.'

The plane leaves are starting to turn and so are the maples, and a leaf drifts down, because nobody has told the trees that the world has ended. The children's Monday-afternoon voices twine into a thread as they walk in their shabby trails from school, ink-stained and bedraggled, their satchels swinging in the low September sun, because whatever children are used to is how things ought to be. Today, with its

137

golden sun and its crisp air, brings thoughts of beginnings, of pencil shavings and new leather and ink on a fresh page, and this is cruel, because even if you could manage somehow not to notice, if you could skim over the posters and assure yourself they only advertise nightclubs and radio sets and soap, if you took off your glasses so that the boarded shopfronts were just a blur, and the outrages daubed there were rendered soft and indistinct, and if you could step through the empty spaces in the street where there should be actual people, and do it without shivering, then all might seem almost to be well, and fresh, and hopeful. But the tumour's already threaded into the flesh. It taints the blood, it poisons everything.

He taps lightly on the Pérons' door.

'Alfy. Good afternoon.'

'What's wrong?'

Where to start. He jerks his head. 'Come for a drink?'

Alfy glances back into the apartment, calls out to his wife, 'Back in a few instants, *chérie*,' and a reply is heard, though the words are indistinct. Alfy grabs a jacket and ushers him out.

They walk briskly; they talk about the new academic year and some of the boys Alfy's teaching, because of course Mathematics and French and Philosophy still go on, just as the leaves turn and fall and the earth spins round the sun. There are, of course, changes to the curriculum. Books are disappearing from the library. At the corner café they sit on the terrace. They lean in, heads together. The sun catches in their beer; it glows golden, cloudy.

'Do you know about Paul?'

Alfy glances round the nearby tables. An old lady in hat and fur coat on such a day is sipping crème de menthe, a small dog at her feet.

'Yes,' Alfy says. 'I heard.'

'The idea of him. That civil, decent man. The very idea.'

'I know.'

'I wanted to find out. What I can do.'

'For Paul?' Alfy says. 'Maybe an appeal, if he is unwell . . . Perhaps his wife . . .'

He sips. He places the glass back on the table. He resists the compulsion to down the beer in one go. The urge is for calories, not alcohol. His hand shakes with it.

He says, 'Actually, I wondered what I can do at all. I thought you might be able to help me.'

Alfy lifts his glass, drinks, and sets the beer back down again. When he speaks next it is in a dimmer tone. 'Why would you think that I would know?'

A bead of water runs through the condensation on his glass like a ladder in a stocking. 'I had rather gathered . . . I was under the impression that you . . .' He wafts away the ineffectual words. 'I'm just sitting on my hands here. Tell me how I can help.'

Alfy looks off along the street, then down at his glass.

'There's someone you need to meet.'

Alfy waves to a waiter, gets out his wallet. 'These are on me.'

He teases out a five-hundred-franc note and tucks it into the bill. His fingertips linger longer than necessary; he taps twice, drawing attention to the banknote and the red ink printed on it. Somebody has typed three words on to the note. They are clear and unequivocal, and as the note circulates the words will pass from hand to hand, day after day, for weeks and months to come. Reminding, reiterating, asserting, saying what simply must be said and yet cannot. The words are *VIVE LA FRANCE*.

He looks up, eyes widening. Alfy's expression is more than usually innocent; he wears that disarming half-smile of his.

'Petty vandals.' He shrugs. 'What can one do? One has to pass it on; one can't simply throw five hundred francs away.'

8

Paris
September 1941

A WOMAN GAZES AT them with large catlike eyes, blinks. He nods at her, rifling for her name, for where he knows her from. That stocky fellow with a moustache: he's also familiar. And that tall queenly woman. *Germaine*, he thinks, *Hélène* and *Legrand*. In fact, glancing round the knots of people as he moves through the lobby and the reception rooms of Mary's house, he begins to suspect that he knows everybody here, more or less. All are friends, or friends of friends, have been nodded to in galleries and at concerts and at gatherings like this down the years. He hasn't seen so many acquaintances in one place since before the *Exode*. If it were not for the making-do worn-shiny clothes, the gaunt faces, he could almost believe that this was a different September, an earlier light.

The drawing room is murmurous; there is music playing on the gramophone: Beethoven, glorious Beethoven, captured in time and preserved in lines and grooves on black shellac, only to have nonsense talked over him. The shutters are open on the garden side of the house; they allow the low evening light in along with the cool air and the moths, which flutter softly through the room and paste themselves to walls and kill themselves in candle flames.

'Why are you frowning?' Suzanne asks.

'I'm not frowning.'

'Stop it, though.'

He sucks his teeth.

Mary comes over to them, kisses first Suzanne then him, a waft of scent and her cheek near his cheek. He watches as, with her curious grace, she pours them drinks. Her hair is falling a little longer now, less sharply cut. The crystal decanter catches the light and kicks it off around the room. He knows now, more or less, what had been left unsaid the last time they met. That she was, already, actively engaged in this.

'I'm afraid it's just corn brandy now,' she says, handing a glass to him. 'It's all that I could get hold of.'

'No less welcome, thank you.'

They exchange enquiries about health, well-being; he asks after Marcel and the words are pond-skaters, treading the surface of things.

'New York, now. Chess.' She smiles, shrugs, bravely non-chalant. Marcel has toppled his king, left the play. This is a game he could see no way to win.

A touch on his arm. He blinks round, frowning – and there's Alfy.

'That someone I wanted you to meet . . .'

He excuses himself, follows Alfy across the room towards a girl in a dark dress who's peering round someone to watch him approach. She, also, is already somehow familiar.

He offers a hand; she takes it, stands on tiptoe to kiss his cheek.

'The Irishman. It is a great pleasure to see you again.'

'Enchanted,' he says, but, truth be told, he is put entirely on the back foot.

Jeannine Picabia. She must be – what? – twenty-four, twenty-five by now, though she still – has the slightness of a teenager. He remembers her at her father's studio, years ago. She sipped cordial and sat on the stairs. They'd talked about the paintings. He remembers the challenge of being soused, and trying to keep his words clear and straight, not breathing smoke and booze on her. Her cool, wry look.

'You must call me Gloria here.'

'Gloria?'

'Other names are for other places, other people.'

That look she gets from her father, at once earnest and playful.

'Gloria,' he says. 'I will forget I ever knew anything else.'

'A selective memory is a very useful thing. Moby also says you can keep a secret.'

'Moby?'

She nods to Alfy. 'Moby Dick here.'

He turns to Alfy, raises an eyebrow.

Alfy smiles. 'My *nom de guerre*.'

'Because of your bitter, vengeful temperament?' he asks.

143

'I think my massive girth. Or perhaps it's my complexion.'

Jeannine fishes out her cigarette case. She offers him, and he takes one. He thanks her, and sets down his glass to light her cigarette and then his. The hit of the Gauloise, after so much parsing out of cigarettes, is like learning to smoke all over again.

'Because most of Papa's friends were all such – I think you say in Ireland – gobshites?'

This makes him snort.

'I mean, they would talk and talk and talk and talk. And everybody's so busy talking nobody's listening to anything at all, all those words and none of them getting heard, nobody ever learning a thing.'

'Artists,' he says. Shrugs.

'That's no excuse.'

She blows smoke, taps her cigarette on an ashtray, lips twisted with pleasure, trying not to show it. One of Mary's beautiful things, this ashtray. Ceramic, swirled inside with inky blue.

'Anyway, you I remember,' Jeannine continues. 'You weren't one of the talkers. You'd gather up far more than you'd ever give away. You have a silent habit.'

He takes a sip of brandy, feels its sting, its dispersal on the tongue. Feels disarmed, to have been observed like this from years ago. To have been already known.

'And this silence of yours is a virtue, like the selective memory, in our line of work.'

'I'm not,' he says, 'a practical man.'

'But I still think you could be useful. Moby tells me that you know German and Italian and Spanish, as well as French and English.'

He tilts his head. This is true. 'Some better than others.'

'And you can type.'

'Not terribly well.'

'It won't matter.' Shifting on her feet a little, she looks up at him, bright and sharp. And he realizes that though they are supposedly in safe company, her voice has been falling, softening all this time, so that now she speaks almost in a whisper and he has to lean in closer to hear her.

'There are risks,' she says. 'What we're doing. It carries the death penalty now. These are anti-German acts. It is considered treason.'

'I know.'

'Are you still willing?'

'I am.'

She studies his expression, unsmiling. Then she says, 'Well, we'll keep you busy, Monsieur. You can be certain of that. It will help pass the time.'

He nods.

Alfy nudges him gently. 'I did not like to ask it of you, my friend,' he says. 'But I am glad that you are with us.'

'And you will need a codename now too, Irishman.'

He catches Suzanne watching them from all the way across the room. She closes her eyes in a slow blink and then she turns away.

What purpose can there be in pseudonyms, when they are all friends and acquaintances, when they have all known each other on and off for years?

They sit, chairs drawn up to a corner of the Pérons' dining table. Mania and Alfy lay out scraps of paper on the table-top. There were plums, brought up by a friend in the country; he has been given one, and has eaten it as slowly as he could. Now the stone is tucked into his cheek, and he shifts it on to his tongue from time to time and turns it over.

'Our job is information,' Mania says. 'We don't try to assassinate anyone; we don't blow anything up.'

'Good.'

'Our network covers the north-western quadrant of France,' Alfy says. 'We're getting information about troop movements, trains and shipping. We watch the Boches. A new corps colour was spotted on troops in Saint-Lô on Wednesday. We had the information in Paris by Thursday afternoon, and over to London by the evening.'

Alfy drags his chair forward. He shifts around the paper slips on the glossy wood.

'We get the information in on these little scraps of paper. Little bits that can be easily kept hidden. We will pass these on to you. Your job is to sort the information. Look for patterns, duplications, where one informant substantiates another. Look for the big picture.'

'I see.'

'Once you've found it,' Mania says, 'you make the big picture as small as possible. Boil it down until you have just the very essence. Because every extra word we send to London increases our exposure.'

'You could do it standing on your head,' Alfy says.

Alfy's broad, good-humoured face. There was the Lycée and then there was the Army and now there is this. Alfy's decisions seem the only reasonable responses to an unreasonable state of affairs. He contributes.

'Then you burn the source material, and you deliver your typescript, we'll tell you where. And that's it, job done.'

He asks, 'How long have you two been involved?'

'A little while now,' Mania says quietly.

'You never said.'

'You didn't ask.' Alfy shrugs. 'And you're a friend. It's dangerous.'

He turns the plum stone with his tongue, feels the seam, the final threads of flesh.

'And you are not native here. So.'

'They try and make it be about country.' He shrugs. 'I don't think it's really about country.'

Alfy leans away. Mania gives him a look, a smile.

'Last chance. If you want to back out now, before you get your hands dirty.' Alfy jerks his head towards the door. 'I'll see you for a beer, and we'll get stuck into that translation and never say another word about this.'

He sits his ground.

'All right,' Alfy says, 'so – and this is very important – just go on as normal, otherwise.'

Mania leans in. 'Really, don't change anything. You and Suzanne, just keep on as normal, and we'll make it look as though your new work is just more of the old. If anybody's watching you, they'll have no grounds for suspicion.'

'Thank you,' he says.

'Why's that?' Alfy asks.

He twists his lips. Shrugs. 'I'll be glad to be of use.'

Suzanne refers to the drawer as the Tinderbox. Things could so easily spark and catch and burn the whole place to the ground.

Alfy comes round to the apartment with his satchel full of typescript and a French–English dictionary. If he's stopped, they are working on the translation of *Murphy* into French.

The translation is getting nowhere.

The paper slips, though, are piling up; Alfy slides them from between the leaves of his dictionary, ruffles them out of his typescript. They fill up the drawer, dry and whispering like leaves.

He works at night, after curfew, the curtains drawn, observing blackout with all due diligence: one doesn't wish to draw attention. He empties the drawer out on to his desk; the paper scraps scatter like a parlour game. He slides them around. Looking for patterns. Matching them. Finding echoes.

Cigarette papers, a torn-up flour-bag. Some of them have been folded tiny and are now criss-crossed with creases, others have been rolled up into tight cylinders and must be rolled back on themselves to be flattened out. Sometimes there is a square of lavatory paper – quite a sacrifice – or the margin of a book, or a strip of advertising poster, the writing on the reverse, with the blocks of colour leaching through. Assembled there on the desk, these scraps of paper mark the movement of troops and materiel across the north of France.

And then, one day, on a dirty green omnibus ticket, five words appear in smudged graphite. Two of the same words are scratched on to the ripped-off corner of a menu; one of them is on a bit of paper bag; three are scribbled on to a panel of a cigarette packet. They are padded round and buffered with other stuff, but those same words keep emerging. He pushes his glasses back up to the bridge of his nose. In soft graphite and in neat hard pencil and in school-teacherly copperplate and pragmatic print, the five words step forward to be noticed. They can't be unnoticed now.

Four of the words are German. They are names of ships. *Scharnhorst, Gneisenau, Prinz Eugen.* One name is of a French port. *Brest.*

He sits there, fingertips on the bus ticket.

'What is it?' Suzanne asks. She sets aside her sewing, comes to him. 'Have you found something?'

He lines up the ticket alongside the lavatory paper. She cranes in; he taps the ticket with a blunt nail.

She presses a finger on a cigarette skin and drags it across the table to line it up beside the ones he has already selected.

'Is that what you were thinking?' she asks.

He nods.

He knows the town. Waves slopping against a harbour wall; a round tower; old men dangling lines into the water; children chalking a game on to the pavement. And these words, lined up in front of him now, could conjure

149

aeroplanes out of a clear sky, could bring all hell raining down on it. These words could take a hundred lives. A thousand.

'You'd only be passing it on,' she says.

He nods.

'It's not as if you'd be adding anything, or changing it.'

He nods again.

'And if you don't, and it might have done some good, if it could have helped bring things to an end, saved other lives . . .'

He closes his eyes. He breathes.

'Because you can't be certain, can you?'

He shakes his head to clear it. He lifts a sheet of *tellière*, folds it and tears it sharply along the fold. He scrolls the half-page into his Olivetti. His fingertips peck out the letters, and the letters strike on to the paper, and the letters cluster into words, and the words seethe on the page, and he can't bear this and yet it must be borne. He swallows down spittle, closes his eyes. All he can see is fire and blood and broken stone.

When he's finished – it is only a few lines to type – he slips the sheet between two pages of his manuscript, which is by far the safest place to keep something that he doesn't want anyone to read. He sweeps all the paper scraps together, then he gets down on hands and knees and checks the floor for drifting slips. He drags the table forward to be certain that nothing has been missed. He drops the crumpled scraps into the grate.

He sits back, rubs cold hands together, eases out his neck. 'You want to share a cigarette?'

He holds the flame to a curled edge of paper. He watches it catch and flare, then drops it into the grate. He lifts the match and lights his cigarette.

He feels the smoke fill his lungs and soothe them, and his head spins; he passes the cigarette on to her. The smoke slips slowly from his lips, towards the fireplace, where it is caught by the draw of the chimney. Their drooping tent stands behind them. It's as though they are camping out here on the floor.

With tired eyes, knees drawn up to her chin, she takes the cigarette. They watch the contagion of the flame, the way that black creeps across the white, then breaks into bits and falls in soft flurries.

'Alfy coming for the thing tomorrow?'

He shakes his head. 'I'm to make the drop-off. Him coming and going here so much, it's getting to look suspicious. He's given me the address. Place over near Parc Montsouris.'

She holds her thin hands up to the brief warmth. 'I don't need to know.'

'I know.'

'Just,' she says, 'be careful.'

The paper's gone, its warmth spent, in just a few moments. He lifts a poker, stirs the ashes. The flakes fall through the grate and he pulls the ash pan out to riddle through underneath, so that no word might remain allied to any other. So there is no suggestion that there were ever any words allied here at all.

'Now would be a good time to get raided,' he says.

'It's never a good time to get raided.'

'It's better than half an hour ago.'

'Don't wish it down on our heads, for goodness' sake.'

A little later, she says, 'We should find something else to burn. Burning only paper might look suspicious.' The chill has descended again; her breath mists the air.

'We're burning books, if anybody asks.'

'You could write one, instead,' she says.

'Ah yes. But who'd publish it?'

He leans against her, experimentally. She doesn't shy away. He slips an arm around her shoulders. She shuffles closer on the rug. They smoke the cigarette down to nothing, then drop the nothing in a saucer, so that it can be unpicked and the filaments of tobacco can be teased into a roll-up, later, when the need will come.

There are not too many people in the Métro at this time of day. Which is just as well, since every single one of them is a police informer, and every single one of them is staring at him. Not unreasonably, either: his bag has swollen to the size of a suitcase, and his legs have grown too long for him, and his elbows stick out like coat-hangers. He is a crane-fly carrying a brick. A flamingo in charge of a wardrobe. Who wouldn't stare?

He's on the train now, and it lurches away, and he sits down and lays the bag on his lap and folds his hands on top of it and sways with the motion of the train. The familiar smell of diesel and cigarettes and bodies and perfume and the contained space hurtling through the dark make it feel more like Paris down here than the city above now does. In the corners and margins, if one doesn't look too closely, Paris remains itself; the city lives on in its underground, in its catacombs; it has become its own reflection in the Seine.

He risks a glance around the carriage. A mother and son, neatly dressed, which isn't easy nowadays. They're not looking at him; the woman is murmuring something to the child. Across the aisle, an old lady in faded black sits with her old man beside her in working blue. Their tree-root hands lie in their laps, and they're not, after all, staring at him either.

The darkness rushes by outside; his bag is hot under his hands. The torn half-sheet of typescript lies between two pages of his manuscript translation. And even through the heft of those pages, that one paragraph fizzes. It is charged like nothing else that he has ever written.

'I'll be back by curfew,' he'd promised Suzanne.

'You better had be.'

And she had kissed him, and held him for a moment; then she had broken away and clattered up the steps into the little gallery bedroom and set about straightening up the bed. And he had closed the door on her and gone.

He climbs up the steps now at Denfert-Rochereau, out under the organic arch, blinking into the low sun. Head up but not too up; shoulders down but not too down. Walk as if it's no effort whatsoever. Though his body is a puppet handed to an idiot. All jerks and tweaks and janglings. Nothing is easy or natural any more.

The air is clean up here at Montsouris – there's so little fuel nowadays, so little traffic – and the late-afternoon autumn sun gives a nostalgic softness to the day. In this part of town there's not the scruff-and-scramble of his stretch of the rue de Vaugirard, where a stranger can blend into the bustle; this area is terribly nice and so terribly quiet: he is as exposed as a louse on a bald head.

His heart is pounding by the time he finds the place. Up in the lift – thank God for the lift, so that he can breathe and breathe and breathe, and hold up his hand and watch it shake and will it not to shake, and find that his will has no effect at all on the shaking of his hand. He wishes for a bonbon, a bit of coltsfoot rock to suck, for the comfort of sugar. Ah, the girls, the almost-nieces. The tangled hair and T-bar shoes. Where are they now, this moment, as he stands at the strange apartment door and lifts his shaking hand and knocks in the particular way that he's been taught to knock? Are they safe? For a moment there is no response to his knock, and he thinks, dreadfully, that he will have to go all the way back to the rue des Favorites with that bit of paper scorching a hole in his bag and melting the flesh off his leg. But then the door opens a crack, and there's a smooth young handsome face, and big dark eyes studying him.

'Yes?'

'Jimmy?' he asks. 'Jimmy the Greek?'

The young man says, blank, 'Where's Moby?'

'He can't make it. I'm . . . I'm the Irishman, he must have said. I've got the . . .' He holds up the bag.

The eyes flash wide. 'Mother of God. Don't tell the whole fucking floor!'

Then the door is opened fully, and he is swiped at to come in.

Jimmy the Greek – his name's not Jimmy and he's not really Greek – double-locks the door behind them.

'Right then, let's have it.'

He rests the bag on a knee, fumbles out the manuscript and shuffles the little half-sheet of *tellière* out from between the pages. Jimmy takes the paper off him. It must weigh almost nothing, but he's lighter for it, instantly.

'You should hang around a while.' Jimmy's already heading off down the corridor, the paper hanging like a bit of litter from his hand. 'So it doesn't look so much like a delivery.'

Down at the far end of the hall, Jimmy opens a door on to a heap of domestic clutter: brooms, mops, buckets, oil-skins and duster-coats, tins, a pair of broken boots. Close up, there's a reek of mothballs and shoe polish and borax and paint. A broom shifted out of the way, Jimmy drags the coats aside, and where there should be the back wall of the cup-board, there's a void. Photographic gear is ranged on the shelves, bottles and trays are laid out on a card-table. A little botched-together darkroom. Jimmy reaches inside, lifts down his camera. With all the cleaning products, even the smell of photographic chemicals will be masked.

'Used to be a hobby of mine,' Jimmy says, and shrugs, because now it could get him tortured, and then shot.

In the main room of the apartment, the high windows are hung with voile, screening the room and letting in a cool white light. The young man's hands are deft as he works, clearing the table, smoothing out the white cloth. The cruciform grey shadow of the window frame lies across it. Then, nearby, a floorboard creaks. He swings round – the dividing doors are blank behind him.

'Who else is here?'

'Nobody.'

Then a truck roars along the avenue below, and Jimmy bends over the document with his camera, and the shutter clicks, and the autumn sun and the shadows and a moment's silent time and the words that he has sifted out of all those other words on the paper slips, the words that he has decided are the ones that matter most, the words that he has typed out with his pecking fingertips – *Scharnhorst, Gneisenau, Prinz Eugen, Brest* – are captured on film.

When it happens, it happens by accident. They stumble their way into sex, too cold, too tired, too hungry to set out for it deliberately, and yet too starved of other pleasures to deny themselves or each other this. Sex has become more acquiescence than an active choice; a *why not* shrug, rather than an urgent *yes*.

Few clothes come off. Perhaps a scarf, but only when it twists too tight and a little slackness must be tugged into it before things can continue. Buttons are undone. Fabric is parted, rucked up, pushed aside. Only what is necessary is uncovered; there is no will or energy for more. Underneath

156

the clothes, new downy hair is growing on slack skin. Fleshless, the body insulates itself against the cold.

Movement disarranges the blankets; skin prickles with gooseflesh. She grumbles, tugs at the covers. He mumbles an apology and rolls away from her, and she sighs, and it is over, and it will have to do.

Planes climb into the sky; they grind over the chalky hills and crumbling shores and out over the creases of the waves; glazed with starlight, their muzzles slip through banks of muffling cloud, and back into the clear. They press towards the lip of this other land, where it juts into the sea.

The two of them lie in stillness, spent. The wet of his eyes is cold when he blinks in the darkness. The apartment is quiet. The street outside is quiet, after curfew; nobody is about. They breathe. Underneath the blankets, she tugs her skirt back down again. He pulls his combinations back and buttons up. They lie unspeaking, thoughts chewing on themselves.

Three hundred and twelve miles away, the night is torn in shreds; it streams with flame, and metal screams and splits, and bricks slither, and the water burns.

And he lies awake. He blinks up at the ceiling. She turns on her hip and is breathing softly into sleep. His thoughts are tangled, will not resolve themselves. Hunger and fatigue and the ache in his chest, and the cold and the old man in the song, dancing barefoot on the ice. And the harm that might come. From what he's done, from the words that he has chosen, and for the direction in which he has sent them.

*

Alfy brings the papers.

The papers pile up, and fill the drawer, and lie there dry and silent as fallen leaves. He spills them on his table, slides the scraps around. Matching them. Finding echoes. Looking for patterns. He translates, redacts, transcribes. He burns up the little slips. He takes the document to Montsouris, to be photographed, or Alfy takes it.

And Alfy brings more papers.

The papers pile up in the drawer. He pours them out, shuffles them around, a puzzle to be solved.

They go on as normal. They don't change anything. They go to concerts together at the Opéra; he takes himself off to exhibitions. He buys a new notebook – a pre-war, silken thing – and tries to write. He goes to see Alfy, because he's always gone to see Alfy. From time to time he passes the same man on the landing or stairs. A priest: fleshy smile, black soutane, and an incongruous whiff of cigars. He doesn't think to mention it to Alfy. There are many other apartments in the building; most likely a priest would be calling on somebody else. Life becomes a parody of itself: the walk to the shops, the drink in a café, the sketchy meals taken together, the conversations about anything other than what presses hardest on them. It is all self-conscious and unreal: there is always the possibility of an audience; everything is open to scrutiny and question. As he considers, in the Galerie Louis Carré, hands behind his back, some recent paintings by Rouault, he knows that he too might also be considered. The pictures are few and small and good, and he is captured by *L'Hiver*, where the roads are white and the land is dun and yet seems to be back-lit, glowing; the trees stand like gibbets by the roadside; figures trudge through the winter landscape, heads bent and hooded, rag-shod, all in couples apart from one shambling man who trudges off alone. The world is cold. He closes his eyes; the image is there like the afterburn from a bright window, exquisitely bleak. He takes a deliberate moment to remember it, to store up its loveliness. He is hoarding. These are famine times.

When he opens his eyes again, he turns his gaze to the parquet, resists the urge to cast around him. If he is being watched, let them make of this what they will. There are some needs he won't subdue.

And a year passes. And it goes on. His hands shake less now when he goes to make the drop. The bag no longer swells to the size of a wardrobe. And it all becomes normal, more or less, because anything can become normal, more or less, given time.

9

Paris
August 1942

A TELEGRAM IS a dreadful thing.

The flat is empty. It's the emptiness of a tea-tin; there are fragments, flakes of what's usually there caught around the seams: a pair of gloves, a hairpin on the mantelpiece, a needle-case.

Suzanne did tell him where she was going; he knows she did. He had looked up from his book and he had said, *Till soon*, and *Take care*. But he hadn't really listened and he really should have really listened, because it matters now, this coming-and-going, now there is a telegram icy in his hand, and the boy is staring at him boggle-eyed, and he doesn't know where Suzanne is, and if he had listened he would know, and he needs to find her now this minute. He needs her here already. Jesus Christ.

He counts coins into the dirt-creased palm; the boy blinks at him, then clatters off down the stairs, a clumsy gait, the wooden soles of his shoes flashing with nails. To have growing feet at a time like this. To want to run, and to be stuck with those wooden things.

He strips away the envelope.

She'd been standing at the door, putting her hat on, checking her reflection in the little mirror. She'd said, *I'm just popping out to . . . I'm calling round at . . . I'll be back by . . .*

His hands are shaking. He doesn't want to open it.

The printed words are clear; he stares and does not see; he refuses them, and yet they prickle through and make themselves known.

ALFRED ARRESTED BY GESTAPO

PLEASE TAKE THE NECESSARY STEPS TO CORRECT THE ERROR

MANIA PERON

Alfy.

Oh good God, Alfy.

He'll go to Mania. And the boys. There must be something he can do. God knows what, but he'll – there must be—

He is scooping up his keys, stringing his scarf round his neck, the telegram now crumpled in his fist – but then stops. He flattens out the paper, stares at the printed tape again, because –

The telegram doesn't actually say what it might have said.

It doesn't say, *Come and help me.*

It doesn't say, *Go and help him.*

It says, take steps to *correct the error.*

· 161 ·

He chews his lip. What does she mean?

Because Mania is sharp as a knife. And she will be thinking fast, and she'll be furious, frustrated, just as he is, because they don't have a code, they didn't even think to agree a code for this, or for any emergency. Everyone knows the telephone lines are tapped. Even a telegram is read by both operators, and by anybody standing at the operator's shoulder. Mania is trying to communicate with them without incriminating anybody – not them, not herself, and least of all Alfy.

What error?

And where is Suzanne? He grabs his coat and heaves it on, but then stalls. If he goes out looking, he might miss her, and then where would they be? She'd be here waiting for him while he was dodging round the streets and friends' apartments, while the Gestapo were putting on their gloves, straightening their caps and getting in their cars.

Time. Happening everywhere and all at once. It is a bastard for that.

He chews at a hangnail, pulls it off between his teeth. His finger bleeds.

Suzanne. Come on, Suzanne. Come home.

'They've taken Germaine too, and Legrand.'

'Christ.'

'We are betrayed.'

Suzanne's face is open as a wound. It doesn't bear thinking about. Perhaps their names are also on the list. Perhaps the

Geste are already on their way round here. He goes over to the window, peers down at the street. And even if they are not yet on the list, then they will be soon. So many friends arrested. A dark room; chains and pliers. None of it bears thinking about, and yet all of it must be thought.

'Anybody out there?' she asks.

'Not a soul.'

He realizes now what it was, that error that must be corrected. It is the misapprehension under which they had been living all along – that they could just go on like this, that it would continue. They had not realized that the world would one day just crumple up and blow away. But the apartment is made of paper, and the streets are botched-up stage-flats and the wind blows right through it all and it creaks and strains. It's not safe here. It never was. That's what they must correct: their deluded sense that things will just go on.

'Do you think Alfy would . . . ?'

His stomach heaves. Yell my name the first chance you get, Alfy old son, spill the fucking beans, cough it all up. Give 'em chapter and verse, inside leg and shoe-size, before you lose a single fingernail on my account. Don't you take one cigarette burn for me, God love you. Alfy. God love you.

'No. I don't know. But he's only one. So.'

'We have to warn everyone,' she says. 'Everyone we can. And then we have to get away from here. I'll run round to Hélène's.'

'I'll phone Jimmy and the others.'

'Watch what you say.'

'Of course.'

She shoulders her bag. He crouches to knot a broken bootlace.

'Have you any change?' he asks. 'I gave my last to the telegraph boy.'

She fumbles in her purse, tips coins into his palm.

'Be careful,' he says.

Suzanne opens the door out on to the dim landing, then pauses on the threshold and looks back at him, in all this rush and fluster, as he gathers up his things.

He raises an eyebrow at her. What?

'I keep wishing you had not come back,' she says. 'I wish you weren't here, you know. Every moment. But I still don't want you gone.'

He huddles in the telephone booth. It smells of polish, tobacco smoke and other people. He dials number after number. Number after number rings out unanswered, in rifled apartments with overturned desks and papers half-burned in the grate, where the rugs are rippled by struggles, by sliding feet; its ringing can be heard on landings, where a door, forgotten in the tussle, has been left ajar.

He asks the operator for the number Jimmy the Greek had given him. Only for emergencies. He listens to the clicks and fuzz on the line. Then it rings.

The phone rings and rings and rings and rings. And there is no reply.

And then a clatter at the other end – the mouthpiece lifted.

'Hello?'

'It's me.'

No reply to this.

'The Irishman.'

The stark insufficiency of that pseudonym. He can hear Jimmy's breath on the mouthpiece, listens for a click, a hum, some indication that the line is being tapped. No code, no fucking code; how can they have got this far without a code? What he would give now for a word that to just the both of them meant, *The Gestapo are on to us, destroy the evidence, get your things together and get away.*

There is just the thin glass panel between him and the lobby. The concierge is very carefully not looking at him, very deliberately not noticing. She is pushing a broom around the floor. He clears his throat, speaks into the receiver.

'I telephoned to let you know, my friend, I find I am very busy at the moment.'

Jimmy's voice comes intimate and soft. 'What a coincidence. So do I.'

'And I think I must expect to be so for the foreseeable future, so I shall not be available—'

'I believe that will be much the same for me.'

'Many of my acquaintances are also very busy at this time.' Another pause. 'Mine also.'

'Well, until we are more at our leisure, then.'

'Yes,' Jimmy says. 'Until then.'

'Goodbye,' he says. 'Good luck.'

He sets the mouthpiece down on the stand, rests his forehead against the panel above. He lets a breath go. Then he fumbles in his pocket for more change. He begins again to dial.

He closes the apartment door behind him and it is sugar-glass. It is barely there at all.

'Suzanne?' He hears the shake in his own voice.

She clips down the steps from the mezzanine, her coat on, piled clothing in her hands, shopping bag on her shoulder. No time for courtesies, endearments. She sets the folded clothes on the arm of the sofa, says, 'Where's your bag?'

'Eh?'

'You know, that dreadful old satchel thing of yours.'

He finds it – he didn't know she didn't like it – hanging on a peg underneath his other jacket. He hands it to her. She slides his manuscript from the drawer into the bag.

'I was too late,' she says over her shoulder.

'What?'

'They've got Hélène.' She turns back to him. Her eyes are brimming, but she is still all briskness. 'The Geste were there, in her apartment, when I arrived.'

'Jesus.'

He moves towards her; she just shoves his bag into his hands.

'But they let you go . . .' he says.

'I played the innocent. I said I had called round to see about her cat.'

'Oh God, that bloody cat.'

She lifts the pile of clothing from the arm of the settee. 'I sorted this for you. Underwear, sweater, shaving gear.'

166

'Thanks.' He just stands there, holding his bag in a bundle, feeling the weight of his manuscript.

'Clothes. Now. Please.'

Yes. Of course. He opens up the bag so that she can stuff them in.

'Are you going to be all right in those boots?' she asks.

He glances down at them. 'The others are worse.'

'Right then. Well. They'll have to do. Come on.'

He follows her out on to the landing. He fumbles with his keys, turns back to the door. He locks up. His hand shakes. His face feels tight and hard. He wonders if they will ever be here again. They head down the stairs. Brisk, light, but deliberately not running. They might pile straight into the Gestapo coming up to find them. They must not look as though they are trying to escape.

'We're popping out for a stroll, we'll stop at a café,' she says back over her shoulder. 'Tell yourself it's an ordinary day.'

Their hands skim down the banister.

'Where will we go?' he asks. 'Do you have any notion?'

'A friend of mine; he'll help us.'

'What friend?'

Even in all this, that little sour twist of jealousy. They're in the lobby. She drops her voice still further, speaks over her heaving breath.

'You've met him, at those evenings. Michel. You remember?'

He shakes his head. Maybe.

'It's what he does. He helps people.'

Right. He holds the *porte cochère*, peers out. The street is clear. She ducks through; he follows. He offers his arm and she takes it. The door slams shut behind them on the lobby and the staircase spiralling up seven floors to the flimsy door locked on silent space and the dust falling on books, and on the floorboards, and on the heavy dark hand-me-down table that Nora Joyce had given him, on *Mein Kampf* and his battered coffee pot and his ashtray dusted with tobacco ash, and the drooping canvas tent and the Turkish rug.

They walk along the street together, their arms linked, carrying shopping bag and satchel, as ordinary as the day itself. They don't know where they're going, but they go.

Part Two

Purgatory

10

Paris
August 1942

THE GRANDFATHER CLOCK ticks. One weight sinks, its chain mumbling through blunt teeth, teasing cogs around. Somewhere in its innards something clunks and shifts, and it begins to chime the quarter-hour.

Which makes it a quarter past three.

He fans his toes, flexes his ankles.

Which makes it a quarter past three, on Friday, the twenty-first of August, nineteen forty-two.

If the clock is right.

He rolls his head softly side-to-side. He can still make these small movements. And while he can, it seems important that he does. When he turns his head to the left, there is light pouring down through a knothole, and beyond it shafts through the gaps between the boards, where sometimes dust too falls in tiny streams. When he turns to the right, there is a black rectangular patch over the floorboards, and this is the rug, which covers the loosened planks where they can clamber out, at those times when they can be out. There is all this, and there is the old man lying next to him.

He's got used to the various and mingled smells by now. The old man's and his own. He barely notices the body odour, the bad breath – it's only when one of them lets out a particularly rancid fart – bad food, and the acid from not having enough of even bad food that makes your stomach eat itself and turns your guts to treacle – that a smell is particularly noticeable. Interesting, to see what one can become accustomed to.

The old man has an enviable capacity for sleep. His breast, under his white beard, falls and rises softly. His face is fascinating: the way the skin slides from his cheekbones and forehead and gathers in concertinas at his ears, leaving the skull visible at the eye sockets and the bridge of the nose. Raising his head a little, he can peer down the length of their parallel bodies and see the old man's feet, bootless, one yellow toe poking through a grey sock.

Sometimes the old man snores. He lets him snore and does not nudge him.

He can himself, sometimes, if he's very lucky, drift out of consciousness for a bit. A swooping fall, a card-sharp rush of images, one replacing the other before any single one of them can be understood. Then he's jerked back, blinking at the boards above his head.

He raises his shoulders to his ears, the blades sliding up the boards beneath him and back down again, like failing wings.

It is not so bad, not really. It is not so bad.

Sometimes, when the old man is awake, he combs his beard with his fingers and mutters to himself. He's Russian. What he's saying could be prayers, or he could be telling stories, or he could simply be reminding himself of better days. But the old man has a listener, alert for patterns, names, anything familiar, trying to pin the sounds down into sense.

He is learning Russian in the gap between the ceiling and the floor.

It is not going quickly.

But then there is no rush.

It is a relief when the old man starts up his muttering. It helps to pass the time.

Other things are passed too, down there between the ceiling and the floor. A bottle stands between them. She leaves it down there empty, retrieves it once it has been used. One unbuttons one's fly and shuffles about and inches up on elbows and pisses with great difficulty, while the other fellow turns his head away, or is, often enough, already asleep. He finds that, all in all, he feels fondly towards the old fellow. He is a gracious pisser and a courteous sleeper; he does not fart as much as might be supposed. If one must have company, this is not bad company to have.

There are also hours spent in the house itself, with the wireless on, the wife and husband home and nobody else expected. The old man sits in the corner by the grandfather clock, and he himself, a fifth wheel, tries to stay out of the way as well as stay away from the windows. This is when the day is done, the shops downstairs empty, and it is to be expected that there will be people at home. Even the slightest out-of-the-ordinary occurrence is questionable now. It only takes a word from a concerned citizen about strangers in the building, or figures moving around a supposedly empty apartment, and they are done for.

So they talk in hushed voices; he stretches out his legs, eases the clicks out of his knees. They share their bad food with him. He joins them at the table for sulphurous stews of turnip and cabbage and beans. He eats little, is constantly hungry. Hunger is normal. You can get used to it, to its incremental twist. In hiding, he can no longer claim his rations, and beyond a little money for off-ration things like blood pudding and root vegetables, he has nothing to contribute here. He just consumes, and excretes, and is dependent on the family to deal with both. He feels the indignity of that; it renders him just animal.

He shaves at the stone sink. He looks at himself in the scrap of mirror, at the angles of his bones. He's no more than a few miles across town from his apartment, but it might as well be another country, since he cannot go back there. He sees in himself now a quality of the patients he'd met at the Bethlem hospital, that time Geoffrey Thompson had taken him to look round. They'd roam the corridors, disoriented and hopelessly lost, but never more than a few yards from their beds.

Geoffrey Thompson. How he's getting on, now? He'll be busy; he'll be rushed off his blessed feet, now that the whole world has gone mad.

He scrapes away the stubble, leaves his top lip unshaven. He is growing a moustache. It's good to have a hobby.

For Suzanne, he wishes daylight, air, the occasional cup of coffee. He wishes her to be safe. They have been separated, so as to be less conspicuous. They will be returned to each other when their new, fake papers have been achieved.

He listens to the Russian but he thinks in French, in its uncompromising precisions, and in German, its words fitting themselves together like links in a necklace, and in Italian, which falls through his thoughts as smooth as drops of water. He strokes that new moustache and thinks in English too; his thoughts assemble themselves in its measured blocks. An English sentence is a brick. To build with, yes, a solid structure; something one can inhabit. But also a dividing wall, a closing-off; a limitation.

The chap has a mouse-brown suit and an old Mossant fedora gone dark around the band where he has sweated through it. His chin is shaven shiny. He hands over the new papers, then dabs at his forehead with a handkerchief; his line of work is enough to make anybody sweat. They step out into the corridor. He glances back – the apartment is empty for the day. The old grandfather is asleep beneath the floor. He closes the door behind him. He will not have the chance to say goodbye. To say thank you. For the bad food, and the floorboards, and the risk that they have undertaken on his behalf.

He pockets his papers. They clip down the stairs and out of the doors into the street.

'Where are we heading?'

'Hotel in the Fifteenth.'

'Will Suzanne be there?'

A brisk nod. A gesture of impatience: they have to get a bloody move on if they are to get there before curfew. They also have to look as though they're not in any hurry whatsoever.

They are approaching a tram halt when they spot the Gendarmes on board, checking papers; they duck down a side street. But then there is a checkpoint on the rue des Ombres, which they swerve again to avoid. There's a long loop round through back streets and alleyways, and they find themselves in the leafy haut-bourgeois Sixteenth, not far from the Bois de Boulogne, where nobody is ever in a hurry, where women snuggle into their furs and feed their tiny dogs on black-market ham, and time ticks slow and weighs a ton, and half the apartments are locked up and empty, their owners gone to the country.

He knows that they look very out of place indeed. In their worn and grubby suits they look like a couple of housebreakers. Unsuccessful ones.

The shadows are long and the sun is low; the air is filling up with darkness like smoke.

'Today's Tuesday . . .' he says.

'Yep.'

And so the world goes on, and time keeps passing. Ticktock. Tuesday slides into Wednesday, and Wednesday crumbles into Thursday and for a good while Thursday seems solid and secure, but inevitably it too shivers and falls and Friday is triumphant, and what he really needs to do is notch it up, note it down, tick it off, keep a tally of the days, to notice time as it is passing, because he fears he is losing his grip on it, and there can be no break, no abeyance, no lacuna: time ticks by and it is their time, his and everybody else's, and what they do in it, and with it, is not separate and distinct from before and afterwards; it is a continuation, and it must be acknowledged as such; time will have to be reckoned with eventually. And so he must check and clarify and notice. He will not let himself come adrift from it.

They turn the corner.

'Oh, the cow.'

There's a checkpoint. Police glance at papers, ask lazy questions of two plump matrons in their furs.

'Nice area for it.'

'Bluff it out?'

Sucked teeth. It's a risk.

Their stride is already shortening, their pace slackening off. The matrons will soon be sent on their way: they can't have anything to hide. There's money in their purses; they're wearing furs. Of course they're law-abiding; the laws suit them.

'C'mon,' the chap says, and they turn and cross the street. 'We'll head through the park.'

Between the trees it's already so much darker. Gravel crunches underfoot.

'Which way?'

'If we head round to the Place de Colombes, then double back, we should be all right.'

'Good. Come on.'

The man's really sweating now, trotting to keep up alongside his lope. The setting sun shafts through the trees, and over the open glades a faint mist rises. There's just their ragged breath – he has no stamina nowadays – and the crunch of gravel, and birds settling in the trees, and something rustling through the shrubbery.

'With any luck,' the man says, 'people will think we're out chasing whores.'

'That still happens here?'

'More than ever. If there's any truth to rumour.'

But luck is an unlucky word; said out loud it just dissolves. Because only a moment later they hear the dogs.

Barrel-chested barking. A pair of them, at least; maybe more. These are not some sclerotic old pugs out for an airing. These are big dogs, hounds.

'You hear that?'

'It's nothing.' They come to a fork in the track; he heads towards the left-hand path. 'It's not to do with us.'

But a hundred yards further on, they hear the voices. Somewhere ahead and off to the right: between them and the maze of city streets. They are speaking German.

'Last seen headed across the Place de la Porte . . .'

They stop dead. He can feel his breath dragging in his chest. He presses a hand to his scar.

'. . . must presume they entered the park.'

He looks to the little man, who shakes his head; he doesn't understand. 'What are they saying?'

He waves a hand to shush him, listening.

'. . . start by the lake and sweep across. We'll send the dogs round the other way.'

The little man raises his hands, nonplussed. What to do?

He finds himself in charge. A low jerk of the arm: come on.

One of the dogs lets out a howl and others join it. Voices call back and forth between the trees. There are footfalls on the track behind them: more than one person, gaining on them.

They peel off the pathway, duck under the low boughs, dodge between the trees. Fallen leaves, dry branches: the noise of their passing is agonizing. It is impossible, though, to go silently.

They slip round the thick trunk of a sycamore and hunker down. The colour is seeping from the world.

'Split up?' the man breathes.

'Do you think?'

'Halves the chances of being caught.'

'Doubles it?'

A dog bays; they flinch down, speak very low.

'Closer.'

'Think so.'

'Have you got anything?'

He doesn't follow. 'Cigarette?'

'No. If they get their hands on you.' A heave of breath. 'For that.'

'Oh. No. Have you?'

A nod. 'I don't think mine will stretch.'

The man leans back against the trunk, his belly heaving like a frog's, and closes his eyes.

He, though, hunkered down in the fallen leaves, looks round him, rubbing at his arms. He feels the chill. He doesn't want this. He can't face this. The words feel childlike, *Boy's Own*:

'We could swim the lake,' he says. 'Doesn't that put dogs off a scent?'

The man's eyes open, his irises black in the half-light. 'And if we got away from this lot, we'd just get picked up by the next patrol. Soaked through, in the Sixteenth.'

'There is that.'

Then eyes widen: boots thud past behind them along the footpath they've just left. They hold their breath. Just one man, going at a run; he's gone, and the breath slides out of them again.

'Have you got much you can give them?' the man asks.

He swallows. 'A bit.'

'That's the problem, isn't it? People. People you can hurt.'

'People are always the problem.'

The fellow sinks down off his hunkers so that he's now sitting on a root. He draws his knees up. The noise seems to be coming from all directions now, men and dogs, and with it the scrape of torch beams through branches, tree trunks, the failing light. They're done for, surely.

'I can't see how we can be worth all this madness.'

Still on his hunkers, he rests a hand, fingers tented, on the bole. He peers around through the trees; he glances back towards the path. They can't move. They can't stay where they are. They can't both kill themselves, and he for one finds that he would much rather survive the night. Suzanne is waiting for him, and will be annoyed if he does not show up. So what's left? The grained, elephantine bark beneath his fingertips. His eyes slide upwards, through drooping branches and the fading rusty leaves, right up into the canopy of the sycamore. It is dim in the gathering dusk and still thick with foliage. Head tilted back, his balance fails and he has to steady himself. The set of his features changes; the lines shift around his eyes.

He turns back towards the little man, taps knuckles against his arm.

Eyebrows up, his expression: what?

He jerks his head upwards.

The man twists his head to peer up along the rising height of the tree. His Adam's apple rolls down then back up his throat. 'I don't like heights,' he says.

He, though, unfolds himself, looks upwards, dusting off his hands. A moment, then the other man gets stiffly to his feet. They stand side-by-side, a pair of schoolboys considering the climb. There are strong drooping branches, but they're only low enough to get hold of at some distance from the tree, leaving one out, as it were, on a limb. Close to the trunk, nothing's within easy reach, at least for the smaller man. So the only thing for it: back set to the tree, a cup made of his palms, he offers a boost. The other fellow swallows queasily, but sets a boot in the hands and is heaved upwards. A grab for the lowest bough, a foot on his shoulder, then the weight is gone and the other fellow's scrambling up amongst the branches. He leaps for the lowest branch and pulls himself up after, satchel swinging.

The little man clambers up a few branches and then stops, and shakes his head at the notion that he might go any higher. A pat on the shoulder, and then the reach and swing that is so long ago and so familiar, the memory buried in his muscles and his nerves. Even the sting of the palms. He remembers that.

Perched high above, his back to the trunk, astride a beam, he tucks his dark muffler over the pale line of his shirt collar, tugs his sleeves down over his cuffs; they are more grey than white but they would still show up in a flashlight. He hooks his arm around a higher branch, tucks his bag close and ducks his nose down into his scarf. It's all right, actually.

Across the woods, saplings and undergrowth shiver with movement; he can hear the crunch and thrash of men through the brushwood; flashlights swipe across the dark.

He chews at the inside of his cheek. He closes his eyes. Takes himself away to this: the white road gleams under the travellers' ragged feet, and the dun field glows, and the sky above is a translucent slate-blue; the delineation brisk, the outlines strong; the whole thing is as luminous as a stained-glass window. The light of that other world beyond shines through for Rouault, as it cannot shine for him.

When he opens his eyes again, he can still see the bundle of the man below him, clinging to the trunk like a fungus.

The dark gathers; it rises from the earth like groundwater. Above, the stars prick through. It's getting cold. He shifts, resettles himself. He eases out the ache in his neck. The wind stirs the tree, and the branch heaves and the trunk sways and the leaves rustle and clouds scud across the sky. The voices come and go. The dogs are distant, then nearer again. He dozes, wakes. Suzanne will be annoyed. He lays his cheek against his arm and dreams.

He falls, arms spread, through the painless brush of branches and the soft caress of twigs and needles, and it is all perfectly pleasant while he falls, but when he hits the ground he will be dead.

He blinks awake. His eyes open on the drop: fifty foot to the bare ground. He has slumped forward in his sleep, his whole weight hangs from that one arm. Between him and the root-troubled earth is the hunched form of his friend, still clamped to the bole. It's lighter now; the night is fading into day and they are both still there. Still ticking on.

He shifts his grip, struggles himself up. His arm has gone to sleep and his chest aches. He clambers down until he is alongside his friend, one hand on a higher branch, one foot dangling, perched neatly.

'How's it going?' he asks.

The man peels his face from the trunk; he blinks. His cheek is printed with bark. He smells musky. He doesn't speak.

'You stiff?'

A slow blink. The fellow's eyes are glazed; he doesn't seem to be taking anything in.

'All right, old chap. Help you down. If you could just—'

But his friend just lays his face against the trunk again, and does not move.

But it is really, really time to go. Before the early-morning dog-walkers notice them; before the search party turns up and has another go. What to do? He climbs down one branch so he is below now, and turns his face away from the smell of urine.

'Just give me your foot, there's a good chap. Just in my hand.'

The man shakes his head.

'Come on now; it's a simple affair. I used to do it all the time as a boy; I bet you did too.' This is something of a lie: he climbed *up* trees all the time. He rarely had to trouble himself with climbing down.

The voice is tacky and dry. 'I don't like heights.'

'I know, I know, I see that. But . . .' The boot in his hands now. 'Try.' He coaxes the boot off the joint of branch and trunk where it is wedged, and pulls it lower. His friend remains stiff and resistant.

'All right?'

'No.'

But the foot shakingly descends.

They inch their way, foothold-handhold, foothold-handhold, down to the lowest bough. He drops loosely to the ground and turns to coax the smaller man to drop; he staggers backwards with him in his arms.

'And there we are. *Terra firma.*'

The man looks around him vaguely. He rubs his face, digs at his closed eyes. 'We'll go . . . we'll go to . . . the hotel.'

'One moment.'

Leaving his friend there by the sycamore, he strides off into the bushes, unbuttons, and pisses long into the mulch.

*

They scuff through the dawn streets. He unkempt, unshaven, self-conscious and on the *qui vive* and trying not to look like it. The other fellow is shuffling along half a pace behind him, walking stiff-legged because of his damp and chafing trousers, and he can't be made to keep up. He's muttering to himself now, and from time to time waving an arm: we go this way; I think it's this way – no, I don't know. Oh shit, I don't know, what are we going to do . . . ?

It's not good, wandering. One may walk, of course, but one must have a purpose to one's walk. The tramps have all gone; the *flâneurs* have given up. One walks to get where one is going, or one stays at home. Which is why the two of them – he a great gangling streak of piss, his friend a waddling puddle of it – make as conspicuous a couple as Laurel and Hardy in these Paris morning streets, and are drawing almost as much attention from the street-sweepers and the bin men and the delivery boys.

They find a café just off the rue Grenelle and order coffee. He mentions the inconvenience of having missed the last train home the previous evening: it really breaks his feet, you know. His friend just drinks his barley coffee in hot mouthfuls and won't be coaxed into better spirits. Hotel, wash, a change of clothes and a comfortable bed; a good sleep; feel so much better after that. No response beyond a blink, a nod. They settle up, and they stumble out again into the cold daylight.

'Now then, my friend, not far.'

But what if Suzanne is gone? And what if she is still there, and furious with him?

The hotel is the kind of hotel you'd find on any street in Paris. The paint is faded and peeling, and the windows are filmed with street dirt. A thin woman in a dull dress slips in behind the counter and opens up the register; a girl pauses with her broom to watch them pass. She sucks a finger.

His head is swimming with fatigue. His eyes feel as though they have been sandpapered. The woman hands him a form to fill in. He takes the stub of pencil. He can't remember what his name is supposed to be.

The little man shuffles up beside him, licks his lips. 'Your papers.' Meaning, the new name is there and he can copy it.

He fumbles his card out and lays it open on the counter, facing the receptionist. He reads his new name upside-down, licks the pencil tip and glances down the list in the guest book – and there it is. Suzanne's handwriting; a new faked name. Signed in yesterday and – he scans across the column – out again early this morning. While he was swilling ersatz coffee in that steamy little café, she was taken on somewhere else, Lord knows where. When he finally catches up with her, she is going to be so cross.

He prints; he signs. What to do now? How does he go about finding her?

'D'you have any matches?' the other fellow asks, out of nowhere.

He frowns round at him.

'Matches. You used to see them, didn't you, in places like this? Bowls full of matchbooks, just lying out on the counter. And sweets sometimes; heaps of bonbons.'

He slides the guest book over. 'I'll give you a light in a minute.'

'Your room will be on the fourth floor,' the woman says. 'It's nice and quiet.' She turns back with the key, then barks past them, 'Marthe, don't stand around gawping. Hop to it, girl!'

The girl jumps. She shunts the broom along.

They climb long slow stairs to their room, getting light-headed with the climb. But the room is a room, and so much better than a tree for being comfortable in. It is full of light. They close the shutters, and close the windows, and close the curtains, and shut the daylight out. He unlaces and pulls off his boots. He sinks back on one of the narrow beds; it creaks and sags into a pit.

His friend perches on the end of the other bed, nearer the window. The counterpane creases under his weight. He is still wearing his damp trousers. But he is busy smoking now. He finishes his cigarette and lights another from the glowing tip of it; smoke spools upwards, oozes from his lips. You'd think he didn't know about the rationing. The little man is smoking as though there's no tomorrow.

He, though, just lies back on his bed and looks up at the ceiling, with its faint repeat of embossed diamonds and flowers, and conserves his energies and his cigarettes. He counts the dead flies in the frosted-glass lampshade.

'Do you know where she'll have gone, Suzanne?' he asks, after a while.

The man shifts a little on the bed. 'Someone will contact us.'

She could be holed up in a basement, or in someone's maid's room, or be staring at the ceiling in a different hotel. She could be miles across town or she could be just a street or two away. Anxiety tugs out the knots and snags and smoothes over the roughnesses; it leaves things simple, easy, clean. Right now, even if she's fuming at him, at this moment he would call it love.

'Printer by trade,' the man says. 'I was. Before all of this.'

He lifts his head a little; chin compressed, he looks down the length of the bed at him. 'Were you now?'

'Posters, mainly. Handbills,' he says. 'Circuses and fire-sales, concerts and lectures, all that kind of thing.' He lifts a hand, shows it. The fingertips are grimed and grey, the nails stained. 'Mark of Cain,' the fellow says. 'You can always tell a printer by his hands. Printers' ink. Does not wash off. A trade will do that to you: it'll mark you some way.'

'Good work, was it?'

'It wasn't bad. Before the war.' He raises his shoulders. 'Now it's shit. It's money and it's a job and that's not to be discounted. And it helps in one way because all the time I'm printing their devilry I look like I'm on their side. It's cover. And maybe I do this in part because I must also do that. To redress the balance.'

The monkey-clawed rabbis; the kind Nazi soldiers with children on their shoulders.

'I had a copy of *Mein Kampf*,' he says, by way of consolation.

The other fellow nods, understanding.

'So what – we just wait?'

'Madame downstairs – she'll get word back that we've arrived.'

'Oh.' He reconsiders the girl, the woman; remembers pale skin, fragile bird-bones.

'Someone will come.'

'Someone?'

Then his friend turns away and lights up another cigarette.

He lies back, hand behind his head. The bed, sunken and narrow, is nonetheless a marvel. He lifts a hand and looks at it. There's a dent in the side of his middle finger where his pen rests, and his fingertips are slightly bent and flattened from thumping on his typewriter keys. That's what a trade will do.

The day lengthens. It stretches and spools. He drifts in and out of sleep. There are daytime sounds from the street below – both French and German voices – and he is gone and back again, and there's the chime of a municipal clock, and he counts the chimes and hopes that he missed a couple of the strikes in his sleep, since otherwise it's only ten in the morning, even though an age has passed already in this room.

The light sharpens and the shadows deepen; sun slices through the shutters and streaks the curtains. The man

189

mutters under his breath and from time to time utters something out loud. The sound jerks him out of sleep, but he fails to catch the sense and he drifts again.

Later, he wakes, and props himself up on his elbows. The man is still there, hunched on the end of the other bed. Another cigarette has burned itself to ashes between his inky fingers.

He blinks at his watch, wipes his lips; they're tacky with spit.

'They should have come by now,' the man says.

He raises the watch to his ear, listens to its tick, then winds it.

'They should have sent word by now, at least,' the man insists.

He sits up, swings his legs over the side of the bed. He rubs his forehead. 'Did you sleep?'

'No.'

'Maybe they did send word. Shall I go and ask?'

'She'd have come and told us. It's the network. They're blown, I reckon.'

'No.'

'Or they'd be here. That's what I'm telling you.'

'Maybe someone's bike's been stolen, or they've got a flat tyre. Or they've got lost. They've forgotten the address.'

Out in the street, distant at first – rounding the corner and the noise increasing – the sound of diesel engines: two, three. The man stiffens; his eyes widen.

'It's them.'

'No—'

'It's the Geste.'

'No.'

'I'm telling you. German car – two trucks. It's the Gestapo.'

He pushes up from the bed, springs jangling. And then just stands there. The noise gets louder, the vehicles approaching – and then passing, and rounding the corner, and gone. A breath released. The man crosses to the window, edges back the curtain. They peer down together through the closed shutters; their faces are raked across with stripes of sunlight. In the street below, there is quiet, not even a pigeon strutting. The passing-by has swept the place quite clear.

'Do you know what they do if they get hold of you?' the man asks.

He tilts his head. He has heard stories.

The man nods slowly at something going on inside his head. He says, 'When she was expecting our first, my wife wasn't at all afraid. Our first child, I mean.'

'Oh.'

'She thought she could just, you know, stand it. That she would be brave and strong and that it would be all right. Second time, though, she was terrified. See, the thing is, you can't imagine pain. You can't foresee it. You think you can still be yourself, endure it and go on, but you can't. Pain makes an animal out of everyone.'

'You should sleep.'

The man just looks at him. His eyes are red.

'Really. It'd do you good.' He sinks down on his bed again and peels off his socks. They are stiff and stinking. He bundles them up and stuffs them into his trouser pocket. 'Lie down, at least,' he says. 'We just have to wait it out.'

A long look, and then, 'I don't know how you can stand it.'

'It's better than the tree.'

His friend blinks acquiescence. He leans closer to the window. Peers out again.

The hall is dim and stuffy and smells of old polish. It's wearing on the nerves, of course it is, being stuck together like this. He leaves the other fellow to himself for a while.

He finds the little room with its high cistern and dangling chain. Outside a fire-escape switchbacks down into the courtyard, past guano-streaked brick walls and a blanket-stitch of pipes. He runs a bowl of water, soaks his socks and rubs them with a slip of hard green soap. Sounds rise up from the yard below, bouncing and echoing in the shaft – women's voices. The neighbourhood chars are lost in recollection. It's almost pornographic. One lusts for vanilla sugar, for a coffee Liégeois, for, oh my God, warm June strawberries and cream; another craves savoury foodstuffs; the seashell salt of *pistaches*, slippery fresh oysters, a briny crumb of Roquefort.

He leaves his socks marinating in the cloudy water. He unbuttons and sinks down on the lavatory seat.

The problem is, of course, not just the fear; it's also the being dragged out of normality. Sleep, yes, and space, and clean clothes, and food – all these things are reassuring because they suggest that everything is as it should be. He

192

hopes the fellow's sleeping by now. He'll spin it out a bit, his absence. He'll wash, and then he'll go downstairs and ask if there is anything to be had. A fried kidney; a gorgonzola sandwich. Where would the old man have gone anyway after the *Wake*, where was there left to go – the last book that Paul Léon had wanted, was there ever any chance of that? – but to the grave, God help him, and ill for so long too, permanently unwell, if only fifty-eight.

He tugs a square of old newspaper from the copper wire and wipes, and stands and pulls up his breeches, flushes, buttons, dips his hands in the soapy water with the socks, and rubs and twists and rinses them and wrings them again and shakes them. He drapes them over a pipe while he strips to the waist, runs fresh water, douses his face, puffing at the cold. He rubs round the back of his neck and under his arms, and dries his prickling flesh with the crusted loop of hand-towel. The socks gather up what's left of their wetness and drip it on to the tiles. He squeezes them out again into the basin.

He is crossing the landing, barefoot, socks in one hand, boots in the other, when he hears the voices welling up from the lobby. Both are speaking French; one accent is German.

Bare bony feet fanned out on the worn matting, he stands stock-still.

There are some rooms occupied, she is saying. There always are. She has a lot of businessmen here, up from the provinces. She always has had. They are busy men; they come and go. Sometimes they leave their keys, sometimes they forget. Men can be so careless; they have other things on their minds.

'And there has been nothing of late that seems at all suspicious?'

'Things are as they always have been.'

'Of course. Because if there had been anything out of order, you would already have reported it.'

A silence. It can only be supposed that she nods.

'I shall need to see the register.'

Upstairs, on the landing, he takes a step, breath held, towards their room. He thinks: fire-escape, courtyard, away along the back alley and put distance between themselves and the hotel. Where next, he doesn't know. His friend will have some idea.

He eases the bedroom door open.

And the light is brilliant; it dazzles him; it makes no sense. The curtains billow, and there's fresh air on his face, and the window is open, and the shutters wide, and it makes no sense at all. And his friend stands there, framed in the wide-open window, his back to the room; he is silhouetted against the autumn sky.

'Hello there—' he calls, but he doesn't have a name to call him. 'Hey, my friend—'

He sees the blank panes of the building opposite reflecting the sky, the potted red geraniums on a balcony, a pigeon shuffling itself along a balustrade. He sees his friend put a foot on to the little wrought-iron railing, and step up, and spread his arms wide across the light. He sees his friend dive out into the empty air.

The pigeon flaps away. He sees the scarlet blotches of geraniums, the gunmetal windows, the drenching white light.

Then there's a crunch like a sack of coal fallen from the coal wagon. And then somebody screams.

And then there are other voices. Yelling.

Two strides to the window and he peers down. His friend lies like a comma on the pavement. A woman stands, her hand to her mouth, frozen. Others run towards the body, but then they stop short. A circle forms. Nobody goes closer, nobody hunkers in to check for breath. Nobody will touch him.

People look up, though, to the window, so he steps away, out of sight.

He stuffs his wet socks into his pocket and snatches up his boots. He grabs his bag, his jacket, his coat and muffler. He is out of the room and racing down the corridor. In the WC, he tugs up the window and folds himself out through the narrow gap. The fire-escape creaks; the air is sour with rubbish; the metal gantry sways queasily underneath him. He clambers down barefoot to the dustbins and the scratting pigeons and an empty yard, the cleaning women and their voices gone.

He treads into his boots there, on the dirty stones. A dimpled window just beside him gives on to the lobby; he can see movement inside, scattered smears of grey uniform and flesh-pink. In German-accented French: *Check all the rooms. Question everyone.*

The sounds of hammering footfalls and doors flung open.

And then, softly and nearby, just beyond the grubby, distorting window, the woman begins to sob.

He walks out of the yard and down the alleyway, to where it opens into the avenue, a block down from the front of the hotel.

A glance thrown back as he steps out of the alleyway. His friend lies curled on his side on the road as if he has laid himself down there, finally, to sleep. A Gendarme stands over the body, but people steer around it anyway; they keep their distance, afraid of contamination. Blood pools between the cobblestones.

He turns away. He sets one foot in front of the other.

There's a touch on his arm. A young lad – pimples, faint moustache, the contact they had been waiting for – who jerks his head down the avenue and says, 'Shall we go?'

He makes himself walk. His legs are puppet's legs. His arms are wood.

He squints into the low sun. Distance gathers behind him. The unknown boy walks at his side.

His boots chafe; his feet hurt.

This is good. The discomfort of the flesh. Its scourging. Its continuance.

There is a bed. There are four walls. There is a window. There is a little china vase on the washstand and it has dried corn-flowers in it. Tomorrow there is a train south: they will try to make it across into the Zone Libre.

They are together. By a conspiracy of kindness, they are returned to each other and given an hotel room for the night.

They have a towel, soap, water in the jug. He can get up and sit down and stretch out, and there is daylight sliced by the shutters.

She is not angry with him, after all. Why would she be angry? He is not to be blamed for what has happened. Rather, to be consoled.

Suzanne turns away to unbutton her blouse; she fumbles at her stockings underneath her skirt. Her hipbones show even through her slip.

He gets up and goes to the washstand. He scrubs his nails, he takes off his collar and unbuttons his shirt and scrubs his neck and under his arms. He gives her time.

And then they lie, half-dressed, unspeaking, smoking, and they do not know quite how to be together; they don't know what is allowed and what is wanted any more. A touch elicits a shiver. An innocuous word will give offence. How did they used to do this, simply get along?

But now she lies sleeping in her slip beside him, the sheet twisted, the mattress dented under their slight weight. His thoughts drift and skip like falling leaves, and he follows them down towards the harbour water and is sinking through it.

Then blinks awake. 'Oh. Hell.'

She surfaces. 'What?'

'Oh God.'

'What?'

'The register.'

'What?' She's up on an elbow, staring at him.

'When I signed the register. I think I used my real name.'

197

She looks at him. ' "Think"?'

'I know I did.'

She closes her eyes. She breathes. Then her eyes open again and she swings her legs off the edge of the bed and scrambles for her clothes.

'I'll pack. You shave.'

'What?'

'I'm not going anywhere with you looking like that.'

He touches his moustache. 'It's a disguise.'

'Brothel of shit is it a disguise. It makes you look like a British officer.'

She starts tugging at her stockings, then stops herself and rolls them slowly on, because even right now at this moment stockings are far too precious to risk.

'We'll have to find something else,' she says, furious. She tucks her blouse into her skirt.

'I'm sorry.'

'I know,' she says. 'It doesn't help.'

11

En route
September 1942

IT SEEMS AS THOUGH they are making good progress for a
while – the countryside is spinning past, it's a brilliant
blue autumn day; beyond the window there's a blur of saplings, brambles, browning fern. She stares out of the window;
she sleeps. She isn't really talking to him yet.

The last time they'd run, they'd run like horses run, or
sheep; they'd run because they were spooked, because everyone else was running. They had run to his friends. First
Shem in Vichy, then Mary and Marcel in Arcachon; there
had been wine and sea-bathing, sunshine, and a fear that
seems, looking back on it, so painfully innocent. Nobody
had been killed; nobody had been arrested then. Not one of
them was in immediate danger. They were on nobody's list.
It seems strange now that they had thought it worth their
while to run at all. Because now they are alone and racing
through vast darkness, and with only a tiny patch of light to
aim for, and that distant and uncertain.

The train slows; it creeps past wooded banks and gravel, past warehouses and stalled goods wagons and sidings and factories and the smoke rising from high chimneys into a wide blue sky. They are inching south.

Crawling towards the shred of light they have been offered. An isolated little town, where the roads are so bad and the buildings so cramped and ramshackle that nobody bothers with it much at all. Roussillon. Her friends, the Lobs, are scraping by all right there, unmolested, even though he is Jewish. But it's a long way off, and there's still the border to get over, and every mile they travel seems to take longer than the mile before.

And then the train slides aside from the main track and stops, between the workshops and warehouses and the small-holdings trailing with dead beanstalks and the still-green creep of pumpkin plants.

Time ticks. The light fades. The air is full of cigarette smoke and body smells. Nothing happens.

A woman sits with a basket on her knee; her two boys had wriggled and complained and played *mon p'tit doigt me dit* for a while, but are now slumped against her, caps askew, asleep. It's not them snoring, though: that's someone else. And further down the carriage a woman just keeps on talking – a thick sound to her voice, as though her throat is clotted. A long low spool of talk, winding on and on and on. On and on and on.

On the main line a train goes thundering by; a stream of green and yellow. And then it's gone.

Theirs doesn't move. The shadows deepen. That woman, he notices, is talking about her hens. How her son used to look after them, how they were his pride and joy, how they were marl and blue and red.

He looks at his watch. Raises it to his ear. Looks at it again. He winds it, his eyes following a flight of starlings as it dips and weaves across the orange sky.

And they had a red rooster who could stare down the Pope, eyes like elderberries, peck at your ankles when you went in to fetch the eggs. But with her son, never gave him any trouble at all. Adored him, did that rooster.

The sun slides beyond the buildings, melon-pink. Suzanne's head sinks on to his shoulder. His cheek rests on her hair. He blinks. This might be the beginnings of forgiveness.

'Do you remember,' she murmurs, 'in Cahors? All that rain.'

He nods, his cheek ruffling her hair, the stubble snagging.

The electric lights do not come on. The woman talks about her orchard, how the boy would scramble up to pick the apples, and she would have scolded him, but what was the point? He would just have gone scrumping elsewhere and got into worse trouble for it.

He blinks slow blinks.

Then a train door slams. And there are voices. New voices. Suzanne jerks awake. He touches her hand. They listen.

Compartment doors slide open; brisk requests, replies; doors slide shut. Papers are being checked – and the woman continues, buzzing like radio static, while they strain to hear over her. His hands grip, his jaw tightens, but it will be fine, of course it will be fine: their papers are good. They have been told that they are good. So much trouble has been taken, so many risks have been run on their behalf.

The voices are closer now. Individual interactions: the demand, the moment's pause with fumbling, the proffering of papers; a silent scrutiny, then questions. To what purpose are you travelling? Where have you come from? What is your ultimate destination? Whom exactly are you intending to meet? But their papers are good. They are supposed to be good. The papers will stand up to scrutiny. Won't they?

'We have to—'

She nods. She's on her feet, hefting her bag.

They thread their way out of the compartment and along the corridor. They pass the woman. Back of a grey head, a maroon felt hat. She is talking about a bicycle now: her son worked for months washing pots in the café in town to save up for it; he would go out riding in the country lanes, his head skimming along higher than the hedges.

He glances back and sees the woman's mouth moving, the tears streaming down her cheeks; a bubble swells at her nostril. He had not known, had not realized that the thickness of her voice was tears. It pushes after him, even as they heave the train door open and dip down for a toehold. The boy had had a puncture, too bad to mend there on the spot, had to push his bike back to the garage. Back after dark, and worried sick, she was.

He drops down on to the gravel, drags his bag after him. Suzanne reaches out a hand and he helps her down. There's a smell of oil and dust and urine. He pushes the door to after them.

'Someone might say.'

'Yes.'

He jerks his head: *come on.* They dash across the tracks, then scramble up the bank and in amongst the trees. Brambles tear at clothes and skin. He blunders through a clump of nettles. He swears under his breath, carries on.

They reach the top of the bank breathless. The air is cool; it's twilight. There's a fence – he, long-legged, swings across, and helps her clamber up and over and down the other side. A lone horse ambles across, snuffing at them.

The field is bare and scrubby and exposed. They turn and scud along the field edge, keeping to the shadow of the trees; the horse trots alongside them. There's a gate but it is tied shut and the knot doesn't give so they climb the bars, and then they're in a lane, the horse left behind. The lane is hedged at first, and then there are fences and then buildings and the way narrows between high walls; there's a smell of tar and the sound of their clattering footfalls and their rasping breath. Something stops and stares, its eyes reflecting red; then a blink and it's gone. Their hands, linked tight, are hot and damp together; they can only go single-file now between brick walls, he doesn't know when they joined hands. His arm is stretched back to her; she's tumbling forward to hold on to him. It's uncomfortable, constraining, it might be better to let go. They don't let go. His chest hurts; the scar pulls and he can't catch his breath.

At an intersection between alleyways they stop in un-spoken accord; she bends double, gasping, a hand to her side. He leans against a damp wall, his belly heaving. There's a little light left. It's grainy and crumbling.

'Are you all right?'

She says, 'I'm all right.' Then, after a moment, 'What about you?'

He nods. He'll live. Though his eyes swim with stars.

'Does your chest hurt?'

'Does it hurt?' He laughs, but the laugh collapses into a coughing fit. When he can speak again, he just says, 'Yes.'

He fishes out his cigarettes, lights up, takes a drag, then turns the cigarette around and proffers it. She takes it off him, smokes. Perhaps she has forgiven him.

'What will we do now?' she asks.

'Keep on. Make that rendezvous.'

'On foot.'

'Well, yes.'

'Oh, the cow.'

'You don't want to walk?'

'I'm fatigued, you know I am. You are too. We were tired before we started this.'

'You could have stayed on the train if you wanted to. You should have said.'

She narrows her eyes at him. She takes another drag on the cigarette. Then: 'So which way is it, genius?'

He looks up at the thin strip of sky overhead; it's a deep evening blue.

'We could tell by the sun,' he says. 'On the train, it was going down on the right.'

'But that was on the train.'

'Yes.'

'And now we're in an alleyway.'

'Yes,' he says.

'And we can't see the sun. And we're all turned around. So.'

'What then, toss a coin?' He fumbles in a pocket.

'What good would that do?'

He shrugs, takes the cigarette off her. 'It'd be something. It'd be a start.'

'Hardly.'

'So we'll just stay here, then.' He takes a drag and settles down against the wall.

'Shut up,' she says. 'Idiot. You break my feet, you know.'

He shuffles his shoulders, chilly brick against his back. 'You know, I like this alleyway. I think we could be happy here.'

'Oh, I've had enough. Come *on*!' She grabs his arm.

He heaves himself off the wall and stumbles after her, his breath sore in his chest: cross-country runs, bare corn-beef legs, the rawness of autumn in Enniskillen.

They emerge into an open space, a woodyard, smelling of sawn timber. A crow flaps overhead and makes them jump. They cross the yard and slip past a boom-barrier on to a wider gravel track, past a parked wagon and a strip of waste-land, past factory gates, and then on to a metalled road; this is becoming the outskirts of the town. He walks beside her then, his breath easing. Softening to her, he catches her hand. He doesn't glance round at her, but even so he knows that she has pulled a face.

The woman lies on the cobbles, her head resting on a curved arm. Her coat is open on a thin blouse and her skirt riding up to expose her stocking-tops. Suzanne crouches to twitch the fabric down. She gets back up and her cheeks are flushed. She slips her arm under his and clings close. Her breath comes in misty billows.

'Her eyes are frozen,' she whispers.

'What?'

'The wet of her eyes is frozen.'

A man is lying flat on his back. They pass him, their footfalls echoing in the evening square. A cat slinks away at their approach. They can see the dark wound in the man's cheek: a hole where there should be skin and muscle. The side teeth are bared in a snarl, a bit of bone glows white and the tongue slumps heavily sideways, hanging out. It's all just there, just open to the world: the quiet internal spaces.

Outside the Mairie, the police are at work. They are rifling pockets, making notes on clipboards; they are lining up the bodies and laying them in the back of a truck. Soon everything – everybody – will be processed and cleared away; it will be as though nothing ever happened here.

He doesn't want to look. He has to look. This has to be looked at, square in the face, right in the hole in the face – the policemen with their breath fogging the evening, the corpses with the air clear and unclouded above them. Words fail him now; they keep on failing; he is as speechless as a corpse himself.

He squeezes Suzanne's arm tight into his side; her chin is crumpled and her gaze fixed. Dry-eyed, they slip into the bus station; it is cold and it is busy. They find a bench. His skin feels oily with disgust. 'Excuse me.' He leaves her sitting there and strides off to the gentlemen's lavatory. There, hunched over a filthy toilet *à la turque*, he heaves up nothing, then some bitter yellow bile. He is left shaking. He feels no better for it.

He goes back to Suzanne, tilts his head at her enquiring look. He is fine. Girls, women, men in working blues gather at the stands. They stand stiff and shivering, coats buttoned up, collars turned, with their baskets, cases, packages; the buses swing in and doors are clanked open, and the people shuffle themselves on board and the buses heave away. Two German soldiers cross the forecourt and leave a wake of silence. There is something vulnerable about their exposed ears, their shaven napes. They take up a position near the rear wall. It makes the back of the neck burn, the desire to look round, the necessity of not doing so.

'How long until the bus comes?'

He checks his watch, turns his wrist to show its face to her. She nods, sits stiffly, hands folded in her lap. He remains silent. He rubs at the back of his neck; it's prickling.

'Who will bury them?'

She speaks low and without turning towards him. He looks round at her, the better to make out what was said. She is grey under the eyes.

'I mean, who will pay for it?' she adds.

'Suzanne—'

'Will they do it? Will the administration pay for the funerals?'

'Suzanne, please.'

'Or the police? Is it their job to organize the . . . the disposal? I mean, they don't actually do anything to stop people being killed, so they must at least deal with the results.'

'Suzanne—'

A bus pulls in at a nearby stand; the engine idles, phlegmy. People file on-board. Some of the passengers are looking at them.

'Or the town hall? The municipality? Is it their responsibility now?'

He slides an arm around her. He pulls her tight, hard; she lets herself be drawn in against him, but just stares down at her worn-soft shoes and shakes her head, and talks almost to herself.

'Or will the families have to? Because—' A blot falls on to her lap, and then another. She sniffs. 'Yesterday all those people—'

He rubs her arm. He whispers, '*Whisht.*'

Her head hangs; she skims her eyes with the flank of her hand. She blows out a long breath. She is trying. She is really trying to stop. And one mood can set aside another. Irritation helps.

'I don't know how you stay so calm,' she says.

Another bus pulls in, rattles near them. Diesel fumes and tobacco smoke.

'I'm not calm.'

Pink-eyed, she glares at him. 'Well, you seem it. Calm and quiet.'

Maybe one day there will be words. Maybe silence will be all that there ever is.

'I can't think about it now. I can't do it justice.'

After a moment, she asks, 'Aren't you scared?'

'Yes.'

'You don't look scared.'

'I'm terrified.'

Her lips are pressed tight; her eyes are wide and sore-looking. 'You're impossible.'

A bus pulls in at their stand. The door heaves open. He gets to his feet and offers her a hand.

'Come on,' he says. 'That's us.'

Later, much later on, they are shown into an afterlife of broken chairs and crates, of empty bottles worn misty at the shoulders. The *patron* goes back into the little locked-tight café and sets about chinking glasses and softly singing. A few bentwood chairs have been drawn round an upended barrel, where there's an ashtray and a candle burning in a bottle. That's all the light there is. Even the air feels crowded, the smells of smoke and stale wine and old coffee jostling together. She sinks on to one of the chairs; he folds himself down on to another. After a moment, he picks a cigarette end out of the ashtray, examines it, then puts it back.

He gets up again to help Suzanne off with her bag, and she manages to lift an arm, to tilt her head out of his way. He sinks down on to the little creaking chair and takes the weight off his aching feet again. It is an act of will not to bend down and start taking off his boots.

The *patron* comes through with three tumblers of red wine, rims pinched together in his fingertips, which leaves his other hand free to carry a plate of *charcuterie*. He sets all this down on the barrel-top. And now they're bolt alert. They glance at each other, then at the *patron* as he ambles across to the stacked crates in a corner. Then they stare at the plate.

The *patron* shifts boxes, chairs; there is air-dried ham and blood-sausage and an unspoken exchange between them – Should we . . . ? Could we just . . . ? – then there's a creak. Behind them a door opens and there's a gust of cellar air. Then he sees, and her name is on his lips – Jeannine – *Gloria*. Her face is shadowed, lined: she is ten years older than when he saw her last, just months ago. They clasp hands.

'Good evening,' he says.

She kisses him. He feels the scratch of his unshaven skin against her cheek. 'Irishman.'

She dips down to kiss Suzanne too.

'My God,' Suzanne says.

He speaks lightly. 'Who else have you got tucked away in there?'

The *patron* shrugs, pleased; he rolls a cigarette with yellowed fingertips.

Jeannine sinks down on a chair; she reaches for a slice of blood-sausage. She is thin and tired, but then everybody is thin and tired. There is something different about her now. A hardness to her that was not there before the cell was blown. The lines of her face are grim.

The ham is cool and leathery and salt. It falls into flakes on the tongue; it is so good he doesn't want to swallow it because then it will be over. Questions suggest themselves but are dismissed; he does not know how to begin.

Suzanne manages though, simple, warm, a way that he must learn. 'How are you? How has it been for you, all of this?'

Jeannine juts her chin, unforthcoming, noncommittal.

'And your family?' he tries.

'Safe. For now.'

'What happened?' he asks, and then rephrases the words almost as soon as they are spoken. 'Do you know what happened?'

She reaches for a second slip of blood-sausage, folds it; it crumbles along the crease. The *patron* lights his cigarette. There's the tiny crumbling of tobacco-and-paper as it burns.

'We were betrayed.'

'By whom? Do you know?'

'A priest.'

'There was a priest?' Suzanne asks.

'In another part of the network. He came to us, said he wanted to help. We took him at his word, and we were wrong. We lost so many good people because of him.'

'But a *priest*?'

Jeanine tilts her head. 'They're just men.' She speaks round her mouthful. 'But maybe he wasn't even that. He'd

211

come along with the Geste when our people were arrested. He came to watch. He liked it.'

'Name of God,' says Suzanne.

He sits back, says in English, 'Fuck.'

'We were foolish,' says Jeannine. Her face is a white mask in the candlelight. 'Recruiting friends, and friends of friends.' She looks at him directly for the first time with those sloe-dark Italian eyes. 'Do you not think, Irishman, that that was wrong?'

He thinks, rather, of a priest. A fleshy smile, a black soutane, and an incongruous whiff of cigars. Passed on the landing or the stairs, in Alfy's building. And exactly where would a priest be getting hold of cigars, times being what they are? Cigarettes are hard enough to come by. 'It was not you who betrayed us.'

'Forgive me, please,' she says. 'I don't yet have a full account of who is still at liberty and who is not. I was uncertain of your situation until Monsieur here told me he expected a Frenchwoman and an Irishman, travelling together, to pass over the border. Once in the Free Zone you have somewhere to go?' She holds up a hand. 'No details, please.'

'Friends of Suzanne's,' he says.

Suzanne says, 'Where they are, they say it's a decent place to be.'

'Good. Good.'

'And you?'

'One picks up what threads one can, and one carries on. Which reminds me. I have something for you.'

She lifts a package out of her bag, a manila envelope with a rectangular block wrapped inside it. The edges are softened with wear. She unfolds the package. She takes out a stack of banknotes. Without counting, she divides the stack, slips two-thirds of it back into the envelope. She holds the remainder towards them. They look at the money. Nobody says anything.

'Go on,' Jeannine says.

'It's very kind of you,' he says. 'But no.'

'What?' Suzanne says.

'I insist.' Jeannine says.

'Others will need it more.'

'Have you gone quite mad?' Suzanne asks. 'Have you not noticed how things are for us?'

He doesn't look at her.

'That priest screwed us for thousands,' Jeannine is saying. 'This is an apple and an egg in comparison. Take it, please. I'd give you more if I could, but I need to keep some in reserve, for the others.'

The *patron* says, 'I can give it a good home.'

'Here.' Suzanne reaches for it. 'Thank you.'

Jeannine passes the cash to Suzanne, who fumbles it into her bag. He looks away, uncomfortable.

'Thank you very much,' Suzanne says.

'Well.' The *patron* draws up a chair, drops his tobacco pouch beside the plate. He nods at it. 'Go ahead, help yourself. Roll up a couple to take with you. We'd better get our plans in place.'

*

213

Their footfalls clip along the empty street.

'She was *offering* us the money; she *wanted* us to have the money; we *need* the money and yet you refused to take it.'

'Softly, please.'

She tugs at his elbow. 'You know how things are for us. You must have noticed. This is not easy. This is not – good.'

'It had not escaped me.'

'What is it? Why can't you let yourself be helped? Why do other people deserve your help and you won't let them give you anything?'

He blows out a long breath. He says, 'What do you think happened to him?'

She stops dead in the road. 'What?' But he continues on with that long lope of his, and she has to break into a trot to catch back up with him. 'Who?'

'The boy.'

'What boy?'

'The boy on the train,' he says.

'Those little fellows with their mum? I don't see why anything—'

'No, no. The woman on the train, the talking woman – the one who just kept talking. She was talking about him. About the boy. Her son.'

He has stopped in his tracks now. She has to turn back to him. He is just a grainy shape, unreadable. 'Oh,' she says. 'Her.'

'D'you think he's dead?'

Her own heartbeat is a thick throb, making the darkness pulse. 'I don't know.'

She steps up to him and pulls him close, and holds him a long moment. Bones and flesh and long-worn threadbare clothes, the smell of unwashed bodies and the cold of the night on their skin, and the gritty tiredness of not being young any more, and the brief warmth held between them. Then he pulls away. And they walk on.

'Are you certain?'

He glances at his watch. He lifts it to his ear. He listens to the tick-tick-tick-tick-tick. He winds it anyway, glancing around. The sun is setting again; the sky is flushed with orange over there, in what must be the west. And it's getting cold.

'It looks more like, I don't know, a shrub.'

'It's a tree. It's a willow. He said a tree, a willow.'

'It's half-dead.'

'Yes. It is. It's a half-dead willow.'

There's a wide verge, which rises to become a bank, and at the top of the bank a fence runs; the tree forms part of this fence, like a post that's taken root and grown. Bleached roots claw down into the earth; above, the trunk is slender, and two slim boughs stretch up to form a Y. A few blunt twigs, a handful of leaves. It is by no means impressive, but it is distinctive. It is the kind of tree of which to make a landmark. Of which one might readily say, *You can't miss it.*

'It's quite small,' she says, still doubtful.

'It's discreet.'

'But how can you be certain it's a willow?'

'He said that it would be. The *patron*. He said to wait by the willow tree and that fellow would meet us and bring us along.'

'But that doesn't mean that this is it.'

'Well, no, I suppose not.'

With tired sore steps, she clambers up the bank and goes right up to the tree. She peers up it towards the branches, and then down at the roots. She gives the trunk a little kick. The whole thing shakes, and one of its few last leaves falls off and skips down to the ground.

'Well,' she says. 'I don't know. I don't know about any of this. I don't know what we're doing here at all.'

He sinks down on the verge. He begins to take off his boots. 'There's a name for them in English, for that kind of willow.'

She watches him as he strips his laces. 'If you get them off,' she says, 'do you think you'll ever get them back on again?'

'What is it now? I can't remember.'

'Your feet will swell up,' she says, 'like pumpkins.'

'"Goat willow"!' He heaves off a boot. 'I don't know if it's the same in French – *saule de chèvre*?'

She sits down beside him, stretching out her thin bare legs. He eases off the other boot and then peels away his socks.

'I never heard that before,' she says.

There is a bramble scratch traced across her left shin. Her stockings are long gone. She wears a pair of folded-down old tennis socks now. The effect is schoolgirlish. He plants his

216

bare feet in the grass away from her. He spreads his gnarly, blistered toes. That one nailless stump with its knuckle missing. Bits cut off and bits falling off and out of him, the shambles that he is.

'Isn't it cold?'

He shrugs. After a minute he says, 'My father used to know the names of all the plants and trees.'

He leans back on his hands. The last of the evening sun is warm on his face; the ground is cold beneath him. Starlings gather noisily in the branches of a nearby copse.

'It will be all right when we get to Roussillon,' she says.

The starlings lift. He watches as they turn in a shoal across the sky.

'We'll get by all right there,' she says. 'We'll get work; you can get your allowance sent. The Lobs have had no trouble there at all.'

'I know. You said. That's good.'

'We'll be comfortable in Roussillon.'

'Yes.'

'We can wait out the whole thing there.'

He nods. If it can be waited out. If waiting is a thing that can be done for sufficiently long, if circumstances permit it. Then: 'What do you think it's called, this place?'

'This place?'

She glances round at the sweeping fields, the verge, the dried stems and seed-pods of last summer's flowers. 'This isn't really a place. Why would it be called anything?'

'In Ireland every hole in the hedge has a name.'

'I didn't know that.'

217

'A name and a story to go with it as to how it got its name. A story that'll go on as long as anyone will hear it.'

'Well, that wouldn't work in France. France is far too big for that. We'd get into a real muddle if we behaved like that round here.'

Ireland is sticky, ink-stained, grubby in the creases. France is clean and freshly washed and soaped.

'You should put your boots back on,' she says.

'They're crucifying me.'

'What if someone comes?'

'I'll put them on then.'

'I don't mean him. I mean, someone else.'

'Who else?'

'I don't know. Police. Border patrols. The Geste.'

'Place like this, we'd hear them coming a mile off.'

He grinds his heels into the cold earth, the grass between his toes. She watches, envious. Then she sighs, and then she bends forward and tugs her own laces loose. She toes off her shoes, one and then the other.

'This man, this contact,' she says, tugging off her socks. Her feet are patched with red, and blisters have formed, and popped, and been worn clean away again, leaving the skin raw.

'Yes.'

'How will we know that it's him?'

'Who else could it be?'

'But that's the problem! That's what I'm saying. It could be *anyone*. We'll be sitting here waiting, and we'll watch someone coming down the road and before you know it they're here, and then maybe it turns out they're not the contact, they're the Gestapo.'

'Gestapo travel in packs, like – I don't know, hyenas. They don't ever go anywhere alone. He'll be alone; just him himself.'

She nods at this, looking across the road towards the wide-open fields, the bare trees, the fading sky.

'I don't like it here,' she says.

'It's only for a little while.'

'Just being here looks suspicious. There's nowhere to hide; nowhere to blend in.'

'That's true. But we can't just go. If we go we miss our contact and we don't have any help at all.'

She rummages in her bag, pulls out a crumpled package, unfurls the paper wrapping. Two biscuits.

'That's all that's left?'

She nods.

He takes one. 'Thank you.'

She leans in against him, clutching her own biscuit. He puts his arm around her. She shuffles closer. Elbows, shoulder blades.

'I don't like it,' she says. 'Not one little bit.'

'You don't have to like it. You just have to get through it.'

He feels the movement of her arm under his hand, and then her jaw against his chest as she bites and chews her biscuit. His turns to powder in his mouth, and then to glue. He swallows, and then takes another bite.

'I'm tired,' she says stickily.

'Then go to sleep.'

'What if he comes?'

'He won't.'

'Don't be facetious.'

'If he comes, I'll wake you. If I'm asleep too, he'll wake us. You won't miss out on anything, I promise you, by sleeping, so have a sleep. But put your socks back on first, though, or you'll get chilblains.'

'I'm thirsty.'

'We've nothing to drink. Do you want a sucking stone?'

'No.'

Suzanne shuffles around, wraps her coat around her and curls on to her side. Above the open fields, the starlings wheel and turn and cry. For a moment, they settle in the trees, and then by some unfathomable assent they lift shrieking into the air again. He sings, softly, in German:

> *Nun merk' ich erst, wie müd' ich bin*
> *Da ich zur Ruh' mich lege*

She shuffles irritably. 'Huh?'

'Schubert,' he says. '*Rast.*'

'Oh, yes,' she says. 'Shut up.'

The song sings on in his head. After a while her breathing changes. He unbuckles his bag and drags out his spare sweater. He drapes it over her. The moon rises. He considers it. Closes his eyes and summons up an image: Caspar Friedrich's *Two Men Contemplating the Moon.* The slumped tree, bare of leaves, its furred roots exposed as it slowly sinks towards the earth. Massive rocks, parched grass; in the sky a white disc, misty, radiant. The two figures, stick-supported, lean on each other. The ancient moon, the ancient rocks, the failing dying ancient tree. The men for just a moment paused to look, to see, as if to give all this meaningless nature meaning.

He finds, in his pocket, that little pebble from the beach at Greystones. He tucks it into his mouth and sucks on it, and the hard thing brings water there.

The cold wakes him. His eyes open on to blackness and he can't make sense of it. Then he sees the stars. He feels the press of the earth against him, pushing at his heels, heaving up against his shoulder blades. His fingers twine into the cold grass, his nails dig into the ground; he is clinging on at the spin of it, the stars hurtling past, the giddy distances, the sick rush of a fairground ride, sticking him flat-backed against this cold earth. Then it thuds right into him: time, the present moment, here. He sits up, drops the stone from his mouth into his palm and retches.

'Is that you?' she asks.

He spits, swallows. 'Usually.'

She fumbles for him in the darkness; her hand is cold on cold skin, the wire and gristle of his arm. She sits up beside him.

'Is he here?' she asks. 'Did he come?'

They sit, side by side, stiff, dew-damp and cold. The sky is faintly light now. The slight tree is silhouetted against the blue.

He says, 'I don't think he did.'

After a while, she asks, 'What time is it?'

He lifts his wrist and peers, but can't make out the hands. He lifts it to his ear and hears it ticking. She shuffles closer, hungry for warmth. He slips his sucking stone back into his pocket and plants a blind, awkward kiss – it lands on unwashed, dirty hair.

'What'll we do?'

'We'll go back to that hayrick, try and sleep through the day.'

He feels the movement as she nods.

'We'll be all right there. No one will be needing any hay yet.'

She sniffs.

'And then Monsieur will surely come tomorrow.'

'It's tomorrow now.'

'I know. I'm sorry. It can't go on like this for ever,' he says.

'No. We'll get to Roussillon,' she says.

After a moment, he says, 'I think it's getting lighter.'

She twists to see the paling sky behind her.

'We'll pass that field again,' she says. 'We can get some of those carrots. You liked the carrots.'

'They were better than the turnips.'

'In a little while.'

'Yes.'

'When there's light enough to see by.'

'Yes.'

'We'll go then.'

'Yes. Time enough till then.'

And then there's a sound.

'Hush.'

Footfalls. Movement in the hedge shadows. Skin bristles.

'Is it you?' he calls out into the darkness. 'Hello there! Is that you, Monsieur?'

The figure stands against the pre-dawn sky. He's just a boy. His socks are crumpled down and his jacket is too big for him. He glances off along the lane. He says, 'Come with me.'

12

Crossing
October 1942

FIGURES STUMBLE OUT of the shaft of daylight and into darkness, blinded by the difference. The door falls shut behind them and they confer in unselfconscious voices, oblivious to the company.

'I can't see a thing. Is that you, Sylvie?'

'It's Agnès, Pascale. Here, take my hand.'

He clears his throat out of politeness. They freeze, fall silent, peer ineffectually around.

Then Suzanne says, 'Good day.' And they soften at the sound of a woman's voice, return the greeting uncertainly.

When he and Suzanne were led to the barn, it was barely morning; their eyes had less of an adjustment to make. The boy sloped off again before they could thank him. They saw the old fellow sleeping in the straw, who stirred and muttered but didn't wake. Later, they were joined by two young men, who were anxious and taciturn and who huddled down in one of the milking stalls and talked only to each other; and then a middle-aged countrywoman, who took a seat on a hay bale, set her basket on her knee, leant back against the bare stone wall and promptly fell asleep. He wondered did the boy bring them, slipping away each time to find someone else before he could be glimpsed?

By now the two of them feel like old lags, and that it is the done thing to welcome newcomers and put them at their ease.

'All's well,' Suzanne says, getting up and limping towards the young women. 'Come in, get comfortable.'

They settle down on bundled fodder. Clothes rustling, coats unbuttoned, bags dropped. And shoelaces stripped; the easing-off of shoes. War, it turns out, is dreadfully hard on the feet.

'You'll never get your shoes back on again, Pascale.'

'Good. They're evil. I hate them. I'll walk barefoot to Avignon if I have to.'

'You'd look well.'

'You say that now, but just wait until—'

The clump of leather hitting the floor, one and then another. A sigh, followed by a wincing exploration of sore places, blisters.

'Anyway, we're stuck here for hours. We know that much. I'm not keeping them on all that blessed time.'

Time passes slowly in confinement. Low conversations, card games, the drifting in and out of sleep; sunlight from a missing slate shafts across the floor, and softens, and goes blue.

He must have been sleeping, because there's a sweep of night air across his face and a slice of starlight that narrows, shrinks and disappears, and he shuffles up on to elbows. He blinks into the dark. Suzanne's already up beside him, properly awake.

'Is it—?'

'Hush,' she says. 'I'm listening.'

The darkness seems fuller, more crowded. There's a whiff of tobacco smoke, and then he spots the red coal of a cigarette and hears the voices speaking low, in the rolling wet accent of the region.

A match flares and for a moment there's a devil's mask, heavy-browed and creased, and the light grows and is touched into a lantern, and it glows on other faces too. These are the *passeurs*. They are nameless. They belong to this place like the local stone.

The lantern draws them from the dark – the girls, one of them limping and barefoot; her friends supporting her, their faces white; the old man, hunched and peering, scratching his groin; the young men approaching too, though wary as rabbits. Suzanne gets up, and he struggles to his feet, and they make their way towards the lamp, lame with wear.

'That's too many. I'd no idea there'd be so many,' one of the *passeurs* is saying.

Around the lantern there's a general sucking of teeth.

'We can't take them all at once, not across the fields.'

'The girls can go in the car.'

'You're kidding.'

'In the boot.'

'All three of them?'

'It's a big boot. We put the dogs in there all the time.'

'They're not dogs, though, are they?'

'No, but it's not like it's the middle of summer. They're not going to suffocate.'

'He has a point. It's not far.'

The three girls stand, just in the glow of the light, in their knee-length skirts and broken shoes. The barefoot one lists slightly to one side. They have their jackets wrapped tight round them, arms folded across hollow bellies.

'Do you particularly object,' a *passeur* addresses them, 'to crossing the border in the boot of this idiot's stinking old Citroën?'

The three of them look at him, long and blank. They're barely more than schoolgirls. The barefoot one says, 'That would be good.' And then the others nod along with her.

Devil-face then turns to his companions. 'Well. There we are, then.' Then back to the girls: 'Better get your things together, my darlings. You're with him.'

The *passeurs* are barely there; they are never more than parts, they exist as synecdoches: a glimmer of moonlight caught on an eye, the turn of a profile against starlight, a pale strip of neck above a dark coat collar. The talk too is scraps and shreds and it drifts away like ashes. He can't put any of it – either what he sees or what he hears – together. He can't make this cohere.

They have been split into smaller groups like sheep by sheepdogs. The girls have curled themselves obligingly into the boot of the car; another party is heading further west across open country. There are patrols and posts on the roads, so their bunch is to go through the fields and cross where the border is more notional than concrete. It is a relief to be told what to do for a while. Not to have to make decisons. It is the relief of a pressure change, a different unease.

They pause at the field gate; the *passeur* says something but it is not quite catchable: a flash of teeth, then this, which he does catch: 'Stay low, tread softly, keep quiet.'

Then the fellow slips into the darkness and they follow. The ground is rough. The *passeur* keeps slipping in and out of sight, as if he is a magic trick: now you see him, now you don't. It makes the heart lurch and hammer, makes the senses strain. Then there's movement, and there he is again, and the skin flushes and the nerves sing out. And underneath it all is the insistent throb of disquiet, of what do we know about any of this, after all? He could be taking us anywhere, he could melt away at any moment. He could lead us right to the Gestapo for the money and the pleasure of watching the arrest. If one man can do a thing like that, so could another. It has become, after all, something that people do.

He is thinking this as he shuffles along, bent almost double, creeping like a toad in the shadow of a hedge. Suzanne, ahead, is a low and silent shape; he can't even hear her footsteps. There is a blond expanse of stubbled field to his left. When a foot strays off the worn-bare path, the cropped stems prod and spike his boot soles. It is a useful reminder of the straight and narrow.

At the corner of the field, they scramble through a gap in the hedge. Beyond, the world is different: the Indian corn still stirs uncut in the breeze, whispering and musty. The path continues on, a narrow pass between the stems.

'. . . silence absolute . . .' the *passeur* is saying. '. . . close now . . .'

He is ushering them by; he brings up the rear, and it's worse then, the sense of fumbling blindly into darkness, through the dry stalks, into who knows what.

Footfalls. The sound of boots on a metalled road. There's torchlight broken into bits by the wicker-weave of the hedge. They hunker low, silent, breath heaving; and then the boots go crunching on, and the light is past and gone.

His heart hammers. His breath is shallow and it hurts. The *passeur* makes a low sound, impatient, subtle, and so they creep on. And everything now seems condensed; everything seems bristling and stark. The grey silk of the corn, the creak of boots, the night air on his face, the smell of rot, the stars above. His calves ache, his thighs ache. Night birds call, clouds bundle across the sky. Down in the mud, they edge onwards, creeping towards a different, deeper darkness.

The little party huddles up against a fence; branches creak in the wind. Whispered instructions: they climb the fence in turn, and on the far side gather under the cover of the trees. No moonlight here; pitch black. With a click of the tongue, the *passeur* leads them off again, this time walking upright along what seems to be a proper path, instinctually known. It is strange to go upright now. The eyes adjust; he can pick out branches against the sky, slender tree trunks.

But then off to the left, there's movement, noises. He stops, bristling, breath caught, and then it's just rustling, snuffling. A badger, or a hedgehog perhaps, making its way through the fallen leaves. And they carry on, treading through the darkness, hands raised against the whip of unseen branches, moving through an entirely different world.

Then the darkness begins to thin; tree trunks are grey against the sky, and the *passeur*'s shape moves across the lightness, and then Suzanne's, and they are out at the far edge of the woods. A stream murmurs to itself; it catches moonlight. Single file, they follow its course upstream, walking between the woods and the water. On the far bank lies the open countryside of the Free Zone.

He sees the moon's reflection on the water. The white disc struggles to disperse and then shivers itself back together, then breaks apart again. He slows, stands, watches. The stone, the water, the moon; he sees himself like Friedrich's painted men, transient, contemplating the enduring, changing, ancient moon. But he is staring downwards here, not up towards the heavens. He closes his eyes.

The schoolgirl limps on raw feet.

The *patron* opens his tobacco pouch.

Paul Léon shambles down the rue Littré.

The priest slides past him on the stairs.

Alfy Péron's blunt fingertip taps a five-hundred-franc note.

Mary Reynolds ushers him in.

Marcel Duchamp lifts his knight.

Lines crease round Jeannine Picabia's eyes.

He opens his eyes again, and the reflected moon breaks, resolves, and breaks, and this is the lie of it, the willing delusion – there is nothing eternal here. Given time enough – and time just keeps on ticking by – even this will cease. The water wears the rock, the rock crumbles, the water dries, the moon itself will fall to dust and there will be no one left to contemplate it.

'*Pssst!*'

He glances round. Suzanne waves him on with wide furious sweeps. He strides to catch up with her.

They cluster at the upended roots of a fallen tree. The trunk lies across the stream; branches stand like ski-poles, hand-to-hand. On the far side lie the raked lines of a vineyard. There's a cluster of low buildings beyond that; the dwellings are in darkness, but the light is gathering at the edges of the sky. The far bank is the Free Zone. They still have some way to go on the other side before sunrise.

Suzanne does not look at him. She is seething with irritation. One would think, now, in the midst of all this, he would at least pay attention, could at least follow instructions. Her shoulders up, her back narrow, she treads across the tree trunk and it feels briefly like girlhood, gymnastics; she hops down on the other side. There she stands in the Zone Libre, while he still stands in the Zone Occupée, under the trees. She peers across as he makes the first tentative steps out on to the trunk, grasping for handholds. He follows her across, into this new place. They make their way through the fields, along the hedgerows and the ditches, in the cold breaking dawn.

His boots are worn to shreds. Her shoes are thin as skin. The autumn sun is too bright, too low, and they are walking directly into it, squinting and sore. He turns the pebble round in his mouth, slips it across his tongue to rest in the other cheek.

'I'm thirsty,' she says.

'I know.'

After a while she says, 'I'm so thirsty.'

'You should get a sucking stone.'

'I don't want a sucking stone.'

They come upon a fall of rocks by the roadside. She halts, sinks down on a boulder and rests her elbows on her knees and her head in her hands. She does not move. He waits, standing, for her to get up again; then, when she does not shift, he sinks down on his haunches beside her and waits like that for a while too.

'Are you all right?' he asks.

Silence.

'Come on, then.'

Silence. Then she shakes her head.

He glances off along the road, then turns to look back the way they've come. Then, fingertips to the ground for balance, he gazes at her hunched, exhausted form. They can't stay here.

He gets up; his joints creak. He offers her his hand.

'Come on,' he says. 'Hop up now.'

She just lifts her head and looks at him. These past days have transformed her. Her skeleton is making a show of itself.

'I thought you wanted to get to Roussillon?' he asks.

A blink, and nothing more. It seems she is beyond goading.

'Once you're up and going, you'll hardly notice.'

'Every whore of a step hurts. How could I not notice?'

He takes her hand then and hauls her to her feet. She protests, but stumbles up. He hooks her arm through his and they take a step.

'Tell me,' he says, 'where does it hurt?'

She starts with her toes: the agony that is her left little one, the raw lump to which it has been reduced. The way her shoes pinch and rub, the way her socks are worn thin on the ball of the foot and the skin worn raw beneath as a result; how her ankles ache; how she has dreadful cramps in her calves, and terrible stiffness in her hip from sleeping on floors and the bare ground. He murmurs agreement and they take another step together; they walk on.

Soon the road beings to climb, a steady, fatiguing slog, and they fall silent once more.

'What about you?' she asks after a while.

'Oh, me,' he says. 'You don't want to hear about that.'

The two of them trudge on through the evening as it falls, and he tells her anyway, about his sore feet and his rickety knees and his burning belly and the twinge of his scar, and his backache and the nerve that fires off in his neck, and the boil on his shoulder blade, the poison of which is making his whole shoulder throb.

She nods silently and they walk on together, sticks and rags, a broken bundle, barely there at all.

The slow unpeeling of the road is a sticking plaster from skin. And each step is the point of severance, each step is to be steeled against and endured. As the light fades he watches his boots, wrecked, as they lump themselves forward, watches the ground as it lurches and sinks and swells away and back. His boots are coated in dust; they are bloody with dust. The dust is red.

In the low light, he lifts his head to see that the roadside banks are crumbling red earth. The cliffs above are veined with rust and blood. The road sweeps towards these cliffs, and as the road rises and lurches upwards like a key change, the cicadas start to sing. And on the top of the cliffs, a little town grows like lichen on the blood-red rocks. They have travelled, through a rosary of days, through a decade of weeks, from one world into another. Roussillon. *Rousse*: of course it's red.

They climb towards it.

It is small-windowed, shuttered, huddled tight, its back turned towards the world. As the two of them slog uphill, the wind grows sharper, more scuddy; it twists this way and then that; it's in their faces, in their eyes, teasing out Suzanne's hair from under her scarf, pulling at their jackets, stirring his beard, spinning leaves and seeds and bits of grass into whirlwinds and blowing dust into dry eyes, and it's too much, really it is too much to contend with now, that the wind should blow full in their faces.

A church clock strikes the hour; the chimes are broken and scattered by the breeze. Suzanne moans in complaint and he nods in agreement.

They shamble past the front of the first house. It is locked tight; the iron homunculi that hold the shutters back during the day are fallen forward drunkenly for the night.

The road is cobbled now. There are sleeping shops, a fruit tree splayed against a wall; the ghost of a clematis climbs over a door; a cat ambles from an alleyway and stops to stare at them. There is a sign. An hotel. Hôtel de la Poste. He tugs on her arm, tilts his head towards the building. She nods. They stumble over the cobblestones towards it.

'We're here,' she says.

'Thank God,' he says.

'Just don't do anything stupid,' she says. 'Don't mess this up now, please.'

13

Roussillon
October 1942

THE DAY IS white and full of clattering, talk: the walls
strain and buckle in the wind.

The two of them lie side by side, still as figures on a tomb,
socks and shoes pulled off, feet patched with blood and
scabbed and stinking. The bed is narrow and their shoulders
touch.

They breathe. Just for a while they are oblivious. The
white light and the noise and the buffeting of the wind do
not trouble their sleep.

When the sun eases in through the slots in the shutters
it makes her surface and she feels the press of her shoulder
against his shoulder and she curls round on her side, putting space between them. Through the thin walls comes
the sound of voices, of a radio, of footfalls, the chink of
glasses and china. Mice rustle beneath the floorboards;
they scamper in the ceiling. He breathes beside her; she
sleeps again.

The sunlight fans across the floor and then begins its slow retreat. Shadows deepen and spread like floodwater.

In the evening, they stir and wake to a blue room, moonlight sliced by shutters. He eases on his boots, wincing, and stumbles out through the hotel yard to the necessary house. The little room is vertiginous and breezy, perched on the edge of a crevasse, a sheer stinking drop beneath.

She, meanwhile, limps out to the town square. She fills the wash-stand ewer at the fountain. The water plummets into the enamel and the spray touches her face and it is cool and sweet. There are lights lit at the cafés, and old men in blue work-jackets drink rosé and talk, and men in shabby city suits and women with faded feathered hats are out taking the air; they give her long low looks and walk on, and murmur with each other, knowing her for a newcomer and one of their own, but remaining discreet in case she does not wish to be acknowledged. And she, for now, is happy simply to be alone.

They take turns washing in cold water at the wash-stand. When they are done, she lifts down the bowl and soaks her feet.

'What,' he asks, 'do you think of the place?'

She scratches at a flea bite, looks at him. 'We know that it's safe,' she says. 'More or less.'

'There seems to be no plumbing to speak of.'

She shrugs. Does it matter? 'What we need to do now is register at the Mairie. Once we've done that we can get our new ration cards.'

'We make ourselves official?'

'I don't see that we can do otherwise, if we want to buy bread. We are in a separate jurisdiction now; we should be all right.'

He whistles out a breath.

'I can't see them coming all the way here to look for us, can you? We don't matter that much.'

He edges in behind her into the hotel dining room. It is packed tight, elbow-to-elbow. Jumbled with noise.

Madame shows them to a tiny table, and provides an off-ration stew of game and vegetables and barley. Globs of fat glisten on the surface. The meat falls to fibres on the tongue; the vegetables melt. It is impossibly good. They are rendered dumb by taste, by the dope of calories.

Suzanne does well; he watches as she does well. They are introduced to the people on neighbouring tables; she manages warm and easy conversation about nothing. He admires this as one might a coin plucked from an ear, or a fancily shuffled pack of cards. He can see that it's done well, but can't ever see himself mastering the trick.

The friends arrive – the Lobs – and Suzanne is delighted, seems astonished by their actuality. Kisses with Yvonne and her brother Roger, Yvonne's husband Marcel leaning in to shake hands but then abstracting himself and standing stiffly back. There is a big old house just outside the town, belonging to the family; they are muddling along together, all very *Grand Meaulnes*. He sips his wine and watches the open gabbling mouths, picks out bits of conversation. The opinions and advice and suggestions about work that might be got, about accommodation that might be sought – they can't lodge at the hotel indefinitely – and introductions that might be made. The bodies press too close, the walls are narrow round him; there is too much noise. He has been too long in silence, too long in solitude, too long upon the road.

He drinks his wine. He lifts crumbs from the tabletop with a fingertip. He nods his assent if his assent seems to be required.

The radio is switched on to warm up. Madame tunes it to Radio Londres and keeps the volume low, and in the packed dining room of the Hôtel de la Poste everyone falls silent, and they listen to the news from elsewhere, to the French speaking to the French.

The wind here has a mind of its own. It billows, blusters, darts, skirls around: you don't know what direction to expect it from. He ducks out of the gritty street and into the post office.

The postmistress's accent is educated but it still has the local wet, rolling *r*s, and a *g* where no *g* is generally required. She is handsome, dark-skinned, dark-eyed, with a flash of grey at the right temple. She smiles at his accent, but it's clear that strangers are no longer strange round here. She makes no remark about its destination, just weighs the letter on her scales with her little row of shining weights, licks a thumb and flips through her book of stamps. Why indeed should there not be easy traffic between the Free Zone and the Free State?

He leaves the post office with a disproportionate sense of achievement – a letter sent to his mother, reassuring her of his well-being, requesting his allowance, which will make things here so much easier – but steps out into stink, and the cobbles tumbling with squares of newspaper – lavatory-cut newspaper – that have already been put to full and thorough use. He dodges his way through them, disgusted, making his way to the Mairie, thinking of the man who'd wanted to shake the hand that wrote *Ulysses*, who was told that there were other things that same hand had also done.

In the chilly formal room of the Mairie, reluctant to sign, he turns the pages of the register and notes the cascade of displaced French arriving from the north, the scattering of foreign names within it. There is even an Irishwoman settled here. A Miss A. N. Beamish.

'The streets are filthy,' he observes to the clerk.

'Ah yes,' the clerk says. 'That'll be the wind. The WCs here empty over the cliffs. This kind of wind, it blows the paper right back up again.'

'Is there nothing to be done?'

A shrug. 'The wind changes. It blows it all away again.'

Freud, he thinks, might have had a thing or two to say about this place.

The next day stray rank papers linger in corners and gutters and shuffle round like last year's leaves. He and Suzanne sit outside the cobbler's workshop, on the cold stone bench, threadbare socks side by side while their shoes are being resoled. They've bought pastries from Gulinis'; they pick off fragments and melt them on the tongue, burst raisins between aching molars. Suzanne gets the hiccups. There's the sound of children playing in the schoolyard below, and the tap-tap-tap of the cobbler's hammer behind them, and the smell of bread and of leather and latrines, while he calculates silently how long their funds can be expected to last at the current rate, how soon his allowance can be expected to arrive: there has been a sharp increase in expenditure, what with the hotel room and restaurant meals and pastries and shoe repairs. They are not living hand-to-mouth on filched turnips and carrots and sleeping in hayricks any more. Their stack of cash is down to a sliver. Work, he supposes, must be found.

'What's up with you?' Suzanne asks.

'Nothing of nothing,' he says.

He pulls at a flake of pastry, and a sturdy woman in tweeds goes by, tugged along by Airedale terriers on leads. She nods, smiles to the two of them. This must be Miss A. N. Beamish. No one ever looked less French.

More people arrive, day by day; they clamber out of packed-tight buses. They slide off the backs of wagons. They come stumbling in on foot along the road. They are travel-worn and bleary, bundled up in crumpled clothes, dusty hats shoved down on their heads, and by their flinching gait it's clear their boots are martyring them. They nag and snipe and cling to each other. And when they spot him there's that wary catch of eye, the nod: he has, he realizes, become one of them: he has joined the community of the dispossessed.

He passes the tweedy woman again, this time in the town square. She has nothing of their hunted, ragged air about her. And the dogs: they make her seem established here. Dogs imply domesticity, permanence, decisions made.

'You must be new,' she says. She speaks in French, formally, but the accent carries Irish threads. 'We haven't met. Beamish. Anna.'

'Enchanted.' He squats to fuss her dogs.

'You are lodging at the Hôtel de la Poste, I imagine?'

He nods.

She leans closer to stage-whisper, still in French, 'Between you and me, that place is a dump.'

The dog rolls on its back. He scratches at its bristly chest. He hides a smile.

'That daft creature would take any amount of that,' she says.

He looks up at the soft underside of the woman's chin as she peers down at him. He says in English, 'We had Kerry Blues. At least, my mother did.'

There is a strange comfort in speaking those actual words in that actual language. The way they are pinned to that particular moment and that particular place: the damp muzzle, the slate-grey pelt under his hand, the sweet old fool of a dog. And his words make the woman's face break into a delighted grin.

'An Irishman!' she says. 'My word!'

He wobbles upright, offers his hand; she shakes it, brisk and vigorous.

'Well, fancy that.' A moment's delighted silence, contemplating him, clasping his hand.

'We've just arrived,' he says. 'We're still finding our feet.'

'Oh, we can help you find them, me and my pal. You'll soon forget your feet were ever missing.' She lets his hand go. 'You'll take a drink,' she says. 'Come on.'

'What do you do here?' he asks. 'I mean, how does one get by?'

'I have my royalties. That keeps us ticking over.'

'Oh. You're a writer?'

She is reaching for the wine. 'Am indeed.'

'I don't think I know your work.'

She wafts away any notion that he might. 'I write racy novels. Educated fellow such as yourself.' She shrugs. 'And anyway, I have a pen name, people think I'm a chap.'

'But they must sell, if you can live on your royalties.'

'They do indeed.'

He raises his glass to her. '*Félicitations*.'

'You're a writer yourself, then?'

Out across the square, the fig tree droops above the stone bench, the fruit already stripped, the leaves heavy and suggestive. He feels suddenly guilty, exposed.

'What makes you say that?'

She smiles. 'There's a tell. Your face . . .' She wafts her hand. 'It did a thing when I mentioned royalties. So I deduce from that, and from the way you speak, that you must be a writer.'

'Writing has occurred,' he concedes.

'Ha!' She leans away, studies him a moment, then reaches over to refill his glass. 'Tell me all your troubles.'

'Ah. Well. You know how it is.'

Inwardly, he is walking through the cemetery at Père Lachaise, packed tight with massive monuments to the brilliant dead. Not a patch of grass on which to pitch his own rotten little tent. No certainty now that he even wants to, not any more.

'No, I don't. How is it?' Miss Beamish asks.

He sits back. 'James Joyce was a friend of mine.'

'Oh no.'

'I used to help him with his work. With whatever he needed, really. I was a secretary to him.'

She shakes her head. Tuts.

'*Finnegans Wake*,' he says. 'I helped him with that, and I worked on the French translation.'

'Oh you poor thing.' Her face is a parody of sympathy. She shakes her head. 'Being friends with a genius.'

She waves the waiter over, holds up the empty *pichet* for a refill. Then she turns back to him, reverting to English.

'But what was this writing that did occur, despite your difficulties?'

He raises a shoulder. 'It never came to very much.'

'Get away of that with you.'

He catches her smile. He knows he will be half-cut and stinking of booze by the time he gets back to Suzanne, and that Suzanne will be cross and say that she isn't cross, and that this state will go on for days, but it is a long time since he has felt so entirely at his ease, a very long time indeed, and it is worth the price that must be paid for its continuance.

'And now,' he says, 'I just can't see the point of it at all.'

'Because of the war?' She tilts her head, considering, as she refills their glasses. 'There's still the oldest and best reason. Even in war, even in any circumstances, really. That still applies.'

'What's that then?'

'Spite,' she says.

He snorts.

'No, I'm serious,' she says, not very seriously. 'You need a bit of spite, a bit of venom, to keep you going. Particularly at the start, when no one gives a damn what you're up to.'

'Well, yes, I suppose so.'

'And then, of course, it's necessary.'

'Necessary?'

'If one is not writing, one is not quite oneself, don't you find?'

And he thinks: the sweaty sleepless nights in Ireland, heart racing, battling for breath. Frank's gentle company the only thing that could calm him. The two things are connected: the writing and the panic. He just had not put them together, until now.

'It's like snails make slime,' she's saying. 'One will never get along, much less be comfortable, if one doesn't write.'

He huffs a laugh.

'So.' She shrugs. 'There you are. You're stuck with it.'

He raises his glass. She chinks it.

'To spite,' she says.

'And slime.'

They drink.

*

245

There are voices beyond the wall; there are voices beyond all the walls: there are voices above the ceiling, and in the adjoining bedrooms and down the corridors and in the lounge. The hotel heaves with people and they are talking, talking, talking, chewing, swallowing, sweating, pacing, pissing, screwing, sniffing, and talking, talking, talking, talking, talking, on and on, endlessly and everywhere, words words words, and bodies packed tight, heaving over and around each other like insects, like grubs and talking swallowing chewing sniffing on and on and on. This place is an anthill; it crawls and hums and ticks and shivers, everyone treading their own shit into the ground beneath their feet. The wind wails and tugs at the shutters and lifts tiles and makes them tap and clatter, and when there is nothing else, when there's a moment's pause in all of that, which is only in the three a.m. pitch-black horrors of the soul, the mice still scratch loud in the laths and the cockroaches click under the skirting boards, and Suzanne still breathes and breathes and breathes beside him. He aches for distance, for space, for silence, for his tiny old apartment back on the rue des Favorites. Where there was solitude and peace, and it was his.

He stares now at the three words he has written. They are ridiculous. Writing is ridiculous. A sentence, any sentence, is absurd. Just the idea of it: jam one word up against another, shoulder-to-shoulder, jaw-to-jaw; hem them in with punctuation so they can't move an inch. And then hand that over to someone else to peer at, and expect something to be communicated, something understood. It's not just pointless. It is ethically suspect.

And yet he needs it. As Miss Beamish said. He has to make the slime that will ease him through the world.

He gleans potatoes left in the muddy margins, apples dropped from the back of the cart. Suzanne, meanwhile, visits her friends. She talks with Madame at the hotel and with the local women. Finding things out. This is, of course, also useful. There is labouring work to be had on a couple of the local farms. Chopping logs, pulling crops, tending the vines. Would he take it? He does not want to take it. He asks when he can start.

The church bell chimes the angelus three times a day. The little cafés shut at ten. It gets cold. In the dark chill room at the Mairie, the blue ink of his signature is shut tight inside the pages of the Register of Aliens. At night, he lies awake while the lost souls twist and mutter in their sleep. All it would take is an outside request for information. An audit. All it would take is for the Geste still to be on the hunt, or to stumble accidentally upon them in the hunt for someone else. He need do nothing to provoke disaster now. It's inherent in their existence here. That it could all collapse to ruins in a breath.

He blunders through to breakfast and Madame has the morning bulletin on. He sips ersatz coffee and stares over Suzanne's shoulder at the dreadful green wallpaper, and Suzanne stares across the room, over her cup, around the people gathered there; they fall silent and they listen. They learn that they are no longer in the Zone Libre: that this has become the Zone Sud. The Axis powers have extended military administration below the demarcation line. The wire has been rolled out round the whole of France. They are all now chickens in a coop, the lot of them.

Suzanne's sharp eyes slip to his and catch. He sets his cup down, reaches out to her, but she doesn't take his hand.

'Chances are they won't come here,' she says.

It is a flimsy enough chance. In the dining room, the guests remain quiet. Madame plods over to the radio set and switches it off sharply, as if it were itself responsible.

'Everyone's in the same boat,' Suzanne says. 'It's just a question of waiting. The war can't go on for ever.'

He nods. He thinks, it doesn't have to. 'Well,' he says. 'I have to get to work.'

There is frost on the ground. His toes are numb in his stupid boots. He walks the long lane down to the vineyard.

The vines are bare, the leaves fallen. The lad, Fernand, is half his age, and is showing him the ropes. The light makes him squint; it is too much. Van Gogh's paintings: those dim muddy northern scenes, the industrial dirt and misery; but then he's bowled over by the southern light, by these sun-saturated yellows, by this exact blue. Art is such a consolation. If he himself could paint – but he cannot paint. He turns the collar up on his coat: the faint whiff of it even now, cheroots and lemon. He is marching down the vineyards with a half-bushel basket, a roll of twine, a knife, wearing a dead man's coat, while the German Army snakes out along the lanes and trackways like poison in the blood, and he daydreams about Van Gogh, and makes nothing happen.

'Come, let me show you,' says the boy. 'You must pay close attention, the knife is sharp.'

The lad is *vouvoyer*ing him, being well brought up: the state he's in, he has hardly earned the formal mode. At the foot of the slope they step in between the rows of vines. Fernand bends, his young fingers feeling through the splayed, sinewy growth.

'Now watch.'

He takes out a stubby, vicious little knife, the steel blade scraped and scored with striations from the whetstone. He makes a swift sloping cut. He lifts away a horizontal arm of vine, dumps it into his basket.

'These ones here, they fruited this summer. They have to go.' He cuts again, lobs aside another sinewy growth.

'Right.'

The lad scrolls out a length of twine, bends the remaining shoots down to the supporting wires and ties them off.

'Like this,' he says. 'One left, one right, spread just so. You understand?'

'I think so.'

The boy smiles. His teeth are white against his tanned skin. It is one of those faces that will be deep in wrinkles by the time he's thirty. He returns to the work and with three deft cuts he finishes the vine, one to the left shoot, one to the right. 'On the central shoot, count three strong buds, then cut.'

He leaves the vine standing like the Cooldrinagh roses in the autumn: neat, abrupt, having been shown who's boss.

'Now, you – this one here. I'll watch.'

The palm-worn haft in his right hand, he reaches into the vine and grips the summer's growth. He copies Fernand's sharp angled cut. The boy nods approvingly.

He ties the stems down, clips them back, cuts away the central shoot.

'Good. If you need me, I shall be off along the next row, over there.'

He gets to work. He bends, cuts, ties, straightens, dumps the waste aside. He bends, cuts, ties, straightens, dumps the waste aside. He unbuttons the coat. Later, he takes it off entirely and lobs it on to the grass and it lies forgotten.

The rhythm of the work loosens his thoughts; they begin to shift and slide. He's no longer where he is; time passes differently: an empty train station, the rub of a blistered heel, and the evening soft, and someone watching and someone being watched. And while he drifts with these thoughts, the blade slips and sheers aside, and instead of grapevine he slices deep into the ball of his thumb.

There is a moment's pause between the damage done and the pain of it. He lifts the knife out of the flesh. He watches as the wound opens like a little mouth: blood beads there and rolls and drips. Blood slides across his hand and falls to the parched winter grass. It's only then that he starts fumbling for a handkerchief, and his head swims.

The boy looks over. The handkerchief is wrapped tight and useless, already red and wet with blood. The boy comes running.

They sit him down in the dim kitchen, where it is warm and smells of woodsmoke and onions. Madame fusses, dabs on alcohol, fixes strips of sticking plaster to hold the wound together, then binds the hand with gauze. He winces. His arm throbs up to the elbow. The blood still comes, though slower now.

Monsieur sets a tumbler down in front of him; it has an inch of brandy in it, and Madame drops a lump of sugar in and crushes it and stirs. She has a round face, red cheeks, her chin sweetly fuzzed with down.

Monsieur scrapes out a chair and sits. He pours himself a drink too. 'Plenty round here are missing a finger or two.'

He nods, but then regrets it. It makes his head swim.

The farmer takes a battered old tin from his breast pocket, and proffers it. 'Cigarette?'

'Thank you.' With his good hand, he teases out a cigarette and tucks it between his lips. It's a ready-made, he notices. He hasn't had one of those in a while.

The farmer heaves himself up to light a spill at the fire.

'It's good?' Monsieur asks when both their cigarettes are lit.

It is toasty and soft.

'That's American tobacco, you know.'

He takes the cigarette from his lips, turns it. Of course it is.

'I have my contacts,' Monsieur says. 'So. We get hold of things.'

'Ah, for God's sake.' This is Madame now. 'Can't you see the poor fellow's exhausted? All the Jews are. They're worn out, the poor things.'

'He's not a Jew. Are you a Jew, Irishman?'

'No, I don't have that distinction.'

Madame wafts a hand. '*Pft*. It's all the same. Just you leave him be.'

She dumps a saucer down between them for the ash. Then she bustles off and busies herself about the stove, riddling the grate, clattering the pans, slamming the oven door.

He sips his brandy and the farmer talks.

'I wonder why you had to come here. Since you are not a Jew. And you are from a neutral country, Ireland, and so you should not be harassed in Paris, you should be able to get by. I don't think you are a homosexual?'

He raises a shoulder. 'I don't think so either.'

'So I wonder what it was that you were up to, up there in the north.'

'This,' he says, 'and that.'

The farmer nods. 'A busy man. You'll be bored here.'

'I have work.'

'But perhaps you'll want other kinds of work.'

He rubs at the back of his neck. He suspects, but is not certain of what is not being said. The cigarette is the clue. Contraband. Supplied by the Allies to the *Maquis*. 'I think my companion would disapprove.'

'Well,' the farmer says. 'You think about it.'

'I'll think about it.'

'Then you tell your companion what you're going to do.'

'Is that how it works?'

The farmer laughs, sets his cigarette down in the saucer. His wife, on the other side of the kitchen, lets out a snort.

'No.' The farmer raises his glass in a toast. They chink. They both drain the dregs. The liquid is thick and crunches with grains of sugar.

Suzanne has wedged a chair in between the bed and the window, for the light. A bolt of thick grey wool is spread over her knees and the counterpane. It's a blanket; she is under commission to turn it into a coat. She is hand-stitching the whole thing. It's trying to the eyes and on the hands. She looks up when he comes in; she says good evening, she notices the bandage. Tuts.

'What did you do now?'

'It's nothing. Madame cleaned it up, so . . .' She doesn't offer any further comment, so he just continues, '. . . it will be fine.'

He opens his bag, wincing, and lifts his supplies out on to the bed. The room is stuffy and cold, and there are voices to be heard from beyond the wall. She gets up and folds the fabric away, stabs her needle into it. Kneading at a shoulder muscle, she inches round the edge of the bed to inspect the haul.

One-handed, he unfurls a parcel of waxed paper. A clutch of olives. He unfolds another napkin and there is a small, fresh goats' cheese and a cube of quince jelly. He lifts out a wine bottle; it's unlabelled, the cork already drawn then shoved halfway back in. He plucks the bottle open, sloshes wine into a tooth glass, hands it to her. He sits. The mattress dips. The nest of olives tips over sideways, the cheese slides downhill towards him and he has to catch it and put it back. She hands him the glass. When he lifts his elbow to drink, she has to lean away. No room to park his arse, no room to lift an elbow, not even certain he can still tell one from the other any more. His head is locked solid with it all, with the weeks of it; the tumblers of his mind are rusted and they're stuck and he can't make them shift, and he can't think for all the closeness, the crowding, everything jammed up around him and yet nothing within reach, everything bundled and boxed and getting under his feet and in his way.

'We are invited over for dinner on Saturday, to the Bonnellys',' he says, rubbing at his eyes.

'Oh. Good.' She takes the glass off him again and sips.

He divides the olives, the cheese, the preserve, on to the two napkins. There is an extra olive so he gives it to her; he breaks the cheese into uneven pieces and sets the larger portion on her napkin. He hands the meal to her. They eat wordlessly, crumb by crumb, pausing to spit pits into their palms. After the last sticky swallow, there is silence between them again.

He holds up the bottle; she proffers the glass. The wine sloshes in.

'They seem to be very pleasant people,' he manages.

'Oh yes,' she says.

'Generous, too.'

254

'Good.'

'All this for just an afternoon's work.'

She blinks at him. 'I am doing what I can, you know.'

'I know.'

'I am going mad here, stuck here, stuck with this. My hands hurt.'

He nods. He knows.

'Just like you to be like that.'

He hadn't realized that he was being like anything. 'What do you mean?'

'Nothing ever touches you.'

She's flushed now. 'In truth, I think it's all the same to you, all of it. If we stay in Paris and die or if we hide in a hole here and go mad, and then die all the same. You do not even notice.'

'I am not finding it easy, Suzanne.'

'Pft.'

'What?'

She looks at him, hard and level, cool with disappointment. She could say: I saw your notebook, back in the apartment, full of nonsense. You spend your time doodling and scratching things out. That is just how you are. You won't make anything of anything at all.

But she says, 'And now we are stuck here, caught like rats in a trap in this dreadful hotel. Even with all the trouble and fatigue of getting here, we are still not safe.'

'We're alive. So we're rather lumbered with the rest.'

'You don't seem to care.'

'You think we should stop, then?'

'Stop?'

'Stop. Just – give up.'

She makes that movement of the mouth, the lips bunched together, the corners turned down, which passes with her sometimes for a shrug.

He could say: I know what stopping looks like. It looks like a man stepping out into the sky. It looks like the ground racing up to meet you. It looks like a black comma on the cobblestones. It looks like a pool of blood.

But he says, 'Is that what you suggest?'

'I'm not suggesting anything,' she says.

'No.' He drinks, sets the tooth mug aside, picks up a crumb of cheese. His injured hand rests limp in his lap. 'I see that.'

She glares at him, brittle and unhappy. Too much store had been set upon the destination. Continuance here, inhabitance – that had barely crossed her mind. Now they're stuck with the day-to-day of it, the day-after-day of it, for as far as the eye can see, and it might as well be eternity; and they are tangled together, twining round each other; they are all elbows, feet and claws.

'Do the Lobs have a piano, perhaps, out at Saint-Michel?' he asks.

'Maybe.'

'Perhaps you could go and play there. That would be good for you. They wouldn't mind.'

She nods.

'Maybe you could even take pupils again. There must be young ones around here who'd otherwise miss out. You've always loved teaching. That would help.'

256

She looks at him. Then she says, 'You're so much better at this than me.'

'No,' he says. 'No, I'm not.'

She nods, though. And then she says, 'Perhaps we can find somewhere more out of the way. A house just outside town. So if the place is raided, we won't be stuck here like fish in a barrel.'

'I'll ask a friend.'

Suzanne blows a puff of breath.

'What?'

'A friend.'

'What?'

'You.'

'What?'

'You and your friends.'

'What do you mean, me and my friends?'

'You make friends like dogs make puppies.'

He frowns at this. Promiscuously? With pleasure? By the half-dozen? He doesn't ask. But Anna Beamish will have an idea or two where they might look for more out-of-the-way accommodation. And he doesn't mention his unsettling conversation with Monsieur. No point in meeting that particular trouble halfway.

14

La Croix
January 1943

THIS IS THE place, then: the little house on the edge of town. He climbs the creaking stairs. The wind rattles the shutters against their latches. He has Shem's old coat on, a muffler drawn up over his mouth and nose and dampened by his breath.

The upstairs room swells wide and dim, slope-ceilinged, with a window in each gable. There is a bedstead, an armoire, a small table and chair. The walls are rose-painted plaster. Beyond the back window, there's just rattling, tormented branches, and black birds tumbling and skittering about. Looking out of the front window, across the road, the ground falls away sharply, so he stands now above the treetops and can see all the way across the valley to the distant mountains beyond. From here, turn right and walk ten minutes into town. Turn left and the nearest house is Miss Beamish's, only just in sight, down at the crossroads.

This is a pool of space; this is a silence wide enough to swim in. If writing could happen at all, in these days, it would happen in a place like this. Here, perhaps, he could make a little slime to ease himself along.

He hears their voices rising up from the garden. Suzanne's, as well as those of Marcel and Yvonne Lob. The professor has been doing great things with the grounds at Saint-Michel; he is not only supplying their own needs, but selling off the excess for a decent profit in Apt. Of course it is the right thing to do, to make the garden here profitable too. But what alarms him is the time that it implies. The waiting. That the seasons will have slid along from winter through spring and summer and back to autumn once more, and they'll still be stuck here, eating garden peas and tomatoes and cooking their own onions in a stew. That by then the worst will not have happened, but then neither will anything else.

This waiting; this *attentisme*. It has become a deliberate decision. Everyone is waiting to see how grand events will fall before they'll take a position, or do anything about anything at all. This is the politics of passivity, and it makes sense. But it is unconscionable. It is not to be borne.

He turns away from the window and clumps down the stairs. Suzanne, at that same moment, is coming in through the back door, her nose pink, her hands clamped under her armpits. There is a brightness about her that he hasn't seen in a long while.

'You like it?' he asks.

'Yes,' she says. 'It will do very well.'

Yvonne and Marcel Lob come in behind her, crowd out the doorway's light.

'One thing you'll have to be sure of is a good supply of fuel,' the professor explains, as if this needed explanation. 'It'll be cold, a place like this, standing all alone. You could freeze to death out here, this winter.'

The wind is bitter; it makes him squint.

He eyes the copse of holm oak. In girth and stature, compared with the common variety, these oaks are barely more than weeds. There are half a dozen or so of them to be cut down, and the wood sawn and split and stacked on to a cart. He'll get it done in a day, he reckons. He has been promised half of the wood in exchange for his work. The little copse means heat and cooking and warm water for the months to come.

They'd gathered wood in the park, they'd broken branches and filched planks. But he's never cut down a tree before.

Still. How hard can it be?

He hefts the axe, swings it. It whacks against the trunk. The haft judders in his hands; the jolt of it travels up his arms and into his shoulders. The twigs shiver, the blade leaves a narrow split in the bark; and that is all.

He sets the axe down on its head, spits on his palms and rubs them together.

He lifts the axe and swings again. The bark opens a little wider.

He takes the coat off and lays it aside.

Later, he takes his jacket off and drops it on top of the coat.

Then he takes off his sweater and his shirt, and lobs them in the direction of the clothes pile. He works on in his singlet, the wind and winter sun creasing up his eyes.

His arms ache. His shoulders ache. His back aches.

It's a different ache from usual. It's not the stiff neck and tired eyes of before, not the tight cramp of study and neglect. And his head begins to clear; his thoughts are smoothed out and they begin to run. There are no knots. No tangles. No sudden snags. There's just the swing of the axe, and the shift and twist of muscle, and the breath in and out of him, and the catch of it, of a deeper breath than usual, on his scar, like the tick forward of a second hand.

He works.

He is at Cooldrinagh, swaying high in a treetop, watching his mother cross the ground beneath him, her shins whacking against the sail of her skirt. He is huddled in his chair in the darkness of his college rooms, cold, deliberately alone. He is drifting in a morphine glow through billowing white curtains, and a line of pain that the blade made in him, waking now to the uneasy thrill of Shem's face, and now to the new comfort of Suzanne's, and now to his mother's pinched visage. He is in that little café on the rue des Vignes watching Shem talk as though the world falling into ruins were some grand conspiracy against him. Two years he's gone now, maybe even to the day – a sting to realize that things are slipping, blurring: he has lost track and doesn't know the date. And if Shem had not died, and if he had fled south rather than to Switzerland, if he were here now, he'd have spread a handkerchief on the bank there and sat himself down on it, ankle on knee, dark glasses covering his eyes, hands folded on the head of his cane, hat tamped down, his good coat laid around his shoulders, watching him work. And he'd be griping. Small-town life, dear God, how does anybody stand it! The dogs following him around, and the food, and the state of his boots on these dreadful roads. C'mon now, c'mon for a glass of wine and a bite of dinner and a few songs, why don't you? There must be somewhere in town where his name is still worth something, where a friend might stand him a drink, where he can caress a piano's keys and sing a few old songs.

He glances down at his palms, at the puffs of unburst blisters, the seams of sweaty dirt, the puckered scar across his thumb where the knife had slipped. You wouldn't catch Mr James Joyce getting his hands roughened. Getting them dirty. At least, not this kind of dirt.

By nightfall, there's a stump in the red earth. It twists its roots deep into the rocky soil.

He has started work on the second tree; he has taken a sappy, smashed bite out of its base. It shudders when he hits it.

He is splitting logs. There is rhythm to this work. His breath plumes and fades, plumes and fades.

The house is silent; Suzanne is out at Saint-Michel, playing the piano. The light lowers, the shadows lengthen, and there is, far off, the sound of an engine from the Apt road. The axe stilled, he listens. The rumbling grows; there is more than one engine. Diesel, heavy, getting closer. He whacks the axe into the chopping block, wipes his palms down his trousers. Gooseflesh prickles on his arms.

Because the roads are so quiet nowadays. Cars moulder in barns. Tractors serve as chicken roosts. Delivery trucks are solitary and infrequent. Bicycles are as cherished as firstborn sons, because there is no fuel now, not for ordinary people. There is only fuel for the government, the Army and the Geste.

He slips round the side of the house and peers out along the road. The rattle of the engines grows, and now there is the gritty peel of the tyres. And then, at the turn, light: the fence is illuminated in stark lines. The headlamps are sloped low and shaded for the blackout. There is no pause at the junction: the vehicles turn towards him with brutal self-assurance. They are passing now, shaking the ground beneath his feet, and he steps back deeper into the shadows, and the trucks thunder into town.

Round the back of the house again he snatches up the coat and drags it on. Suzanne, fingertips shifting their gentle pressure from key to key – no way to get word to her. And in town, the newcomers vanishing as the trucks appear; people slipping down alleyways and up flights of stairs and in through garden gates. If the trucks pull up outside the hotel, if soldiers descend and slam open doors and demand papers. So many people are so vulnerable there.

And if the troops are sent back out this way, to find the Irishman. It would only take a word.

He flits on into the woods, the ground rising, so that he is scrambling up, on hands and feet, through rocks and fallen pine needles. The stream of headlights continues off to his left. The trees baffle the sound and distort it, seeming close, then distant, then right up by him once again. He pulls himself up over roots and shivering dry scree until he reaches the top of the outcrop. His breath hurts; it catches on his scar. He squats down, his back against a tree, and stares out towards the town. He lights a cigarette and shakes out the match and squeezes the black tip till it is cool. He holds the match cupped in his palm: the woods are dry as tinder, even at this time of year. He watches the lights, the flick and smudge of them through the town, and smokes, his hand shaking. Then the lights slither off, along the road that curves away and descends steeply to the valley, and away, and they fade off into the distance. He taps ash into his hand and rubs his palms together. Cigarette clamped between his lips, he gets to his feet and begins the ungainly slither back downhill.

Heron-like, he hunches over his manuscript. He holds his pen in calloused fingertips.

The blankets are thrown back on the bed, the pillows are still dented with the press of their heads; the few clothes he is not actually wearing are slung over a chair. Suzanne is outdoors in the cold, digging over the ground, preparing it for the first seeds.

He has the old coat on, the collar drawn up, the mitts that Suzanne knitted on his paws, his muffler up over his nose. This room is right above the wood-burning stove and is the warmest part of the upper floor, but when the wind blows it whips the warmth away and even here it's cold. He only notices afterwards.

Because the words now come. With a curve and loop and dip and stroke. The words keep happening, and he will not think too much about their coming but just let them come. At the foot of the page, he blows upon the wet coils, then turns the leaf and folds it flat, and on the verso the words go on, loop and dip and twist, as they have gone on now for weeks together. A stalagmite of heavy notebooks grows on the desk beside him.

From time to time there's the cry of circling crows, or the noise of a horse and cart slowing for the turn at the cross-roads. An occasional motor vehicle. People pass from time to time, exchange a few words, but it's there-and-gone and does not intrude on his own words.

And so he thinks of none of it: not the presences nor the absences, neither the wide expanse of sky beyond his window nor the close grain of the wood under his hand, though all of it was necessary for this quiet alchemy to happen.

Writing lets him step aside, and time flows on without him. He sips his just-made cup of corn coffee and it's ice-cold; he looks up from the morning and the light has gone. His shoulders ache. There's a snag in his neck. Then head-lamps blur the dark – and he gets to his feet, but he's too slow to see the truck pass and so doesn't know whether it was a patrol, or if it is one of the few remaining delivery vans, rigged up to run on gas, or wood chips, or old cook-ing oil.

You keep on going, don't you, after all? The horrors build. You keep on doing what you do, out of spite.

He turns away from the window and his desk; he wraps his arms around himself and shivers and clumps downstairs. Suzanne isn't there. He opens the back door and blinks out at her, standing in the chill spring evening, surveying her dug-over patch. Her hands are red with earth.

'Is that you?' she says. She looks round and her face is streaked with red.

'It is,' he says. 'I was writing.'

'We're almost out of firewood,' she says.

Newcomers still turn up in the town. They stumble off buses and hole up in the hotel. He makes friends there, in ones and twos, not by the half-dozen. Henri Hayden becomes a companion over chess; he's an artist, and a blessing. In the evenings, they gather at Miss Beamish's, Henri and his wife Josette, he and Suzanne, Miss Beamish and her companion, also called Suzanne. They listen to the radio.

This is just another bubble. The bubble's shrinking.

A farmer is shot dead. One bullet, neatly through the brain. The blood dries in the red soil. It's known who killed him; it's never spoken of. There's a cloud around the man who did it, a haze of flies. Because this was a neighbour; this was somebody known to them all, over long years, the family over generations. The farmer had found a crate of cigarettes where there should not have been a crate of cigarettes. He reported it. He allowed the information to flow along the proper channels, rather than damming it or forcing it back upon itself, making it flow uphill.

When he sits alone and writes, it is to push against the closing walls of the bubble. The sides flex outward, just a little; he feels that he can breathe. When he blinks, his eyes feel sore against the lids. He's always tired.

The prose creeps. Notebooks fill. A soft evening in Ireland, a redbrick villa, and the elderly and lame and syphilitic. An unseen man upstairs, dishing out pabulum, approval and opprobrium, entirely arbitrarily.

His handwriting shrinks too and becomes more careful. Everything is reduced, condensed. He commits just the essence of the thing to paper. Anything more than that would be a waste.

And when he surfaces to a cramped hand, a crick in the neck, the sunlight shifted across the floor, a sore blink, he knows that even to have written this little is an excess, it is an overflowing, an excretion. Too many words. There are just too many words. Nobody wants them, nobody needs them. And still they keep on, keep on, keep on coming.

At night, when they gather – he and his Suzanne, Miss Beamish and hers, sometimes the Haydens – to listen to the radio at Miss Beamish's house, he notices that the gnomic messages on Radio Londres are increasing. They take up more and more of the broadcast time. The gathered company strain their ears through the noise and clutter of the attempts to block the signal, to catch hold of the surrealist fragments and Dadaesque cut-ups that mean something to somebody somewhere. *The elephant broke a barricade. I repeat, the elephant broke a barricade . . . The blue horse walks on the horizon . . . Giraffes don't wear false collars . . . Aunt Amélie cycled in shorts.* Sometimes, in Miss Beamish's sitting room, a head is shaken at the strangeness; sometimes an eye catches another eye and there's a smile. The poetry of these utterances is intriguing. There are secret parcels and packets of meaning attached to them; they go unseen by all but the intended recipient.

The sun shines, and the leaves unfurl, and the shade deepens blue again beneath the trees, and the grapes swell, and in the streams the fish become fat and sluggish, and the birds hop through the inner storeys of bushes like they do every year; flights of them skim above the houses and through the town, and the boys take potshots at them, sharp-eyed and practised, and the women pluck the moth-light bodies and cook them so that the flesh falls from their greenstick bones.

He has become a creature of wire and rope: muscle twists over bone; tendon shifts under skin; skin becomes as brown as tea. He moves freely, lost in the mechanics of labour, less conscious of his physical self than he has been since he was a child. The stone sits in a cheek, is turned over, sent to rest in the other cheek. In solitude and silent work, his thoughts shift and slide across each other. There are patterns forming; they can be glimpsed in the corner of the eye. It doesn't do to look directly: the pieces drift away like ice. But later, to sit down at his desk, to fill his pen, to trace this across a notebook's whiteness, is to conjure the patterns back. To write is to drift along with the floe; it is to let the floe drift through him.

He walks out with Henri, and they drink a bottle of wine on a café terrace.

At night, he sleeps his black sleep, and it washes him quite clean.

When the day is bright and calm, and the mistral doesn't blow, and there's a warmth to the sunshine, and the air is sweet, and when in the evenings there is light and time and space to write in, it is all too easy to forget that their good luck is just the luck of the crow in the woods, the luck of the merely overlooked.

> Fie on't! O fie! 'tis an unweeded garden,
> That grows to seed; things rank and gross in nature
> Possess it merely.

Henri Hayden can be heard well before he's seen; he declaims the lines as he's coming down the road. Irish and French sounds bulge out of the English verse, along with his native Polish.

He gets up from his seat and peers out of the window. His friend has a *Collected Shakespeare* clamped under his arm and is striding along with the ungainly confidence of the half-cut, having been to Miss Beamish's for an English lesson. Miss Beamish is not a methodical teacher, but she is liberal with her rewards. He raises a hand and Henri pauses in the street, swaying slightly. They talk over the balustrade.

269

'Better keep it down, my friend,' he says to Henri in French. 'You never know.'

Henri wafts the concern away. 'But I must practise my English, so that when the Americans come I can welcome them properly in their own language. It's only right.'

He is not sure that Shakespeare's English, via Connemara, is likely to make much sense to a GI. He drops his voice further still. 'Would it not be wiser to learn German?'

'Oh, they're last week's news, the Germans. They're done for.'

'Henri. Be careful.'

'It's the paperwork, you see. Each new country they go blundering into, wagonloads of new paperwork, all those forms and dockets.' He grins. 'They've bitten off more than they can chew in Russia, now, you mark my words. All that bureaucracy will bring the Nazis to their knees.'

'Maybe they like paperwork,' he says. 'Maybe they relish it.'

'Buggers.' Henri's face falls, but he speaks in perfect English idiom. 'I bet they bloody do.'

In the circumstances, to find oneself still continuing on with all the business of life, to keep on putting one foot in front of the other, taking one breath after the other, while so many others have just stopped, is uncomfortable. It's not as though he thinks he's worth the effort.

He pushes into the post office, making the bell ring, inhaling the universal post-office smell of manila, ink and gum. He catches a glimpse of the post-mistress in the back

270

room, her startled face turned towards the sound of the bell. There's a man there too; he's tucking a sheaf of letters into an inner pocket. A brisk, muttered exchange. She bustles out with a smile and the fellow slides out past the counter and gives him a nod, passing with a cloud of country smell of sweat and wine and livestock. The bell dings and the fellow is gone.

He exchanges courtesies with the post-mistress. She checks the pigeonholes. He leaves with a letter from his mother.

He reads as he walks, past the end of the schoolyard where the children run and shout, past two little girls, who, pausing in their game with marbles and chalk, stare huge-eyed and watch the spindly giant pass, and then snort with laughter when he's gone. He folds the cheque into a pocket.

News of the dogs, and Lily the maid, and Cooldrinagh now sold, and the new place half built – she is even going to call it New Place, which makes him smile – and Frank and Janet, of card parties and coffee mornings and church. Mollie who had walked the strand with him at Greystones, hair blowing, catching in her mouth. Sheila now settled comfortably in Wales with the girls and sending postcards, everybody well. But worried about him.

He turns it over, reads on to her signing-off, then folds it up and stuffs it away. It is warm and it is kind and it is concerned. It seems that they can only be close when they are at such a distance, when the whole of Europe stands at war between them. He should not be putting her through this, all this, all this worry. She is old, she is not well; she is his mother. That queasy umbilical tug. Still, he pulls against it.

He goes past the front of the house. He continues on past Miss Beamish's, through the woods, following the road that winds downhill, underneath the cypresses. He walks as the red road fades to pink, out on to the limestone territory, as the road becomes a white line tracing through the vineyards. The far hills are white with bare stone like a fall of snow. His boots scuff white mud on to themselves.

He takes off his coat, slings it over an arm. Keeps on walking.

He could have stayed in Ireland. To save her this. Getting old and alone and worrying about him.

He is halfway up the slope of the ancient bridge before he notices where he is. Beyond the balustrade there's a twenty-foot drop and white water churns over rocks below. He peers down: it's barely a stream; it must have shrunk considerably over time, to have once merited a bridge like this.

When she is dead, he thinks, will the tug then not be to home, but down into the grave?

His friend just stepped out into the empty air.

The water tumbles, churns, it wears pits into the white rock. Beneath his hard palms, the stone is crumbly as lump sugar.

It had seemed brisk and simple, that step out of the window. But every moment leading up to that moment must itself have been a decision made.

He pushes away from the balustrade. He takes the slow way down, striding along the bridge, climbing the stile and

272

then scrambling down to the water's edge. A wading bird picks its way across the mud, and dips her beak down into it, and sifts the silt for food.

In the looped shade cast by the arches, he eases off his boots and socks and dips his feet into the stream. It is ice; it is vivid and it makes him gasp. His feet are all bones, bunions and blisters and ragged yellow nails as the water tumbles round them, and the one toe with the missing joint, as ugly as sin, and as human. He feels sorry for his feet; he knows what they've been through.

And so one finds one goes on living. One makes slime and one drags oneself along through the world. Because life is an active decision now. An act of resistance. And there is a certain satisfaction in it. One lives, however hard the struggle, to spite the cunts who want one dead.

He walks the dry miles back to the house in silence, skirting Suzanne hunched between her beanpoles, climbing the stairs to his desk. He is already elsewhere. Later she clumps around below, indoors; later still he smells soup. He will go down in a moment. But his pen moves across the page, and two men are contained within barbed wire; they walk parallel, pacing, disconnected and close. Contact, human contact: they crave it, and they shrink from it.

His pen spirals and loops across the paper.

The sun sinks. Then there are voices. Speaking urgently and hushed.

When he comes downstairs, parched and sore-eyed, the room is dim, the lamp not yet lit. It takes him a moment to see Suzanne at the table there, with her friend Yvonne hunched on the other side, her back to him, and Yvonne's brother, Roger, standing in the open back door, smoking a cigarette.

'It's the professor,' Suzanne says.

Yvonne turns round to look at him. Her face is blotted, swollen with tears. The professor is Marcel. Her husband.

'What happened?'

One of those half-breath silences, when someone has to say something that no one wants to hear again. 'He's been arrested.'

He draws out a chair, sits down with them. He feels a rush of sympathy for Yvonne, for the children, for her husband who he's never really liked.

'What can we do?'

Yvonne wipes her cheeks. 'I don't know that there's anything we can do. He wasn't wearing his star or carrying his papers. So.'

'How did they know?'

'He was denounced.'

Roger speaks quietly. 'We'll think of something, Yvonne, don't worry.'

'I don't see what there is to think of.'

'Who denounced him?' he asks.

Yvonne shrugs, fierce. 'We supply fruit and flowers in Apt – I should have insisted that I go instead. But we got too used to being safe. We got to expect that things would just be all right. But someone must have guessed, or suspected, and then . . .' She shakes her head.

It is late when the little group breaks up; it is an unhappy dispersal. They have arrived at no satisfactory conclusion. The professor can't be proven innocent, since he can't be proven not-Jewish. The only plan is that Yvonne assert her remaining rights as a Frenchwoman and a non-Jew; she must kick up as much fuss as possible, as though over some pet dog that has been impounded as a stray. Her man is not to be deported. If he must be detained, it must be in France. If she writes letters, makes appeals, makes a nuisance of herself, then maybe she can slow the deportation process, bog it down in paperwork, until something else happens and things change again. The war can't go on for ever: isn't this what everybody says? That is the professor's best hope, though it is a strange one to find oneself clinging to. That a French camp, like Drancy, with its unglazed windows and bare concrete floors, be considered a good. That his fate is just to wait there, as the war flares and fades around him.

When Yvonne and Roger leave, he goes through the evening rituals, aware for once of what are normally unconscious acts. He draws the shutters, bolts them, his hands old and knuckly and looking entirely alien to him. He is conscious of the barriers' flimsiness, the arbitrariness of the space that they contain. He is conscious too of other spaces: the road down which Paul Léon had shrunk and faded; the concrete and worn grass ringed around with wire and Alfred Péron staring at the sky; a sunless cube in the depths of the Santé where chains hang from the wall; a swaying carriage rattling off towards the east, packed with deported people; his own

275

skull and its pool of darkness, the shiver that grows at the base of it and slithers up into his hair.

Reaching round for the last shutter, he is leaning out into the empty night and is caught by the wide silence here. He feels observed. He goes to bolt the door. They have never been safe here, he knows; they had just failed to notice the danger. All it would take is a few guns, a few dogs, and the crows will be dealt with. Will be cleared entirely from the woods.

He climbs the stairs, rubbing at the back of his bristling neck.

She says, 'I thought you would have heard us.'

'I was working.' He unbuttons his shirt, lifts it over his head. His shoulders ache.

'I thought you would have come down.'

'I did come down.'

Her lips twist.

'You could have called me,' he says. 'If you'd called me I would have come.'

She blinks and looks away.

'Forgive me,' he says.

'We don't all have your excuses. We don't all have your consolations.'

He slings his trousers over the back of the chair, shakes his head, not understanding.

'Disappearing for hours like that.'

'I don't disappear.'

'Even when you're here, you're not really here.'

She turns down the wick, blows out the flame. He climbs into bed beside her in the darkness. She shifts on to her side, away from him, dragging the blankets with her. Her breathing changes.

'What are we going to do?'

'The war will end,' she says. 'We wait for that.'

'We have to do something.'

She makes a muffled noise. He looks at her dark head on the pillow.

'I can't just wait,' he says, 'to see what happens.'

She hefts the covers up over her shoulder. 'Didn't you learn anything from last time? Wasn't that a big enough disaster?'

After a bit, he gets up and smokes a cigarette at the window. Miss Beamish's house is unlit, but the windows catch a little moonlight. Beyond the road, the wind stirs the trees, and far away, over the treetops and across the valley, a light shines on the mountainside in contravention of the blackout. It flickers, flashes. It could just be the play of branches across a window. Or it could be that a message is blinking out into the darkness, that some kind of meaning is offered up into the night.

15

The Vaucluse
April 1944

EASTER SUNDAY. There's a run of farmers, tired women, slow-voiced farmhands, sleepy kids, down either side of the trestle table. It has been a warm and pleasant day, when you could slip into the delusion that, all around, the rest of the world went on just as it used to do. A haunch of pork has been roasted and demolished; scraps lie on the platter and from time to time someone helps themselves to a bit of cooked-crisp skin or a flake of meat. The talk hooks and twists itself together round him, and it is practical and about things and people he doesn't know. He sits back from the table, a little out of the way, cradling his glass of wine. Suzanne sits in, her elbows perched, chin on hands, head tilted, engaged in a diagonal conversation with a woman further down the table.

'You know the family out at Saint-Michel?'

The fellow speaking to him is tipped back in his chair, leaning past the back of the man between them. He's familiar, but then country folk are like that. The same few people swirling round and round and bumping into each other like flotsam in a whirlpool. The fellow sits with shirt-sleeves rolled; his jacket is hanging from the back of his chair.

'Yes,' he says.

'Terrible business.' The fellow offers a hand. 'I'm Bonhomme,' he says. 'I'm a friend of Monsieur there, your employer.'

'The family believes the denunciation came from Apt,' he says, keeping his voice low. They are in good company here, but one must not make assumptions.

The fellow tilts his head. 'It must have.'

He wonders at the certainty. And then he remembers where he'd seen this man: the back room of the post office, pocketing a sheaf of letters, the post-mistress's anxious look on noticing that they were observed. He was going through the mail. He must have been weeding out denunciations, betrayals, reports to the authorities. They could all of them have been informed on many times over, but the words not allowed to hit their mark.

'You keep busy, then?' he asks.

'There is always much to do.'

As they talk, a moth bumps at the candle-lamp, and he thinks of all those letters written, their earnest treachery, their interception and curtailment. The flames that do not catch.

He doesn't notice Suzanne watching them, her eyes narrowing.

Bonhomme wafts the moth away, tilts the candle-lamp and opens it to light his cigarette, then closes the lamp again before the moth can blunder in and immolate itself. He speaks casually, but very low. 'Are you looking for more work?'

'I have enough to get by.'

'Getting by,' Bonhomme says, 'is just the half of it.'

'And the other half?'

'One must add something. Contribute.'

He nods slowly.

Bonhomme looks at him. A long, assessing gaze. He says, 'I think you will.'

The moon is bright and high as they walk home. The cicadas are making a racket. They climb the hill, following the path alongside the vines. They pass through trees, then out into a meadow, where the grass is long and cows stand and stare at them. Above, the sky is vast and bright with stars. Disturbed by their passing, moths rise from the grass, fluttering in ghostly white spirals. It's beautiful; Suzanne feels this as gooseflesh on her arms and a lightness in her chest, at the loveliness of it and its fragility.

He's drunk, and so there's no point talking to him. Hands stuffed into his pockets, he stumbles forward, leaning as though into a ferocious wind. The grass around his turn-ups goes hush, hush. And she knows that no good will come of talking.

'You're drunk,' she says, nonetheless.

He considers this. 'Yes,' he says.

Never sufficient to just take a glass, a taste. Oh no. Heads together with that *maquis* leader all night. And now he is ripped to bits he'll be as unshiftable as an oil stain. The carelessness, the risk; she can feel the fury swell. How dare he do this to them again now, when things are so precarious? No point even saying it. But.

'You were talking to that man,' she says. 'I saw you.'

He stops now too, turns back to her. 'So?'

'He's a *maquisard*.'

'I believe so.'

'I saw the way you were talking.'

'You're jealous?'

'Name of God.'

'Maybe we were talking about the weather.'

She tsks. 'You know nothing. You do not know this place. You have no idea.'

'He says I'll do.'

'Do for what?'

He shrugs. 'Whatever's necessary.' He walks on.

She slumps with defeat. The night air is cool but she feels hot and unhappy and resentful and stuck, in the midst of all this mess, which has been piled so high around her that she cannot move a finger without risking more falling down on top of her. And he just keeps adding to the heap.

But then there's something else – a prickle between the shoulder blades, like being watched, which makes her whip round and search the darkness. He stumbles on, but then notices she isn't following.

'What?'

'Ssh.' She scans the scrubby trees, the hazy night.

'What're you looking for?' He sways slightly, and rights himself. Even as she searches the darkness, she's thinking, *He is going to snore like a pig tonight*. But then there's another sound. So faint at first that it can't really be heard.

'I don't know what you're making such a fuss—'

'Hush,' she says. 'Shut up.'

A low thrum, which builds and grows, and becomes definite and insistent. And is unequivocal.

'Aeroplane.'

The noise is huge, it's bursting.

'Christ—'

Moonlight kicks off Perspex and gleams on the grey blur of the blades. They duck down into the grass. Buffeted with gritty downdraught, crouched low, she can smell the earth, and her own body, and the booze off him, and the sweetness of the crushed grass, and the trail of exhaust coming down on them from a different world. Then the plane is past, and it roars away, and the noise diminishes.

They get back to their feet; she straightens out her skirt.

'Was that an Allied plane?'

'I think so,' he says.

By now the aeroplane is reduced to a thrum in the air and a dark blotch that shrinks against the stars.

'There must be a drop planned somewhere up the valley,' he says. He sounds almost sober now. Her throat constricts; she could cry. Really, if she just let herself, she could cry and cry and cry. Does he not see what a bloody slog all this has been? And now he's going to throw it all up in the air again.

'For God's sake, please,' she says. 'Please. Just wait.'

She studies his face. The moonlight catching in his eyes. The starfished boy in tennis whites, the wounded man strapped down with hospital sheets. He was beautiful, he was brilliant, and he'd needed her. That's what she'd thought. She had thought that it was love.

'Well,' she says. 'That's that, then.'

She wraps her arms around herself, turns away and stalks on. He follows. He could catch up with her in two paces if he wanted to. He could take her hand and slip her arm through his and, even now, he could comfort her. But what is there left to say? He is a disappointment to her; he's a disappointment to himself. He just follows her on through the broken night.

He walks with Bonhomme silently, out along a back lane for a few twisting hairpinned miles; they slope off down a woodman's track that takes them past piled logs and blasted clearings of sawn tree-stumps, mud and abandoned brushwood. They carry on until they're deep into the woods, where the track ends dead. From here all he can see is an untrodden sweep of pine-needles and a maze of rusty trunks, and glancing back, there's just the rutted gash that they've come along. On the left there is a coincidence of gaps between the branches and undergrowth, which might just be a path. At first the signs are equivocal – a bent-back twig here, a scuffed patch there – but as the ground rises the path becomes a worn line through fallen needles, and foot-polished patches on bare stone. As he heaves his way up the final rocky scramble, red stone catches the sun and glows like coals. The rock is skin-warm, crumbling, and as he climbs, it stains his hands red.

Bonhomme is bringing him to the *maquis* camp. It huddles on top of a bluff, deep amongst the trees. Faint smoke rises, but it is soon dissipated by the canopy. A lad nurses the fire, looks up warily; prone figures lie beneath a shelter of canvas and branches and do not move. Three bicycles lean together against a tree. The Boy Scouts, that's what this is like. A summer camp set up in the woods.

Bonhomme nods to the kid at the fireside, who is smoky-faced and looks exhausted.

'We were on a job last night,' Bonhomme says. 'The boys are tired.'

They head on, across the top of the bluff, which is a shallow cup scrubby and soft with fallen pine needles.

'If the Service de Travail Obligatoire doesn't get the lads, they come to us; they can't go home.'

He realizes he's seen the kid before somewhere. Around the town, serving in one of the bars, perhaps. The farmer draws a scrubby bush aside. There's a small, dry space behind, with crates stacked inside; he drags one out, cracks it open, lifts out a weapon.

'Ah yes, now,' Bonhomme says, 'this is last night's haul.'

He watches as deft hands twist the thing, click one part into another and offer the gun up to him.

'Here. Take it. It's not loaded.'

It's surprisingly light. He turns it round, looks at the gaping mouth where the magazine should go, at the grey barrel

284

with its inner twist of mainspring; the stock is an empty metal frame. He tests the shift and clip of the safety catch. Even unloaded it's an uneasy thing. It is cold, brutally simple.

'You have some experience of guns?'

'There was an Officer Training Corps at school, but I tended to stay away from all of that.'

'Shame. This is a Sten gun,' Bonhomme explains. 'Ugly buggers, but they do their job. Except when they don't. Sometimes they jam. Which is a fucking chore. Oh, and then there's this . . .'

Bonhomme levers the lid off another box. A moment's puzzlement in which it seems to be packed with fruit. Steely-green pineapples. The farmer lifts one, and it is a grenade, and he handles it as though it's made of spun sugar.

'You pull the pin out,' he says. 'You don't hang around. You throw the thing. You have four seconds.'

He measures the time out, the beats of it in his head.

'Four seconds and no more, because then the other guy would have a chance to pick it up and lob it back at you. So—' the farmer offers out the grenade; he looks at it. 'Take.'

He lifts it in wary fingertips.

'Don't worry,' the farmer says. 'We've taken proper care of them; you can see they're not degraded. They're quite safe until you pull the pin.'

He looks at him in disbelief. 'We're going to throw it?'

'No. You're going to throw it.'

'Isn't that a waste?'

'The first time you do this, you don't want it to matter too much.'

The firing range is off away from the camp and the store, down a separate gully leading off to the east, the steep sides acting as a natural buffer to noise. He sets the grenade down like an egg before attempting anything with the gun. Bonhomme demonstrates the shift and click that sets the Sten to semi-automatic. He takes the cold thing in his hands, and when he aims and squeezes the trigger a green glass bottle throws itself up into sudden fragments in the air. The noise is hard, the gun bucks in his grip and its heel knocks against his shoulder. It is nasty and efficient.

He hands the Sten back to Bonhomme. He looks down at the grenade, then crouches to lift it. He holds it like a cricket ball, just near his hip, his fingers curled around it.

The grenade is heavy.

After a moment, Bonhomme says, 'You don't have to do it, you know.'

He feels the hatched lines against his sweating palm, the coldness of the metal case. The thing is so self-contained; its hugeness presses out against itself. It's as full of violence as an egg is full of egg.

'You don't have to do any of this, you know.'

'One pulls the pin, and then, four seconds?'

'That's right.'

'What – over there?' Towards a fall of scree from the cliff face, where a scrubby juniper twists out from between the stones.

'See that bush? Imagine it's got a machine gun.'

His lips twist. He hefts the grenade in his sweating palm, turns abruptly and walks away.

Bonhomme frowns after him. 'What?'

'I'll need a run-up.'

He fights the urge to rub the grenade against his trouser-leg. He turns back and fixes his eye on the shrub, and then he goes to pull the pin and fumbles it, hands shaking. It's out. He runs; three long strides, tick, swings his hand up and bowls the grenade out, tick, into the air, tick. He stands, watching, as the grenade spins towards the juniper. As though these were the nets at Portora, or summer cricket fields at Trinity.

He glances round for Bonhomme, but the farmer is just dust and scuffing feet, already gone.

Oh, yes. That.

He has made five big strides when there is an almighty *whumpf* and a thump of solid air hits his back and propels him on. He collides into Bonhomme and they stumble together, come to a halt. They look back. The air blooms with red dust and a shower of rock and grit falls back to the earth. Sound comes blanketed, and a thin ringing pierces through it.

'I should have said –' Bonhomme yells over their deafness. 'If you can manage it, it's a good idea to cover your ears.'

He is taken another way back – along the far side of the bluff and down a dry gully that in winter would be a foaming stream. Their feet clatter over sharp-edged rocks.

'For now, we'll need you to take care of some shipments and conceal some items for us. At the moment we are preparing ourselves, getting things in place.'

He nods.

'But when combat operations start,' Bonhomme says, 'you report immediately to camp. Don't wait around for someone to come and get you, we will need to get to work.'

'How will I know?'

'Do you know Verlaine?'

'Some.'

'"The Song of Autumn".'

'I know it.'

'There will be a quotation, in the messages on Radio Londres. When you hear that, you come and find us. You use the password *Violins*.'

'Verlaine,' he says. 'Violins.'

'And *La Victoire*.'

He rubs his arms.

They reach a footbridge; it cuts across the gully at head height. The ground falls away and there are roofs below, a fence.

'I'll turn back here,' Bonhomme says, his voice dropped low. 'You go up and on; the path will take you to the road. You should know your way back from there.'

They shake hands. He clambers up the bank. At the top he glances round to fix the route in his mind: the footbridge, that sloping tree. Bonhomme has gone; there's a flicker of movement higher up, and that is that.

He turns and heads downhill, following a faint path that gets more definite as it descends. He comes to the dwellings, skirts the side of a garden. There's a gate, and then a lane, and he follows the lane, keeping to the verge, feeling dizzy and conspicuous with it all, like having written, when the writing's going well, or maybe like falling in love.

Those gnomic messages on Radio Londres, carrying their invisible bundles of meaning: one of them will now be addressed to him. A line from a poem that will mean something entirely other than what it means.

At the end of the lane, he finds himself standing on the edge of the main route to Apt. He's only a quarter of a mile or so from home. He stuffs his hands into his pockets, finds his sucking stone and slips it into his mouth. He turns along the road and walks on through the twilight.

Between the coppiced willows, down on their hunkers in the low-growing foliage, they keep out of sight. From the crossroads, one track heads off Roman-straight along the valley floor; the other is a sinuous white line that weaves its way down from the hills behind them and up into the far mountains ahead. There's no settlement at the crossroads, no signpost, nothing but a triangle of woodland, and then open pasture, vineyard, and an owl that goes ghosting past, then settles on a branch, and then flutters off again.

They are waiting to make a pick-up. But no one comes.

They have walked for miles – eight or nine by the time taken and the lick they took it at – out through the pastures and the vineyards beyond Roussillon. At first, it seemed that they were heading for Cavaillon. He followed the other fellow's steady countryman's stride along footpaths and down field margins and farm tracks; there were sudden turns in the darkness, loops to avoid farmsteads where dogs stirred in their kennels, clinking their chains. They climbed fences and ducked through holes in hedges. And soon he was not certain that it was Cavaillon that they were heading for after all. There were no road signs, no milestones to go by, and no landmarks that he could make stick: he thought he recognized a broken tree, a barn, but then as they passed the angle changed and the shapes seemed different, and he no longer felt sure of anything at all.

So that now, huddled in the darkness, the terrain keeps morphing around him, swelling, shrinking, swooping sideways, making different shapes out of itself as he tries to situate himself within it. It's dizzying.

The other fellow, though, seems confident they are in the right place. He seems certain-sure.

'We're early.' A battered tin water-flask is swished in front of his face. 'You go faster than I thought you would.'

He takes the bottle and swigs, expects water, gets brandy, coughs; he takes another drink and then returns the flask.

At midnight, by a distant chime, a cart rumbles down the road towards them, coming down from the hills. It's carrying no light. The other fellow gets to his feet; he follows, his knees cracking. They clamber up the bank out of the woods and on to the road. The dark shape rolls on towards them.

But then something changes. He catches sight of the other fellow's profile – the angled cheekbones, the narrowed eyes – and wonders how he can see that much all of a sudden, and where the light is coming from. He glances round. And then, Christ, there are headlamps coming in a stream along a road further off down the valley. The low, yellowed, half-blindfolded headlamps of military vehicles in blackout. He counts three sets as they bump and weave and slide round bends. He knocks his knuckles into the other fellow's arm, jerks his hand in that direction.

'Brothel of shit.'

The cart is there; the cart is loaded with air-dropped supplies, they should not be out at this time, they're all implicated and it's all too late. The carter scrambles down from his seat: he's a little skinny man, just bone and wrinkles. 'Quick!'

And then it is all ham-handed fumbling and it is so slow, there is a watery clarity in which images hang suspended: the carter's deep-lined temple as he squints down at a buckle, fumbling with it; the silvery muzzle of the donkey, its coffee-dark eye; the raised grain of weathered boards in cold pink hands.

Between them, they manage to roll the cart off the edge of the road and then slither it down the bank into the copse. They heave the wheels over roots, grate through narrow places between trunks. It's become a monster of a thing, lumbering and recalcitrant. The convoy has turned along the valley floor now. Is heading dead towards them.

'Careful!' hisses the carter. He is struggling with the donkey.

They ease the cart-bed down; the crates slide and clunk together.

The donkey brays and pulls against its halter. The carter curses, drags, brings the donkey stumbling after him and into the edge of the woods.

The other fellow's back up on the road, scuffing out tracks, ruffling up the wayside grass.

That sickening rattle of diesel engines. The carter's face is a skull in the shadows: he is dragging at the donkey's halter; she stands splay-legged, head low, unshifting. The other fellow grabs the donkey's halter, wraps an arm around her neck and heaves her over. She drops, collapsing, and he falls with her. She struggles, and he shifts his weight, and she lies still.

'Hey!' the carter says. 'What are you doing?'

'Get down.'

The narrow flickering lights are here. Cheek on mulch, an arm over his head, he feels his chest press against the ground with each breath.

The light races over them. The trees are suddenly green. Headlamps ripple over trunks, silhouette the grasses, make wickerwork of the branches and twigs. The ground shakes. The air is full of noise. Light strokes across the donkey's flank. He sees a blue sleeve, a red scarf, a curve of balding moleskin and the grey haze of hand-sharpened steel. He knows that type of knife. It's a vineyard pruning blade. If the donkey struggles up, he'll cut her throat.

Grit sprays sideways from underneath the peeling tyres. He closes his eyes; he turns his face aside. The noise of the trucks is massive. Lights flash across his closed lids in red striations. And then the noise is fading, and the trucks are gone, and it is over.

He opens his eyes and watches the red tail-lights of the final vehicle. Time ticks on and the lights diminish. And that's it. It turns out that they go on living after this.

'You are a right bastard,' the carter's saying.

The other fellow straightens himself out. The donkey stumbles upright too, unfolding like a card-table. She shakes out her stubby mane and stumbles away a few paces, and stands there with her back to them and craps on to the woodland floor. The blade is closed and slipped away.

'Who'd have pulled my fucking cart? I'd be ruined.' The carter's dusting off his trousers.

The other fellow just looks out after the vehicles. 'Heading north,' he says, frowning, speculative. The lights shrink, and the darkness swells and closes over them, soft as ink.

The carter, muttering, goes off to retrieve and console the donkey. The other fellow turns to the cart.

He follows. He wipes his face. He notices that his hands are shaking.

'All right, then,' the other fellow says. 'Let's get our explosives and get out of here.'

The carter rolls away, muttering curses. They pick their way through the trees, the crate slung between them as they walk. It is heavy. But it's differently heavy to, say, bricks or apples or flour. Out in the fields now, and the moon is up; the countryside is blue and beautiful. But all he can look at is the crate, as it swings there just in front of him like a little coffin.

It could blow them both sky-high. It could blow them into bloody rain. It is a giddy feeling, vertiginous.

Back at the little house, they stow the crate in the dark hallway. It'll do there till morning, when he'll find somewhere better for it. He wipes his hands down his trousers. The other fellow slopes off into the dark; he closes the door on the strangeness of the night.

Indoors, it is as much as he can do to pull off his boots. In stockinged feet he climbs the stairs as though they are a mountainside. He falls into bed. She stirs and half wakes.

'Where have you been?'

'Go back to sleep.'

'Where have you been, though?'

'Nowhere.'

'Tsk.'

'No, really. I don't know.'

She turns on her side, drops back into sleep. He lies on his back, looking up into the darkness as it fades to morning.

Suzanne has been growing geraniums in pots. Miss Beamish gave her the cuttings. The flowers are wafer white, blood-clot red and blister pink – they spread their leaves like magician's hands and are taking over the terrace. So he lifts a pot and sets it gently down on top of the crate, and slides another couple of plants in front of it too. He steps back to consider the effect, his back pressed against the railing. It's still quite clearly and obviously a crate; there's no escaping that. The question is, does it appear to be a benign and innocent empty old crate, the kind of crate on which one might arrange a pleasing display of potted plants, or does it still, geraniums or no geraniums, appear to be what it indeed is – a crate replete with violence, a crate stuffed tight with enormity, chock full of the potential to blow them in all directions at once?

He tilts his head. Considers it. The latter, he decides.

But then it would, because he knows.

From indoors a child's voice sings out her scales, the notes clear and piercing. She has a good singing voice, the kid from the *quincaillerie*, the kind of pure voice that brings goosebumps to your arms. She'd have to leave if she wanted to do anything about it. And where would you go now? Paris? Berlin? London?

It's a pain that Suzanne can't take the lessons up at Saint-Michel, where there is a piano. But Yvonne can't stand the coming and the going any more. Her nerves are shot.

He shuffles another pot along with a foot, then crouches down to tease out the leaves.

'What are you doing?' Suzanne squints out at him through the terrace doors, and then at the flowerpots and the new, conspicuous crate. 'What's going on?' Left unsupervised, the child's voice lingers on a note, and then drops, and halts. 'Are you *gardening*?'

'No.'

She steps through and closes the glass door behind her, so that she is outside with him on the terrace. Down on the street below, an old woman with a headscarf and basket stares up at them. Suzanne raises a hand. The woman is obliged to return the wave and walk on. Then Suzanne turns back to him, and her smile is gone.

295

'Don't give me any of your old slush. What's in the box?'

'Nothing.'

'Nothing?'

'Nothing. Anyway, it won't be here for long.'

'If it's nothing, why does it need to be here at all?'

'I was going to put it under the bed, but I thought you wouldn't like that.'

'Why?'

'Look, don't worry about it. It'll be fine. It's only for a few days.'

'I didn't ask how long it's staying. I asked you what it is, and why it's on our terrace.'

'It has to be kept safe and dry.'

Suzanne's face freezes. The girl's head appears between the curtains. Suzanne waves her furiously back: the child drops the fabric, disappears.

'Name of God—' She speaks low, furious, her eyes narrow and hard. 'You don't have the sense that you were born with, do you? What's in the box?'

'They needed somewhere to store it.'

'Do you even know?'

Then Henri swings into view, coming back into town from his lesson with Miss Beamish. Suzanne turns away to hide her fury, but does not leave, while he raises a hand in greeting and Henri stops in the street and they lob words up and down between them. She stays put, arms folded, and waits it out. Henri ambles off with a wave and a cheery promise of drinks.

'You're not leaving it here,' she says, as soon as Henri's gone.

Down at the end of the garden, there's a hollow in the bank, almost a cave. He can't keep such a close eye on the crate there, but it's well out of the way, and it's dry. He bends to shift the potted plants aside. He lifts the crate and staggers sideways past her, back into the house.

'Just coming through,' he says, to her outraged glare.

The child stands, big-eyed and silent, uncomprehending, her fingers spread on the edge of the tabletop. He raises his eyebrows at her. Suzanne snaps, 'Carry on!' and chivvies him towards the back door. She opens it for him. The child opens her lips and fills her lungs and climbs her way up the scale again.

He goes through the doorway gingerly. She speaks in English, because of the child. Suzanne's English is limited and brittle; it can't last for long.

'What, after all, is in the box?' she asks.

The English word is too close to the French, so he says it quietly. 'Explosives. Sorry.'

Suzanne's eyes widen; her lips part.

'I think the mouldable kind,' he adds, more generally. 'They make these sausage things out of them. Charges.'

Suzanne sucks in a long preparatory breath. He slips out into the garden before she can actually explode.

Suzanne feels for the pins in her hair, but the other Suzanne, Miss Beamish's Suzanne, is reaching for them too, and their hands brush together, and Suzanne lets hers drop and leaves the other woman to remove the hairpins for her with her almond fingertips. The deftness is soothing; the pins' release eases the pressure from the back of her head, like a problem that just disappears. The hair falls in a coil down her back and the other Suzanne teases it loose. She lets a breath go with it and her shoulders soften.

'I hadn't realized how long it had grown,' she says.

The other Suzanne just smiles and tucks a towel around her collar; she gestures her over to the sink.

Leaning in over the stone basin, the stale smell of unwashed hair around her, she feels the stove-warmed water eased on to her scalp, feels the other woman's hand guide the wet into her hair and soften it, slowing the water's fall so that it is not wasted.

'Good?'

'Yes, thank you.'

There is a rummaging as the lid is removed from a pot and a handful of soapflakes scooped out. A shallow palm is cupped low for Suzanne to catch the scent.

'Lavender,' she says at the unexpected pleasure.

'Mm.'

The other Suzanne takes the hand away and shares the flakes between her two palms, and rubs them into foam. She strokes this on to and then massages it into Suzanne's wet hair.

Bent over the stone basin, tendrils hanging down around her face, she feels the other woman's fingers tease; they tweak at knots, scrape lightly across the scalp, eliciting both discomfort and pleasure. A tingling exposure at the back of the neck, where a run of water escapes. She thinks of what else these hands will do, these fingertips; where also they will brush and tease. The other's body is just beside her own, the feel of her breath, her own hip pressing against the other's thigh, and the other woman's breast touching, soft, against Suzanne's shoulder. It occurs to her that the other Suzanne is not wearing a brassiere, and her thoughts slide and become warm.

I am hungry for this, Suzanne thinks, as she is guided upright, her hair gently towelled, as she is brought back to the chair and settled there, vulnerable and tousled as a baby bird. I am just starving.

Through the window comes the hush of the cypresses, and the birds singing, and the other Suzanne moves round her, combing out the tangles, her breath on Suzanne's ear, on her bare arm, on the washed-thin fabric of her blouse. Suzanne's head moves with the insistence of the comb, leaning this way and then that. The hair is tugged out straight in a curtain round her. She closes her eyes as the other Suzanne begins to cut.

Against the summer sun her eyelids glow red. There is just other woman's breath and warmth, and the snip of blades through the curtaining hair, and the sounds of the trees and birds from outside, and voices further off in the street. Suzanne opens her eyes and sees the halo of her own fallen hair lying on the tiled floor. The other Suzanne moves round in front of her and leans in close; she parts the hair in front of Suzanne's face and gives her a smile. Three deft strokes of a comb and then, 'I think you'll do,' she says.

Suzanne returns the smile. They are like that for a moment, face to face, smile to smile, the other woman's lips mushroom-soft, and then she says, 'Well . . .' as she turns away and bustles at the dresser, chinking glasses. A little laugh over her shoulder. 'I'm afraid we're just out of setting lotion.'

She pours wine, and Suzanne turns her head from side to side, feeling the coolness and the lightness, brushing the new-cut ends with her fingers, her own body feeling soft and light and warm, and she is, briefly, relaxed and happy. Then Anna comes in from the garden, with those snuffling little dogs around her feet.

'Oh yes,' Anna says. 'Very nice.' And she takes a glass of wine from the other Suzanne. 'Very nice indeed.'

There is an ease between the two of them, the casual press of hip against hip, of warm soft flesh against warm soft flesh. They fit together, and it makes her ache.

'Thank you,' Suzanne says. 'It feels very nice.'

The other Suzanne hands her a tumbler, but her focus is on Anna now, as it should be. Suzanne takes a sip of wine. What she has felt – this warmth, this softening – it is the gratitude of a stray dog for a casual kindness, a knuckling of the ears, a morsel.

What she wants more than anything is just an arm around her. This easy come-and-go. A kiss.

'Well,' she says, and takes a sip of the wine and sets the glass aside. 'That was most kind of you.' She gets up to go. 'Very kind indeed.'

A soft knock at the back door that evening just as they're thinking about going to bed. He's up and going to answer it

300

before she can respond. The men are in their working blues and battered tweeds, dressed to go unseen in the twilight. Two more appear out of the darkness, pushing bicycles, which tick along comfortably, then stop.

'Have you got our gear?'

'This way.'

They pick their way down towards the hiding place. The evening is loud with cicadas. He crouches to get inside and hauls out the crate. He dusts his hands, while others move in to lift the load.

'Any news?' he asks.

A shaken head, pursed lips. 'Just wait,' someone says. 'Listen out. It can't be long now.'

Anna Beamish bunches up by the radio and twists the dial with the concentration of a safe-cracker, squinting with effort; there's a fug of interference and then a wince-inducing screech.

It is the fag-end of a blazing June day. There are wine bottles standing round the room; cigarette smoke drifts in skeins. He should not be drinking, not really, not now that things are so imminent, but things could go on being imminent indefinitely, and he faces what is coming more with dread than anticipation. Things will have to be done. It's an uneasy thought. And it is so much easier to drink than not to drink, so his head is already swimming with rough wine when Beethoven's Fifth throbs through the static and the noise and distortion flung at it by the German transmitters in their attempt to block the signal. He is straining for the music out of hunger for it, through the radio-fuzz and his own furred senses. For the Morse-like patterns of the notes. *Da da da dum*. It brings a tingle to the back of the neck. That's V, isn't it? In Morse code. That's V.

This is London; the French speaking to the French.

Henri and Josette Hayden listen, heads bent. Suzanne sits in silence too. She had been giving him looks every time his glass was refilled. She wants to go home, but he has been ignoring her because they do not have a radio set at home, and either she has given up on the looks or the more he drinks the better he gets at not noticing.

Before we begin, please listen to some personal messages.

Anna Beamish perches on the arm of a chair; her Suzanne leans in against her, her dark head resting softly on Anna's flank. Around them, the strange utterances slip and drift, unresolvable and haunting.

It is hot in Suez.

One of the dogs butts her head into his hanging hand, and he runs his palm over her fuzzy round skull and then knuckles at her cheek.

The dice are on the table.

The dog drops to the floor and rolls on her back; he can't reach her there without moving and he can't bring himself to move.

Jean has a long moustache.

The dog stretches luxuriously, oblivious, and makes little happy groaning sounds. Outside, beyond the window, cicadas buzz.

Wound my heart with a monotonous languor.

And that's it. His fingers dig into the upholstery. That is the line from Verlaine. That's the message to the *maquis* that they are to begin combat operations. His skin bristles. Now it comes: the chaos of splintered timber and shattered brick and bursting shells and bullets and dust and blood and broken bodies. Liberation.

He finds that he's on his feet and that everyone is staring at him.

Suzanne looks up, her face grey.

His heart races. This is hope, he realizes, and it's horrible. He sinks back into his seat. Hope implies the wire peeled back, and revelation: the crows in the woods, the fowls in the coop, the gamekeepers with their guns and chopping block – what they all will have become. The words continue from the radio, and he doesn't know what to do with himself. His seat creaks, and the dog gets up and nudges her muzzle into his hand again, and he strokes her.

The broadcast over, Anna Beamish crosses to the radio set and turns it off, and the room falls entirely silent.

Then Anna says, 'Well, that was illuminating.'

She lifts a bottle, ambles round, sloshes wine into glasses.

'So are you at liberty to tell us what that was all about, then, old top?'

'Hm?'

'What your keen ear detected there?'

Josette and Henri are looking towards him still, as is the other Suzanne. His Suzanne, though, is studying her shoes.

'Oh, nothing,' he says. 'Nothing much at all.'

303

One of the dogs starts to whine, and there's another sound beyond that. It takes a moment to notice, and, having noticed, to make sense of what they're hearing. It's an aeroplane – not close this time, way off across the valley. The engine noise gets louder, and then it begins to fade, without ever having got properly close at all.

'It's like Piccadilly Circus round here,' says Henri, and Anna beams at him, proud of the vernacular.

'Well then,' Anna says. 'We'll drink to nothing, and wish you all the best of nothing, and swift success with nothing much at all.'

She raises her glass, her lips already stained with wine.

He drains his drink. He sets the glass down. Then he turns to Henri and Josette. 'Could Suzanne come and stay with you for a few days?'

Suzanne speaks quietly, after their kind offers of hospitality. 'Why would I go and stay anywhere?'

'You'd be very welcome here.' Anna leans in a little blearily, touches her knee. 'We do have plenty of room.'

'Thank you, but I am quite all right at home.'

He says, 'I don't want to leave you on your own.'

She looks at him, finally. 'Then don't.'

A walk out through the gorgeous June night, out along the Apt road, his hastily packed bag hanging at his hip. Cigarettes, a box of matches, a notebook, a pencil and his fingerless gloves. He could probably have packed rather better for war: on reflection, these things do not seem to be particularly martial. He takes the lane that leads up across the hillside

304

and fades to the path that skirts the dark house and garden. He reaches the gully and slithers in, barking an ankle on a rock. Blundering up the dry bed, he clatters over stones, lurching along, arms outstretched. It's darker under the trees and the night see-saws around him. His head is not, perhaps, quite as clear as he had thought it.

He is stopped well before he reaches the camp, before he even reaches the bottom of the bluff, by a voice.

'*Qui vive?*'

'*Violins?*' he tries.

A shape steps forward from the side of a pine trunk. It's the boy from the camp.

'I thought it would be you,' the boy says. 'You sound like a herd of elephants. Keep the noise down, eh?'

Chastened, he passes by, catching the outdoor musk of campfire and unwashed body. He treads softly. And this, after all, is what must be done, so that the boy can get on one of those bikes and cycle home to his mammy and be a boy again, as though all of this was just a summer's camp, a nonsense, and not a thing of life and death at all. And that too is hope.

16

The Vaucluse
Summer 1944

THE CRACKLING CODES are conjured out of darkness by Bonhomme's radio set, which he rigs up in someone's attic or the back of a barn or workshop, or up amongst the trees, draping his aerial over the tiles or branches, and then packing it all away briskly and moving on.

The cell sets about making these words flesh.

Allied forces have landed in Normandy. This appears to be a truth. Not even the collaborationist papers and radio deny it. But, still, it is half a world away.

They walk the long country paths and the quiet roads at night. In June it never seems to be fully dark. They divide up ammunition and explosives, dig caches for their own gear, in the woods and in field margins and by the edge of the valley road. They lug the rest to the hidden camps across the countryside, to the forest clearings and exhausted quarries and caves high on the mountainside, where the lean men wait for them and nod approvingly over the new supplies.

There are supplies too for the thin, dark wives, the hungry children, the hard old folk. The families that the men have left behind.

The Allied forces land near Fréjus. It is not half a world away; it is a few hours' drive from here.

Out in the field, everything becomes vivid, vital. He is ravenous at the offer of food, falls down dead and sleeps when provided with a bed or an approximation of a bed. He'll sleep till the sun's shining right on his face or someone shakes him awake. Then he pulls on his wrecked boots over his stinking socks and clambers out of whatever shelter it had been, at whatever time of night or day, and gets on with whatever he is required to do.

Because life is happening here, now, conspicuously, in the farmsteads and barns and in the woods and fields and gullies. The grass stretches itself towards the sun; vine tendrils curl themselves around their supports. Gunfire clatters. The birds are outraged at each other. Cows breathe sweetness, drip milk; lambs quiver and leap; and one lamb lolls, limp, head staved in and oozing. It roasts over the woodland fire and then is jointed into equal shares, its flesh fatty in the fingers and on the lips, becoming a darkness in the belly, and nausea. Heads start up at a hollow boom, and then another and another echoing out through the night. These are charges they supplied, dished out to another cell who are blowing up the railway line. They're sending it sky-high.

Hope. He's sick of it. Sick to the stomach of it. The wire is snipped, though, bit by bit.

*

In the kitchen of the empty little house, he drinks water, cup after cup, poured from the sweating earthenware pitcher. In the jug it seems black as ink, but when he pours it it catches the light and twines and glimmers.

Through the night comes the distant sound of bombardment. And over to the south, the sky glows.

He finds a dry end of bread, dips a bit into his cup and gnaws at it awkwardly, trying to avoid the worst teeth, the ones that ache, the ones that sting, the one that now rocks in its socket. Outside, trucks go by, their low blackout headlamps skimming through the little room, their engines rattling.

He ducks down, out of the line of the window.

When he takes off his boots they have dried as stiff as wood. His socks stick to his skin. He knows he stinks. Sometimes he catches the smell of himself and it is raw and animal. Barefoot, footsore, he climbs the stairs to his empty bedroom and lies down on top of the covers. A slow blink. He is alone. A clattering of gunfire somewhere in the distance. A slow blink. His knees ache. His feet ache. Muscle softens against the mattress. A slow blink, and the lids flutter but do not lift. And the satisfaction of useful work, for once, undertaken; of something underway.

17

La Croix
1944

Miss Beamish's dogs, locked up in the scullery, are barking fit to wake the dead. But it wasn't the dogs that alerted him to the soldiers' presence. It was the gunshots.

The first shots jolted him out of sleep; the second burst made him register what had smashed his sleep apart. They seemed close, but the way that the sound would bounce around the valleys, bluffs and outcrops here made it hard to tell what direction they had come from. Sten gun, he'd have laid money on it, set on automatic: somebody was making very free with their ammunition. He reached out for Suzanne, but Suzanne wasn't there; of course, she was staying with Josette and Henri, so he just lay sweating, alert, listening to the birds cawing to the sky and the empty echoes down the valley, waiting for whatever happened next.

Nothing happened next.

So he got up, crossed to the window and opened the shutters. In the pre-dawn blue, there was just the pale road and the dark trees and the burnt-paper scraps of birds settling back into their roosts, so he closed the shutters and pulled on his shirt and trousers.

He was downstairs when the milk cart rattled past the front of the house, going at an unusually brisk trot. He trod into his boots, drew the bolts and headed out into the lane. He glanced in both directions, but there was nothing going on, so he went a little way into town at a tired amble, keeping to the shadowy edge of the lane beside the sprawling wild roses, under pollarded limes. The dash of a rat made him jump, but that was that.

The town itself was peaceful: just the early-morning unshuttering of shops, the bakery glowing, the scent of bread making his stomach clutch. So he turned back and headed the other way, out of town, passing the front of the little house and on towards Anna Beamish's, and still there was nothing to be seen in the raising light but the dusty road and the trees and the dry grass and the snails trailing their way across the verges and weighing down the stems. Back to bed, if nothing's doing. But then a farm cart came trundling round the corner, down past the side of Anna's place, and the horse jibbed and sidestepped, and it was all the driver could do to keep the old cob steady, and they clattered on past him, and the driver had his gaze fixed dead ahead and didn't even nod.

And that was when he peered along the lane and saw the soldiers.

They were a grey heap up against Anna's fence, but he brought himself to move towards it. Then there was the smell of blood. He stared down at stockinged feet, a hand curled in the dust, the dark inside of a fallen-open mouth. Skin was pale blue; blood was black; a button, though, caught the morning light and glittered.

He stands now, and he looks, and his tongue presses against the back of his teeth, and a tooth gives, and it hurts, and he stands, and he looks, and he stands, and he looks, and the dogs are barking.

And then someone comes out of Anna's house. He hears the door go. The dogs come tumbling with her, beside themselves. The door falls shut.

'Is it yourself?' she calls.

He nods. His gorge rises. They are in trouble now.

She comes striding down the path towards him, the dogs barking and twining around her ankles; she's knotting the cord of a tartan dressing gown.

'For God's sake, *whisht*,' she says, and scoops up one of the creatures and holds it to her.

'We heard,' she says. 'But we thought it best to stay inside. One thinks one should telephone to someone. But who does one telephone these days?'

'There are two—' The words stick in his throat; they have hooks. He turns back to look at the heap. 'Bodies.'

'Definitely dead?' She peers over the gate; her question's answered. She puts the dog down again and slips out to join him, leaving the creatures there to yap and whine. 'Damn damn damn damn damn.'

She frowns, scans up and down the road. Death itself has become contagious; they could catch it here themselves. 'We'll have to do something.'

'Call the priest?' he suggests.

'If they get taken into town, the whole place would be implicated.'

They stand in silence.

'We came through a town,' he says, 'where there'd been reprisals.' The woman with the frozen eyes. The man with a hole in his cheek, his jaw on show.

'We can't just leave them lying here,' Miss Beamish says.

'No.'

She becomes brisk. She's off back through her gate, yelling at the dogs, striding up the path, while he stands there with the dead. Up at the house, the other Suzanne is trying to get the dogs indoors. Voices are raised over their barking: *What is it? Oh Good God, what are we going to do?* He looks at a foot, the hole where a toenail has scythed right through the wool. The soldier's gaiters are lying loose on the dust nearby. The killers took the boots.

It's early yet. The road is quiet. Few people pass this way. They might get away with it.

Anna rejoins him. She has thrown on slacks and a polo-shirt and brings two garden spades, sloped together over a shoulder. She has also brought a bottle.

'My pal suggested this.' The bottle is lifted for inspection. Brandy.

'She is very wise.'

'She is. She really is.'

312

They consider the men. Slavic, high-boned faces, one softer than the other, younger, with a scattering of freckles like a pancake. The eyes are open and they're grey, and the corneas are creasing as they dry, and the flies gather to sip away the wet. The Armée de l'Est, serving here, were recruited from conquered countries; they were prisoners of war.

'State of them, poor lads.'

She hands him the bottle. He uncorks it, swigs brandy, hands the bottle back.

'Where'll we . . .?'

They glance around.

'Over there,' she says with a nod. There, the verge is wider. Wide enough for a grave.

They go past the bodies.

'Russians, do you suppose they are?' he asks.

'Could be. Could be Poles. Took their chances, didn't they? Either this or a labour camp. You can see why.'

The other is darker and seems a little older than his companion, a little harder-looking. Sunburned.

Anna turns her face away. He follows her on to the wider scruffy margin before the trees. He wants to say something consoling, something useful. There is nothing consoling or useful to say.

Her voice is dry; he hears her swallow. 'Here?'

'Here's as good as anywhere,' he says.

They shunt their spades into the ground. They begin to dig.

*

It takes a long time to dig a grave. As the diggers sink lower into the earth, the inner surface grows blood-red, damp, veinous. Paler rusty topsoil trickles down inside. He turns his sucking stone over in his mouth, tucks it down alongside his back teeth; the nerves sing like wires.

After an hour or so, Anna clambers out, careless of her clothes, and goes back to the house. No one passes; no one comes to investigate the gunshots in the night. He is grateful for the isolation of their little houses, for the self-preservation that is keeping their few neighbours at a distance.

When Anna returns, the other Suzanne comes with her, frowning, worried, carrying two bottles of beer and a biscuit tin. They drink the beer and eat in silence, squatting in the dust. The other Suzanne offers to help with the digging, but there is no room really for another in the grave, so they wave her away; also, the fewer people tainted by association, the better. They swig more brandy, swipe at flies, and get back to their work.

They dig as the sun climbs into the sky and the heat grows, and the flies buzz loud and the smell gets worse. He runs with sweat.

'That'll do,' she says, breathless. 'Won't it?'

They climb out.

He turns his face aside as he hauls the boy up by the armpits. He is much heavier than he looks. Flies buzz around him, but he no longer has a free hand to swat them away. Anna huffs down to grab the feet, and between them they lug him over to the edge of the pit. They lay him down beside it.

'How do we do this?' she asks.

'I don't know.'

'Swing him in or roll him?'

Neither seems appropriate. They do not move.

'Right.' She bends to grab the feet again. 'Come on.'

He just stands there.

'What?'

'I don't like it.'

'No. I know. I don't either.'

He hunkers down. They grab handfuls of grey-green serge, drag on limbs, heave and push. The body thumps over on to its side; a hand dangles in. They shove again; there's a fall of dirt and the body tumbles and scuffs down the side of the pit. It lands awkwardly at an angle, feet higher than the head. The sides of the grave are too oblique, the base not flat enough for dignity; the boy's neck twists back and he is profiled on the dirt.

The two of them straighten up. He's about to wipe his mouth, but then lets his arm fall, shakes out unclean hands and wipes them one against the other.

'We've made a poor show of this,' he says.

'We haven't much experience,' she says.

'I've only buried dogs before.'

'It's not the same, is it?'

'No.'

They stand, looking down at the body in the pit.

'There's the other fellow.'

They turn and go back, and lift him too.

By midday, the bodies are swallowed up and gone. All that's to be seen is a darker patch on the pale earth, and that is drying out in the sun. They should not be left here. They should not rot into this red earth. Theirs should be the black tilth of home, years from now, decades on. Half a century or more, they could have had. They could have seen the next millennium in, if this century had not turned out to be the shambles that it is.

He wipes his face with his handkerchief and it comes away smeared with red. Anna's grey Aertex shirt is powdered with red dust and patched with sweat; the sweat and dust make a red mask of her face. She sinks down on the edge of the road and just sits there in the dust. Her head hangs. He folds himself down beside her. He hands her the brandy.

'I'm too thirsty for brandy.' She uncorks the bottle, drinks anyway. 'That was a bad thing we did there.'

He nods.

'I feel disgusting.'

'I do too.'

Anna raises the bottle. 'To the end of all of this whore-house mess,' she says. 'To the end of this heap of fecking bollocks, this pile of whorish shit, because I have had my fill and more of it, so I have.'

The bundling forth of French and Irish swearing makes him smile, despite himself. She takes another slug of brandy. She goes to wipe the bottleneck, then, having nothing clean on her, not even an inch of sleeve, just hands it over as it is.

'To the end,' he says, and lifts the bottle, and the brandy burns and warms, and seems for a while to help.

*

316

That evening he has barely drifted into sleep before he's jerked out of it like a fish on a hook. A whistle in the street. He slips out of bed, leaves Suzanne sleeping. Her lashes long, her hair tumbled and damp. He hadn't known – or if he had, he had not remembered – that she would be there. Does it mean something that she is there?

From the window he can see a large group of *maquis* waiting in the street.

Someone yells up: 'The sons of whores are on the run! Come on down. We're to give 'em what for.'

He grabs clothes and boots, runs downstairs to join them. They march down the middle of the road in the blue evening; they talk, they laugh, they make themselves conspicuous. What, after all, do they have to hide? The balance of the world is shifting; everything is sliding and shivering and settling into different patterns once again. This is their land, this is their home; their noisy footfalls are reclaiming it. He finds himself watching their feet as they plant them on the grit; he watches the slow circle of the cycling boys' legs and he cannot partake of their joy, their comfort, their sense of ease. He is looking out for German low boots on a farmhand's feet.

The group clumps along the cart tracks; they pick up others at crossroads, they call at cottages; the crowd grows. They descend towards the main road along the valley floor, where an arms cache has already been dug. They drag away bushes; they unpack the wares, divvy up ammunition, pace out the gaps between charges and lay them. Bonhomme hands him a cold Sten and he hefts it in his grip and recalls

317

the green wine bottle flinging itself in fragments up into the air.

Somebody is dishing out hand grenades. One is placed in his palm like an apple. He puts it in his pocket. It weighs his jacket down, makes it droop.

From the south comes the thud of shells, and distant gunfire. Aeroplanes grind invisibly across the sky. The Armée de l'Est is expected to retreat this way. It has tanks and trucks and artillery and an urgent need to be elsewhere. The *maquisards* have a few charges, a few rifles and a hand grenade each. They have their own self-righteous outrage to compel them: *la patrie, le terroir, la revanche.* He can feel none of this. We are fleas on a dog's back, he thinks; the most we'll do is make it stop and scratch.

He lays the rifle down beside him on the bank and it catches a guilty sheen of the half-light. The hand grenade lies cold against his thigh. His own blood throbs next to it. He supposes he will throw the thing, if he is obliged to. He is not certain that he can bring himself to throw it accurately. In the half-dark, there are shiftings and sighs. To the south, the skirmishing continues. Someone snores.

He drops off the edge of wakefulness and into harbour-water sleep, livid with dreams, with swaying treetops in blue sky, with the stomach-swoop of falling. He dreams his mouth is full of earwigs and he is chewing them up and swallowing just to be rid of them, but they are bitter and he spits and spits and spits, and still he cannot be rid of them. He runs a stick along the railings, and up in the Dublin hills they are blasting granite: *boom.*

He wakes to the faint crackle of gunfire, the crunch of artillery. He gets up stiffly and stalks off for a piss. Someone smokes a cigarette. It is dawn already and it is cold, and if the Armée de l'Est did retreat last night, then they did not retreat this way.

'Here.' He slips his hand into his pocket, draws out the hand grenade and hands it back.

The *maquis* walk home in the early-morning cool, rifles shouldered. The boys are skittish, jostling; the older men tramp solidly and speculate. The Armée de l'Est must have got entangled with the Yanks, must be fighting harder than you might have thought conscripted POWs would fight. Or they must have taken another route, out towards Avignon or Aix. But this talk is soon stitched through with hopes for this year's vintage, the promise of a puppy from the best gun dog's next litter, a game of *pétanque*. He walks with them, but is not of them; the talk winds round him while he is silent, and his footfalls land on earth that was never to do with him. At his gate, he swings the gun from his shoulder and hands it back to Bonhomme. Who takes it and claps his arm and says, 'Thank you, my friend.'

And then the crowd of them are on their way again, on into the little town.

In the dim kitchen, he wipes off some of the dirt, empties a pitcher down his throat, shovels in cold stew. Then he climbs upstairs and falls into bed, turns on his side, and sleeps.

Suzanne, having lain awake in his absence, and listened to the voices in the street and then him blundering around below, now slides out from underneath the covers. She treads barefoot round the house, chewing at her cuticles. The place already feels unfamiliar, as if they had never lived here. She picks up her mending, drops it again. She shunts her bare feet into espadrilles and scuffs out into the sun. Absently, she picks grapes from the trailing vines and eats them, warm with sunshine and not yet ripe, the sourness making her shudder. They turn to dust over her tongue and teeth, and yet she cannot wait for ripeness, sweetness. She picks another grape. She grows accustomed to the bitterness. *Aigre*, she thinks. It is not actually unpleasant. It is not difficult to bear.

And then, across the quiet, she hears the tear of an engine. She lifts her head to listen. It's coming from out along the road and heading towards them. She straightens her shoulders and goes round to the front of the house.

She can feel the thrum through the ground. Above her, at the upper window, the shutters slam back, making her wince and glance up. He steps out on to the balcony in his vest and dust-stained trousers, his weak eyes searching into the distance. She shifts her gaze to follow his. A vehicle rounds the bend. It takes a moment to realize what she's seeing. A rugged open-topped car – a jeep – burns up the road towards them. It is packed tight with men; the men are big and solid and they are dressed in fatigues. Soldiers. And, incongruously, Henri Hayden is perched on the back of the car. Spotting them, he waves and leans forward to speak to the driver. The car stops in front of the house, the engine churning. White grins on dirty faces. And all of Henri's preparation, all those English lessons with Anna Beamish, are forgotten in

320

this moment of unalloyed delight. He yells in French: 'They were just going to pass us by!'

There are words exchanged between the soldiers in red, rich American English. The driver shunts the car into gear; Henri leans back as they pull away.

'It's over! Good God, can you believe it? It's all over! This fucking whore of a war! We're *liberated*!'

And the jeep batters off up the road into town, flinging up a cloud of red dust. Suzanne raises a hand to shade her eyes. Henri disappears into the billows. Then the dust roils and settles, and the road is empty.

Suzanne turns to look back up to the balcony. Foreshortened by the angle, he is a darkness standing against the brilliant blue and she cannot make him out. He looks into the distance. He lifts his hands and presses them to his face. Then he turns away, and goes indoors.

She wipes her eyes with a flank of a hand. She sniffs. She shakes her head, and turns, and goes back to her garden.

And that is it.

Part Three

Beginning

18

New Place, Foxrock
Summer 1945

IRELAND IS GREEN. It is lush and livid under the heavy sky. After the parched redness of the south, after the greys of battered Paris, his eyes strain to adjust.

Not just his eyes. His attitude, expectations, posture, stomach, nerves. He is out of kilter here more than he ever was.

Milk, for example.

He has become obsessed with milk. He follows the jug as it progresses from hand to hand, watches the white cord as it twines into the cups, watches the gobs of fat shine on the surface of the tea. The mixture is lifted to bristling lips and sucked; throats spasm, lips roll in on themselves and then unstick and stretch and pucker with speech. The milky tea is supped and sucked upon, as though it were something and nothing, as though its continuance were guaranteed; as if it were not, like everything else, as vulnerable and fleeting as the snow, that can be gone with just a change in the weather.

New Place, for example.

The big old house, Cooldrinagh, is sold, and she is in a modest bungalow just across the street from it. Of course she mentioned this in her letters, but it still comes as a surprise. It's wrong, this house. It's all edges, corners and awkward angles. It is delicate unstable ornaments and vases. The ceilings feel too low, the corridors narrow and full of turns. He stumbles around, stooped and cautious, haunted by the openness that had been here, the vacant plot of his childhood where the grass blew and cats fought and mated and he and Frank whooped and tumbled and trod in dogshit. He can hear voices from the old place, and the metronomic tock of a tennis ball. The larches stir themselves in the breeze, and one of them is already turning gold, and maybe there'll be a child up there, clutching a high branch, swaying with the wind. The old house looms over the new; it has prior claim upon the sunshine. He lurches and ducks through the bungalow, but he is peeled into pieces: he drifts through other places, other times, can't make himself be fully here.

Alfy is dead. And all this goes on.

Tea on the lawn should not be so difficult. It should not be utterly intolerable. The cairn of bread-and-butter, the heap of scones, the cake: they are not horrors in and of themselves. That poor spinster his mother has prised off the shelf for the occasion, God love her, and the friends and neighbours: he's known some of them for years. But he just cannot get the hang of it again. If indeed he ever could. Not the rituals, not the conversation, not what is expected of him. He has gone tone-deaf to it. His mother tongue has disowned him.

Alfy died in the care of the Red Cross, the day after being freed. Maria's letter is brief. It chokes him. And he is marooned here, islanded.

He sips his tea black and tries not to notice, but when his mother sets her cup down, it rattles against the saucer in uneasy timpani. When she speaks it is with a tiny shake of the head, as though negating every word even as it's said. He tries not to notice, but he can't not notice. There are too many negatives to ignore.

She passes him a tremulous plate. He takes a slice of bread-and-butter, passes the plate on. He cuts his piece into halves, into quarters, into tiny squares and then into triangles again, the famine habit still hanging hard on him. His mouth is bitter with decay. His jaw throbs. His tongue probes at carious, sharp-edged molars, at the incisor that rocks in its socket and bristles with pain.

The conversation swells and grows, and he lifts a fragment of bread-and-butter and slips it between his lips and tastes the fat and salt and sweetness of it.

He blinks, and the red inside his eyelids is the red of Roussillon; and there are tumbled stones, the hair-cracked road, and dusty broken boots shuffling along it.

He opens his eyes at the blank white linen tablecloth. Paris walls are pocked with bullet holes. Marble counters in the shops are gleaming and empty. Milk is a miracle. Bread is made of sawdust. The Péron twins all bones and shadows, and not growing as they should. Suzanne stands shivering in a queue. And he should not have left them all to that. He should not have brought himself here. Where he is entirely surplus to requirements.

But nonetheless, something is expected of him: he has been addressed. The pale old faces are watching him.

'Sorry. What was that?'

Smiles. A throat cleared. He has, of course, been through a good deal. Allowances must be made.

'Here.' His mother proffers a plate.

He looks down at a thick wedge of sponge. Under the pressure of the cake slice, the jam and cream have been extruded in a pinkish ooze, like bone marrow. It is an offence, an insult to her, his thinness. That he preferred France and famine to her, and this.

Her shake is bad. He takes the plate and sets it down. He looks at the cake. His teeth throb. He should force down a forkful, a few crumbs, a bit of jam; even if it makes him gag, makes his teeth sing out like little birds.

'Back in France—' he says.

Someone lifts a teaspoon, someone turns their saucer slightly; someone reaches for the sugar.

'My friends are getting by on next to nothing. On turnips and sawdust.'

The cake stares up at him, bloodied and gross; his finger-tips recall the glide of paper scraps across a tabletop, the patterns forming. He blinks and he sees the floorboards inches above his face. The crate swinging at his knees along the country path. The clotted blooms of geraniums. His hands clasp and he feels the cold Sten gun in his grip. The haft of a shovel, the grave dug in the red earth. He is not here, he is not really here at all, he can't figure out how to be.

'One hears that things are very bad,' someone concedes, 'in France.'

His mother tugs at the edges of her cardigan and glances up at the sky and says, do you know, she thinks it might be coming on to rain, and someone says that it certainly looks that way; and conversation gathers round this thread like crystals and accumulates, as though everything were normal here and as though the world was the same all over and looked like this; as if there was tea and cake for everyone, and one last patch of sunshine on the lawn before another summer's done.

And for now, what can he do but accept the fiction, however temporarily, and comply with it. He lifts his cup, swallows his tea down. He forks the cake into bits, and crumbs, and spears a fragment and places it in his mouth. It dissolves there like a communion wafer. It is good. He clears his plate.

She watches him discreetly as he eats, a glance and then another glance; a smile caught on her neighbour's smile, the happiness that must of course be felt to have him home again. But underneath it all, underneath every swollen moment of his presence here, there is an ache for him that begins in the middle of her chest and rises to her throat and squeezes out her breath. To see him now, like this, a gaunt, worn creature made of rope and sticks, it has her heart turned sideways in her. Always the hardest path. Always the highest tree. He'd fall, and having fallen, would dust himself off and climb the tree again. When the tree itself had no need to be climbed at all; when there were lawns to run on and games of tennis and croquet and company; when there were so many other, more comfortable things, if he could simply choose them. But falling never knocked that strange determination out of him, and neither could she.

So she must learn. She will not win this war. But perhaps there can be peace.

He goes. Down the pavement and across the road; simply going, making distance. Even now after all these years he could still be hastening to catch up with his father, to fall in step with him in silence, walking away from this tangled mother-love, up to where things fall clear and the track rises through the cotton grass and the curlews calling; his father, gazing at the ground, would stop, and dig up a small stone with a fingernail and rub it clean, and pocket it in case of later need.

He searches out his own small stone in his pocket, the precious one a child's clean eye had selected from all the stones at Greystones. He turns it over in his fingertips.

He misses Paris. Paris under any circumstances. Paris with its bones sticking through its skin, he'd take that over this unruffled plump buck Dublin that is making him gag on butter and milk and cream. That will not let him leave. There are no travel permits to be had, not for failing feckless writers. His teeth hurt like hell, his joints are full of grit, he's short of breath, and he knows he is in no shape for anything, and is no good to anyone at all, and that France in ruins needs him less than she did when she was whole. France needs doctors, nurses, surveyors, engineers. The likes of him would only clutter up the place.

Today has been difficult.

He must grant himself that.

One would think these things got easier with practice, but they don't. Failure still takes some accommodating. Over time, that stab of shame will dull to a low guilty ache, and he'll go on with it like that, and get used to it. His book, the book written in Roussillon, the book that kept him sane, the book that, as Anna Beamish said, he had to write like snails have to make slime. *Watt*. Nobody wants it. Nobody will publish it. Yet another rejection came this morning. Nicely worded, and on not bad paper for the times that are in it. But a rejection nonetheless. And that, after all, is the thing about slime. He might have to make it, but nobody else is obliged to buy it off him.

He presses on. The breath heaves in and out of him. If he can tire himself sufficiently, he might just manage eventually to sleep.

Rigid in the dentist's chair, his skull pressing hard against the headrest, his jaw is locked open. He can taste his own rottenness, smell it as he breathes. His mouth crawls with silvery pains; they're everywhere, like ants.

The dentist's face is practically in his mouth; Ganley pokes and tugs with his little wire sickle and the pain sharpens and turns red. The eyes narrow; the wire digs in under gum and he grips the armrests. This is nothing really;

whatever happens here, however much it hurts, this is nothing very much at all.

'So you were in France for the duration, I believe?'

He swallows spit, open-mouthed. There are three fingers and a metal scraper in his mouth: he can't even nod.

'Uh.'

The wire scrapes in below the gum again and the pain is brilliant, and he tastes blood, and it doesn't matter.

'And you haven't had these looked at, during all that time?'

It didn't even cross his mind. 'Uh.'

Ganley chinks the scraper down on a metal tray.

Released, he fumbles out his handkerchief, dabs his lips.

'Rinse, please.'

He rinses. The pinky-purple fluid stings. He spits into the bowl. The white ceramic streaks with blood; the blood oozes towards the plughole. He has known for a while that things in his mouth are not as they should be; the snags and edges, the deep throb of nerve, the tender itchy gum: there was more going on than there should have been. The clank and clatter of a sucking stone around his mouth can't have helped. It had kept him going, but at a deficit. He will pay for it now.

'We see a lot of this at the minute,' Ganley says. He's at the basin, scrubbing his hands.

'What's that, then?'

'These accumulated problems. Soldiers and POWs have mouths like yours. Neglect, poor diet – over time, well, there's just massive decay and infection. One sees it in country folk too. They'll come up to town with twenty years' worth of rot.

It'll already be wearing you down and affecting what you can and can't eat. Isn't that right?'

He nods.

Ganley dries his hands, sets the towel aside. 'And every day you go on like this you're risking septicaemia, and then, well, all bets are off. So what we need to do, and in pretty short order, is clean things up in there. A good few of these will have to go . . .'

As the dentist talks, his tongue slides around his teeth, up the smooth fronts of his top incisors, one and then the other; it presses into their concave backs. They'd been serrated, keen, pressing through the gum when he was seven years old; now their edge is worn flat and blunt and chalky-porous. And the right one gives under the pressure of his tongue. Like a tree with the roots dug out from underneath it.

'. . . pain, but we'll put you under,' the fellow's saying. 'You'll be sore for a while afterwards, but gum tends to heal pretty well once the source of infection's gone. We'll get some bridgework fitted and you'll be grand.'

He swallows. It doesn't matter. Not the pain, not the loss. It's tiny. His mite dropped into the kitty, his little bit of suffering to help pay off an outraged, vengeful God.

'And the charge for that?'

'You'll need to talk to Miss Cavendish. She can take you through the payments.'

He nods. He hasn't properly gathered what will be removed and what will remain; it hardly matters. His mother will have to be consulted; he won't be able to afford it without her help. He will be leathery and cadaverous, scarred, toothless, already decaying, staggering along to get into her grave before she can.

Now his stomach is sick with blood, and the inside of his mouth is cavernous and far too wet, and his tongue has become a strange mollusc that is living in it. His lips are dry and cracked and overstretched. He should have accepted Frank's offer of a lift. He's still dazed with nitrous oxide and here and there his gums are stitched and prickly, and there are craters too where the blood congeals and lifts in lumps and his slug of a tongue will not leave anything alone, and the street is busy and the sky is a bitter pearl-grey and he is stumbling along making a show of himself, he's sure of it. It's as much as he can do to walk a straight line, to not vomit blood into the gutter. The pain is distractingly various. He aches, he stings, he throbs, is sore. This has been a very expensive and thorough assault upon his person. He may as well have been mugged.

'Hey! Hello there! Hey! Hold on!'

He flinches, but stumbles on, one foot in front of the other, in the shoes his mother bought him. Bloody Dublin; just a big village. There's always somebody who knows you. Whoever it is, they'll give up, with any luck. But no luck: a hand lands on his arm. He stops, looks down at it. A small, smooth gentleman's hand. He looks up.

'There, see. I knew it was you.'

A light-boned, boyish fellow grins at him. It has been a while, but he is instantly familiar. He swallows down the bloody wet.

'Alan.'

His voice is slushy, indistinct; he lifts the handkerchief to his ragged lips. Dr Alan Thompson, who has been busy making his mother proud. Still boyish and light on his feet, and a decent chap, and a medical man; so he won't faint or run shrieking at the sight of him.

Hands are shaken.

'Good to see you,' he manages.

'Good to see you too.' Alan frowns, though, peers in. 'What's up? You're in a bit of a state.'

'Dentist,' he says.

'Butcher, more like. Extractions?'

He nods. 'And fillings.' When he speaks, his whole skull aches.

'Come by the office. It's probably not just your teeth needing attention.' Alan takes his arm. 'In the meantime, I can see you require a calmative and a restorative, and those gums could do with an additional disinfectant.'

He can't face any further procedures, not today. And anyway, he can't afford it. He demurs.

Alan smiles. 'No, no, I insist. What you need, my friend, is whiskey, and a good deal of it. That's my professional opinion. I'm buying.'

It is the best thing he has heard in days. Alan steers him round, and off and into the Bleeding Horse.

It is all settled within the hour, within half a bottle of Jameson's.

The smoke spools up to the ceiling and the drinkers press elbow to elbow at the bar. The first sip of whiskey sears, the second stings, the third he cups warm on his tongue and waits and looks to Alan, and his eyes crease at the company. He swallows, lifts his glass again and looks at the piss-gold stuff.

'I feel so much better. I don't know why I didn't think of it myself,' he says.

'Well, you're not yourself right now, you know.'

They have the gist of each other's recent lives. On closer inspection, time has had some small effect on Alan. He's not quite the boy he used to be. His hair is receding a little, and there are lines at the corners of his eyes and from nostril down to lip. But overall, the years have handled the boy gently, compared with how they've battered him. He feels ancient; he feels shambolic. A broken-down old tramp. A mummy.

'Are you still at the writing?' Alan asks.

'I would be, but I can't. Not here. Not at Mother's. Never could.'

'You must be keen as mustard, then, to get back to France.'

'I have friends there. I'm worried.' He nods over his glass. 'But only essential workers can travel, so—' A lifted shoulder. He is stuck.

'Lookit,' Alan says, leaning in closer. 'Here's something might interest you.'

He leans in too, already bleary, struggling to focus through the aftermath of gas and pain and shock and the current blur of whiskey.

'There's this Red Cross venture I'm involved in,' Alan says. 'We're taking a hospital to France.'

'A what?'

'A hospital. It's going to a little place called Saint-Lô; the town got flattened during the liberation. So we're taking them a hospital. We're getting our supplies together now and will make the crossing in August.'

'With a hospital?'

He sips, nods. 'We have to take everything with us. Everything from syringes to marmalade to lino. There's nothing there at all. We have to get hold of what we need here, sort it, store it, ship it off to France. And then get it all set up when we're over there.'

'That is quite an undertaking.'

'Indeed it is. And we aren't yet fully staffed. And so I thought. See, we're looking for a quartermaster. Someone to take care of the logistics this end and then sort it out over there in Normandy.'

'I see.'

'And so, I was thinking, why not you? Because with your language skills, you could be our interpreter too. Some of us have schoolboy French, but . . .'

It doesn't sound like the kind of thing that he could do. But then nothing ever does.

He raises his glass and sips. And then he nods.

'Good,' Alan says. 'So then we're agreed. And you'll take another drink.'

He is overseeing the unloading of refrigerators in the Red Cross warehouse when Mrs Hackett comes in with the evening edition and waves it in front of him. He reads the headline without understanding it. He stares at her.

'That hallion is dead,' she says. 'Took his own life, can you imagine? That's it.'

And so the war is over. He wipes his hands down his dungarees. He thinks, I am wearing dungarees, Hitler is dead, and the war is over.

It is a blossom-heavy bloody day in May, and it's impossible to feel anything simple.

He does not go back to his mother's house in Foxrock, but instead walks along the banks of the Liffey and up into the congested heart of town. There are aimless angry crowds on College Green, and a Union Jack smouldering on the gates. He keeps on walking. He ends up in a bar that he doesn't normally go to, in the hope of seeing nobody he knows, but this being Dublin he just stares at his drink to make doubly sure. He downs whiskey after whiskey after whiskey, while all around him Dublin scratches and yelps and shivers at its old sores.

When it happens, there is nothing grand about it, nothing sublime. There's no gale, no tossing waves, no spray in the air; it is not a storm-torn sky above him but the low ceiling of his mother's bungalow. There's no pathetic fallacy here. It might be the moment when everything changes for him, but that doesn't oblige the world to notice, or do anything particular to mark the occasion.

It's early evening. The electric fire is eating all the air. A dinner of pap uneasy in his belly, his mouth still raw, the

338

radio on, he is writing to Suzanne as his mother studies a seed catalogue in the armchair and turns rustling pages. His tongue explores craters, jellied blood. He tells Suzanne about the Red Cross work, a salary, some hope of paying back Valéry Larbaud, his hope too that he will be returned soon to France, though not yet to Paris; he will come and see her as soon as he gets leave. Suzanne is a vein of guilt running through all the other manifold discomforts. His thoughts slip into that former life: his old apartment, and the cool solitude through which Suzanne would twine like a cat; her naked belly under his hand; a brilliant smile; eyes closed at the Opéra, there and gone, and gone sometimes for days. He doesn't see that it can ever return to that. Something or other will have to be done. Because, by rights, Suzanne should be here, getting fattened up on butter, milk and cake; she would be, if they were married. It would be a coin into the kitty if they were.

His mother glances up from the lists of bulbs and corms and tubers; in the spring, they will brighten this new bleak wilderness of hers. She regards her boy. There is grey in his hair. There are lines around his eyes. She can see the old man that he will become and her heart aches for him. No comfortable desk in the family firm, no children on his knee, nothing so simply good, not for him. His weak eyes straining always on impossibilities.

She watches as he finishes his letter; he blows on it, then folds it up. There is a line between his eyebrows as he looks towards her. Perhaps he's noticed the palsy in her hands, the way it makes the paper shake. She sets the catalogue aside, meshes her fingers and presses her bundled hands down into her lap to stop them trembling. She will not let him see that she is ill.

She fakes a shiver, says, 'It is getting rather chilly, don't you think?'

He colludes in the deceit. Speech still sounds strange and wet from his reordered mouth: 'Shall I fetch you your shawl?'

'Lily can get it. I'll call her.'

'No need.' Hands on knees, he's pushing up to his feet.

'In my room, then. On the dresser.'

Beyond the stuffy electric heat, the hall is cool. He switches on the light, still uncertain of his way. He treads along to her door and pushes it open. The light from the hallway streaks past him and casts his shadow on the carpet. He flicks the bedroom light-switch and the shadows bolt.

The quilted coverlet is tugged square and straight, valance skirts brush the floor; the curtains hang in tidy folds, undrawn; the panes of glass reflect the room back at him. Her shawl lies folded neatly on the dressing table. As he moves towards it, his reflection in the window ambles up to meet him, faithful as an old hound. Long limbs, smoothed hair, glinting glasses, creased slacks. He lifts the shawl and his image copies him. He turns his back on it, lopes away. At the bedroom door, he switches off the light and glances back.

His image has vanished from the uncurtained window. Reflected there now is the bright oblong of the doorway and his blank silhouette within it; through the darkened glass he can see out across the garden and over the hedge, and on the far side of the street to the topmost storey of Cooldrinagh. The sky is filled with prickling stars; and up there, the nursery casement glows, and inside a child is perhaps kneeling to say their prayers. He watches the weave of larch branches as they stir across the light; he watches the lace they make.

And then the blind is drawn down over there, and the warm nursery is cut off, and all that remains is the pool of night that swells between the old house and the new. And his silhouette, angular and black and blank, framed by the bright doorway.

There is nothing grand about it; no waves, no wind, no briny spray. The world is not and never was in sympathy with him, nor with anybody else. But this is the moment when everything changes, the moment when the wide chaotic chatter and stink of it, all that wild Shem-beloved hubbub, falls away, and his eyes are trained on darkness and his ears on silence. On that stark figure, framed there on the threshold, unknowable and his.

He turns away. He closes the bedroom door behind him. He switches off the hall light: his fingertips trace along the wall, his heart racing.

He can find his own way now, in the dark. He doesn't need the light.

19

Normandy
August 1945

CHERBOURG IS GREY under the blue August sky; the coast-line is encrusted with buildings like a rock-pool is with limpets. He leans against the railing, peering out.

All the crates and boxes, the equipment and supplies he had received, unpacked, repacked, stored and accounted for in the warehouse back in Dublin – the bandages, tinned ham, syringes, soap and cigarettes – are now nearing their destination. It had seemed abstract for so long, too big to conceive. He had focused on the parts and not the whole: all these months in the warehouse, with every labelled parcel stacked on every numbered shelf, with every crate he'd nailed shut and wheeled into its own exact spot in the stores, he had kept from his mind the vastness of the undertaking. It had been, simply, a way to get back to France.

But now, with landfall, that sense of his own desire crumbles and he absorbs an understanding of the work that is to be done.

The ship churns in past the harbour walls: the damage here seems geological. Those tumbled boulders, that rust-streaked stone, all of it massive and massively broken, as though it were the wear of centuries, of millennia of weather, as though it were the shrug of tectonic plates.

The quayside, when they reach it, is a lunatic forced into a straitjacket: chaos twitches beneath the surface and wriggles out around the edges. Rubble has been swept back; there are drifts of broken brick and stone and bent steel and copper piping and splintered beams. Work weaves around it all, between the temporary wooden huts and the idling trucks and the remains of the railway line, as if this were quite reasonable, as if the broken and twisted crane lying half in, half out of the water were just part of the natural scenery of this place, and the box car hanging with the ground gone from underneath it, the rails twisted across a crater, sleepers splintered, had somehow just grown there like a buddleia from the gaps between the stones.

He creeps down a swaying gantry. On the dockside he just stands as others jostle by him. He is overwhelmed by the rank smell of broken drains and diesel fumes, by the powdered brick under his feet, by the heaps of rubble and the carious bits of wall like broken teeth.

A hand clasps his shoulder.

'If you think this is bad,' Alan says, 'just wait till you see Saint-Lô.'

He grimaces. He fishes out his cigarettes. He does not see how anything could be worse than this and still be. He lights up and struggles to fit himself back into himself. His boots

343

are wrong. His tunic, trousers, puttees, are all wrong. He feels his eyeballs when he blinks. The world is in flitters, in bits and shreds. He has to work out how he can be in it, and move through it, again.

Alan beckons him along. He does his best to arrange his face.

'There's a lift waiting for us,' Alan calls. 'Come along, old son. Chop chop.'

He can see it in his mind's eye, the dot dot dot of their progress across the map, as he sits in the back of the car, the wind in his eyes, the dust crunching between his remaining teeth. He does not have to do anything but wait. Crossing the French countryside like this, at thirty, thirty-five, forty miles an hour – watching the speedometer over the driver's shoulder, the needle ticking upwards even while the driver veers round potholes and rattles over the rough – changes everything, so that thistles and teasels are a dotted blur, and the stands of Queen Anne's lace are brief pale clouds; on foot, he'd have seen them grow from a distant haze to up-close snowflake precision. A burned-out tank stands in a field, sooty and scorched and grown around with this summer's nettles. And then it's gone.

'You all right there?'

'What?' he has to yell over the noise of the car.

'You all right?'

He nods, turns back to the window. They thunder through a settlement – church-café-crossroads-and-it's-gone. He's left with an image of blowsy overblown roses, rank grass, charred beams, a crow perched on a fencepost, an empty window frame like a crucifix.

Then they're out, and they rumble over a Bailey bridge, and there's a flash of blue sky-reflecting water, and he glances off and up along the river and through the wide emptiness of the Normandy landscape, which manages somehow to be at once lush and bleak. He fishes for his cigarettes.

He holds the packet out to Alan, who takes a cigarette, eyes narrowed in the bright sun. He taps the driver's shoulder, holds the pack for him to see. The driver shakes his head. There are two hundred miles or so between Cherbourg and Saint-Lô. They sit and smoke past deserted towns and farmhouses and neglected fields and burned-out barns and abandoned gear, and nobody talks. The emptiness gets inside him, like the cold.

A bank of cloud slid in overnight, while they slept, comfortable and oblivious, at their digs outside town; this new morning feels more like November than August. As they drive in through the dripping green, the damp makes his chest tighten; a cigarette soothes, and there are more cigarettes, cartons of them, crates. For once he can be certain, thanks to the generosity of Gallahers, that he will not run out of cigarettes.

The car crawls into what is left of Saint-Lô, along a road cleared through the rubble. There's no colour here; it has been bleached out by the bombs. Dead trees stand skeletal against the grey sky. Mounds of rubble rise and fall into the distance. The town has become a desert of grey dunes, glittering with shards of glass. Here and there stand slabs of remaining wall, calling to mind those ruined English abbeys, the still, sad music of humanity, though these ruins stand not on grass but knee-deep in drifts of broken stone. *Bare ruin'd choirs, where late the sweet birds sang.*

And all of it done in a day by the circling Allied planes. A necessary evil is an evil nonetheless. They don't need a new hospital here; they need a new town. There can't be anybody living here as it is. He yells it over the rattle of the engine, over the rumble of the tyres on the rough road: 'There can't be anybody living here.'

Alan nods in contradiction.

'How?'

A shrug, a smile. 'It's desperate, though, you can see it is.'

He turns back to the window. This place is not human any more. They lurch along with the motion of the car and he stares out at the wilderness of stone, a shiver gathering at the back of his neck. The road itself is not real. It has been cut through the rubble. They're rattling through ghosts of houses, backyards, shops and streets. It's a film, black and white and grey, flickering past the window; at any moment it could just snap. Flicker out into blank white and be gone.

But then colour: red, a punch of it. They're past now, rumbling along. He cranes round to look back.

The red is hanging from the bones of a tree.

He turns right round in his seat, stares out of the back window. He can see a bundle of flesh and grey and glowing scarlet, and for a moment it's an atrocity. But then it coalesces and is . . . a child's red pullover, a boy in shorts, and an older

346

lad in flannels, his arm wrapped around the younger child. The two of them are huddled together on a tree branch in a casual embrace, legs dangling, watching the vehicles roll into town.

The figures shrink, and slide upwards to the top of the rear window, and are gone.

That instinct to take oneself up and out of the adult world, to get that distance. What they may have observed from there, these past years. The tanks rolling in and out again. The planes droning up the valley. The first bombs beginning to fall.

On the edge of town the road gains clarity, begins to know itself again; it slips into old habits and rises over the hillside and is gone. They park up beside a government Citroën. Everybody gets out. There's talk, handshakes, gestures round the empty plot. On the far side of the road, a fine glossy horse stares out over the fence.

'The stores will be set up at the stud farm,' the Colonel says. 'We've requisitioned the attics.'

The farm. A handsome building; long and low, to accommodate the horses on the ground floor. The walls are hazed with bullet holes. Not a windowpane seems to have been left unbroken.

'First job there will be to make the place secure.'

Nods. People are desperate, and there will be temptations here. Penicillin is, right now, worth more than diamonds.

'And the hospital itself,' the colonel says, 'the accommodation huts and walkways, will be over here.'

They pace it out; they talk. From this point, on the edge of town, the devastation is even starker. The lush Normandy fields, the hedgerows thick with flowers and foliage, and then just turn your head and everything is grey, broken, done with. They are wasting their time – he almost says it out loud to Alan and the colonel. They have made a mistake. How can anything they do here help with this? How can anything be retrieved from here? They may as well pack up and leave. But then, grey on grey, along the rubble-swept road, something moves. A figure – a woman. Wearing a drab greenish dress, she carries a basket hooked over her arm, and carries also her distended belly in front of her like a medicine ball. He stares, and then remembers himself and goes to greet her. Explains what they are doing there, in the emollient courtesies of French. She has big famine eyes. Her hands are twigs.

'We know. We are very grateful you have come, you Irishmen. You are very welcome.'

Then she takes a bottle from her basket and hands it to him. 'God bless you,' she says, and then she turns and walks away.

'And you, Madame.'

He's left there, standing, the bottle in his hands, watching her go. From the back, she is narrow. Skinny legs, the wings of her shoulders visible even through her clothes: no hint at all that she is expecting. Fifty feet away and she pauses. He thinks she might be about to turn back, as if there's something more she'd like to say, but she just stands there, head bent, hand to her back, catching her breath. Then she straightens up and just walks on. As though tomorrow is worth the trouble that it takes to get there.

*

The prisoners of war are marched there from some draughty detention camp a little further out along the road. French guards march with them, though they do not give the impression of being eager to escape. They all walk with the same fatigued, uncomfortable gait, as if their feet are broken. Their uniform is faded to the grit-grey of the ruins. They are the boys who should not have had to be soldiers, they are the old men who should not have had to be soldiers again. They are the very young, they are the very old, they are whoever was left to guard this stretch of the Atlantic seawall when the storm broke.

Markers for the foundations are laid out already: stakes hammered into the ground and tied with string. The architect is pacing, talking, pointing, showing around the man from the Ministry of Reconstruction. While this discussion takes place, the prisoners are allowed to fall out and rest. Overlooked still by the guard, they sink to the ground in a cluster, quiet and acquiescent.

He wanders over to them. He squats stiffly down.

'I don't know what you've been told,' he says in German. 'About the work you will be doing here.'

A look, a quirked eyebrow, bushy as a hedge.

'We have cleared the rubble here, we dug the graves. I think we can manage to build this little hospital for you.'

So these are the men who cut the ghost roads through the town. He nods. 'You have building experience from before the war?'

The old fellow bunches his lips, shakes his head. 'I don't. But I know hospitals. I was a doctor.' He lifts his hands and

349

turns them for inspection. Deep grained with grey, the nails blunt and matt with wear. 'You wouldn't know.'

He keeps his interpreting work brisk but loose, moving from French to English to German and back again as he turns between the French surveyor, the Irish staff, the German labourers. The challenge is to maintain the register as meaning is decanted out of one language and into the next; courtesy is all too easily spilt. And if it's not there already, he might drip a little in. It's not professional to moderate the tone like this, but then he is not a professional interpreter. And it eases, it soothes; there was a time when courtesy was a normal thing, and it helps to recall it. The ditch will be a metre deep *if you please*. It will be half a metre wide, *if you would be so kind, sir.*

The labourers take off their tunics; they work bare-chested or in vests. Thin, greyed bodies; bones on show. The staff take to handing out tea and biscuits, cigarettes, bread-and-jam. He feels that he is rich indeed. He becomes promiscuous with his cigarettes.

The prisoners of war begin to talk amongst themselves while they work, and it feels much better than that exhausted silence. Sometimes they address a remark to him. The talk makes the guard edgy, but it makes him feel at ease: the fact of it, the normality. To speak another language is to step into the other fellow's boots. It erases difference. He tells the guard, 'They're remembering the dinners that their wives and mothers used to make.' And the guard raises his eyebrows, but nods, can understand.

Up at the stables, the windows are being boarded up, the locks fitted, the shelves clapped together out of packing crates.

Striding across the waste ground, his eye catches on colour. High up, on a windowsill, in a tooth of remaining wall, the two boys perch, legs dangling, looking down on the work going on there like little gods. He watches as the younger tugs at the elder's sleeve; they slither down and scramble away. They leap from the end of a buried bedstead, tight-rope round the rim of a fallen window frame, thunder over a flattened door. The blot of red shrinks, then disappears amongst the ruins.

The men are piecing together the flat sides of the first hut like a gingerbread house when it begins to rain. The water dots and darkens the wood. The roof goes on in slabs, seals off the space beneath it, changes its nature from outdoors to in. The rain chills the skin; it soaks through tunics and trousers, it traces streams upon the gritty earth, teases in between the rubble, makes white runnels of plaster dust and broken-up cement.

His boots sink into the clay, suck out of it. Rain streams down his face and into his eyes and brings with it the salt of his skin and makes his eyes sting. The men take their boots off at the door. They pad across the boards in damp socks. The beds are hustled in, the bedding unpacked and rolled out. A chair, a locker, a bed each. One simple room for the eight of them to sleep and eat and write and read in, till all the other rooms are built. The rain runs off the new pitched roof and into guttering, and away.

Elsewhere, the rain drips through botched-up roofs and oozes in through heaped rubble and trickles down into cellars so that women go barefoot to save their shoes, and there is nowhere safe to put the baby down.

He writes a letter, wraps a parcel to Suzanne. Biscuits, coffee, a small packet of powdered milk, gleaned from his rations. He doesn't need as much as he is given. He barely draws on his salary here; he is saving hard to repay the Larbauds.

That night, he lies awake in the dark, listening to the breathing of the sleeping men. Listening to the scratch of rats through heaps of broken stone.

By day, the site is an anthill, a Babel tower. Bricklayers hoist hods and slop cement, a team of Algerians rolls the hardcore flat between the huts; there is the smell of cut timber, and the grate and sigh of the saws, and the spooling out of cable and setting in of pipe, and voices raised in different languages and in heavily accented attempts at others. Fights do not break out. Sometimes, though, already, laughter does.

The stores, housed away from the main site, up above the stables, are bustling. Supplies arrive and are sequestered; people come with chits and dockets that must be filled and filed and the duplicate returned. Below, the horses thud hooves against their wooden stalls. Rain drips where a slate is missing, rain spills gurgling from a blocked gutter, wet footprints darken the floor. But, despite all the come-and-go, this remains a solitary place. It's his.

Though there is company here today in the form of a prisoner who is wiring the place for light.

'Here,' the prisoner says in German. 'Do you want to see how it's done?'

He watches blunt fingers manage surprisingly delicate operations, tweak and twist bright copper strands, fiddle in tiny screws. The work is deft and precise and there is a clear logic to it, a followable flow.

'I see.'

The prisoner inclines his head, still squinting at the work.

'My gaffer always said,' he says, 'gas light's kinder on the ladies, but electricity's sharper, electricity's the thing.'

'He was right.'

'He was always right. At least, he was until he wasn't.'

Then the prisoner clips the casing closed and twists in another screw to hold the whole thing shut. He flips the heavy switch. Light leaps; it scatters itself through the maze of shelving and slaps itself on to the stacked packing crates. It casts the prisoner's thin face in deep shadow.

'Job's a good one.'

He proffers his cigarettes. The two of them sink down, side by side, backs against a packing crate. He strikes a match; they lean in. The electric light is a brilliant cone over them.

'Only use the lamps when you really need them,' the German says, gesturing upwards. 'Or you'll run out of diesel in no time.'

'Good point.'

The refrigerators hum and the lights fizz and the generator rattles and the boards are hard beneath him, and the lamp burns down on them like a spotlight, and he's aware too of the sweat-and-tobacco stink of the man beside him and the heave of smoke into his lungs, and its slow spool out of him, and the reality of all of it is insistent, demanding to be noticed. He wants, oh God, he needs. Time, a locked door at his back, and time. Pen and paper and an empty notebook and no concern as to what the end will be, but the means, please God, he needs the means, he needs to write, he needs to shuffle the cards, tamp down the pack. He needs the quietude that it brings. He needs to learn.

He heaves himself up, pads over to switch off the light.

He hears the puck of cigarette from lips. 'It used to be beautiful,' the fellow says. 'Where I'm from, I mean. My town. But it's all been bombed to shit like this place too.'

'I'm sorry.'

'Thorough, your lot, when it comes to that kind of thing.'

'They're not my lot.'

'Which lot are your lot, then?'

He shrugs. 'I don't have a lot.'

The other says, 'I'm not going back.'

'You mean, home?'

'I wrote to my wife, I always did since I was conscripted, but the moment that I heard about the bombing I wrote. I've written to her thirty-two times since. After the first three letters and nothing back, I started writing to my mother-in-law too, and when nothing came of that either, I sent notes to friends, the neighbours, and to my daughters' schoolteachers, and then to the priest, and then the doctor. I sent a postcard to the grocer, asking how business was, letting him know how things were going here.'

He rolls his cigarette along his middle finger with his thumb. He looks at the fellow sidelong, waiting.

'They don't reply. But I keep on writing, and I'm never going back. So. There we are.'

He gets to his feet, leaves the other fellow sitting. Through the maze of the stores, he makes his way to where a box is tucked in behind a bigger box, and he fishes out the bottle of Jameson's and two enamel mugs. He brings them back, sinks down and pours large measures for them both. They sit in the shadows, and they drink.

At the outpatients' department, people queue for half the day. They bring scabies, bronchitis, arthritis and tuberculosis from their damp and overcrowded dwellings. They bring burns, scalds, contusions and raw open wounds wrapped in grubby tea-towels and handkerchiefs. Tired people are clumsy, and everybody's tired here: who can sleep with the rain dripping in on them, with their stomachs growling, with the kids coughing all night long? And everything is botched together, provisional, unsteady here, and so accidents happen: there is nowhere safe to cut up a potato, or put a hot pan down.

And children play in the ruins, since there is nowhere else to play. Masonry falls in showers on them. Cellars cave in underneath their feet. They pick up detonators in a grubby palm and call their friends to see. They get caught up in twisted rusty wire, and fall on broken glass.

Even in the countryside, people are not safe. Farm labourers are rushed in from the fields, only a tourniquet and their own cussedness to keep them from bleeding out in the back of their neighbour's car. There are landmines everywhere, and all sorts of unexploded ordnance, and there is not another hospital for a hundred miles.

As well as blood and flesh and phlegm and parasites and bacteria and shattered bone, the people bring flowers, fruit, eggs, bottles of Calvados and live chickens. They press these on the staff. Treatment is free, but there is a need to express gratitude, to offer some kind of payment. And so they give chickens, and Calvados, and fruit, and often tears.

He signs out the streptomycin, the syringes and suspensions and suture-silk and dressings and tea and cigarettes and sugar and marmalade and tinned ham. Others manage their application. He hands the packages over to the practised hands of nurses, orderlies and caterers, and ticks the items off his list, and when the new stocks arrive he shelves them, and notes them down, and hands over the receipt. What he is managing here, he likes to think, is the flow of decency. That it flows in this direction is long overdue.

Suzanne's letter is slow in coming too, and when it arrives it is slight and strange and he reads more between the lines than is written on the paper. She thanks him for the biscuits and the coffee and the milk. She is surprised that he could so easily spare them. She wonders when he will next be in Paris. He will see how things really are for everybody there.

But paper is scarce, and the sheets are small, and slight as tracing paper, and he'll forgive her if she doesn't squander a second sheet on this. But then she doesn't even fill the first one.

He takes his turn to patrol the stores at night. For all the work that has been done to secure the place, it's still vulnerable. And so he paces out the old vaulted attics with a flashlight, the lights left off to conserve fuel, listening to the scratch and squeak of rats in the stalls below, and the horses as they step and blow and huff, and the clatter of the generator that keeps the refrigerators humming even when the lights are out. A loaded revolver is strapped against his ribs; it lies hard and it makes his skin twitch like a horse's. If someone breaks in, and isn't scared off by his mere presence and a flashlight, he is expected to fire.

Between patrols, he sits under one light, his back to a tea-chest, his coat buttoned to his chin, feet drawn up towards him. He sets the gun aside. He opens a book. A quick choice from the crate supplied along with the cigarettes and whiskey, the Scrabble set and table-tennis, for the leisure hours of the Irish volunteers. He turns pages. The words skim by and do not settle. Instead, he feels the press of his own thoughts, the swell of the dark space at the back of the head from where the images start to spill. He's lost: the broken boots, the stiffening limbs, the sun sinking, rising, sinking; a country road, a tree. This is a waterfall that he is falling with, these are dream-thoughts on the edge of sleep; they slip away and turn to mist when he looks at them directly.

A noise. His head jerks up; he sets the book aside. A thud – something fell. And then a metallic clattering, scuffling and rummaging: someone has broken into the stores. He reaches for the gun. The darkness stretches out across the countryside from here. The hospital is more than a yell away. He is all by himself with this. The scuffling continues.

He unfolds up from the floor.

All is as black as backstage; his torch picks out patches as he moves through the stores. He clicks the safety off. He must defend a million cigarettes. A ton of jam. Fifteen crates of whiskey. And sterile dressings, bottles of stinking yellow iodine, and those milky, opalescent little ampoules of penicillin, snugly packed into their boxes, the boxes stacked in their humming refrigerators. In purely utilitarian terms, penicillin, perhaps, is worth shooting someone for. His hand is sweaty – he switches the gun into his left, wipes his palm down his trouser-leg, swaps the pistol back again, fumbling the torch. He treads softly down between the crates.

He slides round the corner. A carton lies sideways on the floor, tins tumbled out, the lids burst off some of them. Something dark writhes over the pale spillage. He doesn't fire. He reaches for the light switch, flicks it. And the rats scatter. He lets a breath go. Then he goes to fetch a dustpan and brush. He sweeps up the powdered milk that has been spilt and pours it into the bin. He rights the remaining tins and sorts through them, and puts the untainted ones back on the shelf. There is, after all, no point crying over it.

Later, the gun handed over to the next watch, he walks back to the barracks through the blue pre-dawn, smoking a cigarette, not knowing quite where to put his feet, since the path itself seems to be heaving. A whisk of tail, a dart, a flash of eye; dozens of them, scores, bold as you like. Their usual runs and haunts have been blown out of existence in the bombing; the warehouses and stables and farmyards are no longer there – and so the rats spill everywhere, and seek out new shelter and new sources of food. Just like anybody would.

To the east the sky is paling, and soon another day is going to happen to him, but first there must be sleep. He toes off his boots outside the door, carries them along the row of sleeping men. At his own bed, he flops his greatcoat across the low cross-tie of the roof. He unbuttons his tunic, steps out of his trousers, clambers into bed. He lies, blinking in the darkness, his tongue exploring the spaces in his mouth, the remaining teeth like monoliths, the smooth bald gum. Out there in the darkness there is a scratching and a scuttling, and the almost-too-high-to-hear squeaking of the rats, and something must be done about that, before they taint everything and take over the place entirely. In his mind, he assembles another package, composes another letter. He thinks, a tin of butter, a tin of ham, a tin of peaches. What else can he glean, for Marnia and the boys? He blinks. He blinks. And then he's gone.

20

Paris
October 1945

THEY'RE RATTLING DOWN a boulevard in a Red Cross car. He has brought a bag of pears with him from Normandy; it sits on the parcel shelf. And this, oh God, this is Paris again, look at it, and there's money in his pocket, look, there are people on the terraces, a tram swings round the corner. He's driving through the city. His uniform-issue boots are sound and sturdy; he has a bag full of sweet and bulging pears. The war is over and so things should be good, but there is still so much that is lacking now. And this is an uneasy anticipation, seeing her again.

He spins past the Arc de Triomphe, along the Champs-Élysées and through the Place de la Concorde, so that his passengers can see the city. The open spaces of it, spinning with bicycles, rattling with buses and even a few official cars. And, what is more – and is more striking – an absence of German Army vehicles. There are no big fair men in grey-green, no bunches of Green Beans on the terraces or clusters strolling down the streets in civvies with their cameras. This is not somebody else's city any more. The bunkers and the checkpoints have been dismantled or turned to other use. Pigeons flutter upwards. He follows their flight past a broken window patched with a board, and a spray of bullet holes in a pale stone wall. There are scars left here too. Marks of harm. His eyes follow the pigeons up into the wide clear sky.

'Watch the road, eh?'

He swerves on to the Pont de la Concorde, and they are rattling along through the Left Bank. He drops his passengers at their lodging on rue Jacob – the quiet loveliness of the rue Jacob – and then he goes – well, he goes home, he supposes. This is the nearest thing there is to home. Back through these narrower streets, where an occasional bicycle wobbles aside, and a pram is bumped up on to the pavement, and a few commercial vans are loading and unloading. And as the moment of return approaches, things slow and become thick with apprehension.

The lift is *hors de service*. Trudging up seven storeys, breathless, to the apartment, and she is there – he knows it instantly. Though it is not warm, nor lit, she is there, her presence filling up the space like water. And he is gooseflesh and unease with it, not knowing even now what kind of return this will be.

'Suzanne?'

Her belly contracts. She drops her sewing aside, gets to her feet. Because coming in through the apartment door, there he is, out of nowhere, like a magic trick, and just as exasperating. All this time his world has been expanding, and has become busy and bustling and full to overflowing, while hers has contracted to a pinprick. She is hunger, body, tiredness, the slog of simply scraping by. She has nothing left for him.

And now he is looking around the flat, and then looking at her, as though it were something and nothing. As though it were inevitable he'd be there, now, this minute, and why would it be a surprise to her at all?

'Well,' he says.

'Well.'

And in uniform! Trust him to spend the war in hand-me-downs and hedgerows and then deck himself out in conspicuous uniform just as everybody else is shedding it. The new gear – greatcoat, cap, trousers, puttees, tunic – is it that that makes him seem all the more contained, unknowable, and just – different?

She stands up, takes a step closer, looks him over, trying to read this new iteration of him. He has a kitbag hanging from his shoulder; the other holds a small calico sack. It bulges with something, with lots of somethings, small and rounded and smooth somethings.

'How are you,' he asks, 'my flea?'

'Oh,' she says, unsettled by the endearment. 'You know, it goes.'

He drops his kitbag and reaches out an arm and she steps into the space. He holds her there a moment, the both of them like boards. One arm is wrapped around her.

'You're thin,' he says.

She can hear the rumble of his voice in his chest. She nods, her head sliding up and down against serge. Everyone in Paris is thin. His flesh, though, has filled itself out. He is more solid than he used to be. She wants to say, *I am happy to see you*, but the truth of it is not quite as clear as happy. There has been too much wear and tear for there to be straightforward happiness now. There is not the substance, the structure left for that.

Now, he pushes her gently away and goes to unbutton his coat, which makes him remember the calico sack.

'Here,' he says. 'I brought something for you.'

She swipes at her eyes. More bounty from his better life; it makes her feel sour. But the mouth of the bag opens on a clutch of pears and offers up a cloud of scent, floral, sweet; her mouth floods.

'Oh, the cow,' she says.

She dips in a hand and lifts out a fruit and hands the bag back to him. The pear is heavy with juice; between her fingertips the skin is grained and toad-like. She presses her mouth into the soft flesh, her eyes closing. She eats, wordless, the wet sweetness of it astonishing, while he sets the bag down and slides off his coat and hangs it up and looks around the scant little apartment, and twists his head to peer up at the sleeping loft above. She sucks the last of the flesh from the strands of the core and drops what's left into the wastepaper basket. Juice has gathered under her lower lip and she wipes it upwards with the flank of her hand. Then she notices him, noticing her.

'Excuse me,' she says.

'You're hungry. Have another.'

'I'm sorry.'

She dips her hand in again. Her cheeks flush. She bites carefully. Little fractions of wet flesh and grainy skin. Turned and lingering on the tongue, while he climbs the stairs to the little sleeping loft and looks around. Like a dog circling its bed.

He calls down to her. 'We'll go out for lunch,' he says. 'If you'd like to.'

She pauses, swallows. 'Can we?'

'Yes,' he says. 'Why not?'

She tilts her head, unseen, considering the new authority in his voice. This is having money, she supposes. A salary that just happens to him every month. This is having more than enough, rather than substantially less.

'I'd like that,' she says.

She drops the threads of the second pear into the waste-paper basket. She fetches her shoes and sits down to put them on. Her hands are cold and sticky with juice. He clumps back down the stairs. She does not look at him. You have brought me pears, she thinks, but this is what I have brought for you: this is all that I have in abundance. We have had a glut of horrors here.

'I don't know what you've heard,' she says.

'What's that?'

'About our friends,' she says, and then she pauses and has to clear her throat, because after all there is scant satisfaction in sharing this.

'What do you know?'

'Different stories.'

He looks away; she follows his gaze across to his book-shelves, his desk.

'Not yet,' he says.

'What?'

'Later,' he says. 'Just not yet.'

She stares at him. Unseen, she shrugs. 'Well.'

He can do as he pleases. He always will. She is too worn out with it all to care.

They eat lunch in a little local bistro, where they used to eat before. Frayed cuffs on the waiters, who are men he doesn't know; washed-thin dresses on the ladies, bare legs. He recognizes the sisters who used to run the hairdresser's. There is bread, since bread is no longer rationed, and he has rillettes and cornichons, and they have a *pichet* of wine to share. They are quiet; the whole place is quiet. Life goes on, after all. It insists on it.

The meal is expensive. It is three times what they would have paid for something rather better before the war. But it is welcome. And the coffee, when it comes, is real, and strong, and good. It makes her shudder.

'Will you be back,' she asks, 'do you think?'

'To Paris?'

'Yes.'

He casts his gaze around the restaurant, taking in the scuffed tiles, the thin faces, the empty mirrored shelves where there had once been bottled spirits and liqueurs.

'Where else would I go? My contract ends in January.'

She nods. She is making those little moves – napkin laid aside, bag hunted for and opened, peered into – that signal departure. 'Well, I'm teaching this afternoon, so . . .'

People still learn to play the piano, then. And children still sit their exams, no doubt. They go on holiday, and celebrate their saints' days and their birthdays. For all it still feels so sketchy and provisional, they are now living in a world where a Jewish boy's baccalaureate counts for something again.

'I have to return to Saint-Lô tomorrow,' he says.

'I see.'

'I'm only in Paris to fetch rat poison. It's not easy to get hold of, not out there.'

'Right.'

'I'll send you something when I get back. What would you like? What do you particularly need?'

She closes her eyes and half smiles at his entire failure to understand. She needs everything; she has nothing but needs. Some can be kept at bay, others are impossible to assuage.

'A bar of soap,' she says. 'A toothbrush. A lipstick. Anything at all.'

He walks with her to the Métro. By the square, a small child picks up horse chestnuts from the pavement; a woman watches, having watched him all the way through all the war. He recalls the baby in the pram being bumped along the cobbles, that razor-clear autumn of '41, when he'd carried the typed-up information across town to Jimmy. And

Jimmy – he wonders, how did Jimmy fare? Did he get through it all and out the other side?

At the steps down to the station, Suzanne kisses him on the cheek, brief and cool. 'What happened to your coat?' she asks.

He looks down at the clean green serge of his Red Cross greatcoat, with its white and red armband, then back at her, nonplussed. Nearby, a pigeon scrats in the gutter. It is an ugly battered thing, peg-legged. Pigeon pie.

'No,' she says. 'Your other coat.'

'Oh, yes. I left it behind, in Ireland.'

'Why did you do that?'

He'd hung it up in the wardrobe in his mother's spare room. With his father's still-cherished overcoat and shoes, her fox fur, the stink of camphor. He'd closed the door on it and turned the key, that same evening, in that same darkness, his mother's shawl still over his arm.

'It seemed like the right thing to do. Anyway, they gave me this one, so.'

'Will they let you keep it?'

'Oh. I don't know.'

She tsks, shakes her head. 'What'll you do, then, when your contract's up?'

He shrugs.

'What do you think a new coat would cost, right now?'

'I have no idea.'

'Well,' she says. He is still himself, for all he's changed. 'You'll find out, I suppose. Till I see you.'

367

Then she kisses him again, because it seems the thing to do, and she turns away, and she clips down the Métro stairs.

Now that she is gone, he could go back to the empty apartment, to the peace and solitude of it. He could turn the key on the rest of the world and let him and the silence warm to each other; he could find a notebook, start to write. But instead he walks, hands stuffed into his pockets, turning the pebble round and round in his fingertips, the collar of his greatcoat scratchy at his jaw. He presses on through the half-broken, skin-and-bones, scraping-by life of the place, through the city clattering with footfalls and pierced with voices and rumbling with drays, past the men in old coats and shoes worn to shreds, and young women in threadbare dresses and bright lipstick, and the old ladies in black clothes who have shuffled their way through the war with shopping bags and hairnets intact. The blue paper has gone from the street lamps. They have torn down all the German signposts, and the yellow placards from outside the Jewish shops. And the city, ticking over, ticking on, is nonetheless thick with loss, as infested with absences as the hospital is with rats. Walking in Paris, in October 1945, is the loneliest thing in all the world.

He takes his cigarette packet out and touches the one remaining cigarette. He puts the packet back.

He will get used to it, just as he has grown accustomed to the missing teeth, the missing toe, his scar. He will learn to accommodate the loss.

There are places, even in the ruins, that are touched by grace. Saint-Lô at night, and a little window is warm and lit. It is curtained with an old lace shawl to disguise the new and dimmer substitute for glass and the figures that move around on the other side.

Because inside the small front room, there's a piano and a tumbler of Calvados, and there's music playing, and it is all quite pleasant and comfortable and people do like to be there. Men like to be there. That Calvados on the piano-top is his, and he sips it whenever the music allows him to, because it is him playing the music, popular and sentimental songs. One of the girls leans against the instrument and watches him play. He is surprised, rather, by the ease of the music after so long an absence; his fingertips find their way without much need for thought. The Calvados may be helping with that, since he is not concerned about the performance; he just performs. The old upright is practically in tune, though the middle C key has gone mute. Which is not bad, when so many other pianos are now tangled wires and splintered teeth.

The prostitutes wear cardigans over their slips and frocks. They have boots and slippers and bare legs. They shiver and huddle into themselves; their skin is blueish. There's something familiar about the girl who's watching him play; he can't quite place her, but then he's half-cut, and the uncut half is taking care of the music, so that doesn't leave anything very much for working out where he has seen the prostitutes before.

Late on, blurry with drink, he's obliged to leave the piano and amble off to find the necessary. He opens an inner door expecting a back room or the kitchen, but there's night air

369

and stars above, where the walls and roof have been blown clean off. A man is pissing up against a heap of broken bricks. Finished, the fellow buttons up and slips past him with a grin, heading back indoors. He takes his turn out in the night and adds his water to the musky pool. As he pisses, he lifts his face to the rain, closes his eyes, enjoys the easy sway of his own Calvados-adjusted senses.

The door shut behind him, he returns to the piano, and people are talking and laughing and going on as if there were a whole house standing square around them, not just a few chancy habitable rooms. This is what the world is liable to do nowadays – collapse in ruins – and people go on behaving as though it were nothing very much at all.

He sips from his cigarette, one hand keeping the rhythm going; then his smoke smoulders and fades out in a saucer, and a girl tops up his drink, and when the woman leans closer as a song ends, he gets up to hear her, and someone else slides into his seat at the piano, and his head reels and the woman takes his arm and smiles, and says his French is sweet.

'Come upstairs with me,' she asks, 'why don't you?'

And so she leads him off upstairs, and it turns out that he is drunker than he'd thought he was, or that the stairs are out of kilter: they pitch him sideways, so that he has to hang on to the banister and clamber up them like a mountaineer. Perhaps what's familiar about her is just hunger: the pinched look, the stick-thin, bones-on-show appearance makes sisters of them all. French women just look like that now.

Upstairs with her, the door shut behind them, and she peels off her cardigan and steps out of her slip, and he can see the press of hipbones through the skin and the dip like salt cellars in her collarbone, and when she lies down her breasts fall away sideways from the bones of her ribcage, and her breasts are so soft, very soft, and traced with mother-of-pearl stretchmarks, and he rolls a prophylactic clumsily on and is inside her, and it is only just as he comes that he remembers her, heavy with pregnancy, handing him a bottle of Calvados and telling him he was welcome here.

A pack of boys races down the newly surfaced roads; smaller kids huddle together on the corner, hovering over a concoction of mud and leaves. Girls have chalked a game on to the ground and are skipping through it. He walks, clipboard in hand, beside the colonel.

'On the whole, successful, I'd say.'

'And the corpses dealt with?'

'Incinerated, yes. You know what the kids are like here. Play with anything.'

They stop short to allow a pack of little children to thunder by.

'This is a hospital, not a playground!' the colonel yells after them.

They hurtle on, joyous, heedless.

'This place is getting lousy with them,' the colonel says. 'Worse than the rats. Someone's going to get hurt.'

The building work continues. Trucks grind back and forth; there are staff cars, locals' cars, and half a dozen ambulances that hurtle in and out of the site at all hours, day and night. The children do stand a good chance of getting hit.

'Their mothers send them to play here,' he says.

These are kids who are missing fingers, who have brutal scars beneath their clothes; these are kids who are also missing parents, brothers, sisters, friends. For all the risks from traffic, they're safer here than anywhere else for miles and miles.

Things are getting better. Things are becoming sound. There's asphalt on the roads and on the paths. There's glass, or something like glass, in all the windows. There's lino on the labour-room floor – since there is breeding still, even now, even in this devastation. There are curtains round the beds, and clean sheets and warm blankets neatly tucked in. The operating theatre gleams with aluminium and sterile steel. The rain doesn't drip through, the wind is kept at bay, the rats are in retreat. There is tea and there are biscuits and there is bread-and-jam when it is required, and it is often required. There's kindness here. There's decency amongst the ruins. It is something to behold.

21

Normandy
December 1945

JUST A QUICK run, they said. Just out to Dieppe and back. You're well used to the route, sure you could do it in your sleep. Pick up the new matron and that's you. On you go. Your time's your own after that.

But the ship is delayed. And he's an idiot because he didn't even think to bring a book. And now it's snowing. And that's just the fucking marzipan, that is. Snow. Snow is general all over Normandy.

The hut is all steam and cigarettes. He looks at his watch, considers how bad the roads will be if she arrives now, if she arrives in ten minutes, half an hour. An hour. Two. For fuck's sake. The wind buffets the windows and the stove blows back smoke. He finds an abandoned copy of the London *Times*, sits, unbuttons his greatcoat, tries to read.

Then he's up again, newspaper hanging, to peer out of the window at the snow as it scuds in flurries round the holding yard. He buttons his coat up and tucks his muffler in. He looks at his watch.

He's half gone already. He's back in Paris, seven flights up on the rue des Favorites. And he's here, in a prefab in Dieppe, watching the snow build on the windowsill, watching it fall thick on the yard beyond, pristine as a ream of paper.

At the hatch, the girl gives him coffee and bread-and-margarine and an apology for it, though he's happy enough with such frugal stuff. He eats, smokes, drinks coffee. Picks up the paper again, thumbs through it, hands it over to an English doctor waiting for his passage home, who settles into it readily. It belongs to the world that the doctor is returning to, not this one, where he remains.

When the ship finally enters the harbour, the throb of it can be felt through the quayside building. He steps out into the night. He turns up his collar, pockets his glasses; snow whips into his face. The vessel heaves and groans as it lines itself up along the quay. The closer it gets to actually being here, the more things seem to slow. It takes an age for moorings to be secured. Another age for the gangways to be lowered. The passengers creep off as though they are half-dead.

She looks exhausted. He shakes her hand and takes her bag and ushers her over to the truck. She shivers inside her cape; he holds the door open for her and takes her arm to help her in. It takes some restraint not to chivy her along.

'Thank you.'

They drive into the night, snow swarming in the headlights. Away from the coast, the wind drops and the snow falls heavily. The windscreen wipers shunt it into wedges; lumps fall off and fly aside. The snow makes a dazzling tunnel of the headlights. The darkness beyond is absolute.

'How far is it,' she asks, 'to Saint-Lô?'

'A hundred and seventy miles, give or take.'

They are both illuminated, briefly, by the flare of a passing vehicle. The road ahead, caught suddenly in their merging lights, looks as smooth as a pillowcase, and then the other vehicle has passed and their truck rackets along, lurching into potholes, through ruts and across debris, all hidden by the blanketing snow. He winces, but doesn't ease off. She shifts in her seat, glances at him; he remains in profile, eyes on the spinning dark.

'Is it necessary,' she asks, 'to go quite so fast?'

'It's not as fast as it looks.'

After a moment, he fishes his cigarettes off the parcel shelf and offers them to her; she takes one, then takes his rattling matches off him too and they lean together so that she can light his cigarette along with her own.

'You should try and have a sleep,' he says.

'I don't know that I could.'

He glances across at her. 'It'll make it go by much more quickly.'

She shakes her head. Her free hand grips the edge of her seat. She clearly feels that this is quite quickly enough.

'Careful!'

He slams down a gear for a bend. They make the turn and hurtle on through the winter night. The darkness has become a solid thing and it's racing away from his headlights, retreating from them as fast as he can drive towards it: he is chasing after the dark, and he will slam right through it, into whatever it is that lies beyond.

They burn through scattered dwellings that here and there coalesce into settlements, and there are lights sometimes, and the smell of woodsmoke, and then they're in a square, where there are a few lights lit, which have a tired and faded look about them, and he knows that by the time they reach the next town everything will be shut. He'd prefer not to stop, but she must need some refreshment. He eases off and pulls over and yanks the handbrake on. She visibly relaxes.

'Two ticks,' he says. 'Stay here and keep warm. I'll go and see if I can rustle something up.'

He leaves the engine idling. In the café, the *patron* is locking up for the night, but seeing the man in Red Cross uniform there he starts to draw the bolts again and ushers him in, past the empty bentwood chairs set on the tabletops, into the end-of-evening smell of smoke and wine, which brings to mind a plate of *charcuterie*, the memory of Jeannine, and thence that priest, and that brings him out in gooseflesh. But they have nothing they can give him here. There will be *viennoiseries* in the morning, but until then, there's only coffee and brandy to be had.

'That'll work, thank you.'

He lights up, leaning on the zinc, twitchy, running a fingernail back and forth along a scratch. The *patron* fills the percolator, heats milk and reaches for the cognac on the almost-empty shelves. This place, this little café in this little town, the scar along the countertop – this is

376

everything for the moment. While outside in the cold cab, breath pluming in the air, the snow gathering on the windscreen, the press of a hairpin into her scalp, is also everything. And the coffee bowls and brandy bottle lifted from the shelf, the other side of the zinc, the stubble-blued chin scrubbed at with a hand, is everything again. These small worlds, overlapping and impenetrable.

He returns to the cab with a coffee that is getting cooler and more dilute with snow. She has fallen into a doze. When he opens the door, she is startled awake.

'Thank you.' She lifts the drink to her lips and then, catching the scent, hesitates.

'Drop of brandy. Keep out the cold.'

'I don't drink,' she says.

'I'm afraid there's nothing else.'

She pulls a face.

'Consider it medicinal,' he says. If he could just take the bowl back, then they could be on their way. 'For the good of your health.'

She hesitates, then drinks it straight down. She hands him the bowl. 'Where will we stop for Mass?'

'Mass? Tonight?'

'It's Christmas Eve.'

Of course it is. Of course. 'I'll get you to Saint-Lô in time.'

She grimaces.

He pulls to a halt outside the ruined church of Notre Dame in Saint-Lô. She swallows queasily after the twisting, jolty journey here.

'All right?'

She fumbles with the door.

Inside the church, candles have been lit; they glow through the fragments of stained glass still clinging to the cames.

He turns the engine off and gets out to help her down, but she is already sliding from her seat. She straightens her skirt and settles her cape around her shoulders with a distinct air of relief.

'Well,' she says. 'Here we are. Thank you.'

From inside the church comes the sound of violins, thin and icy. The snow still falls.

'Will you join me?'

He pulls on his cap. 'I'll wait on you here.'

He leans back against the truck.

She goes up the steps and in through the doorway. That'll be an hour or so, Mass. He listens to the priest's incantation and the low murmur of the congregation, and then the priest again. One doesn't need to hear the actual words; the shape and pattern of them is instantly knowable. Her footprints fill. Snow gathers on his shoulders and his cap. He brushes it off and lights another cigarette. Violins begin to play, and then voices join them. Cigarette in lips, he treads over to the door to peer inside.

The church is open to the sky: the priest stands, vestments pulled over a bulky coat, bald head bowed, and snow falls on him. Snow carpets the stone flags, covers the altar with a blue-white pall. Snow drapes the edges of protruding masonry and the scorched and broken timbers. The candles flicker and fizz as the snowflakes hit them.

They are gathered there, all of them; they sing. The colonel, the volunteers, the ancillary workers, the new matron with her cap and cape. The Catholic contingent of the prisoners of war are with them in the snow. He thinks he catches the bristly profile of the German doctor. And the thin women from the ramshackle bawdy-house. And children, small ones held sleeping, older ones bundled up in jackets and scarves. Near the back, a youth with a small boy pressed into his side, heads tilted back to bawl out the hymn together.

It's impressive, that conspiracy. That insistence that everything means something, that happenstance will be made to fit a pattern, for all that the pattern cannot be discerned from where they stand, human, their feet upon the earth. That everything must be referred upwards, into the empty sky.

He turns away, back into the night, the snow falling. He gets back into the stuffy crampedness of the cab and finishes his cigarette. It's a kind of homesickness, he suspects. But then he never entirely felt at home.

Movement at the cab door: she climbs back into the truck with a cloud of cold and thumps the door shut behind her.

'Beautiful,' she says. 'Thank you.'

'Good,' he says. 'I'm glad.'

The engine clears its throat, and clears its throat again, uncertain: diesel doesn't like the cold. But it settles into its plegmy rattle and he stamps on the clutch.

'Not far now,' he says. 'Just on up the road.'

He shoves the gearstick sideways, then shunts it forward; he releases the pedal and they lunge away again, through the broken town shawled in snow.

'You must be tired of ferrying people around at all hours.'

'I've put you through it tonight,' he says. 'I'm sorry.'

He swerves round on to the road that leads up to the hospital; here the snow is worn to slush.

'Oh,' she says. 'No.' She grips the door handle and the seat as they take the bend.

'My contract's up. I'm afraid my mind's elsewhere. And you wanted to get to Mass, so . . .'

He turns down the main drive, passes a row of huts. They pull up outside the women's barracks.

'We shall be sorry to lose you, I've no doubt,' she says.

'The place is all set up now, so, they're grand.'

'What will you do next?'

He yanks the handbrake on and clumps the gearstick back into neutral. 'Start again,' he says. 'I suppose. Just like everybody else.'

The white huts are almost pretty, with their curtained windows warm in the twilight, and he walks along the clean frosty pathways to where his lift is waiting for him.

There are footfalls indoors as the nurses do their rounds; there are murmured voices, there are those hard ungovernable coughs of the tubercular patients. He can hear the buzz of chat from the rec hut, the pock and tap of the table-tennis balls. He has made the necessary farewells. He doesn't want to make any unnecessary ones, has no desire to linger.

He runs his tongue round his mouth, the gaps and the smooth places where the decay was halted and the voids were filled. The absence of pain is a thing in itself, though not painlessly achieved. Like this place, this scraped-clear bit of earth where the rubble has been brushed aside and something sound is made of it.

It's temporary, of course; everything's always temporary. Decay is paused, not halted; ruin is always incipient. One day, before you know it, all of this will be half-rotten, streaked with green and crawling with woodlice. But that doesn't mean it wasn't worth the doing.

The new matron steps out of the women's ward and comes walking down the path towards him. Her eyes are tired but her expression is light; she actually looks happy. She sees him, kitbag and coat, heading to the cars.

'Are you going right away?' she asks.

'My lift's waiting.'

'Hang on just two minutes before you go.' Her hand is on his arm, she is drawing him back.

She leads him into the women's ward, up the step and indoors. One corner is curtained off. At the far end of the hut, a woman sleeps, curled on her side.

'Come, see.'

She eases back the curtain and there is a row of little cots. He knows these cots. He has an invoice filed away for them back up at the stores. In one, swaddled in white linen and tucked in tight under cellular blankets, is a tiny raw-looking thing, patched with flaking skin. Its birdlike breast barely lifts the covers, but it does lift the covers, and, as he watches, it keeps on doing so. Impossible tiny little breaths in a creature not yet used to breathing. A being not yet used to being.

'Is it all right?'

'Oh yes. Perfectly. He's just a few hours old.'

'And the mother?'

The nurse nods, and in her smile is the knowledge of a job well done. 'She's doing fine.'

The infant stirs; its lips move. It doesn't cry. Its eyes open, and they are dark and bluish and alien.

'It isn't crying.'

'They don't always cry,' Matron says.

He looks down at the small creased thing, which stares back at him with an ancient calm.

'They do keep on being born, don't they?'

'Hm?'

'People. Babies.'

'They rather insist on it.'

'Poor little scrap,' he says.

'New life, though,' she says. 'It gives you hope.'

'Oh, don't say that,' he says. 'That's not fair.'

He considers the curled-up creature there, the years that it will have to live through, the best outcome at the end of it all. Why would you do that to someone, out of love? And aren't they supposed to cry? *When we are born, we cry that we are come to this great stage of fools.* It's just a natural reaction.

'Well,' he says. 'God bless.'

A big, lovely smile from her, as if he has expressed some kind of approval, as if something has been agreed between them.

'God bless,' she says.

He shoulders his kitbag and slips out through the door. Hope is not a thing that he can bring himself to consider. It really does not agree with him at all.

22

Paris
January 1946

'I'LL WALK FROM HERE.'

He slides out at the corner, slams the door, raises a hand in thanks. The vehicle rattles away. There is ice between the cobblestones; there is frost on the railings. He turns his collar up. His coat now is worn to fit his body, it has softened to him. Made itself be his.

The street-market is busy on the rue de Vaugirard, but the stalls are thinly stocked. A few winter cabbages, half a barrow-load of potatoes, a pile of chestnuts; everything is sad and slight and mean-looking, and there is a conspicuous absence of bread, since it's back on the ration. A few pewter-grey fish lie cold in the cold air. The housewives are pecking grimly through these offerings. He notices the prices chalked on the little boards and winces. It is going to be impossible to live on his allowance. It was stupid to walk away from a proper salary, ridiculous to leave behind the chickens and the Calvados and the jam and the nice warm little huts, to

384

try again at this impossible thing that nobody cares whether he does or doesn't do, and for which no payment is to be anticipated. It was stupid, impossible, ridiculous, and absolutely necessary.

He peers up the face of the apartment building. His little casement is unlit; behind it waits a pool of calm and quiet. If Suzanne is elsewhere. He goes in through the lobby door. The lift is still out of order; the stairs twist upwards, into shadow. His head is too full to accommodate the possibility of her, to accommodate anything other than what has to happen next. The cupboard in the back of his mind is ready to burst open, and all the mess that has been shoved in there will spill out on to the floor. He has to have the space, the quiet, to let that happen, to deal with the mess, sort through it and shape it into something.

There is a strange push-pull to this, an urgency and a dread. He grabs the handrail, heaves himself up three steps at a time, striding his way up the spiralling helix. He can't let himself think too much about the doing of it; it must just be done.

Suzanne halts two steps above him. She is fastening her glove. They are caught out by the suddenness of the encounter, their eyes locked. She is struck, again, by the brightness of the blue; he is caught by the warmth of her eyes, black-coffee-brown. Her gaze slides away, and she glances over his furrowed forehead, his furze of hair, his cold hand curled round the strap of his bag. She feels an instinctive tug towards him, but there is too much, just too much heaped up now between them. She can't go over, she can't go round, she can't just blunder through.

'It's you,' she says, and her voice sounds dry and strange.

'Yes, it's me.'

She is rendered conscious of her stockings – her best pair, though darned at heel and toe. Her patchy pumiced legs. He has seen her worse. But he doesn't see her now; she knows it. He is here, but she can tell that he isn't really here at all.

'Well,' she says, and she doesn't know what else to say.

He steps up and kisses her on the cheek. The smell of her, of old coat and body and a faint whiff of perfume, which she must have been eking out so carefully. If they could get back to where they left off, to that stupid lovely summer five years ago, when her body was sepia-printed from the sun and they had been easy together; if they could drag themselves back to that, claw their way along through mud and dust. But there is so much territory, so much cooling space between them. There is so much wear and tear.

No point pinning it with words, he thinks. Let it flutter by.

'You're back,' she says.

He nods.

'And that's that, is it?'

He says, 'That's that.'

There is maybe more that he could say, phrases he could conjure up and offer out to her that would help, but his eyes drift past her on and up the stairs, into the shadows.

'Good,' she says. 'Well. I missed you.'

Then she just slips past him and goes on, clipping down and round the stair, going briskly. He watches. She turns again and she is gone. Her footfalls fade out, and the *porte cochère* opens and then slams behind her.

She pauses in the street. She touches her eyes with a gloved finger. There is time, she tells herself; they have been granted that, at least. But is more time really what they need?

The circling stairs twist up into the shadows. His chest aches; his scar hurts. Perhaps he should go after her. He hefts the bagstrap up his shoulder and begins again to climb.

Inside, he drops his bag and locks the door behind him. The apartment is cold and dim. He unbuttons his greatcoat but keeps it on. He moves around the room, touching things into place, going into the kitchenette to set water to boil. He hunkers down by his bag to rummage out his notebook, a new bottle of ink, his fountain pen. The pan begins to rattle as he lays his materials out on the tabletop. He goes to make coffee, brings the things back through. He draws out the chair and sits. In silence and in solitude, he folds open his new notebook. He flattens out the page. He dips his pen into the ink, and fills it, and wipes the nib. The pen traces its way across the paper. Ink blues the page. Words form. This is where it begins.

Author's Note

I FIRST READ BECKETT during my MA in Irish Writing, at the Queen's University of Belfast. I was at once unsettled and fascinated – those battered, persecuted characters, scraping by in the margins of a hostile world. This was like nothing else I'd ever read. Beckett's work seemed to float free – I had no reference points; I felt lost.

Until my tutor, Dr Eamonn Hughes, pointed out that Beckett had been stuck in Occupied France during World War Two; he'd had to go into hiding. It was a light-bulb moment: a modern eco-bulb; a slow-growing light. I began to get an inkling of where these characters came from, the nature of the world they inhabited. The context of Beckett's wartime experiences was not, by any means, *the* way to understand his complex and allusive work, but it was a light by which to peer at bits of it.

Because the war years did mark a major change in Beckett's work: he was already a published writer when the conflict broke out, but the work sometimes feels like that of an (albeit brilliant) adolescent, overburdened by his influences. There are indicators of change beforehand, but those years in Occupied France seem to have established many of the key themes, images and preoccupations of Beckett's later work. They also marked the start of his paring away at language: a stripping-back of Joycean wordplay and polyphonic extravagance, towards bare bones, and silence. Beckett experienced, in the direct aftermath of war, an epiphany. He understood, fully and for the first time, the kind of writer he would be. This revelation occurred not when confronted by the wild darkness of a storm-torn sea – as *Krapp's Last Tape* might seem to suggest – but with appropriate-for-Beckett bathos, at his mother's suburban bungalow in Foxrock.

The war was not something that Beckett just drifted through; it presented him with a series of extraordinary moral choices. And in impossibly difficult situations, he consistently turned towards what was most decent and compassionate and courageous. He chose to face the war with his friends in France, rather than sit it out in neutral Eire. He chose to give his subsistence-level rations away to those in still greater need. He chose to resist. He chose to survive. And then, after the devastation, he chose to aid with the rebuilding.

In short, he grew, as a writer and as a man. Afterwards he would go on to write the work that would make him internationally famous, and for which he would be awarded the Nobel Prize for Literature. Work that still resonates powerfully with us today.

A Country Road, A Tree emerges from a profound sense of admiration for both the writing and the man; it is an attempt to offer up a fictional version of this story, because it casts a particular light on both. But there is also a personal connection here. Beckett and I had a mutual friend. Barbara Bray was a literary translator and a drama producer. She was a great supporter of my husband's – the playwright Daragh Carville – and mine when we were starting out as writers. I'm so grateful for her kindness, for the warm, supportive correspondence, the lunches and drinks she insisted on treating us to when we were young and broke. I sent her a copy of my first novel when it was published; she sent us a present – a pair of beautiful hand-made pewter coasters for our writing desks – when we got married. I didn't know, at the time, the extent of her involvement in Beckett's life. She was not, after all, just a friend to him, but she was a good and valued friend to us.

I am also grateful to James Knowlson for his magisterial biography *Damned to Fame: The Life of Samuel Beckett* (London, Bloomsbury, 1996): spending time immersed in this extraordinary book has been one of the chief pleasures of working on *A Country Road, A Tree*. The other biographies, Deirdre Bair's *Samuel Beckett: A Biography* (London, Jonathan Cape, 1978) and Anthony Cronin's *Samuel Beckett: The Last Modernist* (London, HarperCollins, 1996), each offered their own invaluable perspective on this phase in Beckett's life. Whilst there is little in the way of wartime correspondence, the Cambridge University Press edition of *The Letters of Samuel Beckett*, edited by George Craig, Martha

Dow Fehsenfeld, Dan Gunn and Lois More Overbeck, provided key way-markers and essential detail throughout the writing process. I also found myself turning again and again to Phyllis Gaffney's *Healing Amid the Ruins: the Irish Hospital at Saint Lo* (Dublin, A&A Farmar, 1999) for its fascinating account of the Irish Red Cross in post-war Normandy.

In shaping this novel, I have drawn on accounts in the biographies and references in the collected letters; I've found clues in Beckett's own novels, poems and plays; I've drawn from other memoirs, from fiction and histories of the period, from art and music, from the various languages spoken and the places inhabited and the places just passed through. I'm immensely grateful for the advice and information and nudges I've been given along the way. The resulting novel, I know, is a partial, incomplete and limited thing. I always knew it would be. But nonetheless, I had to try.

Jo Baker was educated at Oxford and Queen's University, Belfast. She lives in Lancaster with her husband, the playwright Daragh Carville, and their two children. She is the author of the bestselling *Longbourn*, which is due to be made into a film.

LONGBOURN
Jo Baker

'If Elizabeth Bennet had the washing of her own petticoats,' Sarah thought, *'she would be more careful not to tramp through muddy fields.'*

It is wash-day for the housemaids at Longbourn House, and Sarah's hands are chapped and raw. Domestic life below stairs, ruled with a tender heart and an iron will by Mrs Hill the housekeeper, is about to be disturbed by the arrival of a new footman, bearing secrets and the scent of the sea.

'A reimagining of *Pride and Prejudice* from the point of view of the servants . . . a joy'
Guardian

'A really special book, and not only because its author writes like an angel'
Daily Mail

'A genuinely fresh perspective on the tale of the Bennet household'
Sunday Times

'A fascinating insight into the harsh working conditions of life in a grand house two hundred years ago'
Good Housekeeping

THE BALLROOM
Anna Hope

1911: Inside an asylum at the edge of the Yorkshire moors, where men and women are kept apart by high walls and barred windows, there is a ballroom, vast and beautiful. For one bright evening every week, they come together and dance.

When John and Ella meet, it is a dance that will change two lives for ever.

'Moving, fascinating'
The Times

'A tender and absorbing love story'
Daily Mail

'Heartbreaking and insightful'
Sunday Express

'Fiction at its finest . . . the reader is utterly transported'
Irish Independent

WAKE
Anna Hope

Remembrance Day 1920: A tragic secret connects three women: Hettie, whose wounded brother has been struck dumb; Evelyn, who still grieves for her lost lover; and Ada, who has never received an official letter about her son's death, and is still hoping he will come home. As the mystery that binds them begins to unravel, far away, in the fields of France, the Unknown Soldier embarks on his journey home. The mood of the nation is turning towards the future – but can these three women ever let go of the past?

'Superb. Beautifully crafted'
Irish Times

'Tender and timely'
Chris Cleave

'A moving novel about the aftermath of the 1914–1918 conflict . . . Unlikely that many will prove better than Anna Hope's *WAKE*'
Sunday Times

THE ORPHAN MASTER'S SON
Adam Johnson

Pak Jun Do knows he is special.

He knows he must be the son of the master of the orphanage, not some kid dumped by his parents – it was obvious from the way his father singled him out for beatings. He knows he is special when he is picked as a spy and kidnapper for his country, the glorious Democratic Republic of North Korea. He knows he must find his true love, Sun Moon, the greatest opera star who ever lived, before it's too late.

He knows he's not like the other prisoners in the camp. He's going to get out soon. Definitely.

'An addictive novel of daring ingenuity'
David Mitchell

'Fast-paced and intriguing . . . will remind readers of David Mitchell's *Cloud Atlas*'
Financial Times

'Deserves a place up there with dystopian classics such as *Nineteen-Eighty-Four* and *Brave New World*'
Guardian

'Excavates the very meaning of love and sacrifice'
New York Times

FORTUNE SMILES
Adam Johnson

Adam Johnson takes you into the minds of characters you never thought you would meet – a former Stasi prison warden in denial of his past, a refugee from North Korea unsettled by his new freedom, a UPS driver in hurricane-torn Louisiana looking for the mother of his son.

Love and loss, natural disasters, technology, and how the political shapes the personal, these tender tales from a giant of American literature show us humanity where you might least expect it.

'An epic storyteller'
Zadie Smith

'Unputdownable is an overused word, but at their best these stories are completely gripping'
Sunday Times

'Ironic, witty, super-intelligent'
The Times

'Formidable, meaty tales that cling on and don't let go'
Independent

ALL WE SHALL KNOW
Donal Ryan

'Martin Toppy is the son of a famous Traveller and the father of my unborn child. He's seventeen, I'm thirty-three. I was his teacher.'

Melody Shee is alone and in trouble. Her husband doesn't take her news too well. She can't tell her father yet because he's a good man and this could break him. She's trying to stay in the moment, but the future is looming – larger by the day – while the past won't let her go. What she did to Breedie Flynn all those years ago still haunts her.

It's a good thing that she meets Mary Crothery when she does. Mary is a young Traveller woman, and she knows more about Melody than she lets on. She might just save Melody's life.

'Worthy of a Greek drama'
John Burnside, *Guardian*

'To his raw, wounded and grieving characters Donal Ryan says: If you are still breathing, you can be redeemed'
Colin Barrett

'Ryan's strongest work to date . . . an exquisite account of womanhood, friendship, prejudice and tradition that is both intimate in scale and awesome in achievement'
Irish Independent

THE SPINNING HEART
Donal Ryan

'My father still lives back the road past the weir in the cottage I was reared in. I go there every day to see is he dead and every day he lets me down. He hasn't yet missed a day of letting me down.'

In the aftermath of Ireland's financial collapse, dangerous tensions surface in an Irish town. As violence flares, the characters face a battle between public persona and inner desires. Through a chorus of unique voices, each struggling to tell their own kind of truth, a single authentic tale unfolds.

The Spinning Heart speaks for contemporary Ireland like no other novel. Wry, vulnerable, all-too human, it captures the language and spirit of rural Ireland and with uncanny perception articulates the words and thoughts of a generation. Technically daring and evocative of Patrick McCabe and J.M. Synge, this novel of small-town life is witty, dark and sweetly poignant.

'Extraordinarily accomplished'
Sunday Independent

'A modern literary masterpiece'
Ryan Tubridy, *RTE*

'I can't imagine a more original, more perceptive or more passionate work than this. Outstanding'
John Boyne

'Unexpectedly tender . . . compellingly humane . . . an exciting, relevant and believable contemporary novel about the lost and the wounded'
Irish Times